TIME-MARKED WARLOCK

SHAMI STOVALL

Thank you
for reviewing!
Shami Stovall

Published by
CS BOOKS, LLC

Cover Design: Chris McGrath
Editors: Nia Quinn, Celestian Rince

IF YOU WANT TO BE NOTIFIED WHEN SHAMI STOVALL'S NEXT BOOK RELEASES, PLEASE VISIT HER WEBSITE OR CONTACT HER DIRECTLY AT
s.adelle.s@gmail.com

To John, my soulmate.
To my patrons over on Patreon, because they're amazing.
To everyone who read an ARC copy, thank you so much!
To Drew, for being a great agent.
To Soundbooth Theater, for doing the audio!
To my Facebook group, for all the memes.
And finally, to everyone unnamed, thank you for everything.

CONTENTS

CHAPTER
ONE

I t was extremely important to note that Adair Finch woke at exactly 4:34 a.m.

Someone was banging on his front door.

Finch opened his eyes and immediately reached for his phone on the nightstand. Most warlocks wouldn't have cared what time it was, but Finch wasn't most warlocks. He marked the time with his magic, threw off his blankets, and then stood from his bed, his vision blurred. Finch crept out of his tiny bedroom, the banging echoing throughout his otherwise silent abode.

If a random passerby had managed to glance into Finch's apartment, they would have assumed Finch lived with four undisciplined children. Dirty dishes covered every available surface. Clothes piles decorated every corner. The only thing missing was crude crayon drawings across the walls.

But Finch lived alone. He had for a long time.

The banging on the front door grew frantic.

"Help," a muffled voice from the other side cried. "*Help! Please! I need help.*"

Panicked shouting wasn't a common occurrence in the

Applegate Apartments. Most everyone kept to themselves, which was the way Finch liked it.

No one had come calling for Finch's help for many years, though. Who was at his door now?

Once close, Finch peered out the spy hole and stared out into the hallway, his vision distorted into a fisheye perspective. A young girl paced back and forth, just beyond the boundary of his apartment. She stopped in front of his door, her shoulders shaking, her dark brown hair a mess. She grabbed at the long locks, her unsteady hands twisting into a tight grip.

How old was she?

She wore a black hoodie and a pair of faded jeans. Her sneakers, worn and scuffed, weren't marked by any designer or brand. The girl seemed plain. Perhaps too plain.

Finch assumed, given her short stature and small size, she was twelve or thirteen. Which also made him suspicious. Why was a child banging on his apartment door?

Her muffled sobs betrayed her earnest distress. Even if this was some sort of elaborate ruse, Finch couldn't bring himself to ignore it.

He opened the door, but he kept the chain lock in place, allowing only a small crack's worth of space to peer into the corridor.

"Who are you?" Finch asked, his voice rusty.

When had he last spoken to anyone? Had it really been *weeks*? DoorDash and Amazon had significantly cut down on his need to interact with magicless mortals.

The girl whirled on her heel, her eyes red and puffy. She rubbed at her face and practically slammed herself into the door, obviously thinking it would fly open. The chain rattled as it held in place, keeping her at bay.

"I need help!" she cried. "Are you Adair F-Finch? Or

Carter Finch? I need to find them! Please. *Please*. I need the help of a warlock."

"*Shh*," Finch hissed the moment she uttered *warlock*. "Keep your voice down. *I'm* Adair Finch. Where're your parents?"

"That's why I'm here! Please, there's not much time!" The girl pushed on the door, rattling the chain a second time. Tears streamed down her reddened face. "Mum w-was... and... Papa..." All her control left her. She sobbed louder than before.

Finch closed the door, removed the chain, and then opened the door wide. He grabbed the girl by the shoulder, pulled her into his apartment, and slammed the door shut afterward, hoping she hadn't disturbed the quiet residents of the Applegate Apartments too much.

The girl ran both her hands over her face and cried, her shoulders bunched at the base of her neck.

Finch flipped on the nearby light. The bulb in the kitchen flickered to life, revealing the many food safety violations that made up his cooking space. He moved over to the counter and then unceremoniously swept his arm across a small portion, shoving the garbage and discarded fast-food containers to the side.

The girl's muffled sobs grew weaker, but she still couldn't speak.

Finch opened several cupboards until he found a single coffee mug. He grabbed it, filled the thing with water, and then placed it on the counter. Then he opened a wooden bread box near the stovetop. There was no bread, only packets of tea that most magicless mortals had never heard of in their life.

With a sigh, Finch riffled through them. He plucked out one—the last of that flavor—and dropped it into the coffee mug filled with cold water. Then he snapped his fingers over the container, and the water instantly heated, bubbles sprouting to life a moment later.

Steam lifted from the mug, filling the small kitchen with a pleasant aroma.

Normally, Finch would never use his sorcery in front of random strangers, but the girl obviously knew about warlocks, or else she wouldn't have been shouting for one. No need to hide his abilities now.

Finch handed her the coffee mug once the water inside had cooled just a tiny amount.

"Drink this," he demanded.

The girl flinched at his gruff and rather hostile tone. It didn't help with her crying.

After a moment of tapping on the side of the warm mug, Finch took a deep breath and tried to remember how to interact with other human beings. In a forced, but calm, voice, he offered her the mug a second time.

"This will help soothe your nerves."

The girl sniffled. She rubbed at her nose, and with a shaky hand, she took the mug.

Finch turned his attention to the living room. If a family of raccoons had broken in and started nesting, no one would've been able to tell the difference. Finch stomped his way over to the second recliner. *His* recliner was clean, and positioned next to the TV, away from the window. The second recliner wasn't in the best of shape, and most of last week's clothes were piled on top.

He shoved all the laundry onto the floor. Something *clanked* when it hit—something metal bundled inside the dirty clothes—but Finch ignored that.

"*Here*," he said, his gruff tone back in full force. "You can sit here."

The girl made her way to the recliner. She barely glanced around as she took a seat on the very edge of the crusty cushion. After another sniffle, and a rub at her eyes, the girl sipped her tea.

It only took the magic leaves a few seconds before their calming effects kicked in. The girl exhaled, her body relaxing, her tears drying up. She took another sip, and then another, each drink longer than the last.

Finch turned his recliner to face the girl's and then took a seat.

He glanced at the clock on the wall.

4:41 a.m.

Seven minutes had passed since Finch had marked the time.

The girl placed the mug on her lap. Her face, still puffy, had been wiped clean. Her striking blue eyes would've been beautiful if not for the bloodshot red around her irises. She panned her gaze over her surroundings.

After a deep inhale, she glanced down at her mug. "What was in this?"

"Midnight raspberry leaves," Finch stated.

And while that sounded like a scent of candle found at *Bed Bath & Beyond*, it was actually a rare type of plant that only witches grew on special occasions. Midnight raspberries were said to cure nightmares, and the leaves, when brewed, brought with them a supernatural level of calm. That was, until they were fully digested and left the body. Then all nightmares and anxieties would return.

"What's your name?" Finch asked.

"Bree," she muttered. Then she finally met Finch's cold stare. "And you're *really* Adair Finch?"

"That's right."

Bree glanced around the apartment a second time. "Are you sure you're not a hobo pretending to be Adair Finch?"

"All right," Finch said with a groan as he stood from his recliner. "Get out."

"N-No, wait!"

"I'm not here to be judged by children. There's the door." Finch pointed.

Bree held up a hand. "Please. I'm sorry, it's just... Mum always said the Finch brothers were powerful warlocks. *The* most powerful warlocks she knew. I didn't think... you would live like *this*." She gestured to their surroundings. "Or wear clothing like *that*."

Finch scratched at his outfit. His ratty T-shirt had more holes than a colander, and his sweatpants had stains that only magic could cure.

It likely didn't help that he hadn't cut his dark coppery hair in quite some time. It practically reached his shoulders. And the stubble bothered him. He scratched at his chin, making a mental note to correct the problem.

Finch begrudgingly sat back down.

"I don't know what to tell you, kid," he muttered. "That was a long time ago."

"Y-You're still a warlock who helps witches, though, right? Mum said you were a PI and that I—"

"I'm retired," Finch snapped.

"Oh." Bree fidgeted with her mug. After a strained moment of silence, she asked, "What about Carter? Mum said your brother was—"

"He's dead."

Finch had made the statement with all the emotion of a dictionary entry, but that was the only way he could talk about his brother anymore. Just facts. No reminiscing.

But the information didn't seem to sit well with Bree. She stared a hole into her mug, her unblinking gaze becoming watery all over again.

Finch leaned forward. "Why don't we back up? Why were you wandering around, shouting about warlocks? If your mother knows me, she must've *also* known to tell you to keep quiet about my profession."

"I had to yell," Bree whispered. "She told me that if I was ever in trouble, I needed to find Adair and Carter Finch as quickly as possible."

"Who's your mother? What's her name?"

Most people who knew the names of warlocks were also one of the magical themselves. A witch, or another warlock, or even a mortal under the power of a curse—something. If Bree's mother knew Finch's name and profession, he likely knew of her in turn.

"My mum is Vera Blackstone."

Finch's eyebrows shot for his hairline. "Vera? Really?"

It had been a long time since Finch had seen her. The last time was at her wedding. She was an interesting witch, one who loved to mingle in the affairs of the magicless. She always had the latest scoop on all the dealings of mortal men.

"Why isn't Vera here with you?"

Despite Bree's midnight raspberry tea, her lip quivered. "Th-That's why I'm here..."

"What happened?"

"Someone... broke into our house." Bree sipped the last of her tea, tranquility returning. "A man. I think. He snuck in. He was waiting in the kitchen when... when I went downstairs."

"Who all do you live with? Tell me everyone who was in the house at the time."

"It's just me, my mum, and my papa. The intruder was someone else."

"Vera married a warlock," Finch stated. He narrowed his eyes as he tried to recall the name. "L *something*. Lark. Or—"

"Papa's name is Liam."

"Yes. *Liam.*"

Finch remembered him. Liam was a warlock who had

made pacts with household spirits. A smaller man who loved crafting, who was always working on something new. That was how he'd met Vera. She had gone to him looking for magical devices to use in her garden.

Finch rubbed at his chin. "If someone broke into the house, Vera probably knew about it."

"She didn't," Bree muttered, her gaze unfocused.

"Trust me, kid. She's a witch who takes special care of her house."

"Mum *didn't* know. The man came out of nowhere."

Finch scoffed. "Look—"

"The intruder was there!" Bree shouted. She stood from the recliner, her mug spilling to the floor. More tears welled in the corners of her eyes. "I saw him. *I saw him.* He…" Bree grabbed the bottom of her hoodie with both hands. "I n-need your help because… the intruder killed Mum. And then he took Papa. And… and I'm afraid he might come back for me, too."

Finch glanced at the clock on the wall.

4:47 a.m.

CHAPTER
TWO

"W hen did this happen?" Finch asked, his voice low.

"A few hours ago," Bree whispered as she sank back onto the recliner. Her hands shook as she brought her knees up to her chest. After a deep breath, she closed her eyes. "I ran away while Papa fought the intruder. I… I didn't know where to go, or who to talk to. The mortal police won't know what to do. And Mum said to find the Finch brothers if ever there was trouble. She said you and Carter would help."

Damn.

Finch rubbed his temple, his eyes still on the clock. If only he had marked the time before going to sleep, instead of right when he woke. If he had done that, he might have been able to undo the whole situation, but as it stood, Finch didn't have that ability.

"Will you please help me?" Bree whispered.

"Had your mother angered someone?" Finch asked, ignoring her question.

Bree perked up, her eyes wide. "So you *will* help me?"

"Just answer my questions. Had your mother angered someone? Or something?"

Bree quickly shook her head. "No. She hadn't angered anyone."

"Had anyone been coming around the house who hadn't before?"

Again, Bree shook her head.

She held her knees tighter against her chest and scrunched her eyes shut. Although she had the magic of the calming tea in her system, the situation obviously still got to her, especially with intense questioning. Finch sighed and tried to think of simpler, easier questions.

"Had anything happened yesterday that was out of the ordinary?" Finch asked. "Before the intruder arrived, I mean. Anything at all? Even the slightest incident might be important."

"No," Bree whispered. "It was a normal day. Nothing had happened."

So there were no leads and no suspects? Finch exhaled harder than before. He had solved murders with less information in the past, but it had been arduous. And with a child involved, he suspected the ordeal would be more painful than it needed to be.

Bree opened her eyes and stared. "So... you *will* help me?"

"The city police have a warlock or two under contract to help them solve crimes when they involve witches or other magical phenomenon." Finch met her gaze with a cold one of his own. "They work right alongside the detectives. They'll help you just fine."

"Mum said the mortal police, and those who work for them, are incompetent." Bree gripped her pants. "If you can't help me..."

But she never finished her statement.

And the warlocks who worked for the city typically *were* incompetent, but Finch wasn't about to say that.

The clock on the wall was the loudest thing in the room. It ticked incessantly, grating on Finch's patience. He didn't want to get involved, but he couldn't say *no*, either. The girl clearly needed help, and once upon a time, when Finch still left the house, he had been friends with Vera. Perhaps, with his magic, he could *help* the local supernatural division of the police force get on the right track and then leave Bree in their care.

"I'll help you," Finch drawled.

Bree's eyes went wide. "Really?"

He stood from his recliner. "I'll do some preliminary investigations to help the police catch the murderer. But I'm not going to do anything else, understand?"

The halfway agreement didn't seem to sit well with Bree. She stayed seated on the recliner, her gaze falling to the dirty floor. After a quiet moment of contemplation, she finally nodded. "O-Okay. Thank you. I just... I really need your help, even if it's just a little bit of it."

Finch glanced around the living room, regretting all the life choices that had brought him here. Then he sighed. "We need to go to your house so I can look around."

Bree leapt off the recliner. She fidgeted with the sleeves of her hoodie as she said, "The police are probably there already. I think... the neighbors might've heard everything. There were sirens when I was running down the street."

Damn.

"They'll be looking for you," Finch stated.

Bree tensed, her posture stiff. "Please don't send me with the mortals. *Please.* I... I'm worried. If the intruder comes back, the mortal police won't be able to protect me."

That was probably true. If the murderer had the means to kill a witch and subdue a warlock, he was probably too dangerous for a normal police officer to handle. Would the murderer return for Bree, though? Since Finch had no idea what the man's motives were, it was difficult to tell.

"You'll stay with me," Finch stated.

He could protect her if she was close, even if he hated the thought of traveling around with a sad child the entire time.

Then Finch reached for a pile of laundry. He dug through the clothes, tossing aside anything he deemed irrelevant. Then he found the coat he needed. Finch tugged it free from a wad of gym clothes and brushed it off.

"If we go to my house, won't the police take me?" Bree whispered.

Finch tossed her the coat. It hit her in the chest, and Bree wrapped her arms around it in an awkward catch. Then she turned it around and frowned.

It was a thick, brown coat favored by rangers or particularly burly hikers. The fur-covered collar gave it an extra rugged feeling, but all the manliness was defeated by the streak of glitter on the left sleeve. The shimmery, almost rainbow stripe sparkled whenever the light hit it just right.

"What is this?" Bree asked.

"Put it on. The magicless won't see *you*. They'll see someone who belongs." Finch grabbed some semi-clean clothes from the next pile over. "If you're in a crowd, you'll just be another nameless face. If you're next to me, they'll see you as just my assistant. No one will see *Bree Blackstone* as long as you're wearing it."

"What if we run into a witch? Or a warlock? Or someone else magical?" Bree slipped her thin arms into the huge sleeves of her new coat. "What will happen then?"

"They'll see the real you. And they'll think you're wearing a stupid coat."

Once Bree was dressed, Finch realized the coat was about ten times too big. Bree could swim around inside it. Hell, the coat could double as a tent. Despite the fact that it was oversized, it would still work, that Finch was sure of. The coat's magic would shield Bree from the eyes of the mortals, which meant Finch would only have to be on guard when dealing with the magical.

"It smells like dirty socks," Bree whispered, her nose scrunched.

Finch huffed a sarcastic laugh. "That's probably the best-case scenario in this situation."

He stormed over to the bathroom and slid inside. Within a few seconds, he changed into a pair of wrinkled slacks, a button-up shirt, and a black coat. Then Finch grabbed a pair of boots off the bathroom counter and slipped his feet into them.

It was already 4:57 a.m.

Finch had twenty-three hours and thirty-seven minutes before he would need to reset time.

―――――

The drive across Stockton was a dreary one.

Gray mist rolled across the grimy streets, painting the city in gloom. Finch hadn't used his car in a few weeks. The old fast-food wrappers had fermented on the back seat that entire time, filling his Toyota Celica with a musk that was difficult to describe without using the word *rancid* more than once. He kept the window down, despite the bitter cold.

Bree shivered in her gigantic coat. She kept her arms folded over her chest, her attention on everything beyond the passenger-side window. Her breath fogged the glass, she sat so close.

The radio played soft pop music until a grating commercial killed the peace.

"*Are you ready for* Princess Problems Eighteen? *Gather the whole family together for this fun, animated adventure! Poor Princess Attica is at it again when—*"

Finch slammed the power button.

The fact that there were *eighteen* movies in a franchise called *Princess Problems* clearly proved they were all living in a simulation no one was maintaining. Finch couldn't stand listening to the preposterous sales pitch for something so trite.

"Mum took me to see *Princess Problems Sixteen* when it was in theaters," Bree muttered. She never turned to face Finch. Her breath coated the window so thick, it was impossible to see out of, yet she stared directly into the fog regardless.

Finch hated the commercial even more for stirring up such memories. If he was going to watch Bree while investigating, he needed her to remain calm, cool, and collected.

"Let's focus on the task at hand. You said your house is over this way?" Finch turned the vehicle toward an orchard, far from the bustle of Stockton's high-traffic areas.

"Yeah." Bree pointed to a road leading away from the highway. "Go that way. Just keep driving. It's the last house on the road, by the single streetlight."

Finch did as she instructed. The roads through the orchards eventually led to a street surrounded by trees. It was as though they had entered a forest, where the canopy of leaves overhead blocked out the small amount of dawn trying to pierce the fog.

The police tape told Finch which house was Vera's.

A whole gaggle of police cars surrounded the house, with three in the long driveway, and three parked on the sides of the street. Finch recognized the field forensics truck just beyond the single streetlamp. The police were still gathering evidence and evaluating the crime.

Perfect.

Finch parked his Toyota a good two hundred feet from the first police car. Then he switched off the engine and slid out. He turned his attention to Bree. "Stay here. This will only take a moment."

He shut the door and headed for the house.

Once Finch stepped onto the sidewalk across the street, he stopped and patted the pockets of his coat. Technically, Finch had once worked alongside the Stockton Police, aiding the supernatural division. That had been before he went private, opening an agency with his brother. The police chief at the time—someone in the know about all things supernatural—had insisted Finch keep his badge and permissions, and even called him from time to time to help with difficult cases.

Where was that badge now? If Finch flashed it to the beat cops, he could slip into the house and glance around, perhaps even speak with the police force warlock on duty.

He had left it in the car. In the glove compartment.

Finch turned on his heel and stomped over to the passenger-side door. He opened it, only to be greeted by Bree's sniffling.

She wiped tears from her eyes as she glanced up.

A long moment of silence stretched between them.

"What're you doing?" Finch demanded.

Bree swallowed and then managed to whisper, "I was just... thinking about Mum. I'll never see her again. And what will happen to Papa?" She glanced at the fog dancing between the trees and clasped her hands tightly together.

Finch silently cursed himself for thinking he could leave the girl all alone in a car. Even with the nerve-calming tea, she was still shaken by the recent events, and scared of her surroundings. Leaving her alone would only intensify her anxieties.

"You don't have to worry anymore," Finch said in a gruff and matter-of-fact tone. He grabbed the glove compartment and opened it up. Inside, he found his badge and a black Sharpie. "You've got me now, remember?"

Bree furrowed her brow. "But… the man who broke into our house… He… He was really strong."

Finch glared down at her and frowned. "Your mother said I was a powerful warlock, didn't she?"

"Yes."

"That's because I am."

Bree slowly turned her gaze to the moldy Burger King wrappers on the back seat, and then to the stained napkins on the floor of the car. With a frown, she glanced back up at Finch. "You're sure?"

Finch knelt next to the passenger-side seat. Then he uncapped the pen and motioned for Bree's arm. She hesitantly offered her right hand. Finch pushed up the sleeve of her coat and hoodie, and then placed the tip of the marker on her skin.

"Do you know how warlocks get their magic?" he asked as he drew a single straight line across her skin.

Bree half nodded. "Papa said he made pacts? With spirits? But I didn't learn much. Mum said I was going to become a witch, so I didn't need to use cheap tricks."

Cheap tricks.

Finch snorted as he drew a second straight line next to the first. "Warlocks get their powers from making pacts with *anything* magical. Spirits. Demons. Fae. Even old gods. If someone *has* magic, a warlock can make an agreement to gain access to that creature's abilities. Understand?"

"Yes."

Finch drew a third line on her arm. "The stronger the magical creature, the stronger the magic they can gift a warlock."

Bree nodded again. "But don't they ask for more in the pact? Papa said he didn't like spirits who were too powerful, because they asked for too much."

"Hm." With a steady hand, Finch drew a fourth line through the other three, creating a mark that resembled a line of lowercase *T*s. "That's true, but don't worry about that bit. All you need to know is that I made a pact with something very powerful."

"What?" Bree's eyes grew wide, and her fear waned.

Finch pointed to the mark he had drawn on her arm. "Do you recognize this?"

She shook her head.

"This is the *Mark of Chronos*. And now that I've drawn this on you, my magic will work twice as well." Finch stood and slid the pen into his coat pocket. "If your mother's killer is foolish enough to show himself while I'm around, he's a dead man."

Bree grazed her fingers over the mark. "Who is *Chronos*?"

"A powerful manipulator of time," Finch stated.

"What if…" Bree glanced up, her hand shaky. "What if the intruder is a warlock who also made a pact with Chronos? What will we do then?"

Finch chuckled at that question. It was a logical thought, but she didn't have to worry. "Chronos has only ever made pacts with two warlocks. Me, and my brother."

The information settled over Bree. She took a deep breath and then relaxed a bit into the seat of the car. Finch held out his hand, and she stared at it.

"C'mon," he said.

"You really think everything will turn out okay?" she whispered.

"If you're with me, nothing bad will happen."

Bree lit up as she grabbed his hand and leapt out of the vehicle. She jumped to his side and remained quiet, the stripe on her coat glittering, even in the fog, like a magical safety device.

Determined to see the scene of the crime, Finch headed toward the police tape around the driveway of Vera's home.

CHAPTER THREE

Vera had done well for herself.

Her house, situated in a small suburb of unique dwellings, had everything someone might want. A garden, a swimming pool, enough bedrooms to raise a large family, and a tree that provided shade without shedding too many of its leaves.

The neighbors were too close, though, but that was a universal problem in California. The backyards were long, but not wide.

Finch ducked under the police tape and headed for the front door, Bree close at his side. A half dozen police officers jumped from their vehicles, but the moment Finch flashed his badge, they stopped their panic and waved him through. A couple of them gave Bree odd glances, but no one said anything about her presence.

Finch entered through the front door. Bree slowed her pace, her face pale.

Her mother had died in this house, and supposedly, Bree had seen it all. Surely, she didn't want to wander back into the scene of the crime.

"You can wait here," Finch said.

Bree nodded once. She held her gigantic coat tight across her body, her gaze slowly losing focus as she clearly retreated into her thoughts.

The entrance hall wasn't long. Finch came to a T intersection and then turned left to enter the kitchen and dining room. An old clock hung on the wall, ticking away as he passed. The time was 6:57 a.m. Later than he would've liked.

Several forensic officers were already deep into their work all throughout the house. They took pictures from every angle, placed markers around anything they suspected as evidence, and carefully combed through Vera's belongings. The kitchen was especially busy, mostly because of how large it was.

A kitchen island stood in the middle of the room, one with a butcher block built into half the counter. It was obviously the site of the murder. Two built-in burners were positioned at one side, both stained with blood.

With just a quick glance, Finch suspected someone's head had hit the edge of the island. The other half of the countertop was made of stone, and last he checked, skulls didn't do so well in a matchup.

Blood also stained a large segment of the wooden floor. If Finch had to guess, Vera had been slammed against the stone portion of the island and then left on the floor to bleed out. Had she been stabbed? Likely. The bloodstains were large enough to point in that direction.

According to Bree, a strange man had been in the kitchen when she entered. Then her mother was killed, and then her father taken. It was dark. Bree hadn't seen many details. Had Vera been caught by surprise?

A man wearing jeans, a black shirt, and a matching black coat stood near the kitchen island. While the forensic team continued their detail-oriented work, the plain-clothes man stared at the blood and frowned. He was clearly a detective with the Stockton PD. They all wore casual outfits when on the job—at least all the higher-ranking ones.

Finch frowned.

He had met this detective before... What was his name?

The detective turned, his face set in a permanent glower. His brown hair was cut in a severe way—a part in the side of his hair so deep, one could see his scalp—and his chin was free from all stubble, though not from razor burn. He looked as though he had punished his face for merely existing.

That was when the name came back to Finch.

Rhett Jenner.

He had been a low-level detective back when Finch still actively worked with the police.

Detective Jenner glared, took a deep breath, no doubt preparing for a tirade, but then his eyes went wide. "*You?*" he asked, clearly dumbfounded.

"In the flesh," Finch quipped.

The other officers glanced up from their work. It was unusual for random people to stumble into a crime scene. They regarded Finch with suspicious glances and then turned their attention to Jenner, obviously waiting for his command.

Detective Jenner's face reddened slightly. He rubbed his jaw, his eyes narrowing. "You're Adair Finch. One of the *special* detectives."

Ah. Finch understood. This man knew he was a warlock, but didn't want to say it in front of the other officers, but he also needed to make everything seem legit.

Everyone resumed their work, even if they occasionally gave Finch a sidelong glance.

Before Finch could ask any questions, Detective Jenner waved his hand in the air. "Clear out," he commanded. "Take fifteen, and then come back and finish what you're doing as soon as possible."

The forensic crew—still halfway through their documentation—grumbled in irritation. The camera man turned, his mouth open, probably to protest, but Jenner snapped his fingers, and no one uttered any further objections. They cleared out of the kitchen and dining room, muttering observations to themselves as they went.

Once alone with Finch, Jenner shook his head. "We don't need your magic," he growled under his breath. "Me and my boys are capable of solving this without mumbo jumbo."

Finch huffed as he ambled around the butcher block.

There were a few on the police force who hated witches or warlocks helping out with their investigations. Some had damn good reasons, too. There was no way for mortals to double-check the investigation of the magical. They couldn't reproduce the results since they had no way to use the magic themselves. Therefore, they just had to take the witch's or warlock's word that everything was in order. And what if someone was lying?

On the other hand, criminals *using* magic to murder or cause mayhem couldn't be caught by mortal means. At least, not usually. Sometimes they could, but it was rare. So, in order to stop those criminals, magic had to be used to fight magic.

Detective Jenner followed Finch around the kitchen, keeping his distance. He moved with tense steps, his focus unwavering, his eyes following Finch's every glance.

"I thought you had retired," Jenner stated. "Last I heard, you were rotting away in an apartment somewhere, waiting for the sweet embrace of dementia."

"I'm only thirty-seven."

"Is that so? Heh. You might want to see a doctor."

Ignoring the commentary, Finch stopped next to the

stains on the floor. He knelt to examine the marking. Vera's body had already been removed, which was rather quick. Stockton PD wasn't known for their haste or efficiency.

"Who's the homicide sergeant overseeing this?" Finch asked.

"Sergeant McGregor is outside. I'm the lead detective. You can direct all your questions to me."

"How did Vera die?"

"You knew the victim personally?" Jenner pulled out his phone and tapped away at the screen. "I wasn't aware of that…"

Finch stood, his mind on the kitchen. Nothing else was out of place. Nothing was broken, there weren't other signs of a struggle, and besides the blood, the floor seemed clean enough to eat off.

And there was no real trace of magic.

If a handgun was fired, it left discharge residue. It was the same for most forms of magic. Finch had trained to detect the subtle changes in the air after large amounts of magic were used. The only sorcery he sensed was from the cupboards. He opened a few and found mason jars filled with strange liquids.

Witch's brews. All unlabeled.

But no evidence they had been opened anytime recently.

"Was any magic used at all?" Finch crossed his arms as he glanced around the kitchen for the fourth time. Surely Vera would've attempted to stop the killer with some form of magic. But perhaps she had been caught completely off guard? Magic was often difficult to perform when in distress or crippled by agony. If the killer had stabbed her, and then thrown her into the butcher block, she could've been knocked unconscious.

She wouldn't have the ability to use magic then.

Jenner scoffed. "Listen, this isn't the kind of case that

requires your skill. As far as we can tell, no magic was used. Victim died of five puncture wounds to the chest. The knife was recovered from the floor. Husband disappeared afterward, along with their preteen daughter, and his vehicle. I've seen this all before."

"You have?" Finch asked, dry and almost sarcastic.

"Of course. It's *always* the spouse." Detective Jenner tucked his phone away in his coat. "The neighbor to the north overheard the victim and her husband arguing an hour before the time of death. Before you showed up, claiming to know the victim, there were no other leads or hints to anyone else other than the husband."

Arguing?

Bree hadn't mentioned that part of the story.

Finch faced the detective with a sneer. "Wait, now *I'm* a suspect, is that it?"

"All you kooky *Harry Potter wannabes* get yourselves into trouble with each other all the time. I wouldn't be surprised if you turned up here just to hide your tracks."

Jenner walked over to the fridge and examined the business cards stuck to the surface. One was for pizza, but one had no name or logo—just a number. Those were the types of business cards warlocks and witches used. Plain. Not conspicuous. And Jenner must've known the trick, because he pulled out his phone and took a picture of the whole front of the fridge.

"You have no idea where Vera's husband went?" Finch asked.

The detective shook his head. "Since the man wasn't very social, we haven't had many leads. Plus, we're concerned someone might be hiding him. And since he is *also* a weird magic-wielding degenerate, he's probably in an invisible basement, far from our grasp."

"Huh. Then you might need my skills after all, right?"

Jenner turned to Finch with a hard-set expression that bordered on a challenge.

After a long stare, Finch half smiled. "How about you point me in a direction so I can help you find the invisible basement Liam is hiding in? That's my job, after all." Finch flashed his badge.

Jenner exhaled.

His expression never softened, though. He was tense. He had been the entire time. Jenner never showed even a slight hint of relaxing.

Jenner tucked his hands into his coat pockets. "The victim's husband, Liam Blackstone, is some college professor despite the fact he's another weirdo with a pointed hat, just like his wife. He works at the University of the Pacific. Other than heading to the campus, the neighbors say he doesn't get out much. Apparently, he was seen burying a couple cats in the backyard a few weeks ago."

"And that's why you're certain he's the killer?" Finch asked, lifting an eyebrow.

"The man has more red flags than the Beijing Olympics. Who else would it be?"

Burying cats in the backyard? While that was a strange bit of information, Finch figured it could be related to Vera's or Liam's magical research. Witches often needed blood or other body parts for some of their brews. And she had a lot of brews.

Then again, Liam could just be a man lacking empathy, whose lust for blood had finally hit a dangerous tipping point. Cats no longer satisfied him. Finch didn't really know Liam, not like he had known Vera.

"Thanks," Finch muttered. He walked around the butcher block and headed for the hallway. "If I find anything, I'll let you know."

"Locating the victim's daughter is our number one

priority," Jenner stated. "If you see her—or even discover a hint she's alive and well—you tell us immediately, do you understand?"

"Sure. I'll do that."

Detective Jenner stepped close to Finch before he exited the kitchen. He pulled out his own card, one embossed with the Stockton PD's symbol—a deer standing in front of a boat. His name was displayed prominently on the right-hand side.

"*This isn't a game.* If you're still a master at solving crimes, you'll focus all your efforts on the victim's daughter." Jenner thrust the card toward Finch. "She's twelve. Shoulder-length brown hair. On the smaller side. She answers to *Bree*. Got all that? She may be in serious danger, and I'll be damned if a kid dies on my case."

Finch tucked the card away. "If I find her, I'll call." Then he headed down the hall, turned toward the front door, and spotted Bree leaning against the door handle.

She glanced up as Finch approached, her eyebrows knitted. "Did you figure out who did it?" Bree whispered.

"You didn't tell me your parents were having an argument," Finch said, ignoring her question. He opened the door and stepped outside.

"I didn't think it was important." Bree leapt to his side and matched his pace. She kept her arms crossed and her gaze on the ground. "They were just arguing about Papa's work. It wasn't anything."

As they left the driveway and headed for the neighbor's house, Finch huffed. "You're *certain* there was a strange man in your house? Are you sure it wasn't your father in the dark, and you just didn't recognize him?"

"There was someone else," Bree said, no hesitation in her voice. "He was waiting in the kitchen. Mum and Papa were back in their room. I'm super certain."

Finch mulled over her statements. Was a twelve-year-old

reliable? No. Definitely not. They were often confused about details, and easily frightened, which led to misinformation. Finch had once questioned a small boy who had sworn there was a monster in his closet because he heard strange noises. Turned out, the pipes in the wall had broken, and the splash of water was the "monster" he had heard.

What if Bree had seen her father, but the trauma of the event made her think it had to be someone else entirely? It was possible. Stranger things had happened.

"Did the stranger try to attack you?" Finch asked.

Bree frowned. "The man attacked Mum and then Papa. I… I ran away after. I think the man chased me, but once I was outside, he didn't follow."

Another new detail. And another indicator that it was probably her father. Liam didn't want to kill his little girl.

As Finch stepped onto the neighbor's long driveway, a series of eerie caws drew his attention upward, to the branches of a tall oak tree. Fat ravens sat between the leaves, perched up high enough that no human could reach them, even with a jump.

One of the ravens stared down at Finch with unnatural, red eyes. When Finch met the creature's gaze, he stopped and tensed. Bree stood close, her brow furrowing the moment she caught sight of the strange beast.

"What's that?" she whispered.

"A *corpse biter*," Finch replied. "A shady spirit drawn to dead bodies."

CHAPTER
FOUR

"**D**o you have a minute to spare, spirit?" Finch asked, keeping his volume low. He didn't want to draw the attention of the police officers next door. While most would never see the corpse biter, they would find it odd that Finch was talking to a group of ravens.

The corpse biter tilted its bird-like head. Without blinking its red eyes, it cawed out a laugh. "What do you want, warlock? Do you wish to make a pact?" Its voice was raspy and quiet, almost lost between the noises made by the many corvids all around.

"No," Finch quickly stated. "I want to know if you've seen anything."

"Anything? I've seen many things." The corpse biter tilted its head to the other side.

"A witch died here last night."

The corpse biter fluffed its black feathers and cawed another laugh, this one crueler than before. "I know. I smelled it."

Bree clenched her hands tightly into fists. She said nothing, but she grew stiffer with each passing moment.

"Did you see who killed her?" Finch asked.

"I did not." The corpse biter smoothed its black feathers. "I arrived after she died. I came for her garden, but I had hoped to see her body. The humans took it away before I could feast."

"You came for her garden?"

"Oh, yes." The ravens around the corpse biter cawed with enthusiasm. "Her garden is filled with bodies. So many delicious bodies."

All the color drained from Bree's face.

"*Human* bodies?" Finch asked. Corpse biters didn't care where they found undead flesh. They just wanted something rotten and decayed. The body of a human was just as good as the body of a crusty fish.

"No. Only cats. Disgusting, vile cats."

Again, the ravens cawed, their jubilation heard in the high-pitched cracks of their calls.

Detective Jenner had mentioned that Liam was caught burying a few animals. Finch was still convinced it didn't have much to do with Vera's murder, but he couldn't rule it out completely. Therefore, he wanted to know more. "How many cats are buried in the garden?" Finch asked. "Two? Three?"

"Sixty."

"*Sixty?*" Finch balked. "Six-zero?"

"Yes, warlock. That's what I said."

A couple cats could be explained away, but *sixty*? Finch didn't have an explanation for that. Why would Liam butcher so many cats and then bury them in his backyard? Perhaps he really was a psychopath.

It was looking more likely by the second.

"Do you know why your father would kill cats?" Finch asked as he turned his attention to Bree.

She fidgeted with the long sleeves of her coat. "Papa

didn't kill cats. There's no way. He's really kind and nice. You have to believe me."

Either Bree wasn't telling him the truth, or she just didn't know the truth. Either way, Finch wasn't about to get the information he needed from her. He rubbed at his chin, trying to make sense of this new information.

The ravens continued their incessant cawing. The corpse biter didn't join in. It just stared at Finch, waiting.

Done with the conversation, Finch headed up the driveway to the neighbor's house. The spirit watched him go, its unblinking red eyes following Finch's every movement.

Bree hurried to stay close. "Why didn't you make a pact with that spirit?" she asked. "Don't warlocks want to make pacts with as many things as they can? Then you'll have more magic."

"Firstly—when I make a pact, I have to do something for the spirit. Either give them something I own, which can include things like *body parts*, or do something they ask of me, which is usually tedious or sinister. Nobody has time for that shit." Finch hesitated after the last word. He glanced over at Bree. Her eyes had gone wide. "Pretend you didn't hear that."

She stared at him with a sardonic glower. "I've been on the internet longer than thirty minutes. I've been exposed to worse things than the word *shit*."

Damn kids these days. "Whatever." Finch shook his head. He went straight for the front door. Gnomes were stationed all along the grass under every windowsill. If he had to guess, he would say the place was owned by someone well above their seventies.

When they reached the door, he stopped and said, "Secondly—corpse biters don't have many useful magical abilities. Perhaps if I wanted to eat decaying flesh, I'd make a pact then. But unless I'm stuck in a ditch, surrounded by gangrenous bodies, I doubt I'll need the ability."

"You know what abilities a corpse biter can offer?" Bree whispered.

"Of course." Finch scoffed. "I've been a warlock for decades. And corpse biters are quite common."

"That's so cool." Bree crossed her arms and half shrugged. "Papa didn't talk to me much about spirits and demons and things. I think it was because Mum told him not to."

"Witches have their own innate magic. You'll develop your own abilities."

"I know... I just think it's awesome to make deals with creatures and get all sorts of interesting powers."

Finch held up his hand. "Enough of this. I need to question your neighbor. Don't talk unless I address you, got it?"

Bree glanced at the door and then back to Finch. With a frown, she said, "This is Miss Baker's house. She doesn't like it when anyone visits."

"This'll be quick," Finch stated. "And then we're going to head to your father's work."

The information slowly settled over Bree. She returned to her quiet state, her attention on the ground. Finch wasn't sure what she was worried about, but he didn't want to think about it, either.

Finch banged on the front door to Miss Baker's house. When no one answered, he did it again, only louder. Bree shuffled closer to his side. The sun was rising into the sky, burning away some of the fog.

The front door finally opened, but only a small amount. An elderly woman poked half her head outside, her thick glasses resting on her large nose. Her schnoz dominated her whole face, actually. The perfect body part for consuming cocaine, though Finch kept that joke to himself. The lady wore a floral dress, and her glasses were secured around her neck with a silver chain. She wasn't the type to vacuum up a bunch of drugs with a single inhale.

"Who're you?" the woman asked. Her gray hair was tied tightly behind her head in a neat bun, and she smoothed it as she creaked open the door a bit further.

"I'm with the Stockton PD," Finch stated. "Are you Miss Baker?"

"I've already given my formal statement, thank you very much. I'm not in the mood for any more questions."

"This will only take a moment." Finch wasn't a master of charisma. All he wanted was a few minutes of this woman's time, but most people found parting with their precious minutes too much of an ordeal. "I just want to ask you about last night."

Miss Baker frowned. "Hm! This is just a waste of my time. How unprofessional. If you knew what you were doing, you'd read the report the previous detective wrote."

"Ma'am, trust me. This is important. Do I look like a man who would waste your time?"

The old woman gave Finch the once-over. "You look like a man who's legally required to introduce himself to his neighbors."

Finch dragged a hand down his face as he exhaled. He felt like hot garbage, his clothes were wrinkled, and he wanted nothing more than to sleep for three more hours, but he didn't have the luxury of rest until he was done with this. Why was a little old lady one of his obstacles?

Why?

"Miss Baker, please help him," Bree said. She stepped forward. "He's trying to catch Mum's killer. And remember how Mum helped you with all that gardening and—"

"*Mum?*" Miss Baker barked. "Whose mum? Who are you? I've never met you before in my life."

Finch grabbed the front of Bree's coat and pulled her away from the front door. He turned slightly to face her and hissed under his breath, "What did I say about the coat? She doesn't see *you*."

Bree bit her lip. "I'm sorry. I forgot." Then she straightened her posture and glared. "I'm just trying to help."

"Stand right here. I'll handle this." Finch whirled on his heel. "Sorry about that, Miss Baker. We're just passionate about… the law. It would be helpful if you could tell me about your neighbors. Did you hear them arguing?"

"Last night?" The elderly woman rubbed at her hip. "Oh, yes. I couldn't sleep. The weather wakes me. It's been getting cold."

"Uh-huh. If you heard them, can you tell me what their argument was about?"

Typically, if someone killed their spouse, it was one of three reasons. Money, sex, or child custody. If Liam and Vera had been arguing about one of those three things last night, Finch would close the investigation and declare Vera's husband the killer.

"They were arguing about necklaces," Miss Baker said, her own words more of a question than a confident statement. "Vera yelled something about how they had too many. Her husband—a quiet man, those are always the weirdos—shouted something about needing to make them."

Make them?

He made *necklaces?*

Finch stared at the older woman, one of his eyebrows lifting to his hairline. He hadn't been expecting that explanation. Why would they argue about jewelry? And Vera hadn't wanted Liam to make anymore? Had he been getting too aggressive at the local flea market?

What was this?

"Uh… right." Finch cleared his throat. "Anything else?"

"No. Just the necklaces."

"What about them? Any other details would be appreciated."

"Just that Liam was making too many. Didn't you hear me?"

Finch held back a sigh. "One last question. Did you ever see Liam burying things in the garden? Animals, perhaps?"

Miss Baker nodded once. "Lately, he was in the garden all the time at night. Burying things. I told him it was suspicious to do it in the dark, but he just chuckled. I never liked him much."

"Thanks for your time," Finch muttered as he turned away.

He took Bree by the arm and guided her down the long driveway. The crows cawed as they walked by, the corpse biter still perched in the middle of the flock. Its red eyes remained bright in the shadows of the tree's canopy.

"I'm sorry," Bree said. "But I really do want to help."

"Who's the professional? You? Or me?"

"I'm a witch. And it's *my* mum. I figured I could help."

Finch led her to the side of his Toyota and stopped. He wasn't sure how to answer that. He wasn't sure he could.

"And Papa didn't kill any cats," Bree said. She yanked her arm out of Finch's grasp and rubbed at her bicep. "I don't care what Miss Baker or the corpse biter said. He's really nice, and he wouldn't do that."

Finch gave her a sidelong glance. "Remember how I said that some spirits or demons can require bizarre tasks for their pacts? It might be that your father is fulfilling some creature's requirement."

"Really?" Bree crossed her arms. "You think so?"

"I'm not sure. I don't have enough information yet."

"Can we figure it out?"

"If I can talk to whatever he made a pact with. But he might just be insane for all we know."

"He's not insane. We can just rule that out."

Finch opened the Toyota's passenger door. "Let's focus on finding your father. We'll figure out the motives for everything later."

Bree slowly took a seat in his car. Then she tapped her fingertips together. After glancing up at him, she asked, "You believe me, right? That Papa is kind and gentle and he wouldn't hurt anyone? He definitely didn't hurt Mum."

"I believe that's what you think of him," Finch stated.

Bree glanced down at the dashboard. She had no further words for him.

Finch closed the door and made his way around to the driver's side. All signs pointed to Bree's father as the killer. Perhaps for bizarre reasons—like arguments over necklaces —but that was where the case was heading. Finch made a mental note to himself. If Liam's coworkers gave Finch more reasons to suspect the man, he'd give Bree over to the police, watch from afar, and take down Liam himself.

That was probably the best course of action.

CHAPTER
FIVE

The sun burned away the last of the mist. Driving across Stockton wasn't as bad once the daylight had chased away the gloom. It was long, though. Friday mornings were the worst for traffic.

7:32 a.m.

Finch kept his eye on the GPS screen mounted to his car dashboard. He made mental notes about the timeline, and everything he knew so far. From what he had gathered, the murder was rather straightforward.

Firstly, Liam had been killing cats. Too many cats. Even if he was harvesting them for witch's brew, it was too much. One cat could make a year's worth of potions and tonics. Why would anyone need to kill *sixty*? Was it to appease his sick sense of pleasure? Or something to do with his magic? Either way, it was a bizarre facet that Finch needed to consider.

Secondly, Liam and Vera had argued about necklaces the night of her death. Loudly enough that one of the neighbors heard.

Thirdly, Vera had been stabbed to death. Either quickly or by surprise. Too fast for her to use her magic in response.

Lastly, Liam had disappeared shortly afterward.

As Finch navigated the roads to the University of the Pacific, he contemplated heading back to Vera's house. If Liam was making necklaces, surely there would be a few around. Perhaps they would give him some insight into their argument.

But if I find Liam, I can just ask him myself, Finch reasoned.

The silence in the vehicle hadn't bothered Finch. He preferred the quiet. So, when Bree shifted in her seat and turned to face him, even the tiniest of creaks caught his attention.

"Papa surprised me and Mum on Valentine's Day last year. He took us to the ice-skating rink." Bree crossed her arms over her chest. "And he said we were the two most important girls in his life."

"Great," Finch drawled.

"And for Summer Solstice, we all went camping, and Papa made a pact with a woodland spirit so he could talk to the animals. He showed me all the wildlife around the lake. We petted these bunnies, and also some gophers, and all the birds. All day long!"

Witches celebrated all the solstices and equinoxes. They were important holidays since the abilities of witches were often heightened by the phases of the sun and the moon. Camping on Summer Solstice was common for witches and their families.

"Vera didn't have a coven?" Finch absentmindedly asked. Covens often celebrated their holidays together.

"Mum was a *waning crescent witch*. That means—"

"She did all her magic on her own," Finch stated, fully aware of all the types of witches, though he had forgotten Vera's specific type. That made everything more difficult, however. If Vera'd had a coven, they would've helped with the investigation.

Bree turned away. She was quiet for a long moment before breaking the silence once again. "Also, Papa surprised us one night by making cookies. He, uh, let me help make the frosting. And…" Bree rubbed at her face, her eyes growing watery. "And Mum kept pretending she couldn't spread the frosting right, so that Papa would c-come over and help, just so she could kiss him."

She rubbed her face harder than before.

"How about we listen to the radio?" Finch reached over to turn on music, but Bree shot her hand out and stopped him.

"No, I have to tell you all this," she said, defiant.

"Why? To prove your father's a *good guy*?"

Bree nodded once.

"That doesn't mean he's not a murderer."

"I just think you should look for the *real* killer and not even consider Papa. He didn't do it."

"Are you convincing me? Or trying to convince yourself?" Finch glanced over. Bree glared back at him, her posture stiff.

She didn't say anything else. She just glowered, equal parts angry and upset. The midnight raspberry tea would help calm her, but it clearly wasn't potent enough to remove all the powerful feelings that arose from the situation.

Finch pulled the car into the university parking lot, following the signs all the way to the faculty area. The University of the Pacific favored brick facades and old-world architecture. There was a clock tower, several long buildings and auditoriums, and even a damn chapel on the campus. As a private university, it could spend its money in almost any way it saw fit, and appearances was clearly one of their top priorities.

The number of stained-glass windows was unusually high. Same with the number of trees.

It was beautiful, but Finch imagined it would be quite easy to get lost.

Finch parked in the spot marked **DR. BLACKSTONE.**

"This is Papa's spot," Bree whispered.

"If we're lucky, he'll come out to tell us to move," Finch quipped as he killed the engine and stepped out of the car. "C'mon. Let's speak with some of your father's coworkers about his last known activities."

"O-Okay." Bree hopped out of the car and quietly shut the door. She hurried to Finch's side, her attention on their beautiful surroundings. Several fountains were positioned between buildings, most of which were multiple stories tall.

While Finch wanted to speak to a few of the magicless workers of the school, he sensed a wellspring of magical energy close by. After tucking his hands into his pockets, he wandered toward a group of oak trees near the edge of the parking lot.

What a strange place for a creature to dwell.

"Where are we going?" Bree whispered.

"Something is nearby." Finch pointed to the spot between the trees. A small hole—something a normal person would mistake for a gopher dwelling—was near the trunk of the largest tree. "There."

"Is it a spirit?"

They stopped walking once they reached the cluster of trees. Finch held out his hand, stopping Bree from getting any closer. Then Finch glanced around. It was still too early. Not many students were wandering the campus.

"It's not a spirit," Finch muttered. He returned his attention to the hole. "It's one of the fae-folk. A dwarf."

"Fae-folk?"

"That's right. Warlocks have classifications for all types of magical entities. The rule of thumb is: if the creature can sometimes pass as a person, it's probably fae-folk. Elves. Dwarves. You get the picture."

Bree nodded along with his words, her eyes wide. "Papa made a pact with a dwarf."

"Then there's a good chance *this* is the dwarf who knows your father." Finch stepped over the roots of the trees and then knelt next to the hole. He was about to interact with the creature, when Bree hurried and knelt next to him.

"Can I question the dwarf?" she asked.

"Do I have to keep reminding you who the professional is?"

Bree lifted one knee close to her chest. "I really want to help, and… This is Papa's creature he made a pact with, right? I want to know more about it. Maybe since I'm magical, and *it's* magical, it wouldn't mind talking to me."

Finch pinched the bridge of his nose. Allowing her to "help" would only slow things down. Then again, dwarves were some of the friendliest of the fae-folk. They appreciated the ingenuity of mankind, and admired their craftsmanship. Because of that, dwarves made easier pacts with warlocks, and often interacted with humans, though in subtle ways.

Bree stared at him with a slight frown. She said nothing, just waiting with bated breath for Finch's decision.

"Fine," Finch said with a groan.

Bree's expression lit up, a smile appearing instantly. "Really?"

"Go on." Finch motioned to the hole. "If I need to, I'll take over."

Giddy, Bree leaned in close to the hole. She yelled, *"Hello,"* at a volume even the deaf could hear.

Finch grabbed the shoulder of her coat and yanked her away from the opening. *"Keep your voice down!"* he hissed. "What the hell are you doing?"

"What else should I do?" Bree whispered. She pulled her coat from his grip and bunched her shoulders at the base of her neck. "You don't have to yell. If you just *told me* what to do, I'd do it, okay? I've never interacted with spirits and stuff."

She had made that clear, Finch had just forgotten. His tirade died in his throat before he could voice it. This was *his* problem. If he had been clearer, Bree wouldn't have messed up. He dragged a hand down his face and sighed, frustrated with both the situation, and himself.

"Listen," he muttered. "The fae are prim and proper. You have to *knock* at the entrance to their dwellings or else they'll ignore you."

"Knock?" Bree rubbed at her shoulder. With a frown, she turned her gaze to the dirt.

After a long sigh, Finch motioned to the trunk of the tree. "Knock here. Then say hello." Before Bree did anything, Finch held up a hand. "Another rule of thumb. The fae love etiquette and formality. They have courts and rules of social engagement and all sorts of irritating nonsense, got it?"

Bree nodded once. "Wow. Really? That's so cool." She glanced at the tree. "Um, okay. I should say hello?"

Finch glanced at the clock on his phone. 7:43 a.m.

"And use your full name," he said as he tucked his phone away. "The fae trust people who use their full name more than someone who doesn't introduce themselves."

Bree's smile returned. "You really know a lot. Okay. I'll do that." She knocked on the side of the tree and then scooted closer to the hole. "Hello. My name is Bree Blackstone, and this is Adair Finch."

Hot air rushed up from the depths. It smelled of sulfur and copper.

Dwarves didn't like the light. Finch knew the creature

wouldn't venture to the surface, not while the sun hung in the sky.

"Salutations," a rusty voice echoed up from the depths of the hole. "Long has it been since I had new visitors come to call."

"Can we speak to you for a moment?" Bree asked. "About your warlock, Liam Blackstone."

Finch rolled his eyes. She just *assumed* this was the right dwarf, rather than asking for confirmation first. It didn't matter too much, but Finch made a mental note to correct her line of questioning if this ever happened again.

A deep chuckle wafted up to the surface. "Liam is a private man. So am I."

"He might be in trouble," Finch interjected. "You wouldn't want to lose your pact with him, would you?"

No creature wanted to lose their warlock. Making pacts was the fastest way for spirits, demons, and other creatures to get exactly what they wanted. Dwarves always wanted crafting materials. Their pacts involved long-term agreements for supplies. Liam was no doubt dropping things into the creepy hole on a regular basis.

"I'm his daughter," Bree said. "And everything Mr. Finch said is true. My papa is in trouble. Can you help us?"

Another blast of hot air shot from the hole. The dwarf groaned and shifted underground. The nearby trees shuddered. "You smell of his blood. You *are* his offspring. But the warlock with you is… quite powerful. You don't need my assistance when you have his."

Bree glanced over at Finch. "The dwarves know about you?" she whispered.

"My brother and I were well known." Finch shrugged. "That was a long time ago."

"I just need to know a few things," Bree said into the hole. "Please, Mr. Dwarf. It'll only be a moment."

After another rush of hot air, the dwarf replied. "Fine. Ask me your questions. What do you need to know?"

"Do you think Papa is a good man? Kind and trustworthy, I mean?"

The dwarf scoffed. Soot and smoke puffed out of the hole. "The morals of dwarves and mankind do not mix. I know little of Liam. I cannot judge him."

"Does Liam have a pact with a creature to kill cats?" Finch asked, interjecting before Bree could ask more inane questions.

The dwarf chuckled a second time. "No. None of his current pacts require the blood of felines."

As far as Finch was concerned, it wasn't looking good for Liam. He wasn't magically compelled to kill cats. Then why have sixty of them in his backyard? He probably *was* a bloodthirsty lunatic. That was the most logical explanation.

"What was your agreement with Liam?" Finch asked.

"He would provide me with various types of metal. In exchange, I would make it easier for him to craft things. His hands can mold metal like clay. His magics can become permanently affixed to objects. He can sense the purpose of crafted magical items, and use them without instruction."

"And you *only* required metals?"

"Yes, warlock. Metals. I need materials for my forge. Once I've finished my masterpiece, I'll be remembered forever in both song and stone." The dwarf's rusty voice was accompanied by another round of hot air.

"Do you know where Papa is right now?" Bree asked. She scooted closer to the hole. "We're trying to find him."

"I don't. Every fortnight, Liam would leave two pounds of metals by the tree, and I would fetch them once the moon rose. We didn't interact."

Finch stood with a groan. "Thanks, dwarf. We'll look elsewhere."

Bree stood as well, her attention on the hole. "Thank you so much."

The dwarf replied with, "I will speak well wishes to the fire of the forge until his safe return. Farewell."

Then Bree glanced over at Finch. She frowned and crossed her arms. "You *really* think it's Papa now, don't you?"

"Listen, kid." Finch tucked his hands into the pockets of his coat. "Sometimes life is complicated. Maybe it would be best if you stayed with Detective Jenner. He can get you in touch with some of your relatives while the police wrap things up."

Was Finch even required for this murder? Would his magic even help with solving such a straightforward case? Perhaps it was best if Bree just had time to grieve and come to terms with reality. Besides, if her father had killed her mother, she shouldn't be involved in uncovering that horrible truth.

A car drove into the faculty parking lot. A small thing—some sort of black Nissan—and Finch turned to face it. The vehicle pulled up next to Finch's Toyota. With his sights set, Finch ambled over, determined to finish up his preliminary questioning and go home.

I have Jenner's cellphone number. I can call him after this.

A thin man, half broomstick, half coatrack, stepped out of the Nissan. He wore gold-rimmed glasses, a vest, a button-up shirt, and a pair of well-ironed slacks. For whatever reason, perhaps an affront to the fashion spirits, the man had opted for *all brown*. Everything from his shoes to his tie was some shade of brown.

A questionable choice.

His outfit matched his oak-colored hair, at least.

When Finch neared, the man grimaced and leaned against his little car. "Uh, hello?" the man asked. "Is this *your* vehicle?" He pointed to the Toyota. "That's a reserved parking spot. I'll have to call—"

Bree hurried up next to Finch and stared with wide eyes. "Dr. Colton?" she asked.

"Bree?" Dr. Colton asked, his eyes going equally wide. "W-What're you doing here? And with this... strange, homeless man?"

Finch scratched at his chin. Dr. Colton could see through the magic of the coat. "I'm here to question Liam Blackstone's coworkers. I'm a PI working with the Stockton PD." He flashed his badge, but not long enough to actually convey much information, just long enough to seem official. "I need just a few moments of your time."

Dr. Colton fumbled for a moment, patting at the pockets of his slacks. He quickly withdrew his cellphone and tapped away at the screen. "R-Right."

"What're you doing?"

"Oh, um, texting my assistant. I need to tell them I'll be late. It's almost the start of my first class."

"Uh-huh."

Finch didn't believe him at all. Dr. Colton sweated like a sinner in church. The man tapped at the phone screen with shaky and unsteady pokes, hesitation present throughout all of his body motions.

"Are you aware that Liam's wife, Vera, was murdered last night?" Finch asked. He kept his hands in his pockets, trying to be calm enough for the two of them.

"*What?* Oh, my goodness." Dr. Colton shoved his phone into his slacks and shook his head. And then he shook it again. "I had no idea. That's awful." He glanced at Bree. "And... you're here? With *him?*"

"He's helping me," Bree stated. "He was Mum's friend." She stepped closer to Finch. "But how can you see me? I thought..."

The coat protected her from the eyes of the magicless. Something was different about Dr. Colton, though. He wasn't a warlock—Finch was certain of that—but if he saw Bree for who she was, he wasn't *magicless*, either.

"You're right here, in an almost empty parking lot." Dr. Colton pulled his phone out a second time and tapped at it again. "This isn't the time for childish games. I just didn't expect you to be out and about with a detective. Why aren't you in police custody? Safe at the police station?"

"When was the last time you saw Liam Blackstone?" Finch asked, ignoring Dr. Colton's attempts to speak to Bree.

"L-Last night. In the labs. He was working late on some personal project." Dr. Colton glanced back down at Bree. "Are you sure you don't want me to take you somewhere safe, Bree? It seems odd that you're out here with this man, even if he's a great detective."

"I saw someone murder Mum," Bree said, her voice wavering a bit when she said it. "Dr. Colton, you have to tell us all about how Papa was hardworking and kind and how he wouldn't do anything to harm anyone."

Finch shot her a glare. Her trying to influence the witnesses would make his job harder. It wasn't the biggest deal, but he wished the girl would just allow him to do his work. Why was she so insistent?

"You *saw* someone kill your mom?" Dr. Colton repeated, his voice low.

"That's right," Bree said. "I did. Last night. Please, Dr. Colton. *We have to find him.*"

Again, Dr. Colton tapped away at his phone. He shook his head and muttered things to himself. Finch didn't like the man. He was clearly agitated, but not elaborating. Dr. Colton knew something he didn't want to share, and the man desperately wanted out of the situation.

"I think we should go inside," Dr. Colton said, motioning

to one of the far buildings. The red bricks were half covered in green ivy. "We can talk more inside. Quickly."

Finch sighed.

Right as he was about to turn to head inside, a loud *crack* rang out across the parking lot.

Blood splattered across the Nissan. Dr. Colton hit the side of the vehicle and tumbled to the asphalt, a hole in the side of his chest, his brown outfit quickly soaking in crimson.

Another *crack,* and Finch understood what was happening. Someone was shooting at them. Somewhere far off. Only rifles made that harsh kind of *bang* that sounded like something cracking in half.

Bree didn't even have time to cry out. She fell forward, shot in the back, and hit the ground hard.

A third shot was coming, but Finch didn't give the shooter a chance.

Finch manipulated time itself.

Everything froze. The leaves in the trees, the cars on the distant road—even the wind.

Then the color drained from the world, turning it into a black-and-white movie devoid of all vibrancy. The shadows were pitch black, and the sky a pool of pristine white.

One by one, all the nearby objects melted away, unraveled by Chronos's powerful and disturbing time magic. The university disappeared. The cars disappeared. Even the people—Bree and Dr. Colton—until there was nothing left but an empty, white void.

Finch's body jerked. He blinked his eyes.

And then he was back in his bed, dressed in his ratty pajamas, flailing around in the sheets. He sat up, his heart hammering.

His phone displayed the time.

4:34 a.m.

CHAPTER
SIX

F inch leapt out of his bed and stumbled through his dark apartment. He went straight for the front door, unlocked it, and then threw it open. Bree stood out in the dimly lit hallway, her eyes wide, her body shaking.

Bree wore the clothing Finch had met her in. A black hoodie. Jeans. His oversized coat with a rainbow stripe was nowhere to be seen—because it was back in a pile in the middle of Finch's living room.

With her eyes still wide, Bree turned to face him. *"I was shot,"* she whispered. "There was so much blood…"

Finch grabbed her arm and pulled her inside. Bree didn't put up a fight. She muttered disbelieving statements as Finch switched on the light and immediately went for his bread box. Inside, he found a single package of midnight raspberry tea. The last one in his possession. For a second time.

He grabbed a mug, snapped his finger, heating the water, and dipped the bag into the boiling liquid.

"You're fine," Finch said as he waited for the calming brew to finish. "Everything is fine. This is fine."

Bree shivered. Then she rubbed at her arms, silent tears running down her face. "Dr. Colton... He was shot, too."

Once the tea was ready, Finch led Bree into the living room. He shoved the clothes off his spare chair—a metal something hitting the floor with a loud *clunk*—and then Finch sat Bree down and handed her the drink.

"Drink this," he commanded. "And don't worry about any of that. It didn't actually happen."

Bree trembled as she brought the mug to her lips. Finch feared she would spill the drink all over her hoodie, but she sipped the liquid just fine. After a few gulps, Bree managed to control her shaking. She glanced around until her gaze finally settled on the clock hung on the far wall.

"It's... in the morning?" she whispered.

Finch took a seat in his favorite recliner. He ran a hand down his face and nodded. "Yes. Exactly. Everything is great, and we're back in my apartment, far from everyone else."

The clock ticked loud enough to fill the living room with white noise. Bree sipped more of her tea, her nerves clearly calming. She swirled her drink around in her mug before finally turning her gaze fully to Finch.

"You can rewind time?" she whispered.

"That's right," Finch stated.

Bree scooted to the edge of her seat. "Well, then, *rewind time some more*. Rewind it until Mum is alive, and we can stop the murderer!" She gripped the mug too tightly, her fingers practically bone white.

"My ability doesn't work that way," Finch drawled. He had known he would have to explain this at some point, but he dreaded doing it. Few people understood. "Here's how it works. I mark a specific time—in this case, 4:34 a.m.—and I can rewind time to that point, and *that point only*. I can't go any earlier."

Bree's shoulders drooped. She stared at the floor, her

eyebrows knitted. "Oh. I get it. It's like a save point in a video game. And you already saved your game beyond the point that Mum died. Now you can't go back."

Somehow, even though Finch had described this ability to dozens of people, the twelve-year-old girl understood it better than anyone previously. He pinched the bridge of his nose, both impressed and concerned, since he didn't play many video games. *Maybe I should start.*

"Technically, if I allow time to flow beyond twenty-four hours after I marked the time, my marker has to be reset." Finch sighed. "So, I can redo a single day as many times as it takes."

Bree snapped her attention to him. "And everyone remembers? Dr. Colton? Miss Baker? They know time went backward?"

"No one will remember," Finch stated. "To them, this day hasn't happened yet."

"But... why can *I* remember?" Bree glanced down at her mug. "I can even remember... the feeling of the bullet..." She rubbed at her chest, her hand shaking.

Finch stood from his chair, grabbed a pen from the mess on the kitchen counter, and then walked over to Bree. He knelt, gently took her arm, and shoved the sleeve of her hoodie up, exposing her left arm. It was blank.

"Do you remember the mark I drew on you?" Finch asked.

Bree stared at her pale arm. "It's gone."

"I drew the Mark of Chronos so you would remember everything that happened after I rewound time." He uncapped the pen and drew the four lines needed to recreate the mark. "I have to do this every time I manipulate time, understand? If I forget, even once, you won't remember what happened. For any of the resets. It'll all go away."

Bree swallowed hard. Once Finch had completed the

mark, she pushed down her sleeve. "Can *I* draw the mark? That way I make sure I'll remember?"

"Only someone with Chronos's magic can do it. So me or Chronos himself. That's it."

"What if *you* were shot?"

Finch shook his head. "Don't worry about that." He didn't want to tell her the truth.

If *he* died before he could activate his ability, that was it. Finch couldn't recover from that. Like shooting a gun, his magic required that he pull the trigger. If he couldn't pull the trigger, no more rewinding time.

But Bree didn't need to know that. She just needed to recover.

A long moment of silence passed between them. Bree rested back in the chair, her gaze unfocused. She set her mug down, crossed her arms, and lifted her legs up until her knees were close. She seemed completely disinterested in the world, her attention consumed by dark thoughts.

When more tears slipped down her face, Finch stood and exhaled. He wasn't sure what else he could do to help her. Her mother had been murdered, her father had vanished, and now she knew what it felt like to take a rifle shot to the back. Not a lot of people could handle that kind of stress, even with the aid of magical calming tea.

"I can't bring your mother back," Finch muttered. "But I can give you all the time you need until you feel strong again. I have a bed, I'll order some food—you don't need to do anything for a bit, all right, kid?"

———

After eleven hours of sleeping, and two of watching TV, Finch rewound time again.

He pulled Bree into his apartment, prepared his last bag of midnight raspberry tea for the *third* time, and then redrew the Mark of Chronos on her arm. After that, Bree took another nap, Finch ordered some Chinese food, and they repeated the cycle.

For eight more days.

Finch didn't mind. Only Chronos knew how often he had reset a day just to allow his mind more time to wander. If Bree needed a little bit, he would give it to her.

———

While Finch was preparing the last of the midnight raspberry tea for the thirteenth time, Bree stood next to him in the kitchen. "You can do this forever?" she whispered.

"That's right," he said. Finch glanced over. The girl leaned against the kitchen counter, her gaze on the dirty floor. "How about we go outside today?"

"I don't feel like it."

"Just for a short bit. Trust me—I know it helps to get out and see new things. I've been in this position more times than I like to admit."

Bree glanced up through her eyelashes. "You have?"

"My brother was killed. It... took a toll on me." Finch didn't want to say anything else. Perhaps Bree understood, because she didn't ask for any information beyond that.

Once Bree had sipped on her tea, she donned Finch's ugly coat. Finch took that as an acceptance of his proposal. Together, they left his apartment and went straight for his Toyota.

He drove them through Stockton until he came to the downtown mall. Technically, Stockton had two malls—one across the street from the other like they were a *McDonald's* and *Burger King*. Finch parked, and then walked around his vehicle and opened the door for Bree.

"Why are we here?" she asked as she stepped out into the cold fog of the Friday morning.

"Don't teens like the mall?" Finch motioned to the gigantic two-story building. "Go wander around. Buy whatever the hell you want. I don't give a shit." He said everything with the enthusiasm of a coroner examining a fresh body. Malls were some of his least favorite places on the planet.

Bree's eyes widened. "I can buy *anything?*"

"That's right."

When Finch reset time, his bank account would return to whatever it was before. What did it matter what they purchased now?

Bree headed for the front door, purpose in her step. The inside was a vast wonderland of shops—a place spare money went to die. Finch followed behind Bree, his hands in the pockets of his pants. Without a word, Bree went straight for a store called SAINT LAURENT. Finch had never heard of the place, but the moment he walked in, he was greeted by the presence of a million handbags.

"Gigi says these are the best bags ever," Bree said as she walked over to a black one perched all by itself on a pedestal-style stand. "Mum said I couldn't have one until I graduated college."

"Who is *Gigi?*" Finch asked. The whole store smelled of perfume and leather. A particular mix that made him think of *desperation*.

"Gigi runs a YouTube channel about fashion and makeup." Bree gently took the bag from the stand and carefully placed the strap on her shoulder. "I've watched her forever. She's my favorite YouTuber of all time."

"Uh-huh." Finch stopped listening the moment he heard the word *YouTube*.

"I can… have *anything* here?"

"Whatever you want."

Bree bit her lip. She held the black handbag close, and then hurried over to a coat rack. A gray trench coat with a black fur collar sat front and center. That was the one she grabbed. Bree slipped it on and then delicately placed the handbag over the shoulder of the coat. For the first time in days, Bree smiled as she examined herself in the mirror.

A store worker sauntered over to Finch. The sales rep wore glitzy jewelry that bordered on gaudy, and her heels were tall enough to be considered skyscrapers. "Excuse me," the woman said, her smile a little too smug. "But we ask that customers not damage any of the products."

"We're buying them," Finch stated.

"Mm-hm. Sir, I don't think you know what kind of store this is." She gave Finch the once-over, a sneer barely contained. "Perhaps you'd find your fashion needs at the local *Ross?* Or *K-Mart?*"

Finch shot her a glare. "I'm sorry. I didn't hear any of that —I was too busy minding my own damn business."

The saleswoman placed a hand on the collar of her shirt, her lips twisted down in a pronounced frown. She walked away and immediately whispered things to her coworkers as though this were the worst thing she had ever experienced in her life.

After grabbing a thick belt with a prominent silver buckle with the letters YSL on the side, Bree hurried back to Finch. "I can have *all* this?"

"How many times do I have to say it?" Finch growled.

He walked her up to the counter, and the same prissy woman from before ambled over to help them. Bree removed the coat and bag and handed them over. The woman, eyeing Finch the whole time, scanned the handbag.

$4,900.00.

Then the woman scanned the coat.

$4,990.00.

Once Bree handed over the belt, the woman scanned that as well.

$645.00.

Wow. Something under a thousand. Finch huffed to himself. *Back when I was a kid, everyone wanted the latest baggy pants. How much did they cost? Like ninety dollars? What the hell is wrong with kids these days?*

Finch handed the woman his credit card. She tapped it to her screen, her eyebrows raised. When everything was approved, she gave Finch a sideways glance, even going so far as to give him a second once-over.

He tucked the card away and then turned on his heel. "Let's get out of this dump."

With a big smile, Bree donned her new coat again, clasped it shut with her shiny belt, and then wore her handbag proudly on her shoulder. They exited the shop, but before leaving the mall, Finch pointed to the food court.

Bree hadn't eaten much, but after the trip to Saint Laurent, she seemed happier to see all the food options. Finch didn't want to eat in a public space, though.

"Let's just grab some things and head back," he mumbled.

Bree pointed to a *Blaze Pizza.* "I love that place!"

"Sure." Finch then gestured to a *Baskin Robbins.* "You want that, too?"

"Really? Yes. That sounds so good right now."

"Perfect. Let's get an unreasonable amount and head out."

———

Finch and Bree sat in Finch's living room, both in their own recliners, both up to their necks in food. The curtains were shut, and the TV was on, and neither Bree nor Finch had moved out of their seat in the last hour.

Princess Problems Eighteen played on the screen in front of them. Triplets, separated at birth, all discovered through whimsical means that they were actually royalty, but each had come from a vastly different life. Finch stared at the TV while the poor girl traded places with an identical-looking pop singer.

Bree nibbled on her pepperoni pizza. "Princess Coraline is my favorite. In the last movie, she had amnesia. She couldn't remember who her family was."

Finch dunked his sausage pizza into half-melted chocolate ice cream and then took a bite. "Hm. Who's the lady on-screen now?"

"That's Maddie. She's technically Princess Coraline's cousin. She has a claim to the throne, and wants to take it."

"Fuck Maddie." Finch dunked the crust of his slice into the ice cream and took another bite.

Bree snuggled up into her ten-thousand-dollar outfit and giggled. "Does that even taste good? It looks gross."

"Don't knock it until you try it."

"Have you had pizza and ice cream before?"

Finch chortled as he grabbed another slice. "All the time, kid."

"Is that why you look like a bum?"

After dunking another slice into the ice cream, Finch shrugged. "Who cares? Right now, we're doing whatever we want."

But after that statement, Bree's smile vanished. She turned her attention to her own pizza and half-melted ice cream. She had three flavors, each more decadent than the last. Despite her beautiful clothing, all the pizza she could want, and sundaes made of the most flavorful ice cream, more silent tears streamed down her face.

Finch muted the TV. "What's wrong?"

"I just want my old life back," Bree whispered.

With a sigh, Finch sank a bit deeper into his recliner. "Me, too." Sometimes, in the darkness of his apartment, it was easy to forget.

He glanced over to the far wall. With only the TV for light, he could still make out the old photographs. Picture of his brother, and the trips they took together around the world. Those had been the days.

Bree rubbed at her eyes and face, clearing away as many of the tears as she could. Once she was composed, she turned her attention to Finch. "You said… your brother is dead?"

Finch exhaled. "Killed. He was killed."

"Did you ever catch who did it?" Bree asked, her voice so quiet, Finch almost didn't hear it.

"No," he replied. "I never did."

"Then, do you think you'll be able to catch Mum's killer?"

"Definitely."

Bree rubbed her face a second time. Then she sat up straighter in the chair. "How can you be sure if you didn't catch your brother's killer?"

With a half smile, Finch glanced over. "Because whoever killed your mother has already made a terrible mistake that cost them everything."

With wide eyes, Bree leaned onto the armrest of her recliner. "Really? What?"

"The person who shot at us when we were at the university…" Finch sat up, knocked over some food wrappers, and then shifted his weight around on his chair. "They're in cahoots with the murderer."

"The shooter isn't the murderer? How do you know?"

"The murderer didn't try to outright kill you, right? If the man killed your mother without an issue, he could've gotten you easily. I think this shooter is someone different—someone who didn't care if they spilled the blood of a little girl."

Bree's eyes remained wide.

"And we know where the shooter is—and we have an infinite amount of time to get the drop on *him*."

CHAPTER
SEVEN

4:56 a.m.

F inch had once again brewed Bree the last midnight raspberry tea, and then they flew out the door. They weren't headed to Bree's house—they went straight for the University of the Pacific. Finch parked close to the faculty parking lot, but not in it, and then walked onto the massive campus. There were no gates, which made everything easier.

It was chillier than before. Fog haunted their steps.

Bree stayed close to Finch, her gigantic coat on her shoulders, and the Mark of Chronos on her arm. When they crossed the faculty parking lot, she pointed to the dwarf hole by the trees.

"We're not going to speak with him," Finch stated.

With a nervous glance, Bree asked, "Why are we here? What if… I get shot again?"

"If that does happen, we'll learn some more valuable information."

She grabbed the side of Finch's coat and tugged. He

stopped and turned to face her, a frown already set in place. He was prepared to snap at her—remind her who the expert in this situation was—but she stared up at him through her eyelashes and frowned back.

"I don't want to get shot again," Bree whispered.

For some reason, Finch couldn't seem to muster the same level of irritation. He swallowed some of his sarcastic words and sighed. "Listen. You probably won't get shot." He motioned to their cold surroundings. "The sun hasn't burned away the fog yet. It would be difficult to get a good aim on us."

Bree nodded once.

When she didn't seem reassured, Finch pulled her a bit closer. "Trust me." Then he knelt. He pointed to the nearest building. The fog swirled around the red brick walls, but the mist wasn't thick enough to obscure the rooftops. While the windows were practically hidden, Finch could at least see everything he needed to. "Look—this is around where we were standing when you were shot."

Bree stared at him. "Do you... think this is reassuring? Because it's not."

He snapped his fingers and gestured to the fog. "Can you see any windows? Pay attention. What we need to look for are the number of buildings that have a view of this parking lot. See?" Finch pointed to a second rooftop. "That's two." Then he pointed to the last building nearby. "And that's three. There are only three places the shooter could have been when he fired on us."

An icy wind rushed over the empty parking lot. It was far too early for the university's faculty to be on campus, but as some of the fog cleared, Finch spotted a vehicle.

A black Nissan.

Dr. Colton's vehicle.

Which was odd, because Finch knew Dr. Colton would

drive into the parking lot around 7:48 a.m. Finch kept this new bit of information in his mind as he glanced around. No other vehicles.

"You think the shooter is in one of the buildings right now?" Bree whispered.

"He's *somewhere* right now, so let's find out if he was here before we spotted Dr. Colton." Finch motioned to the first building. "C'mon. Let's go."

Together, the two hurried across the parking lot. Once through the fog, they stepped onto a walkway, and then up a set of brick stairs. The first building they approached had a metal plaque mounted next to the front door. It read: STUDY HALL D.

Finch grabbed the handle, but the door shook as he tried to open it. Locked. It was an old-fashioned key lock— nothing fancy, just the way Finch liked it. After a long sigh, Finch rummaged around the pockets of his coat. He withdrew a small tin container and cracked it open.

"What're you doing?" Bree asked.

"I'm gonna pick the lock," Finch muttered as he withdrew two small wires from the container.

"You're not going to use magic?"

"Never play an ace when a two will do, kid."

Finch leaned in close to the door and slowly inserted the wires. Bree stepped over to his side. Then she moved her face near the handle, her eyes practically inches away from Finch's work. He grumbled a complaint, but was the kid going to listen? Of course not.

The lock came undone with a *click*. Finch stood straight, tucked away his tools, and then pushed open the door. "Let's go."

"Can you use magic to pick locks?" Bree asked as she stepped into the building.

"Of course."

"Will we maybe use that in the future? If the lock is too big or complicated or something?"

"Maybe," Finch grumbled.

"Really?"

Finch walked inside and then closed the door behind them. The study hall wasn't particularly impressive. It was a building that had been constructed well over eighty years ago. That was about the time the window requirements on multistory buildings changed. Windows became bigger, and most universities switched to double panes. The windows on the study hall had bars over them.

The wrought iron used to secure the place was as cold and gloomy as the weather outside. Finch refused to switch on the lights, just in case some sort of minimum wage security guard was on duty. The morning light, filtered by the fog, was enough to navigate the study hall by.

Finch quickly did a sweep of the first floor, glancing into each room and studying the layers of dust that coated everything. The building hadn't been used in some time. The perfect place for a shooter.

Finch pointed to the stairs. "That way."

"How do you know?" Bree asked.

"The bullets struck you and Dr. Colton from a high angle, which means the shooter was up a few stories. We should search the rooms with the best vantage point on the parking lot, and then wait until 7:50 to see if we can spot the shooter."

Bree walked next to Finch as they headed to the stairs. "You actually remember what time I got shot?" she asked.

"You bet your ass I remember." Finch opened the door to the stairwell and went for the third story. The steps were hard cement slabs, another indicator the building was older. "I take special note of the time whenever *anything* happens."

Bree took the steps two at a time, effortlessly keeping up

with Finch. "Because your time powers allow you to keep rewinding the day? You keep track of everything so you can, like, change things?"

"Something like that."

Finch and Bree reached the third story. There were only a handful of rooms with windows, and only a fourth of those were facing the faculty parking lot, for a grand total of two rooms. Finch methodically searched the rooms, though all he found were old desks and empty bookshelves. This study hall hadn't been used in some time.

"Will you teach me?" Bree asked, staying within three feet of Finch at all times.

"Teach you *what?*"

"How to be so observant. And how to use magic like you do. And how to be a detective."

He gave her a sideways glance. "Listen. We need to focus. Maybe after, when we're not hunting a killer, I'll give you a few pointers."

"Really?" She hustled close to him. "I would like that. It would be awesome to do all the stuff you do."

"Uh-huh." Finch wanted to add, "*It's all fun and games until someone dies,*" but he didn't have the heart to crush the girl's hopes. He just remained quiet.

Once confident no one else was in the building, Finch set up a monitoring position near the window closest to the parking lot. The fog was still thick, but the sun was working its magic.

Bree sat on an empty desk near Finch and also watched the window.

Time passed slowly. Finch checked his phone every couple minutes.

"You don't think my father is the killer anymore, right?" Bree asked, breaking the silence between them.

Finch kept his gaze out the window. "No."

"Why?"

"I thought your father had killed your mother when this was a simpler case. A *personal* case. But if there are at least two people involved—the murderer in your house, and now a shooter in a tower—that tells me there's a lot more going on here. Far outside your father's *modus operandi*."

Bree smiled. "And you believe my story? You believe he took Papa?"

"Yes."

Although, this was the piece of the puzzle that baffled Finch the most.

What motivations did the killer have to kidnap a grown-ass man? Liam wasn't even a noteworthy warlock. Why *him?* Out of everyone to take, he seemed the least useful.

At 5:31, the fog cleared enough for Finch to see the entire faculty parking lot. At 5:46, Dr. Colton exited a building on the opposite side of the parking lot and hurried to his Nissan. The man fumbled with a few backpacks, almost unable to carry them all by the straps on his shoulders.

His outfit...

Dr. Colton wasn't wearing his *all-brown* attire. He wore a white shirt and black slacks. He opened the trunk and proceeded to load the backpacks one at a time, struggling to get them all to fit.

"Kid," Finch said.

"You can call me Bree." She slid off the desk. "And maybe I can call you Adair? That's a unique name. I like it."

"We're leaving." Finch ignored her comment and headed for the door.

"We are?" Bree kept pace as they exited the study room and headed for the stairs. Even when Finch hustled, she managed to stay right next to him. "What's happening? Did you spot the shooter?"

"We're going to follow Dr. Colton."

The two of them made it to the ground floor in record time. Finch slowly peeked out the front door. The fog had become a weak mist that lingered over the campus like an illness that refused to die. Dr. Colton continued to struggle with his trunk, his focus consumed by his task.

Finch took Bree by the shoulder and quietly guided her out of the building. Together, they headed for Finch's Toyota. Once inside, Finch adjusted the rearview mirror until he had a perfect angle on the entrance to the faculty parking lot.

The moment Dr. Colton drove off, Finch started his engine.

"We're really going to follow him?" Bree asked. She glanced at the clock. "What is he doing up so early?"

"I don't know. We're about to find out."

Bree buckled her seat belt as Finch followed the black Nissan. She scooted to the edge of her seat and placed her hands on the dashboard, her gaze locked on to their target. For several minutes, she seemingly studied the vehicle, her attention never wavering.

"What're you doing?" Finch asked. "You probably shouldn't sit like that. You could get hurt."

"I'm trying to glean information. Maybe I can learn something."

"Tsk." Finch chuckled to himself. "Learn anything yet?"

"Well… I memorized his license plate." Bree scooted back into her seat. "What information do *you* think is important?"

"The route this man is taking. He's avoiding all the larger streets and taking back roads." Finch motioned to their residential surroundings. "I suspect our *professor* doesn't want to be spotted."

Bree nodded along with his words. "Oh. I see." She glanced back at Dr. Colton's car and stared a bit longer.

Once Dr. Colton turned down the road to Bree's home, Finch knew something was wrong. He pulled his Toyota to the side and parked behind a set of shrubs planted in the front yard of a house down the way. Then Finch stepped out and motioned for Bree to do the same.

Finch stood on one side of the shrubs and watched as Dr. Colton parked near the police cars in front of Bree's house.

"That lying son of a bitch," Finch muttered.

Bree poked her head around the side of the massive shrub. "When we met Dr. Colton before, didn't he say he didn't know my mum had been killed?"

"That's right."

"He really *is* a lying son of a bitch."

Finch gave her a sideways glance. Bree just offered a shrug in response. He let it slide. Apparently, kids cursed now. The internet had ruined all innocence.

After a long exhale, Finch shoved his hands into his coat pockets. "Okay. New plan. I'm gonna rewind time, and we're going to investigate the labs at the university. Clearly, your father and Dr. Colton were working on something."

"What about the shooter?" Bree rubbed her arms.

"Kid, we have *time* as an ally. We'll get to everything. And since this will probably be an easy method to gather information, we should go with this first. Fighting a shooter in an abandoned university study hall is the more difficult route. We'll save it for later."

Fighting the shooter meant there was a slight chance Finch could die before using his power. He didn't want that. If he could avoid the confrontation, and gather information in other ways, he'd take it.

Bree clapped her hands together once. "Right. We can do this as many times as we want, right? We can catch Dr. Colton in all his lies? And find out what necklaces Papa was making? And *then* we can fight a shooter in an abandoned building? Like we're action stars in our own movie?"

"You got it."

"That's so cool. Oh, and you can call me *Bree*."

"Sure, sure."

Finch rewound time, draining color from the world. The muted objects around him melted away, leaving him in a white void so bright, Finch had to close his eyes. When he opened them again, he was back in his bedroom, wrapped up in his blankets.

4:34 a.m.

CHAPTER
EIGHT

Once again, Finch brewed his last bag of midnight raspberry tea.

Then he drew the Mark of Chronos on Bree.

This always happened whenever Finch relived a day more than ten times. The routine became ingrained and monotonous. Bree and Finch didn't even really speak as they readied themselves. Bree grabbed her coat, Finch dressed himself, and they met at the front door once prepared.

They could complete everything without even thinking.

They drove in silence through the fog until they returned to the University of the Pacific. Finch parked, and then together, they walked through the faculty parking lot. Dr. Colton's Nissan was in his parking space, just as it had been.

Finch pulled Bree aside and hid behind a cluster of trees. They waited until exactly 5:46 a.m.

Dr. Colton exited the nearby building. Right on time.

He carried his backpacks to his car, exactly like before, and took his sweet time arranging them in his trunk. Once finished, Dr. Colton shut everything, sat in the driver's seat, and then drove away.

Finch glanced at his phone.

5:55 a.m.

Dr. Colton wouldn't return until 7:48 a.m. Until then, they could search the university labs. Perhaps Liam was inside? Finch wasn't entirely positive what was going on, but he was determined to get to the bottom of it.

As Finch headed for the door, Bree walked alongside him. They reached the front door of the building, and Finch came to a stop. This door didn't have an old-fashioned lock like the empty study hall. This door had a card reader. Finch's lockpicking tools wouldn't help him at all.

Bree stared at the card reader. Then she glanced up at Finch. "Are we going to use magic to get inside?" she whispered.

After a short groan, Finch ran a hand down his face. "Probably."

"Really? What kind of magic? What're you going to do?"

The chill of the early morning wasn't helping Finch's mood. He disliked making new pacts, especially in moments like this. Most of the time, if a spirit or creature knew he *needed* something, the price for their power mysteriously went up. And if he was negotiating with a demon…

Demons were the worst.

However, a good rule of thumb was: the weaker the creature, the less one had to pay to use their powers. Finch just needed something puny—a spirit with magic capable of unlocking doors, no matter the technology used to lock them.

A mischief spirit.

"Stand back," Finch said as he motioned for Bree to move.

She hopped to the side and glanced around. When nothing happened, she frowned. "Do you have an ability to open the door?"

"No. I'm going to get one."

"You're going to make a pact with something?" Bree's eyes grew wide. "Right now? *While I watch?*"

"Calm down, kid. You're making this awkward."

Finch took in a deep breath, and then exhaled. When he was younger—when he learned to be a warlock from his father—he had been taught how to summon nearby creatures of magic. He withdrew a small pen from his coat and then wrote lines on the cement walkway in front of the building. Like the Mark of Chronos, there were certain symbols that held power, and the Mark of Summoning could be used by any witch or warlock to call for nearby help.

But Finch couldn't just draw a generic Mark of Summoning. If he did, he would get *everything* in the nearby area, and some creatures weren't friendly. They would demand a price for their time, and if it couldn't be paid, they could become violent.

Finch only needed to summon mischief makers.

So when he drew his Mark of Summoning on the ground, he made sure to include the symbol for tricksters. A smaller symbol between the other lines that limited his message.

Only those with mischievous magic would know Finch wanted to speak with them.

"Can *anyone* become a warlock?" Bree asked. "Girls, too? Not just boys?"

"Yes, anyone can be a warlock," Finch said absentmindedly.

"How many pacts can you make? Can you make dozens and dozens? Or just one? Maybe two?"

Once Finch finished drawing his mark, the earth had a special property about it—an aura of magic that radiated from the ground. Whenever any mark was on the ground, it was amplified. Technically, if Finch drew the Mark of Chronos on the ground, it would allow for multiple people to remember the shift of time, so long as they were standing over it. Like a room or a bubble wrapped in Chronos's protective magic.

"Most warlocks never make more than three pacts at a time," Finch muttered. He stood straight and crossed his arms. Now he had to wait.

"Only three?" Bree frowned. "What if you wanted to make more?"

"You can. But not more than five. Humans can only ever make five at a time."

"Why?"

Finch exhaled as he dragged his hand down his face. Why did he have to be saddled with a child? Did she need to know everything about warlocks? Of course not. This wouldn't help anything.

But they were just waiting for something to answer his summons...

So Finch sighed and decided to fill the time with answers.

"My father told me humans have five important parts to their being. Their *cores*." Finch pointed to his head. "The crown." Then he pointed to his face. "The eyes." Then his chest. "The heart." Then slightly lower on the chest. "The soul." And then he vaguely motioned to the lower half of his body. "And, uh, the *loins*. For lack of a more appropriate term."

Bree nodded.

"When you make a pact with a spirit or demon or whatever, they'll tie their magic to one of your cores. They need one of them to act as an anchor, basically."

"More like piers," Bree said. "And their magic is a boat docked at the pier."

"Sure, yeah, whatever. *Piers*." He shot her a glare. "Who's teaching this lesson? Me? Or you?"

Bree fell silent. She just frowned and stared up at him, her expression worsening the longer Finch said nothing.

He sighed. "Listen, some beings will only make a pact with you if they can tie themselves to a specific core. A succubus, for example, will only ever make a pact with you for the, uh, loins part. You can't make five pacts with five different succubi. They just won't do it. That's not how their magic works. But if you wanted, you could make five pacts with corpse biters, because those things just don't care."

"But not only do they need a specific part of you, they also demand a price in the form of a pact?" Bree sighed. "This seems complicated."

"Yeah, well, I wasn't trying to teach you how to become a warlock." Finch huffed and turned away from her. "Don't worry about it, all right? I know what I'm doing."

Bree stared at the ground. The fog hung close, and her nose was slightly blue. After cupping her hands and blowing hot breath into them, she seemed to regain some of her color.

"Um, Adair?" she asked.

"What?"

"Who all do you have pacts with? Which piers are they docked at?"

She just wouldn't give it up. Finch sighed. He glanced down at his Mark of Summoning. Nothing had arrived yet.

"*Chronos the Manipulator of Time* considers himself a god," Finch stated matter-of-factly. "All those old-world gods—any of them who were worshipped, really—always demand *the crown*. You won't find any warlocks bound to a whole pantheon, because none of those so-called gods will share."

"Is the crown the most important part of a human?"

"It's the most influential," Finch stated. "I also made a pact with *Ke-Koh the Ifrit of Rebellion*. He's tied to the heart."

Bree stepped close and smiled. "Oh, wow. Is that how you make the tea hot every morning?"

"Yes. But don't tell that to Ke-Koh. He would be very…

disappointed. I'm sure he likes to imagine his magic is being used for revolution—not for domestic pursuits."

Finch was even disappointed with himself. When he had made his pact with Ke-Koh, he had imagined many other uses for the fierce flames of the ifrit.

"Is *the heart* the most important part of a human?" Bree placed a hand on her chest, over the breast pocket of her ugly coat.

"No. It's just the greatest source of human determination. Most *power-focused* spirits and demons want the heart."

The snap of a twig ended the conversation instantly. Finch turned, tense and ready. Using a Mark of Summoning was often risky, due to the unpredictable nature of what would answer the call. Thankfully, if Finch had made a mistake, he would just restart the day and try again, but he didn't want to have to redo the monotonous tasks of their morning routine.

A red fox emerged from between two shrubs planted by the side of the building. Its lustrous fur betrayed its supernatural origins. The fog was so thick, no creature's fur should shimmer, yet the fox practically glistened with each movement.

Its black eyes landed on Finch.

"What is *that?*" Bree whispered.

"It's a trickster spirit," Finch replied.

The fox tilted its head. In a playful feminine voice, the fox spoke. "I have a name, you know."

"I am Adair Finch. This is my ward, Bree Blackstone. I summoned you because I want to make a pact. Your name?"

Out of all the supernatural beings in the world, spirits were the easiest to get along with. They tended to have a singular purpose, their pacts were simple, and they were everywhere, even the harshest deserts or the deepest parts of the ocean. They were born from nature itself, and as long as there was life, spirits would always exist alongside it.

The red fox pranced over, her fluffy tail slowly wagging from side to side. She perked her ears up. "My name is Kullthantarrick the Sneak. It has been a long while since I made a pact with a warlock."

Bree glanced between them. "Uh… Kull-than-tar-rick?"

The fox giggled and swished her tail around. "What's wrong, witch girl? You have a problem with my name? You may call me *Kull*. And I will call you… *Bee*. That makes us good friends now. Only good friends share nicknames."

"Okay. I like that." Bree walked over and knelt. Then she held out her outstretched hand.

"*Don't*," Finch barked. He pulled her away from the fox. "Not until I've made my pact." He lowered his voice as he added, "You never know what trickster spirits are after."

"Can *I* make a pact with Kull?" Bree whispered.

Finch glared. "No. Absolutely not."

"Why?"

"You just barely learned about the five *piers* of your being," he said, using air-quotes for the *piers* part. "You don't know what you're in for. Just sit back and watch me, understand?"

Although it looked as though Bree was disappointed, she eventually nodded. Finch appreciated the fact she was reasonable, but it seemed she was determined to learn herself a bit of magic no matter what. He really didn't like teaching, though.

Finch turned back to the fox. "*Kullthantarrick the Sneak*— lend me your power." He knelt and held out his hand, palm up.

The fox trotted closer. "Oh, I see. All business. I like that in a human. I have business I need doing… and I think you might be the perfect mortal to help me."

CHAPTER
NINE

"Adair Finch," the spirit said. "My power is yours, but for a price. I require a body—a *human* body. One empty and lifeless, but whole enough to wear. Unlike other spirits, I've grown tired of my fleshless existence, and I want more thrill."

"Spirits who take bodies forsake their immortality," Finch stated.

Kull twitched her fox ears. "I'm quite aware. But it's worth it."

Spirits weren't physical creatures, even if they could sometimes assume a corporeal form. They were pure magic, untethered to entropy. But the moment a spirit inhabited a body, and took it for their own, they were bound by time's cruel march.

Finch had heard many stories about spirits taking bodies. Most of them involved a spirit who had fallen in love with a human. In the end, the spirit wanted to be with the human so much—have children, grow old together, experience all of life—that they gave up their immortality just to do so.

"A dead body that's still whole is all you want?" Finch

rubbed at his chin. Finding a discarded body was harder than it sounded. Modern medicine, law, and practices meant Finch couldn't just pick up a corpse from the nearest morgue. But there were *other* ways. "How long do I have to find one?"

"Hm." Kull sniffed the air. "You don't fool me, Adair Finch. You're the warlock who made a deal with time itself. I will give you unlimited time to fulfill my request—since you have it already—but in exchange, you must keep me with you. I don't want our pact to be erased through your manipulation of time. You will make sure I remember. That is a requirement for my power."

Finch silently cursed under his breath. Most of the time, he could get away with making a pact and then "undoing" everything once he rewound the day. It was the perfect way to gain minor magical abilities for the specific purpose of whatever he was doing.

Fulfilling certain pacts could be a hassle. Like gathering a corpse for a spirit to inhabit.

But trickster magic was often more useful than one would first think.

With a heavy sigh, Finch nodded. "It's a deal."

Bree softly clapped her hands. She hadn't made any noise the entire negotiation, but from the sparkle in her eye, Finch could tell this was the outcome she desperately wanted. For some reason.

Kull reached out her snout and touched Finch's open palm. A surge of magic pulsed between them, linking them together like pieces of a chain. At the core of Finch's being, he felt the tie—the shackle. His sight faded and then returned, and he understood Kull had laced herself to the weakest part of Finch's being.

The eyes.

Finch stood and rubbed his temple.

"That's all it took?" Bree glanced between them. "Why couldn't *I* do that? It didn't seem hard."

"You're going to find a dead body, huh?" Finch scoffed as he headed for the door locked with a card reader. "I somehow doubt that."

"Well, with unlimited time I could."

Kull trotted alongside Finch, her fox tail swishing. "I wouldn't have given a witch girl unlimited time. Maybe a few years. *Maybe*. It would depend on how generous I was feeling."

Finch stood in front of the door. His heart beat faster than normal, flooded with the additional power of the spirit. Newer warlocks always struggled with learning what abilities and magic they gained from their pacts, but Finch had done this hundreds of times before.

He placed his hand on the card reader.

Computer programs were the easiest to trick. They were equations, basically. If correct key card, then door unlocks. It took no other input, made no other decisions. So when Finch visualized his new magic flaring through the device, and then pressed his power into the door, the computer program was given exactly what it wanted—the correct key card.

The door unlocked.

Finch stepped into a medium-sized lobby complete with a front desk and a few waiting chairs. A plaque under the desk read: **LABORATORY AND STUDY BUILDING C**. The place was empty, and most of the lights off, but not all. The computer at the reception desk was cold, but the camera perched by the ceiling had a red light that blinked after anyone made a move.

Finch didn't care if they recorded his movements.

No one would ever see the video.

"With my magic, you won't show up on recordings," Kull

said. She hurried over to the reception desk and leapt on top. She never made a noise. "Well, unless you want to be recorded. But you don't look like the *OnlyFans* type."

Finch shot the fox a sidelong glance. "Is this how all spirits talk these days?"

"I like the human world." Kull snickered. "Much, much more than my fellow spirits. Why do you think I want a body? What I wouldn't give to take my first breath—to experience the gift you humans call *life*."

"Uh-huh. Trust me... It's overrated."

Bree shuffled into the lobby and glanced around. With a smile, she turned to Finch. "This is amazing. I can't believe you opened that door so easily."

"It's hardly worth getting excited over," he muttered.

"What would happen if you failed any of your pacts?"

"I'd lose the part of my being the creature bound itself to," Finch said, icy and serious.

Bree stopped dead in her tracks, her eyes wide. "You'd lose it? Forever? Your heart or your crown? Or even your eyes?"

Finch walked around the desk and headed for the door to the labs. "The eyes are the easiest to lose. Trust me, kid—this is why I didn't want you making a pact. You don't know what you're getting into. Last thing you need to worry about is losing your heart or your soul."

"Oh..."

Bree dropped her gaze to the floor as she followed Finch deeper into the building. Kull chased after, never making a sound, her fox eyes glittering. When Finch glanced back, he sighed. Walking around with a fox was bizarre.

"You can change shapes, can't you?" he asked. Every trickster spirit he knew had some ability to change themselves.

Kull chortled. "Of course. You don't like foxes? That's

impossible. *Every* human loves a cute fox. They made a whole song about what they say."

"You can't be a fox because you stand out worse than blood on linen. Pick something normal."

The fox stopped in the middle of the hallway. Finch and Bree did the same. In the blink of an eye, the fox curled into herself and then unfurled as a black house cat. The domestic kitty pranced over, her tail and head held high, her eyes bright golden.

"Better?" she said with a slight purr.

Bree smiled. "Oh, wow. Awesome. Can you be a calico cat? Those were Mum's favorite. She had a calico familiar once."

Kull shook her head and twitched her whiskers. "I take the form of the most trickster animal in the family. For canines, it's the fox. For felines, it's the black house cat."

"What about for birds?"

The cat curled and unfurled, and in an instant, feathers appeared where fur had once been. A bird flew around them and then landed on Finch's shoulder.

"For birds—the humble pigeon, of course," Kull said, her pigeon form plump and fluffy. Her gray and blue wings had a glitter to them.

"*Pigeons* are the most trickster of birds?" Bree looked at Finch. "Seriously?"

He shrugged. Kull cooed in protest on Finch's moving shoulder. "I don't know, kid. I don't make the rules. I just begrudgingly follow them."

"Do you think pigeons poop at *random*?" Kull cooed out a laugh. "Silly witch girl. You have much to learn about the ways of birds."

"Oh, wow. I can't wait to learn everything." Bree giggled to herself, smiling more than ever before. Although Finch didn't like the spirit, he was silently grateful for her presence.

Finch continued down the hallway. The dim bulbs provided just enough light to reach the name plaques on most of the doors. Some were labeled as "student labs" and others for faculty. Due to the many pictures and posters of geodes on the wall, Finch assumed this was a geology lab.

That explains why the dwarf would be around here to begin with, Finch thought as his gaze panned over the various materials hanging on the walls. Dwarves loved whenever people gathered different types of metals and minerals. They almost always built their hideaways close to factories and mines.

Kull cooed as she turned her head from side to side, her eyes too far apart to really stare forward.

"Do you have to be a *pigeon?*" Finch growled.

Bree turned and smiled. "I like Kull as a pigeon. And she doesn't look out of place at all. You look like a real hobo now!"

Bree spoke with cheery conviction, not an ounce of insult in her tone, even if Finch hated every word. He pinched the bridge of his nose, wondering why he had ever gotten out of bed to answer the girl's cry for help in the first place.

Fortunately for Finch, he spotted a plaque with the name **DR. BLACKSTONE.** He immediately headed for the door. Like before, it was locked with a card reader. Finch placed his palm on the device, visualized it working, and his trickster magic unlocked everything. Then Finch walked into the lab and caught his breath.

The stench of blood hung heavy on the air.

No lights were on, unlike the rest of the building. It was cold and dark, and Finch ran a hand over the wall until he found a switch.

The lights flickered to life and revealed a gruesome scene. Bree gasped loud enough that it disturbed Kull. She fluttered her wings and cooed.

Three long lab tables were positioned in the middle of the room. Two of them were covered in cat bodies. They were dead, for certain—their throats cut, and the blood drained into the built-in sinks. Other than that, they were perfectly intact. It was disturbing, if only because Finch counted at least twelve scattered around.

Why so many?

"What's going on?" Bree whispered.

Finch glanced up to the corners of the room near the ceiling.

No cameras in this room. Of course not.

"Oh, my," Kull muttered. "You're already living up to your reputation, Adair Finch. Everyone knows you deal with all the worst kinds of crimes." The little pigeon nervously chuckled. "Perhaps I should've thought a little harder about making a pact with you... Maybe I shouldn't have asked to stick around."

That reminded Finch. He walked over to the one lab table with no bodies. He set the pigeon on the counter and then opened drawers in the lab until he found a pen. With a soft touch, he drew the Mark of Chronos across Kull's wings, directly on the feathers. No matter the form she assumed, the mark and magic would stay with her.

"Remind me to write this every time, got it?" Finch tossed the pen back in a drawer and then proceeded to walk around the large room.

Bree followed him, her attention glued to the bodies of the cats. Orange ones. Gray ones. Black ones.

No calico cats, for some reason. Was that intentional? Or perhaps a coincidence? Calico cats were rarer, after all. Finch wondered.

As he walked around, Finch also took note of the papers on the floor, and the number of cupboards and drawers that were just open. The place had been rummaged through.

Cleared out. Finch's thoughts went straight to Dr. Colton and his many backpacks.

The man had grabbed everything he could out of the lab and run. But in Finch's experience, crooks who fled the scene in haste always left something significant behind. Always.

As Finch slowed his pace, he paid more attention to the details—and to the cold chill in the air. Magic had been used in this room. Plenty of it. Like gunshot residue, the essence of magic clung to all surfaces, and especially lingered around the cats. What had happened here?

Finch stopped and examined a large orange tabby. Its eyes were shut, its throat slit. Finch lifted the cold body and moved it to the side. Something was underneath.

A necklace.

"Oh, look what we have here," Finch whispered to himself. "The reason Vera and Liam were arguing the night she died."

CHAPTER
TEN

I t was a strange necklace made of black beads and a silvery chain. Finch gently picked it up, but the instant his fingers grazed one of the beads, he flinched. He dropped the necklace onto the counter, and it clattered across the hard surface.

"Adair?" Bree asked. She hurried to his side. "What's wrong?"

"Nothing."

It had felt familiar. But only for a moment. Probably a trick of the mind.

The inky black beads were devoid of luster and shine. Finch had never seen anything like them.

He picked the necklace up a second time. When he held it in his hand, the magic in the room was more noticeable than before. He wondered why. Obviously, the necklace was heightening his senses, but for what purpose? Finch didn't have a way to identify the exact magical properties of jewelry —but he knew a few people who could.

He pocketed the necklace. "C'mon, kid."

"Bree," she said.

"C'mon, *Bree*." Finch shot her a glower. "Happy?"

She smiled so wide, he thought her face would explode. "Yes! I like my name. A lot. And I'm not a kid."

Finch grumbled his acceptance as he headed for the door. Kull flapped her pigeon wings and flew from the counter. She landed on Finch's shoulder with a soft *coo* straight to his ear.

"You can't forget me," Kull said.

"Trust me, I wish I could." Finch left the lab and strode his way down the hall. Fortunately, Liam's dwarf was nearby. And hadn't he said he had made Liam a better crafter of items? And that he had allowed Liam to identify magical objects? That meant the dwarf could, too.

Finch slammed the front door open and walked out into the cold morning fog. Bree kept close, her steps filled with boundless energy. Once she finally realized where they were heading, she smiled wide again.

"The dwarf? Papa's dwarf?"

Finch replied with a single curt nod. The little grouping of trees wasn't far. If he could solve this bit of the mystery, he was certain it would shed light on the real problem. And the identity of the killer and his shooter friend.

The dwarf's hole reeked of sulfur and copper.

Finch knelt next to it. Bree followed suit. Then Finch knocked on the tree and called out.

"Hello. I'm Adair Finch, and this is my ward, Bree Blackstone."

"Salutations," a rusty voice echoed up from the depths of the hole, just like before. "Long has it been since I had new visitors come to call."

"I'm here because you're one of the fae-folk who can identify magical items." Finch dug the necklace out of his pocket. "I have something I need identified."

A blast of hot air shot from the hole. The dwarf grumbled

something at first, his tone both intrigued and irritated. "You know of my magics? Ah… Of course you do. *Adair Finch*. A warlock with no equal. I'm surprised you need anything from me."

Bree's eyes widened. "He doesn't remember anything," she whispered. "When you rewound time… the dwarf forgot."

"Of course," Finch muttered under his breath. Then he leaned closer to the hole. "Dwarf, I have a necklace in my possession. The beads… I don't recognize what kind of magic made this." Finch withdrew the item and held it close to the entrance of the dwarf's lair.

With a powerful *sniff*, air was sucked into the hole. Finch's hair was tugged by the effort, and Bree giggled. When he shot her a glare, she mimed locking her lips and throwing away the key.

Kull cooed, her eyes practically looking in two different directions.

"Strange is that necklace," the dwarf finally growled. "I don't care for it."

"What does it do?" Finch asked.

"I apologize, warlock. I don't know."

"I thought your magics could identify magical items. This is clearly magical."

The dwarf chortled, his rusty voice wafting to the surface in chuckled bursts. "Yes, yes. Under normal circumstances. But that necklace is vile. I don't know what made it, but I want no part of it."

"I'll pay you in metals," Finch stated.

"Hm. A negotiator. Very well. For two pounds of silver, leave the necklace with me, and I'll disassemble the item. Within a fortnight, I should know all its secrets."

Finch cursed under his breath. His ability to manipulate time was great, but he couldn't allow this investigation to last longer than a single day. If he gave the necklace to the dwarf, the fae creature would never actually get the chance to identify it.

But that was fine.

Finch stood.

There were other creatures in Stockton with far greater power than a common dwarf.

"Thank you for your time, but I can't wait a fortnight," Finch said.

Bree stood as well, but only after waving to the hole. "Thank you so much."

Kull flapped her wings. "You think the dwarf saw your gesture, do you?"

With her cheeks turning pink, Bree crossed her arms. "Well, just in case."

"May your accomplishments be remembered in song and stone," the dwarf said, his voice distant.

———

Finch drove across Stockton, already tired of the Friday traffic that never went away. Until he left this time loop, he would be caught in an endless line of cars.

The sun rose, destroying the fog. Bree stared at the window for most of the drive, but as Finch turned onto the shabby downtown roads, she sat a little straighter. The cracks in the sidewalk had weeds as tall as a large dog growing out of them. Every building was part brick, part neglect, and Finch shook his head when they drove by the run-down apartment building.

Then he turned down a small road and entered a quaint residential area. It was an island of normality in a sea of poverty. Gates separated the tiny homes from the drug addicts who prowled the streets just a few blocks away.

Finch had to drive around a car accident. Two tiny

vehicles were crushed, and a gaggle of individuals hovered nearby. No one looked injured, but there was blood on the asphalt. Not much, but Finch took note.

"Where are we?" Bree asked.

Kull sat in the back seat. She flapped her wings as she stared out the nearest window. "Oh! I see you want to speak with the Occultist. She's a grumpy witch. So much fun to mess with."

"She's a witch?" Bree perked up. "That's amazing. Maybe I can speak with her and—"

"No," Finch interjected. "*I'll* do the talking. From what I've heard, the Occultist isn't a *people person*."

Kull cooed a laugh. "Oh, you've never met her? This will be a treat. For me. Not for you. Definitely not for you."

Finch could only reply with a groan. Why were so many magical beings difficult to get along with? It seemed baked into their nature.

Bree placed a hand on her chest. "She'll like me. Everyone loves kids."

Finch snorted back a dark laugh. "Oh, boy. You clearly have a lot to learn." Then he glanced over at her. "And I thought you specifically said you *weren't a kid*."

"W-Well, I'm also a witch, so maybe the Occultist will like me because of that." Bree narrowed her eyes. "Or maybe she'll understand we really need help because a fellow witch was murdered."

That was a clever angle to bring up. Finch hadn't even considered that until Bree voiced it. Witches did tend to stick together when one of their own was attacked. Even if they weren't in the same coven. Some witches were exceptions— Finch knew a few blackhearted witches—but ever since ancient times, they tended to band together to keep themselves safe from pitchfork-wielding lunatics.

Finch parked his vehicle in front of a small house with a

sign out in the yard. There were no words on it, just the picture of a palm. Most knew it as the symbol of a fortune-teller, but Finch understood the deeper meaning.

He stepped out of his Toyota. Bree quickly followed with Kull on her shoulder. As she ran around the front of the vehicle, Finch glared at the bird.

"No," he said. "Look like something normal."

Kull drooped a bit, her wings hanging by her side. With giant yellow eyes, she blinked at Finch. Bree patted her gray and blue feathers and whispered soothing nothings.

"Please?" Bree asked. "I like her as a pigeon. Witches can have familiars. I, uh, don't know if pigeons are capable of being one, but if the Occultist asks, I'll say Kull is mine."

"What the hell is wrong with everyone?" Finch muttered to himself.

It didn't matter. The Occultist would see Kull for what she was. A spirit. Kull taking the form of a cat would be purely to prevent magicless individuals from paying their little group too much attention.

Finch turned away and stomped up to the front door. Everyone thought he was a hobo anyway. And with an apartment full of drug addicts nearby, perhaps no one would question a dirty pigeon as a companion.

Bree softly clapped and then hurried after him. Kull cooed with delight, and even plumped herself up by puffing her feathers outward.

The Occultist's house was humble, which was just a kind word for *small*. It had a wooden front door painted the deepest shade of blue. Small potted plants of all varieties crowded the porch. Finch stepped around them in order to ring the doorbell.

Within a few seconds, the door opened to reveal a young woman. She wore a tight black shirt, dirt-stained jeans, and a pink silk sash tied around her waist. Was it dirt? Her jeans seemed stained with smears of crimson, but Finch wasn't certain. She wore no shoes, and enough jingling metal bracelets to melt down and craft a bicycle out of.

The woman narrowed her eyes as she ran her fingers through her lush black hair.

"Are you the Occultist?" Finch asked.

She rubbed a hand across her face. "Now is not a good time."

"Please. It's important. I need to speak with you."

The woman gave him the once-over. "You're not from around here, are you?"

"What gave it away? Let me guess—the pigeon."

She placed a hand on her hip. The woman had the smooth face and youthful energy of someone in their early twenties. The Occultist had worked in Stockton for decades. Was this woman really her? It seemed unlikely, but Finch had seen stranger things before.

"I'm the Occultist," she finally said, her voice heated, bordering on upset. "But most decent folk call me Ceija. Why are you here? I don't want visitors."

"This will only take a minute. I have a necklace that needs to be identified. It may be connected to a murder. The necklace has strange magical properties."

Ceija flashed him a glare. "No introductions? Typical. I shouldn't expect much from intrusive strangers."

"I'm Adair Finch," he said, holding back his irritation. "And this is my ward, Bree Blackstone."

Bree offered a single wave of her hand. "Hi. I'm a witch, too." She motioned to Kull on her shoulder. "And this is our spirit. You can call her Kull."

Kull cooed.

The Occultist huffed and slowly opened her door. "Very well. You may enter."

Finch stepped into the house. The overwhelming smell of

incense caught him off guard. He coughed and patted his chest as he made his way into the living room. That obviously didn't please Ceija. She eyed him with a frown.

The walls of her abode were painted in rich, earthy tones. Mostly emerald green with real wood trimmings. The living room was lit almost entirely by candlelight, and Finch wondered why anyone would want to live like this. He knew himself. He would die via house fire if he did anything like Ceija.

Bookshelves packed with leather-bound books were the only real decoration. No pictures. No vases or mirrors. All plants were either outside or positioned on the windowsills.

The house had mastered *ambience*.

A couch and two chairs faced a TV in the middle of the living room. The television was the most modern thing so far, and damn near cutting edge. It was huge—perhaps over seventy inches.

Bree sat on the couch. Finch took a chair. Everything was far plusher and more comfortable than he had imagined.

Ceija didn't sit. She walked around behind the seats, her expression stoney and her frown growing. Was she in a bad mood? It seemed like it. Finch didn't really understand why.

"You three really have no manners," Ceija said.

With a groan, Finch stood from his seat. "You're one of the fae, aren't you?"

Ceija threw back some of her black hair. "I've lived in Stockton for over two hundred years. I remember when people called this place *Mudville*. And in all my years, only pompous warlocks, like yourself, ever call me *one of the fae*."

This was going… poorly.

Finch hadn't seen it before, but the woman had slightly pointed ears. Her black hair wasn't entirely hair, either. Small inky down feathers were woven throughout, giving her volume and an elegant grace that normal humans could never achieve.

She was *part* fae. Still a witch, but with slightly different magics based on the fae-blood in her veins.

And she probably came from a line of fae who were so proud of their bloodlines and lineage, they hated to be lumped together with common fae creatures. Brownies and leprechauns were fae, too, and that just didn't sit right with the others. If Finch had to guess, he would say Ceija was likely descended from a *voibyrd elf*. They were some of the most powerful fae which lived deep in the Balkans. From what Finch could remember, the last of the voibyrd elves had been slaughtered during WWI. But that didn't mean their half-breed children didn't dot the Earth.

"May I please have a seat?" Finch asked.

Ceija glared at Bree.

With a small noise of surprise, Bree slid off the couch and stood. "Um. Can I have a seat, too?"

"What is *this*?" Ceija hurried around to the front of the couch. Her frown deepened as she stared at a white spot on the fabric.

Pigeon droppings. They had the lumpy consistency of spoiled milk and a vile sheen of greenish-white.

Finch shot Kull a glare. The mischievous pigeon cooed as she turned her head to the side, her eyes wide and playfully vacant.

"Get out," Ceija cried. She pointed at the door. "*How dare you* come in here, insult me by calling me one of the fae, and then sully my couch. I won't *ever* identify a necklace for you. Not now, not—"

Finch manipulated time.

The colors faded from the house. The candles became black-and-white. The walls shifted to a muted gray. Once the color vanished, so did all the objects. The couches. The chairs. The house. And then the distant streets and everything beyond. Even Bree and Ceija and Kull.

Until Finch closed his eyes and jerked himself awake.

He sat up in his bed.

Then he glanced at his phone.

4:34 a.m.

CHAPTER
ELEVEN

F inch hurried to his front door and threw it open. Bree stood in the hallway, waiting for him to let her in.

"I didn't tell Kull to do that," she said. "She did it all on her own."

Finch slammed the door and brewed a cup of tea as though on autopilot. With a sigh, he said, "Of course it wasn't you. Kull is a spirit of trickery and mischief. She *wanted* us to have problems, if only to make herself laugh."

"Do all trickster spirits do that?"

"Yes. It's annoying."

Finch handed her the tea and then went to change. While he dressed, Bree dug out her special coat and threw it over her shoulders. She smiled as she waited by the front door, obviously familiar with the routine.

But Kull wasn't here. Finch glanced at his watch. He didn't want to wait around in his apartment, but he *had* to have the damn bird if they were going to continue their investigation. A part of his pact was to keep her with them. If

Finch failed to do that—if he failed to write the Mark of Chronos on her—he would lose access to all her magic.

And his eyes.

Thankfully, a faint tapping at the window drew Finch's attention. He stepped over a few piles of clothing and lifted the window open. A gray-and-blue pigeon flew straight into his apartment, the wings fluttering loud enough to echo down the hall. Creatures who made pacts with warlocks always knew where the warlock was. They were tethered through magic, after all.

Kull panted as she landed on the back of his favorite recliner. "Ah... I made it. I came for you as *quickly* as possible." She stretched out a wing. "Now... draw on me. Paint me like one of your French girls."

Bree stifled a giggle.

"That isn't..." Finch held back his sarcastic comment. He grabbed a pen and started redrawing the mark. While he made the lines, it occurred to him that his pact with Kull really *was* still in place. Which was odd. Whenever Finch rewound time, any new pacts he had made were typically undone.

He shook away the thought.

It was because he had given Kull the Mark of Chronos. That kept their pact in place, even when time rearranged itself.

Finch wondered... If he forgot to write the mark on her spirit body, and he rewound time, would the pact come undone, thus preventing her from taking his eyes? Finch didn't want to test the theory, but he suspected it might be a loophole.

"I feel beautiful," Kull said once Finch was done. "Thank you, warlock. You are much too kind."

"Damn right I'm too kind," Finch snapped. "What the hell

was that back there? We're in the middle of a serious investigation. Keep your cooing, *and your pooing*, to yourself!"

The little pigeon hung her head. Bree walked over and scooped the bird into her arms. "I'm sorry," Bree said. "I'll watch Kull more closely in the future, okay?"

Finch glared at her. "Don't apologize. And don't cover for the damn mischief-maker. It's not your responsibility."

"W-Well... We all have to work t-together, and I just don't want you arguing, okay?" Bree turned away, the pigeon held tight against her chest. "I don't want to think about you getting into a fight."

Finch took in a deep breath, ready to launch into a whole new tirade about how policing his emotions wasn't going to solve anything, but then he stopped. Bree's parents had argued right before her mother's death and father's disappearance. Perhaps this was more of Bree's way of saying she didn't want to relive the nightmares of that event.

Damn.

Finch swallowed his words, and his anger, and let them all go with a powerful exhale. "Fine. No arguing. Let's just get in the car and head to the university."

Bree whirled around on her heel, her eyes wide. "R-Really?"

"Yeah."

"But why the university?"

"We need to get our necklace again. *Then* we need to head back to the Occultist's."

"Do we always have to re-collect everything we found before?" Bree carried the pigeon over to the door. "Like, if we find more evidence? We'll have to get it all and then question people?"

"That's how it works." Finch grabbed his own coat and then opened the door. "Like a video game, right?"

———

At 5:55 a.m., once Dr. Colton left, Finch used Kull's magic to effortlessly break back into the labs at the university. He went straight for the large orange cat, lifted it up, and snatched the black bead necklace. It still surprised him when he first touched it, but he shook away the unease and returned to his vehicle.

With Bree and Kull whispering in excitement the whole trip, Finch made it back to the island of serenity in a sea of drug lords. There was no car accident this time. They had arrived earlier than the collision, it seemed.

He drove by the dilapidated apartments and parked on the road right in front of the house with the fortune-teller sign.

"Let me do the talking," Finch said as he opened his car door.

"Because that worked so well last time," Kull quipped.

Finch turned around in his seat and glowered at the bird. She cooed and then flattened herself on the seat, clearly not sorry at all, just acting stupid to get out of trouble. Bree pulled the bird into her lap in the passenger's seat and nodded. "We'll behave."

"You can't speak for the trickster," Finch stated.

"I'll watch her. Everything will be fine. Trust me."

"Uh-huh."

Finch exited his vehicle, and Bree quickly followed. The early morning mists still lingered. Finch had gotten to the house earlier than yesterday. He wondered if it would affect the conversation, and decided to just test his luck.

He stepped over the potted plants and rang the doorbell.

After a good thirty seconds, Ceija answered. She pulled open the door and stared at Finch, her black hair damp, as though she had just stepped out of a shower.

She also wore the same outfit—a black shirt and jeans—but this time she wasn't dirty. Which was odd, because in an hour from this moment, she would have stains all over her outfit. What was she about to do?

"Are you the great *Ceija*?" Finch asked, awe in his voice. "Thank goodness. My name is Adair Finch. This is my ward, Bree Blackstone, and this is her pet spirit, Kull." He bowed his head slightly. "I'm so sorry to intrude, but can we please take a moment of your time to discuss a serious matter? A Stockton witch has been murdered."

Ceija's expression softened. She pulled open the door and motioned to the living room. "Yes. I see. This is a very serious matter indeed. Please, come in."

Finch stepped into the house. Bree hurried to his side, her eyes wide, but the corners of her lips twitched upward in a knowing smile. While it was amusing to see her impressed, it wasn't a major accomplishment in Finch's eyes. They hadn't gotten Ceija to help them yet.

Before he sat, Finch turned to the Occultist. "May I please take a seat?"

"Yes, do take a seat," Ceija said, motioning to the couch. "I will brew us some coffee and tea, and you will tell me everything while we drink." She smiled as she left, far cheerier than before.

Finch sat, and Bree took the cushion next to him. When the Occultist left the room, Bree couldn't control her giggling.

"You did it," she whispered, smiling ear to ear. "This is going *way* better than it went before! I can't believe it. I thought she would be grumpy all over again."

"When you have time as an ally, anyone can be swayed to your side," Finch muttered under his breath. "We just needed to know the right words." He withdrew the beaded necklace. "Let's just hope she can identify this."

Kull cooed, and Finch shot her a look that could kill. Pigeons were incapable of smiling, but he could've sworn the little bird replied with a coy smirk.

It didn't take long for Ceija to return to the living room. She carried a tray of teacups and gently handed one each to Finch and Bree. Then she took a seat on a chair and smiled at Bree. "You're a young witch. Were you born in this valley? I've been here a long time."

"You've been here for hundreds of years," Bree said matter-of-factly.

Ceija's expression hardened. "Yes... How did you know?"

"Uh, while I would love to discuss the history of our great city, we don't have much time," Finch said. He held an arm out in front of Bree and then offered Ceija the necklace. "Do you happen to recognize this? I don't know what it does, but the murderer dropped it."

Ceija took the necklace. Her frown deepened.

"This is foul," she whispered. "You said the *murderer* dropped it? I can see that."

Bree's eyebrows lifted to her hairline. "Really? You know what it does?"

The woman shook her head. She handed it back to Finch. "I'm sorry, but I want no part of this. I could identify it... yet I feel no urge to do so. Something about this is twisted."

The squeal of tires heralded the *crash* of metal on metal. There it was. The car accident. Finch glanced at his phone. The time was 6:39 a.m.

Despite the racket outside, Ceija said, "There are a great many magical creatures in the world. Their powers are varied, and so are their temperaments. I suspect whatever creature gave its magic to make this necklace, it is a hateful being."

Bree tapped the tips of her fingers. "Did a warlock make a pact with it?"

"Hm. Probably. Only *humans* craft magical items. The spirits, demons, and old gods that walk the earth never make such things."

"Really? I didn't know that."

"We really do need help," Finch stated, trying to steer the conversation back toward something productive. "Please. I can pay you almost any amount of money. I just need to know what it's for."

Ceija shook her head. "I'm sorry, warlock. I don't want this creature's magic in my house, or in my thoughts. I'd rather you take it and leave, frankly."

The urge to tell her that she would forget everything once he rewound time was tempting, but Finch kept that to himself. From his past experiences, telling people he could manipulate time often resulted in negotiations where people wanted to remember everything. Just as Kull made it part of her pact—she had to remember.

So Finch kept his powers secret, to avoid individuals demanding he use his abilities to their advantage as payment for mundane services.

After a long moment of silence, Ceija stood and motioned them to the front door. "I'm sorry. I can't help you. I suggest you seek out another witch. Or perhaps one of the dwarves. They are capable of identifying a great many things."

Finch said nothing as he stood. Bree glanced between him and the Occultist, obviously wanting to protest, but Finch shook his head. They had done everything correctly this time, but that still wasn't enough. He would have to rewind time and try a new tactic. Perhaps if he acted more desperate or—

Someone pounded on the front door.

Ceija hurried to answer it. When she threw open the door, a thin man with shaky hands said, "Ceija, ya gotta come quick. I think it's ya pup. There's been an accident..."

"My dog?" Ceija's eyes grew glassy in an instant. "Cauldron?" She hustled out the front door, forgetting all about Finch and Bree.

Finch followed her outside. He watched as Ceija traveled with the gangly man down the road for a few blocks. They went straight to the car accident—the one Finch had seen before. And just like he had surmised, the drivers both exited their vehicles unharmed.

But the blood…

That wasn't *human* blood. A dog was being pulled from the twisted bumpers of the cars. It was a smaller thing—no more than eight pounds—perhaps a miniature poodle. Ceija ran directly for it. Her neighbors wrapped the poodle in a sweater before handing Ceija the body. The Occultist took the dog and then jogged back to her home, blood smearing onto her black shirt and jeans, dirtying them as she went.

While most people would've been devastated to see their dog maimed, Ceija had a stiff upper lip. She rushed by Finch and Bree, never really looking at them, and carried the injured dog straight into her home. The door slammed shut behind her.

"Wow," Bree said. "I can't believe that all happened. Why didn't we see it before?"

"We came here too late last time," Finch whispered. He stared at the ground, unseeing. "No wonder Ceija was so upset when we spoke with her before. Her dog had just been in an accident. Perhaps even dead." Probably dead. Finch just didn't want to say it in front of the girl.

"Do you think it was her familiar?" Bree frowned. "Witches have special connections with their animal familiars."

"Well, this is perfect, actually."

Bree wheeled on him. "That's mean. C'mon. Witches

don't want to—" Then Bree cut herself short. She stared at Finch, her expression shifting from irritation to delight. "Oh, my god. We're going to save a dog, aren't we?"

Finch rubbed at his stubble-covered chin and chuckled. "Now you're catching on."

CHAPTER
TWELVE

Finch rewound time.

He slid out of his bed at 4:34 a.m. Then he got Bree, made her tea, drew the Mark of Chronos on her arm, let Kull inside, drew the same mark on her wing, got dressed, gave Bree her coat, and then headed out the door.

The number of steps to take every morning was tedious, but important. Finch made careful note not to forget anything, lest he mess up his own investigation.

At 5:55 a.m., Finch broke into the university labs, took the necklace, and then drove straight to the Occultist.

They arrived at 6:18, parked the car on the street where the car accident would happen, and waited. The crash wouldn't actually take place until 6:39, which meant they had some time to mentally prepare. Finch killed the engine, leaned back in his seat, and observed the local denizens going about their day.

A lot of them were milling around the street corner. Finch silently hoped Bree wouldn't ask him what they were up to. YouTube or TikTok or some other bizarre social media site with two capital letters in its name had probably already explained the concept of prostitutes to her, but on the off chance they hadn't, Finch didn't want to be the one to shatter her childhood any further.

"Why don't we just get out of the car and save the dog right now?" Bree asked. She pointed to a park just down the block. "If I were a dog who got out of my backyard, I would go over there."

"We can't just bring the dog back to Ceija." Finch rubbed his jaw. "We need to save it from a car crash."

"Why?"

"So that Ceija will be more inclined to identify the necklace. If we rescue Cauldron from certain death, I suspect she'll be more willing to help out, even if the necklace exudes strange magics."

"What if she doesn't?" Bree whispered.

"We'll figure out another way to identify it," Finch muttered.

Kull flapped her wings and landed on the center console of the Toyota. She puffed her feathers and blinked her golden eyes. "Couldn't you just break into Ceija's home and force her to identify it?"

Finch slowly turned to face the bizarrely murderous pigeon. He said nothing, because he already knew where this was going.

"I mean, what does it matter if you hurt her?" Kull asked as she tilted her head like only a bird could. "Once you undo time, everything will return to how it was before. Even if you *maimed* Ceija, she would be whole and well the instant you used your magic. So... why go through all this? Why not force the Occultist to help us? It seems like the faster and more efficient method, especially since it won't hurt her at all."

Despite the playfulness of her tone, her words sent an icy

chill down Finch's spine. The spirit was serious, even if she was trying to cover that up with a casual demeanor.

Bree furrowed her brow. She glanced over at Finch and tapped her fingertips together. But she didn't add to the conversation. Her discomfort was written all over her slumped shoulders.

"I could do that," Finch drawled. "But this method will also work." He glowered at the bird. "And what does it matter if this is slower and less efficient? We literally have eternity to handle this matter."

Kull cooed.

The truth was—Kull's instincts were right. Finch had, in the past, strong-armed his way through several problems, only to have time unravel and set everything back to normal.

But Bree was with him. If she weren't here, Finch would've done a lot of things differently. He would've fought the shooter in the tower right away, and then beaten information out of the murderer. Bree was clearly still traumatized by what had happened, however, and Finch refused to leave her alone.

This route to solving the murder would still work. It was just longer and more convoluted. But at least it would be pleasant.

At least, Finch *hoped* it would be pleasant.

The more he found out, the more he suspected something terrible was waiting for them at this end of this route. And it disturbed him not to know what it was.

The three of them sat in silence for a long while.

Finch glanced at his phone.

6:30.

They still had nine minutes. He exhaled and stared at the ceiling of his vehicle.

Kull cooed. "I can't wait until someone asks me, *What was it like solving a murder with the legendary Adair Finch?*" The pigeon chuckled. "I'm going to reply with, *My favorite part was when we abused time to save a witch's poodle.*"

Bree giggled. She held up a finger. "My favorite part so far was when we found a trickster pigeon."

Kull preened, her gray and blue feathers practically glistening.

"My favorite part was the few minutes of silence we just had," Finch said with a groan.

Again, Bree giggled.

But once it became 6:37, Finch opened his car door and headed down the sidewalk. Bree leapt out and followed him, Kull on her shoulder. The chill of the morning air hurt Finch's nose, but he pushed the irritation aside. He kept his focus on the surroundings. Where would a poodle be?

Then he spotted it.

A black poodle, no more than eight or nine pounds, sniffed around a lush raspberry bush directly outside the apartment complex. The little dog walked with a prance in its step, its mouth open, its tongue hanging freely. It looked happy, which was ironic, given its upcoming fate.

"Bree, stand back," Finch muttered.

Hesitantly stepping onto the grass beyond the sidewalk, Bree patted her pigeon companion and just watched. Finch wished he had more of a plan, but the truth of it was he didn't even know how the cars had gotten into an accident in the first place. How was he supposed to save the poor little poodle?

He walked down the road, his hands in his coat pockets, his muscles tense. The ditzy dog sniffed at every crack and strange plant, its black curly pelt a sight to behold. If Finch squinted his eyes, the mutt could maybe be a cauldron. It was fat enough.

And there were a few people around. A woman sat on the windowsill of her apartment. She smoked a cigarette, her eyes on the distant horizon. A few kids ran around in the park. The hookers at their corners chatted with one another.

Finch spotted the thin man with shaky hands who had spoken to Ceija.

The rev of an engine caught Finch's attention.

A car drove through a corner of the nearby park, the tires ripping up the grass in its haste to accelerate. What was going on? Finch watched as the vehicle sped in his direction. On instinct, he glanced over his shoulder. Another car was turning the corner. The driver, a teen boy with earbuds in—and staring at his phone—barely had one hand on the wheel. The teen turned onto the street and hit the gas almost entirely through muscle memory.

Then the poodle stepped off the sidewalk and trotted into the road.

"Adair!" Bree shouted. She pointed to the dog.

Everyone was watching. The woman in her apartment. The kids in the park. The shaky-handed man.

Perfect.

Finch sighed as he lunged for the dog. The vehicles were so close, he could practically smell their exhaust. His heart pounded as he rushed forward, scooped the animal up in his arms, and then kept going.

The *crash* happened so close to him that Finch could've sworn he felt the whip of the wind and the heat of the friction.

This was reckless. Finch scolded himself for that fact as momentum carried him to the opposite sidewalk. He stumbled over the curb and held the frightened poodle tight against his chest. The poor animal's heart raced, but its tail wagged as fast as it could.

"I got you," Finch muttered in the kindest voice he could muster.

He stood straight, and agony lanced through his lower

back. He groaned, his teeth gritted. The worst part about aging was remembering a time when random body parts *didn't* suddenly hurt for no reason. Ten years ago, Finch could've combat-rolled through that car crash, saved the dog, and maybe even backflipped onto the opposite sidewalk.

His brother would've been right beside him the whole way. Maybe even saving the drivers from their cars somehow.

Now Finch had to wait a moment for the pain in his muscles to subside.

Damn.

"Did you see that?" a woman shrieked. "Did anyone record that? It'll go viral! I know it will."

Bree ran across the street, her bright smile a cure all its own. She practically clapped her hands when she jumped onto the sidewalk. Kull cooed out a congratulations. She even fluttered her wings.

"That was amazing!" Bree patted the poodle on the head. "I thought you were going to use magic or something, but instead, you just leapt in front of the cars. It was amazing!"

Using magic…

Finch wished he had some sort of ability he could've used to grab the pooch, but nothing would've worked for this particular situation. Additionally, he was *not* going to make another pact with a creature just to solve a simple problem. Kull had taught him that lesson.

And even if he had been hit, he could've rewound time. The crash wasn't so powerful he would've died instantly. He would've had time to trigger his ability. Finch had been hit by a car before and managed to escape through the flow of time. His hip hurt just thinking about the incident.

"Ya saved that dog!"

Finch turned around. The man with shaky hands hustled over. He wore a tank top, sagging jeans, and an expression so exaggerated, it was like he was part cartoon. The man's eyes couldn't get wider.

"Ya saved that pup!"

Finch held it close. "That I did."

"Here, give him to me, and I'll take him back to his owner." The man held out his hands, but Finch honestly feared he might drop the animal.

And he couldn't hand Cauldron over. Finch needed him.

"I'll carry the dog," Finch stated. "Just take me to the owner. I'll explain what happened."

"Right, right!" Without a second thought—or even a preliminary question—the man ran down the street.

Finch and Bree followed behind him. While the neighborhood gathered out on the street to examine the wreckage, Finch kept his attention on the fortune-teller's sign. If this didn't work, he wasn't sure what would. And who else could he approach about item identification?

Oh, he knew someone else. But it was the *last* person Finch wanted to deal with.

Once they reached Ceija's home, the man banged on the door. Ceija answered within seconds, her eyebrows knitted. "What's wrong?" she asked.

"Look here, Ceija." The man pointed to Finch. "Ya pup was out, and was crossin' the street, and then *bam!* This man jumped out and saved him. Two cars crashed, and the pup would've died, but he was here!"

The man's story was damn near incoherent, but Finch halfway followed the string of events. Ceija must've known the man well, because she nodded along with his words, her expression shifting from concern to relief.

"You saved Cauldron?" Ceija stepped outside in her black outfit, her skirt flowing. "Thank you so much. What a brave thing to do for a stranger's pet." She took Cauldron into her arms. The dog wagged his tail harder than before. He even licked at Ceija's jaw.

"It was no problem," Finch stated.

"But still. Thank you so much. Can I brew you a cup of tea? Or perhaps coffee?"

"That would be much appreciated, actually." Finch bowed his head slightly. "And did that man say you were *Ceija*? I'm looking for a woman by that name. That's why I was in the neighborhood, actually."

Ceija replied with a curt nod. "Ah, the fates have intervened this day, then." She motioned him inside. "Please. You have my thanks, and my ear."

"My name is Adair Finch, and this is my ward, Bree Blackstone. Oh, and also, we have a pigeon."

The shaky-hand man did a double take. "Oh my god. It *is* a pigeon. This whole morning was so whack I didn't even realize." He practically slapped himself on the face. "Crazy."

"Perhaps it would be best if you went home," Ceija said to him. "Your mother is sickly, is she not?"

The strange man waved and then took off. No more words. No real goodbye. He just flew off wherever his attention was focused next.

"Never mind JJ," Ceija said. "He's kindhearted." Then she motioned to her living room. "Please. Join me. I do wish to repay you in any way I can."

Which was perfect, because that was exactly what Finch had been betting on.

CHAPTER
THIRTEEN

F inch stepped into Ceija's house and was once again assaulted by the incense. He waved his hand in front of his face as he followed Ceija into her living room. Before taking a seat on the couch, he asked, "Would it be okay if we sit?" He rubbed his lower back, digging his knuckles into his muscles, hoping they would loosen.

"Of course." Ceija set Cauldron down and then headed for the kitchen. "Let me get you something. It's the least I can do for someone who saved my dog."

Bree sat down next to Finch, Kull on her shoulder. With a small smile, she leaned over and whispered, "You're such a good actor. You look like you're in a lot of pain, even though that car never touched you. You're so fast!"

Finch forced a grin. "Yup. All an act. To gain her sympathy."

My fuckin' back is going to kill me.

The tiny poodle walked over and wagged his tail. Perhaps he knew Finch was his savior, because Cauldron sniffed Finch's pants and nuzzled them afterward.

"He likes you," Bree whispered.

When Ceija returned to the living room, she genuinely smiled. Then she set down both coffee and tea each for Bree and Finch, along with small trays of cookies. Ceija had a third cup—one thick and made of hardened clay. It had a green sheen, and she placed it on the side table next to Finch.

"A brew," she said. "It will ease the pain."

Finch took the cup and threw back the contents in one swig. He knew witch's brews. They all tasted awful. Always. They were made with all sorts of foul ingredients. Finch had learned his lesson long ago to never ask for a list of the contents. Spider legs, blood, liquid from strange places—they were all common sources of ancient spirit magic only witches really understood how to manipulate.

Even though he drank it in one go, a bitter taste of dead grass lingered in his mouth and throat. Finch coughed and tapped his chest. Then he threw back the coffee and burned himself.

It was one of those mornings.

The pain in his back damn near instantly began to fade, however. It helped.

Ceija took a seat on a chair, and just like last time, offered Bree a smile. "You're a young witch. Were you born in this valley? I've been here a long time."

"I was born here." Bree pointed to Cauldron. "Is he your familiar? I love mini poodles."

"Oh, no. He's my pet and companion, but Cauldron isn't suited to be a familiar. He's much too adventurous."

"Does he play fetch?" Bree scooted to the edge of the couch cushion, as though ready to run outside and start playing. Finch held back a sigh. They had an investigation to finish.

"Cauldron likes fetch, but his favorite game is to pout until you give him more bologna."

The dog ran to Ceija, wagging his tail at a furious rate. He clearly understood the word *bologna.*

Finch held up a hand. "As much as I love dogs, I came here to speak with you on an extremely important matter." Finch dragged the necklace out of his pocket and handed it to Ceija. "Do you happen to recognize this? A witch was murdered last night, and I'm in the middle of the investigation. The killer dropped this, and I need it identified."

Ceija stared at the necklace. "I see. Well, clearly this was destiny. You are carrying a tool made using vile means. The killer you seek is wicked. I will gladly help you."

Her declaration eased the last of Finch's worry. "Thank you," he said.

"Give me just a few minutes." Ceija stood and left the living room, her attention on the black beads the entire trek.

———

Bree sat on the floor, playing with Cauldron. She giggled and patted the poodle's head. Occasionally, the pooch licked her face and hopped around her in cute little circles. Finch wanted nothing to do with him, but he was glad it made Bree happy. She needed it.

With her eyes skewed in two directions, Kull waited on the armrest of the couch. She cooed whenever the dog got too close, scaring him away.

"I like Cauldron," Bree stated. "And it's a good thing we saw where he was going long before the accident."

"Why?" Finch said as he rubbed his eyes.

"Because now we can save him really quick early in the morning whenever you undo time."

Finch huffed out a single laugh. "What? I'm not saving the dog again. We only needed to do it the one time."

"But…" Bree glanced up at him. "If we don't save him, he'll probably die in the car accident."

"You don't know that for certain. Ceija is a witch. She might have a brew to fix him."

"He'll be really hurt, though. And sad. We can easily save him. We can leave your apartment, drive down this street, pick up Cauldron, and drop him off before continuing the rest of the investigation."

"No," Finch growled. "We're not doing that. It's a waste of time."

"But you said you have *infinite* amounts of time!" Bree stood, her eyes glassy.

Finch stared at her. Why was she getting so emotional about the dog? He wasn't even hers. He was just a random pet owned by someone Bree had just met.

"You're right. I do have time. But it's also a waste of my patience and sanity, and I have *very* limited amounts of those these days." Finch pinched the bridge of his nose. He couldn't believe he was even entertaining this idea. The dog didn't matter.

Bree wiped her face with the sleeve of her giant jacket. She took a seat on the opposite side of the couch, ignoring all Cauldron's attempts to play with her. Kull cooed, but said nothing, one of the pigeon's gold eyes on Finch.

It didn't matter if Bree pouted. Finch knew the investigation came first and foremost.

Ceija returned to the living room. She held the necklace with only two fingers, and carefully brought it over to Finch. She offered Bree a brief glance and then asked in a hushed tone, "The witch was her mother, wasn't she?"

Finch nodded.

"Well, I've identified the killer's necklace," Ceija said at her normal volume. She took a seat in the same chair and crossed her legs. "The purpose of that item isn't as foul as I originally thought. Whoever holds the necklace can see through magics that trick the mind. Illusions. Befuddlements. Even a glamour, if it's weak enough."

"That's all it does?" Finch furrowed his brow.

"Yes." Ceija sighed. "But it was made with a bizarre set of magics. A dwarf was involved, or perhaps a warlock bonded to a dwarf. And something else. I want to say a demon, but it might be more powerful than that. I didn't recognize it."

Bree glanced up. She sniffed but cleared her voice before asking, "Did a cat have to die to make that item?"

"Something had to die," Ceija said. "You see, magical items have life spans, just like humans, but inanimate objects don't really live and breathe, so the creator must *give* them life. When forging a magical item, you kill a creature—their remaining years are transferred into the object. This necklace has about eleven years before it will break and cease to work."

"Really?"

Ceija nodded. "Yes. That's why the witches, warlocks, and sorcerers of old hunted tortoises for their most powerful magical items. They wanted something that lasted long enough to pass from one generation to another."

"Modern magical item creation just uses sharks," Finch stated. "They live for a few hundred years, and killing one won't get you into any sort of trouble. Well, some species, anyway."

Ceija waggled her finger. "No. Only the learned and educated witches and warlocks use sharks. The back-alley brewers and talentless crafters grab whatever animal they can find to create their flimsy items."

"Why not use clams?" Bree whispered. "They live for five hundred years. That's what my biology teacher said."

Ceija offered Bree a kind smile. "Only vertebrates will work, young witch. The spine is the thread that holds the cores of one's being, and you need the cores to ground the magic in the item."

"O-Oh."

Liam had been killing cats by the dozens. Had every dead cat produced another one of these necklaces? That would make sense. Vera had been arguing with Liam the night she died. She had said he was making too many necklaces.

But why mass-produce them?

Finch still didn't understand. *Had* Liam and Vera been struggling financially? It didn't look like it. And if Liam had a position at the University of the Pacific, they definitely had legitimate sources of income.

But it was worth investigating. Perhaps Liam was selling the necklaces on the side.

Finch would need to ask the lead detective. They would have Vera and Liam's financial information—bank accounts, holdings—and could quickly tell Finch if something in the numbers was suspicious.

However, if they were struggling to make ends meet, wouldn't Vera *want* Liam to make more necklaces? Why argue to stop? That didn't make any sense to Finch.

Unless Liam was being strong-armed into making them. For some reason.

"Adair Finch…" Ceija brought a delicate hand up to her chin. "Are you the private investigator everyone spoke about ten years ago?"

"Probably," Finch muttered, his thoughts wrapped up in the investigation.

"I was told you died a violent death."

"No. That was my brother."

Ceija's eyes widened. Then she exhaled, her expression returning to something soft. "I see. Well, from what I heard, you helped countless witches. You never turned anyone away, even if they couldn't pay for your services. Is that true?"

"It's true."

In reality, it had been Finch's brother, Carter, who never turned anyone away. If someone was in distress, nothing else mattered to Carter. He didn't care if they had money, what race, creed, or gender they were—Carter wanted to help them. Carter wanted to bring justice to anyone who asked.

Finch always went along, of course. Every murderer they caught, every kidnapped child they located, every strange magical artifact they recovered—it was an adventure that made the world a slightly better place. A wild ride with a feel-good conclusion. What wasn't there to like?

There was nothing Finch wouldn't give to get those days back.

"Thank you so much for helping all those people," Ceija said, bringing Finch back to the present. "I'm so happy you're still here, even if your brother has moved on. Witches have always had it rough throughout history. It's nice to see you're helping to catch another killer of our kind."

"Think nothing of it," Finch muttered. He stood from the couch as he jammed the necklace into his coat pocket. "I should be thanking you. Now that I know what this necklace does, I have a better understanding of what's going on."

"The crime rate has been increasing. Not the mundane crime of the magicless. Crimes involving witches, either as victims or as the criminals themselves." Ceija rubbed her hands together and then smoothed the collar of her shirt. "You should be careful. The necklace makes me think the murderer is someone with powerful ties to magic."

"The necklace helps someone see through low-level illusions," Finch muttered. "No one powerful needs that as one of their tools." But Finch didn't elaborate further. The killer hadn't dropped the necklace—that was a lie to quickly get Ceija to identify the item. The piece of jewelry was just something tangentially related to the investigation. Finch wasn't ready to conclude whether the killer was magical or not.

"The local covens have been more active. From Stockton to Oakland, there are witches fighting for territory. Heinous uses of magic." Ceija shook her head. "They're the kind that give us all a bad name. Murder. Drugs. Political scandals."

Finch had been checked out for over a decade. He knew little about the goals of local covens, even though he had once been very familiar.

He filed this new information away. Perhaps he would need it.

Ceija stood. Then she walked over and opened her arms. Finch stared for a moment. When he didn't move, Ceija stepped closer and embraced him. He awkwardly patted her back, confused.

"That's for saving Cauldron," Ceija said with a grin. Then she released him. "Thank you."

Finch forced a smile. "Uh. Sure." Then he motioned for Bree. "We should be going."

Bree stood and followed him out of Ceija's house. But she didn't speak. Kull didn't say anything, either, not even as she flew from the living room to Finch's shoulder. She landed and cooed, but otherwise remained quiet.

They walked down the street, no one bothering with conversation. Then they piled into Finch's Toyota. He started up the engine and drove away, the sadness in the car as thick as peanut butter.

A few minutes into the drive, Bree sniffled. She rubbed her eyes, her lip quavering.

"What's your problem?" Finch growled. "It can't possibly be the dog. It's not even your pet. A few days from now, you won't even remember it exists."

Silent tears streamed down Bree's cheeks. They rolled to her chin and then dripped to her lap. She said nothing.

Finch came to a stop at a red light. The rumble of his older vehicle filled the cab with noise, but it didn't distract him. He glanced at the radio, but when he realized Bree's crying was intensifying, he just gripped the steering wheel.

"Listen, if you don't stop this, I'm going to start leaving you at my apartment during these investigations, do you understand?"

"I..." Bree took a deep breath and steadied herself for a moment. "I couldn't save Mum. I had to watch, b-because I couldn't do anything. Now I can't even save C-Cauldron. He's just... he's going to die, and there's nothing I can d-do."

Bree pressed her face into her giant sleeves, her quiet sobs muffled.

The light turned green.

Finch didn't move the car. He watched as the light switched to yellow, and then back to red. It was still early in the morning, away from the busy streets. No one was around. It was just him, Kull, Bree, and his overwhelming sense of guilt.

"The dog might not die," Finch eventually stated, his voice strained. "I told you. Ceija might save him."

Bree continued to sob, the sleeves of her coat pressed hard into her face.

After a long exhale, Finch said, "Sometimes things die. Most of the time, that's out of our control. That's just an aspect of life."

Bree caught her breath. She removed the sleeves from her face and turned to him, her eyes red, her breathing shallow and irregular. "But this is different! We *could* save him. We c-could! But I can't d-do it on my own! *I need your help*, and, and *I wish I didn't!* I just want to s-save him. I want to save *something*. I want..."

She wiped another stream of hot tears from her reddish face.

The light changed to green again.

Finch ignored it.

They were arguing about a dog. A stupid, tiny dog. Not even Bree's dog. A stranger's dog. That loved bologna. Whether it lived or died in a car accident, it wouldn't change anything about their investigation. Finch already had the information he needed. He would take it with him when he rewound time—he no longer needed the Occultist to identify the necklace.

But Finch remembered the clawing dread of helplessness after Carter died.

He couldn't save his brother.

Even thinking that brought the dread back.

"Fine," Finch said, his voice quiet. He sighed. "We'll save Cauldron."

Bree rubbed her eyes for several seconds. Then she glanced up at him. "R-Really?"

"Yes."

"Every time you rewind time?"

"We don't need to do it every time. Just the *last* time is all that matters."

"But you might forget!" Bree's lip trembled. "And while we're out investigating, Cauldron will be hurt. Doesn't that upset you? We should save him so he's not suffering somewhere. We have to."

There was no arguing—Finch felt it in her words. Bree was desperate to make sure the dog suffered nothing, not even a temporary injury. With a curt nod, Finch said, "Fine. *Every time.* Happy?"

Bree wiped her face as she smiled. "Thank you, Adair. I think… that will make Ceija really happy. And Cauldron, too."

"Me, too," Kull chimed in.

Finch flinched and snapped his attention to the back seat of his car. He had forgotten the pigeon was with them. The damn bird sat in the back like a person. She blinked her eyes at Finch.

"What?" Kull asked. "I really wanted the dog to live. He's a little mischief maker at heart. That's why he escaped Ceija's backyard."

"You can understand animals?" Bree asked, a bit of awe in her tone.

"Occasionally. Depends on the animal."

Finch waited for the light to turn green a third time before driving away from the intersection. "Enough talking about the damn dog. It's decided. We're saving him. No more dwelling on this subject."

Bree lightly clapped her hands together, her genuine joy on full display. And while Finch hated himself for being emotionally guilted into doing what she wanted, he also couldn't deny he liked seeing her happy.

Hopefully saving the dog wouldn't take up too much of their morning. Finch rewound time, draining color from the world and transporting him back to his bedroom. He awoke again, wrapped in his blankets, at exactly 4:34 a.m. on the same cold Friday morning.

CHAPTER
FOURTEEN

F inch opened the front door, pulled Bree inside, grabbed the last bag of tea, warmed the water, opened the window for Kull, grabbed Bree her coat, and then headed into his bedroom to get dressed. He had this part of his morning down to a science. He could complete every task with his eyes closed, and just to keep things interesting, he did just that as he grabbed a shirt and pair of slacks.

Once out of the apartment, Finch drove his car… to save the damn dog.

They drove down the street near Ceija's and parked directly next to the bush the little poodle was hiding in. Finch stepped out, yanked the pooch from the shrubbery, and then carried it down the block to Ceija's house.

Cauldron fought him the whole way, barking in panic. Bree watched from the car, her eyes wide. Kull just laughed. Although Finch couldn't hear the coo-chuckles, his mind filled in all the blanks. The bird thought this was hilarious.

"I'm saving you," Finch growled at the animal. *"Calm down, ya ham-sandwich-for-brains."*

But the dog did the opposite of that. Cauldron thrashed and snapped, his little body filled to the brim with grit and moxie. He hadn't shown this kind of wild determination when he was about to be hit by a car. *Nope*! He had to save it for Finch, like the *intelligent* and *good boy* he was.

When Finch arrived at Ceija's house, he pounded on the front door. The instant she opened it, he shoved the dog into her arms and choked out the words, "He escaped."

"Cauldron?" Ceija breathed. "But how did you know where I lived?"

Finch turned on his heel while she asked the question, barely catching sight of Ceija's baffled expression. She muttered, "W-Wait, I don't know your name!" But Finch didn't bother responding as he stomped his way back to the car, jumped inside, and sped away.

Two blocks down, after Finch shot through two stop signs, Bree grabbed her seat belt and held it tight. "Um," she whispered. "Maybe we can give Cauldron the Mark of Chronos so he remembers who you are and doesn't mind when you save him?"

"*No*," Finch said through gritted teeth. "I'm not giving *the dog* any of my magic. I'm more tempted to give him a chloroform rag."

"Maybe I can save him, then? So he's not scared?"

"This is the fastest way," Finch said. He knew the girl would caress the animal and carry it gently to Ceija's door. They didn't have time for that. The dog could handle a couple seconds of confused transportation in exchange for his life. "Let's just focus on the investigation. Today we're going to follow Dr. Colton."

Finch ran a red light and turned down the road for the University of the Pacific. Although Bree clung to the sides of her seat, her worry written across her face, Finch felt no anxiety whatsoever. He had driven these exact same roads for days. The police weren't here, and neither were any reckless drivers. Finch had seen the same traffic conditions more than once—he *knew* when it was safe to ignore a few traffic laws.

It would all become useless information once this investigation was over, but until then, he used what information he had to his advantage. He made it to the university twenty minutes before Dr. Colton would leave at 5:55 a.m.

Finch parked the car on the road beyond the parking lot and waited. The minutes ticked by in silence.

Kull cooed a little tune in the back, helping to fill the car with some cheerful atmosphere. At one point, Finch was convinced it was the jingle from a chocolate bar commercial.

Bree giggled and glanced into the back of the car. "I love Kit Kats."

"I do, too," Kull said. "Sugar is the most mischievous of ingredients. It gives you quick bursts of energy, while also increasing inflammation and eventually scrambling your mood. What a devious trick. And it tastes so good, who doesn't get addicted?"

"You seem to like a lot of human things." Bree folded her arms. "How long have you wanted to have a human body?"

"Hm. For a while now. It's the only path left for me. I must do it."

"Really?"

Dr. Colton exited the parking lot exactly on time. Finch waved at Bree and Kull to quiet themselves, even though it wouldn't really help with their investigation. Finch just wanted to concentrate. He followed the doctor all the way from the university, back to Bree's house. Dr. Colton parked near the police, and Finch hung back in another driveway behind a line of tall shrubs.

Then he waited again. The morning fog gradually waned,

allowing the sunlight to coat the world in cheer. Finch turned up the AC, hating the bright light that shone off the chrome of nearby parked vehicles.

Kull didn't coo any songs. Instead, she flapped her wings and landed on the headrest of the passenger seat. "Do humans ever experience profound moments of realization? Spirits do."

"I think so," Bree muttered.

"Have *you* had one?"

"No, but I'm only twelve."

"Ah." Kull puffed her feathers. "I'm over four hundred years old. Which is quite impressive, I'll have you know. Spirits are frequently hunted for their magic. Witches, warlocks—even the few remaining wizards that exist—all want spirit energy for their strange rituals and items."

"That's awful." Bree frowned. She tilted her head back so she could stare up at the pigeon. "When I'm a warlock, I won't hunt spirits. Not ever."

Finch shot her a sideways glance. "You mean when you're a fully realized *witch*. You don't need to become a warlock to gain powers."

"But I'd rather be one." Bree sat straight and rubbed her chin with the sleeve of her oversized coat. "Wait. Can I be both? What would you call that? A *witlock*?"

"A *watch*," Kull quipped.

Finch shot them both glares. Bree ducked lower into her coat, but Kull merely chuckled.

"You can't be both," Finch eventually grumbled. He glanced away, keeping his attention on Dr. Colton's parked vehicle. "Remember those cores of your being I told you about?"

Bree perked up. "The crown, the eyes, the heart, the soul, and the loins? I totally remember." She repeated them with such haste and excitement that her volume increased with each word.

"*Shh*," Finch said. "Yes. Those. Listen, when you get a little older, you'll fill those cores with your own witch magic. Once you've developed your abilities, creatures won't be able to tie themselves to you. It's like… you're parking at your own pier. All five of them. At the same time."

"That's a terrible analogy," Kull said.

"*I know*." Finch waved his hand at the bird. "It was the *girl's*."

"Uh-huh. Clearly you lack the gift to teach." When Finch waved his hand again, this time closer to Kull, the pigeon hopped to the side of the headrest, her feathers fluffed.

"Sit in the back," Finch commanded.

Bree tapped her fingers together, her brow furrowed. "So I have to choose? I can either be a witch or I can be a warlock?"

"You can be a warlock first," Kull said as she flapped her wings. "And then later become a witch. But once you finalize your training, and drink moonlight, you will never again have the choice to become a warlock. *You* will become a magical creature. Technically," Kull cooed a laugh as she said, "warlocks could make pacts with you. Though that is rare."

"Which is stronger?" Bree turned her attention to the window. She stared into her own faint reflection in the glass. "Which one will give me the most power? That's what I want."

"Spoken like a true *full moon witch*."

Finch snapped his fingers and pointed at the back seat. "I said, *get in the back*." After Kull complied, Finch glanced over at Bree. She remained silent. "Listen, Bree, the strength of a warlock comes from whatever they make a pact with. There are weak warlocks—"

"Like Papa," Bree whispered.

"—and there are powerful warlocks. But you have to be willing to fulfill pacts. It's a harder life. Magic doesn't *come* to warlocks like it does for witches. You should just stick to your training, and forget everything you see here."

Bree offered no response. She continued to stare, her gaze unfocused. Finch leaned back in his seat. When he glanced over, gazing through a hole in the shrubs, he spotted Dr. Colton hurrying to his vehicle. The doctor climbed inside and drove away from the house, and crime scene, much faster than he had driven in.

Finch started up his car, pulled out of the driveway once Dr. Colton passed, and then followed the man. Finch kept his distance, trying not to disturb the doctor's peace of mind, but it seemed that wasn't something Finch had to worry about. Dr. Colton drove like a drunkard. At one point, he almost smashed into a parked car.

Clearly, Dr. Colton was distracted. Or perhaps flustered.

A few minutes of questionable driving later, they entered a long stretch of road lined by orchards. An ocean of orange trees swayed in the morning breeze as Finch drove by. The scent on the air was pleasant, and filtered in through the AC.

Dr. Colton turned down a dirt road.

Finch parked before the turn.

"What're we doing?" Bree whispered.

"Following him," Finch replied.

"We aren't going to drive?"

Finch shook his head. "All the roads around here are dead ends. He's heading to his house. Or a ranch."

"Perhaps his house is a ranch," Kull offered from the back seat.

Finch opened the door of his Toyota. "Either way, we're going to pay the doctor a visit, but I don't want him to know we're coming."

Bree and Kull exited the vehicle from the passenger's side.

The beautiful morning greeted them with open arms. The aromatic wind played with Bree's brown hair, and she struggled to keep it out of her eyes. Kull landed on Finch's shoulder and hunkered down into her feathers, her head practically disappearing.

The walk down the dirt road wasn't long. Finch spotted Dr. Colton's four-door Nissan parked at the second house on the right, the trunk still open. He sauntered up the concrete driveway and peered into the back of the vehicle. A thick blanket covered the contents, and Finch carefully pulled back one edge to get a better look.

Necklaces with black beads.

At least a few dozen of them.

The doctor had taken them from the lab. But why? And why take them back to his house? Had he gone to Liam's in the hopes of handing them over? But was then surprised to find out he was missing and his wife was dead? Or was something else going on?

After a short huff, Finch threw the blanket back into place. He traveled along the footpath to the front door. The country home had plenty of space on each side, though the fence around the back told Finch this piece of property probably didn't own any of the orchards.

He stopped in front of the door and knocked twice.

The exterior of the house had dark paneling and brick detailing. The dark coloration contrasted harshly with the white picket fences and Easter colors of all the other houses on the same road.

"Why isn't Dr. Colton answering?" Bree whispered.

"I don't know," Finch muttered. "But we know he eventually goes back to the university, so he won't stay here long. We can stand on this porch until then."

A decorative bench sat on the front porch, half the seating

area taken over by potted plants. Bree took a seat and swung her legs.

Finch lifted his hand to knock again, but then it swung open, startling him for a split second. Dr. Colton stood inside the house, now in his all-brown suit like a uniform for a job at a chocolate factory.

"Uh, hello?" Dr. Colton asked as he gave Finch the once-over. "I'm sorry. I don't have any spare change to give you."

Bree leapt from her spot on the bench and took her place next to Finch. "Dr. Colton? Is it okay if we come inside?"

"Bree?" Dr. Colton asked, his eyes widening, his face paling. "W-What're you doing here? And with this... strange, homeless man?"

Again, Dr. Colton saw through the magic of Bree's coat, but now Finch wasn't confused. For some reason, the doctor had one of Liam's necklaces on him. It was clear to Finch that Dr. Colton had cleared the necklaces out of the lab. If he had one on underneath his clothes, or even in his pocket, the necklace would allow him to see through the minor illusions the coat created.

"Can we come in?" Bree repeated.

"I'm here to question Liam Blackstone's coworkers," Finch said. "I'm a PI working with the Stockton PD." He flashed his badge, but Dr. Colton didn't even glance at it.

"O-Oh, I see." Dr. Colton took in a deep inhale. "Uh, well, please come in." He hesitantly stepped aside and motioned them into his home.

Finch went first, his hands in his pockets. He scanned the front room and kitchen and immediately determined the doctor lived by himself. Most surfaces were covered in a fine layer of dust, and personal effects were scattered everywhere. Academy journals, a pair of socks on the armrest of the couch—but the real indicator was the single chair at the dining table. All the other chairs were in bizarre places. One was in the corner of the living room with a potted plant on top. Another chair sat next to the front door with hats resting on the headrest.

The lone chair betrayed Dr. Colton's entire living situation.

It was a quaint house without many pictures on the wall. The most interesting decorations seemed to be replicas of famous pottery, statues, and paintings. The doctor clearly loved history. Even his kitchen table was covered in so many ceramic pots and jars, Finch wondered if he was running a sad *Etsy* store.

"What is this about?" Dr. Colton asked. He stepped close to his dining table and awkwardly stood next to it. He patted his pockets, searching for something. "Because I need to get to the university to teach a class this morning. I'm very busy."

"My mum died," Bree said matter-of-factly, her tone cold. "Did you know that?"

"*What?* Oh, my goodness. I had no idea."

Bree's expression hardened, her glare much icier than her voice. "You're a liar."

Finch held up his hand and stepped between her and Dr. Colton. In a heated tone, he said, "Let's just cut to the chase. Where's Liam? What was he doing? Why are you trying to cover for him?"

"W-What're you talking about?" The doctor backed away and hit the table. A few jars toppled over. Dr. Colton kept his gaze on Finch while using his hands to feel the edge of the table to guide his stumbling as he went around. "I'm not involved. Get out of my house."

The man had the spine of a jellyfish. Finch had seen his type before. Applying pressure typically got answers—or at least interesting revelations that would lead him to answers.

Finch slammed his hands on the table. "I know where you

were this morning. I know you came back from Liam's house just now. I know about the necklaces."

All the color drained from Dr. Colton's face. "Oh, god. You're that... that detective Vera talked about. You're Adair Finch."

Kull cooed a laugh, and in that tense moment, it felt threatening.

"Are you going to cooperate?" Finch demanded. "Because trust me—I don't mind doing things the hard way."

With a shaky hand, Dr. Colton grabbed a ceramic jar and smashed the top on the wooden table. In the next instant, magic flooded the kitchen. The jar had contained a trap—a classic defensive measure witches often made for themselves or others to protect their homes.

Unfortunately, in the half second it took to activate, Finch knew it was powerful... and that he couldn't avoid it.

CHAPTER
FIFTEEN

he trap was a *Witch's Web*.

What felt like barbed wires lashed and tethered Finch's body in place. The restraints were invisible, but as solid as steel. The barbed wire cut through parts of Finch's clothing and dug deep into his skin. Wires wrapped around his arms and his legs, and one coiled around his neck. The barbs dug into his flesh, burning his senses, tunneling his vision.

Blood trickled to the tile floor, but some of it clung to the invisible wires, faintly showing their location. The wire covered most of the kitchen, and blood slid down each one. It looked like the wires had exploded outward from the broken jar, and after wrapping around its victims, had frozen in place.

Kull and Bree were tethered with the same sinister restraints. The pigeon was practically held midair, as though suspended in a spider's web. Bree, who stood at the door to the kitchen, bled from wires that wrapped around her shoulders and legs. She cried out, shocked and confused, her pain evident.

Dr. Colton, free from the trap's imprisoning properties, gulped down a breath and stumbled to the kitchen counter. "Oh god, oh god," he muttered as he pushed over old mail and paper towels in his frantic attempt to find something.

When Finch attempted to move, the barbed wires cut deeper. That was the insidious trick to the trap. It caught people and then slowly bled them to death in the most painful way possible. Witches sometimes wanted the blood for their brews—or sometimes they just wanted a good show.

The blinding agony made it difficult to concentrate, which in turn made it difficult to activate Chronos's ability. Finch took a deep breath, reminding himself it would be over as soon as he calmed down.

Dr. Colton held up something.

His cellphone.

With shaky movements, he dialed a number. The other end answered almost immediately.

"H-Hello?" Dr. Colton said as he held the phone flat against his cheek. *"You told me no one would be looking for me!"*

Someone on the other end shouted.

"S-Somehow Adair Finch is here! *He knows everything!* W-What am I supposed to do?"

Bree half screamed, half sobbed.

The cry broke Finch's concentration. When he managed a slight glance over his shoulder, his chest twisted in guilt. Her blood stained the wires scarlet.

"He's in the trap. He can't move. He…" Dr. Colton hesitated. "But, the girl—"

More shouting.

"Oh god."

The doctor slammed the phone down, sweat dappling his face. He hastily opened a drawer in the kitchen, and then withdrew a Glock 22. A potent 40 cal handgun with at least fifteen shots in the magazine. Dr. Colton held the weapon like it stank of BO, but despite that, he faced Finch.

But...

Pacts tied to the core of someone's crown required concentration. The mind controlled their function.

Pacts tied to the core of someone's heart, however, were another matter. Empowered by emotion—be it sadness, rage, love or anything between—the magical ability intensified whenever those feelings were the most prominent. Finch knew this. He had known since he became a warlock. In his panic, he had just momentarily forgotten.

Because the number of things a person couldn't remember when invisible barbed wire exploded in their face was everything *but* the barbed wire in their face.

On that note, Finch had also forgotten that Ke-Koh, the Ifrit of Rebellion, hated imprisonment and forced confinement. All Ke-Koh's magic and power was made ten times more potent whenever he, or his warlocks, were chained down or held against their will.

So when Finch imagined using Ke-Koh's fire, he envisioned burning the trap, freeing himself, and then searing Dr. Colton just enough to disable him.

What Finch had envisioned was *not* what happened in reality.

He called on the powers of Ke-Koh, and it was as if someone had dropped the *Mother of All Bombs* into the quaint little kitchen.

White and blue flames exploded forth from Finch. The superheated fire shattered the Witch's Web, incinerated the walls of the kitchen, carbonized the table, cremated Dr. Colton, and then violently burst into the surrounding orchards, burning up every tree it touched in a matter of seconds.

If there were any other verbs for *igniting really quickly*, all those happened as well. The oranges, the leaves, the grass, the glass of the window—they were ashed in a matter of moments, the might of the ifrit so powerful, it was as if the sun had touched a small portion of Earth.

A thick stench of burnt hair and smoke filled the air. Only the refrigerator and oven lasted longer, and even then, they were warped and blackened at the end of the evocation.

Everything else in front of Finch was a wasteland of ash and embers. Dr. Colton's house had been demolished down to the structural supports—but only the parts Finch faced. Everything behind him, such as the living room and entrance hall, was untouched.

There was nothing left of the jars and any other magics they may have contained.

Or of Dr. Colton.

Finch swallowed air and then staggered backward into a wall he hadn't leveled. His heart raced, and flashes of flame wafted out his mouth with his breath, Ke-Koh's magic flooding his veins.

"A-Adair…"

When he turned around, Finch spotted Bree on the tile floor. Her coat had been shredded by the trap, and blood ran as freely as her tears.

Now that he wasn't experiencing constant agony, Finch called on his powers from Chronos. He rewound time. Colors drained from the world, then objects, until finally there was nothing left but a void.

Then he closed his eyes.

A moment later, Finch jerked upright on his bed. He opened his eyes and glanced at his phone.

4:34 a.m.

Finch leapt out of bed and dashed across his dark apartment. *What a rookie mistake*, he thought as he reached the front door. *I should've checked the damn house. I should've been more vigilant.* He threw the door open, grabbed Bree, and then slammed the door closed. She trembled in his grasp, her eyes wide. At least she was no longer crying.

I should've been better.

Finch prepared the last bag of midnight raspberry tea and handed her the cup. Then he went to the window and opened it a mere two seconds before Kull landed on the sill. The mischievous pigeon flew into the living room and perched on the armrest of Finch's favorite recliner.

"I'm sorry," Finch muttered as he headed back into the kitchen to get himself some sort of tea. His anger still lingered, even if the world had forgotten what had happened.

Bree sipped her tea. It didn't take long for her trembling to stop. Then she held her cup close to her chest and stared at Finch with wide eyes. "You... burned everything. I didn't know you were that powerful."

"Ke-Koh the Ifrit of Rebellion is not known for his mercy," Kull said in a hushed voice. "He's an angry creature who dwells in the caves of Mount Damavand. Ke-Koh's fire is so hot, they say he could evaporate the Dead Sea." The pigeon cooed. "They also say his pacts are terrible, and he kills warlocks more often than not."

Kull flew from the living room and landed on the kitchen counter. Finch finished his tea and took a sip. It wasn't magically calming, but it did help with his own nerves.

"What did you do?" Kull whispered, her yellow eyes wide. "What sort of awful pact did you agree on to gain the ifrit's flames?"

Finch grabbed a pen and then marked the pigeon's wing with Chronos's magic. "It's none of your business." Then he turned his attention to Bree and drew the same mark on her arm. She continued sipping her tea, her gaze distant. "Are you okay?" Finch asked. "If you want to take a break, we can."

Bree shook her head. "No. I'm fine."

"You're not fine. You were just caught in a deadly trap."

"I've been shot before," Bree said matter-of-factly. "I'm not a baby."

Apparently, she was done being a preteen and ready to become a jaded fifty-year-old.

Bree walked out of the kitchen and navigated her way around a few piles of clothing before clearing her recliner and taking a seat. She drank the rest of her tea, never crying or complaining.

After a long sigh, Finch set down his own cup. He wandered into the living room and took a seat in his own recliner. Then he faced it toward Bree. "Listen—I'm sorry. It was…" He ran a hand down his face, unable to look at the girl as he said, "That never should've happened."

"It didn't happen," Bree said.

Finch glanced up and met her blue-eyed gaze. "What?"

"It didn't happen," she repeated. "You reversed it."

He shook his head. "But it shouldn't have ever happened. Those kinds of tricks are the things I could've prevented if I had been vigilant." Finch buried his face in his palms. "I'm sorry."

Kull flew onto Bree's chair. The pigeon cooed and fluffed her feathers.

"We're fine now," Bree said. "Why are you so upset?"

"*Because I fucked up*," Finch shouted as he stood from his chair, his voice louder than he wanted. "I couldn't have known about the sniper. That was an escalation to this case I didn't see coming. But *this*? That lunatic doctor isn't even a warlock. He's using borrowed magic. Stupid traps. I should've searched the place first. I shouldn't have confronted the man without knowing what he had at his disposal."

Finch turned on his heel and paced a small portion of his apartment. He was about to open his mouth again, to rant about how he knew Dr. Colton had magical items because of the necklaces, but Finch stopped cold. He stared at the pictures of Carter on the wall.

His anger and shame only deepened.

"I should've been more vigilant," Finch whispered, more to the pictures than to Bree.

After a deep breath, Bree slid off the recliner. She walked over to Finch and stood only a few feet away. "I forgive you."

He whirled on his heel to face her, his eyebrows knitted.

Silence stretched between them.

Bree reached down into a pile of clothing and pulled out the oversized coat with a strange stripe of rainbow iridescence on the sleeve. Then she slowly slipped it on. "Are you almost ready to go?" she asked.

Finch huffed a single laugh. "Eager to get back out there? After what just happened?"

"Well…" Bree rubbed her eyes and shook her head. When she glanced back up at Finch, she was practically glaring. "We can't just let Dr. Colton get away with that."

Kull flapped her wings. "Oh, yes. I love me some good vengeance."

"You want to strike back at the man?" Finch asked.

Bree nodded once. "He's a liar and snake, *and I hate him*. He obviously knows where Papa is." She swung her arms as she spoke, wrapped up in her anger, just as Finch had been. "He's not being truthful with us! And then he used a trap that Mum made? I hate him. *I'll never forgive him*."

"Your mother made that Witch's Web?" Finch rubbed his stubbly chin. "You're certain?"

Again, Bree nodded. "Of course. I know Mum's magic. That was *hers*. I don't know why Dr. Colton had it. But we should make him pay."

"He was burned to a crisp last time," Kull interjected, her tone all sorts of sarcastic.

"No, it's not enough." Bree closed her coat and secured it shut. "We should get that trap and use it on him. Then he'll really be sorry."

That was dark. But Finch understood the sentiment. However, something wasn't adding up. He sighed as he resumed his pacing, albeit slower. With each step he mulled over the problem. Both Kull and Bree watched him as he went back and forth near the far window.

He didn't want to keep them out of the loop.

"Dr. Colton isn't the killer," Finch said aloud. "But he does know who the killer is, or at the very least, he knows whatever organization the killer belongs to."

Bree tapped her fingertips together. "He has to be helping Mum's murderer. He tried to kill us."

"But he was also shot in the university parking lot," Finch stated. "I doubt it was by accident. That means the killer finds him useful, but he's probably a liability. The doctor knows too much. However, Dr. Colton clearly thought shooting a detective working with the Stockton PD, and potentially murdering a little girl, was a better option than facing the killer himself."

Kull cooed. "Oh, I see. You suspect the murderer is someone prominent. Or at least powerful." The pigeon tilted her head from one side to the other. "Interesting, interesting."

"And I think Liam was being pressured into making those necklaces," Finch said, voicing all his conclusions. "Which further indicates this is an organization we're pursuing, not a single person."

"Only one person was in the kitchen when Mum… when she died." Bree frowned.

Finch stopped pacing. "Sorry. I know that. I mean, the killer is part of something. Like a gang, or a coven, or some sort of hunters' group."

"It can't be a witch's coven. Only women can be witches, and the murderer was definitely a man."

"But covens can hire or train men to help them," Finch muttered, still mulling over all the facts. Could Vera and Liam have angered other witches? The Occultist hadn't mentioned anything about that when they arrived, and she had Bree's full name. It would've been obvious who had died.

That wasn't adding up.

"Well, are we going to go?" Bree asked, her shoulders squared. "Because I still think Dr. Colton should pay." She stomped over to the front door. "He might not be the killer, but he's gross and awful. Even if you have to burn him a hundred times, it'll never be enough to make up for what he's done."

CHAPTER
SIXTEEN

F inch drove from his apartment complex and headed straight for the dog. He parked, dragged the pooch out of the bushes, and carried him all the way to Ceija. This time, he didn't even say anything. He handed her Cauldron and left immediately afterward, a mysterious hobo who would certainly define her whole day.

Until Finch reset time and did it all over again.

Then he headed straight for Bree's house. The roads to the murder location were easy to navigate, and Finch found himself replaying the scene in Dr. Colton's home several times before he made it to the street with all the police vehicles.

Fog lingered between nearby trees. The chill of the gloomy morning welcomed Finch as soon as he opened his car door.

"What're we doing here?" Bree asked. "We need to catch Dr. Colton at his house."

Finch shook his head. "No. First, we need to search his house. He returns to the university at 7:48 a.m., so that means we can enter his place after that. In the meantime, I'm going to speak with the lead detective again." He reached into the glove compartment and withdrew his badge.

"Why?"

Finch stepped out of the vehicle and pulled his coat tighter around his body. "I'm going to ask him about Dr. Colton. Last time I was here, I didn't think to question the man about Liam's coworkers, or any affiliations Liam might have. I want to know everything the police do before we go deeper."

Bree nodded along with his words. Then she settled herself into the passenger's side. Kull flew into her lap, and Bree petted the pigeon like it was her familiar.

"I'll wait here," she muttered.

Finch lifted an eyebrow. "You're sure?"

"Just be back quick." Bree forced a smile. "I know nothing is around here because we already did this once before, right? I'm safe."

Finch replied with a curt nod. Then he shut the door of his car and headed toward the front door. Just like before, Finch ducked under the police tape. Half a dozen police officers leapt from their vehicles and tried to stop him, but Finch flashed his badge, stopping them all in their tracks.

The quaint house was exactly as Finch remembered it. He traveled down the short entrance hall, turned left at the T intersection, and entered the crime scene—the kitchen and living room. The old clock hanging on the wall ticked as Finch walked by, a steady constant that echoed throughout the whole house.

Forensic officers were deep in their work as Finch approached the island in the middle of the kitchen. The bloodstains on the floor were just as fresh as ever, even if Finch had been working on this case for longer than two weeks.

"You?"

Finch glanced over at the dumbfounded detective. Rhett Jenner wore plain clothes—jeans, a black shirt, tennis shoes—and he had a harsh part in his hair, exposing a part of his scalp. Who could forget Detective Jenner? The man radiated constant discontentment.

"In the flesh," Finch quipped again.

Detective Jenner's face reddened. He rubbed his jaw, his eyes narrowing. "You're Adair Finch. One of the *special* detectives."

There was no need to dance around things. "I already know everything about the case," Finch stated. "So you don't need to bother telling me the mundane details."

"You…" Jenner stared at him, his eyebrows knitted. "You know everything?" he finally whispered.

"Vera was stabbed to death by an intruder in the middle of the night. Her husband is missing. So is his car. So is his daughter." Finch motioned to the other forensic officers. "I can't say more, currently."

Detective Jenner's face reddened slightly as he waved his hand through the air. "Clear out," he commanded. "Take fifteen, and then come back and finish what you're doing as soon as possible."

The forensic crew grumbled in irritation, just like they had before. The cameraman stepped forward, but Jenner snapped his fingers, and no one uttered any further objections. They cleared out of the kitchen and dining room, muttering observations to themselves as they went.

Finch wished they would move faster. He had seen this before, and seeing it a second time just irritated him.

Once alone with Finch, Jenner shook his head. "We don't need your magic," he growled under his breath. "Me and my boys are—"

"*Are capable of solving it without my mumbo jumbo,*" Finch finished, mimicking Jenner's voice. With a roll of his eyes,

Finch stepped around the island and then faced the detective. "Liam was kidnapped. He's being used to create magical necklaces against his better judgment. Probably against his will."

"W-What?" It took Jenner several seconds to process the information, like English was his third language rather than his first. "That doesn't matter to—"

"That's why there was an argument between him and his wife last night. I'm fairly certain the killer is the person who wants Liam to continue making jewelry for him."

"But…" Jenner blinked his eyes. The redness of his face drained until he was pale. His bewilderment stole his words, clearly. "Are you involved in this?" he eventually whispered.

"No, I'm just on top of it," Finch quipped.

"The murder happened just a few hours ago. Unless you're involved, how would you know anything that—"

Finch sarcastically waved his fingers. "All my *mumbo jumbo*." Then he hardened his gaze. "Liam's coworker, Dr. Colton, is in on it. This morning, the man took dozens of necklaces from the university to hide them in his house. Do you know anything about that?"

Detective Jenner didn't move. He didn't say anything, either. He remained stiff, his eyes wide. Was he *that* surprised by all Finch's knowledge? The man looked like he could barely believe what he was hearing.

"Do you know who the killer is?" Jenner asked, his voice low.

"Not yet. But I will." Finch narrowed his eyes. "If you cooperate."

"I…" The detective shook his head. "This is insanity. No magic would give you this type of information. You must be involved in this somehow." He pulled out his notepad and jotted a few notes down. "I'm gonna have to question you."

"Fine. Just tell me what I need to know. Who is Dr.

Colton? And why is he involved with Liam when he's not a warlock?"

Jenner shook his head. "I don't know anything about Dr. Colton," he said, anger in his voice. "And you'll need to come to the station with me. This is too crazy—too bizarre. You think you can come in here and spout information like it doesn't matter? You clearly know something. Weird Merlin wannabes and your lunacy."

"It's too early in the day," Finch muttered with a sigh. He had known this was a possibility. Detective Jenner had barely familiarized himself with the case. The police likely hadn't chatted with Dr. Colton yet, which was why the doctor was going out of his way to hide evidence.

If Finch wanted to use the police to his benefit, he would need to speak to the detective later in the day, *after* the man had gathered whatever information he could. But did Finch have the patience for that? Given how fast he was collecting pieces to the puzzle, there was little need for the police or Detective Jenner.

Jenner motioned to the door. "C'mon. We'll take my vehicle."

But Finch wasn't going to go to the police station to be needlessly interrogated. Instead, he rewound time.

Everything stopped.

The color drained from the world, leaving it black and white, like an untouched coloring book.

Then the objects fell away, and Finch returned to his bedroom.

———

Every morning had the same steps. Finch ran through them with the speed of an expert.

Get Bree out of the hallway.

Make tea.

Get Kull from the windowsill.

Draw the Mark of Chronos on both.

Give Bree her coat.

And... save the damn dog.

Once Cauldron was back in the arms of his owner, Finch headed toward Dr. Colton's house. He couldn't go there yet, because it was too early, so he pulled his Toyota into the parking lot of an old coffee shop on the outskirts of town. It was a run-down joint, with a deserted pet shop on one side, and an empty office building on the other.

Parts of Stockton were forgotten to time, and those were the last few places Finch felt like he fit in. He parked the car and then stepped out into the fog. Bree and Kull exited a moment later.

"Why did you reset time?" Bree asked. "You haven't answered me all morning."

"The detective was suspicious when I knew too much about the case," Finch muttered.

"Okay. But why are we here? Shouldn't we go to Dr. Colton's?"

"We're going to drink coffee and wait until he returns to work before searching his house."

In reality, Finch just wanted the girl to have some peace and quiet after what had happened. Although Bree refused to admit she was shaken, Finch knew better. They would relax, have a pastry or two, and *then* dive back into the investigation.

Kull stayed on Bree's shoulder as the three of them approached *Nico's Brew*, the sad hole-in-the-wall joint that smelled of coffee beans from half a mile away. The windows had thick blinds over them, and the neon 'open' sign blinked at such a frequent rate, it was using Morse code to ask someone to kill it and put it out of its misery.

"The detective is right… I would be suspicious, too," Kull said. "Warlocks are rather shady individuals. I'm surprised you haven't suspected one of them." The pigeon tilted her head, her eyes not even focused on anything as she said, "After all, wouldn't a warlock killer make the most sense? They would know Liam and Vera, and know of their capabilities…"

"The problem is that warlocks don't form covens or have much hierarchy. At least not around here." Finch rubbed his eyes as he reached for the door of the shop. There were other places in the world where warlocks were forced to "license" themselves and join clans, but that wasn't the case in sunny California. That only happened in places around the world with old structures and legacy organizations.

They entered *Nico's Brew* and found it devoid of patrons. The owner, Nico himself, stood behind a small bar. He kept his beans on display, each type, from Arabica to Liberica, packed in bags and sitting on a shelf mounted to the wall. A flatscreen TV hung in the top corner of the coffee shop. The news played, and Nico watched it with undivided attention.

The man, his gut so large it looked as though he were hiding a second person in his T-shirt, didn't even bother offering a good morning. He smoothed his thick mustache and narrowed his dark eyes at the screen. The news anchor reported on a drug scandal, with no mention of Vera's brutal death.

Finch sat down at a booth near the door. Bree sat on the opposite side.

When Kull hopped onto the table, Nico glanced over with an icy glare.

"Is that a *pigeon*?" the coffee shop owner asked.

Bree grabbed the bird. It squawked as she pulled it into her coat. The giant article of clothing had more than enough room for a little girl and an animal, but the bird thrashed about, killing any chance of remaining hidden.

"It's not a pigeon," Bree said, crossing her arms and holding down the mischief spirit. "It's, uh, a cat. My therapy cat. It's a service animal."

Nico stared, his mouth slightly open, his upper lip curled in disgust. He rubbed his eyes, as if questioning his own perceptions. Before he could reply, a black cat leapt up from the collar of Bree's coat. The feline landed on the table with such grace that there was no sound upon impact. Kull had transformed, and her black coat was as lustrous as ever.

Bree wrapped her arms around Kull. "It's against the law in California to send people away if they have service animals. You have to let me keep her."

She was right. In California, individuals with service animals couldn't be denied because of their animal. There were expectations, of course, but the courts of California were just as crazy as their laws. Even if the cat were ripping up the blinds and pissing on the carpet, it was better than dealing with a judge and paying an overpriced attorney.

Courtrooms were where taxpayer money went to die.

"Fine," Nico said with a grunt. He pointed a large finger at her. "Keep it to yourself." Then he exhaled and slowly returned his attention to the TV.

Kull purred and swished her cat tail. "Adair," she whispered, a smile in her voice. "When you get me a human body, can I have one like his?" She pointed with the tip of her tail at Nico.

"You want to be an overweight Italian with diabetes?" Finch asked.

"The body doesn't have to be overweight—I just want to stand out. I want a noticeably beautiful body. Or a strikingly athletic one. Or the tallest one you can find." Kull tilted her head and twitched her whiskers. "I want people to remember me even after a casual glance."

"That wasn't part of our arrangement," Finch muttered, no emotion in his voice.

Bree petted Kull down the back. "Maybe once you have a human body, you can dye your hair? Then you'll stand out."

"It's 2024—everyone dyes their hair." Finch rolled his eyes.

"W-Well, maybe she can wear colorful makeup."

He leaned back in the booth and laughed once. "Have you seen social media? They've resorted to drinking bleach in order to get fifteen seconds of attention. Kull will have to try harder than *makeup* and *dyed hair* if she wants to stand out."

Nico walked over to the booth and slammed a mug of coffee on the table in front of Finch. The dark liquid rivaled the night sky, its contents visibly potent.

"The usual," Nico said, his voice scratchy and gruff from years of smoking. He turned his cold stare on Bree. "And what will you have?"

"I'll have the same thing," Bree stated matter-of-factly.

Both Nico and Finch chuckled. Their amusement didn't sit well with Bree, however. She exhaled and frowned. "What?" she demanded. "I can handle whatever Adair is drinking. That's what I want."

"How about I fill yours with cream and sugar and milk?" Nico rubbed his gut. "Hm? You'd like that? It'll knock the socks off Starbucks."

Bree shook her head. "I don't want that. I want it just like Adair's."

She said nothing else, and made no other arguments. She knew what she wanted. Nico didn't debate the issue further. He shrugged and then lumbered away, clearly too old for any of this garbage.

"We need to be super awake," Bree muttered. She glanced

over and spotted a small napkin container at the other end of the booth. After a short sigh, she tugged a napkin free and held it with both her hands. "We have to catch Dr. Colton off guard."

"Hm." Finch allowed his thoughts to dwell on the doctor's home. He couldn't have *too* much magic there.

"How much can your fire destroy?" Bree tore a small piece of the napkin away from one of the corners. "Could you... destroy this whole coffee shop in a single blast? If you wanted, I mean."

"Yes," Finch absentmindedly replied.

In reality, he had only used a small blast of Ke-Koh's fire. Finch had wanted to just destroy the trap and slightly harm Dr. Colton, not raze the neighborhood. And while he *could* nuke the coffee shop into oblivion, that wasn't going to help them catch the killer. Why would Bree even ask such a question?

"When we find Dr. Colton..." Bree lowered her voice to a serious whisper, her gaze hyper focused on the napkin. "We should burn him slowly. Start with his hands. I bet he'd be really scared if that happened... if he couldn't ever hold or touch anything ever again."

She ripped up the napkin into little bits, practically creating confetti and cluttering the booth table with her destruction.

Then Nico cleared his throat.

Both Finch and Bree tensed and turned. Nico had been standing there for only a few moments, but it was clear he had heard more than he wanted. An awkward moment of silence passed. Nico glared at them with a deep—and very concerned—frown.

"Here's your coffee," he said as he hesitantly placed it on the table and scooted it toward Bree. Then Nico shot a glower in Finch's direction. He said nothing, but the concern was evident.

No one uttered a word as the Italian man stomped his way back over to his position behind the bar. Kull watched him go, her gold eyes appraising. "Oh, yes... So large. So wondrous."

Finch slid his arm across the booth table and collected the shredded bits of napkin. Then he shoved the cup of coffee closer to the girl and leaned onto the table. "You know what? How about we get a few croissants, and you take it easy? *Torturing a man* doesn't sound like something you'd normally suggest."

"He's helping my mum's murderer," Bree intoned. She kept her gaze on his, her eyes glassy. "He tried to kill us."

Finch couldn't disagree. Dr. Colton was obviously a trap at some level. He was either armed, or someone around him was. Perhaps burning him a bit was the only solution. Finch didn't like that Bree was suggesting it, though. She was much too young to consider such solutions.

"Kull is right, you know." Bree glanced away. She stared at the table, her woebegone expression worsening. "Once you rewind time, it won't matter anyway. We might as well torture Dr. Colton, get our information, and never think about it again."

"Maybe." Finch sighed.

Bree didn't reply. She didn't even really blink. The girl just stared, her lip on the verge of quavering.

What was there to say? Finch searched for the words, but they never came. He understood the feeling—all too well—of wanting to hurt everyone who ever fucked with him. But those desires had soured into something bitter. How could he keep that same process from harming a little girl? What advice could he give, or actions could he take, to stop her from ending up cold and hateful?

Perhaps giving her what she wanted was the best solution.

A smash echoed throughout the tiny coffee shop.

Nico, Bree, and Finch all turned their attention to the black cat sitting on the end of the table. In classic feline fashion, Kull had pushed Bree's coffee mug off the edge. The white cup was shattered across the floor, the black liquid splattered in all directions.

Kull snickered a mischievous laugh.

"*Get out!*" Nico bellowed, his voice so loud that even Bree's mother could hear it. "Get out, the both of you! I don't want no destructive psychopaths in my shop. You're banned! *Banned.*"

CHAPTER
SEVENTEEN

F inch drove through a Starbucks and begrudgingly ordered a frou-frou drink and breakfast pastries. The price was damn near half his rent, and all his dignity, but Finch didn't care. Bree nibbled her meal, her quiet demeanor still a concern. The cat, on the other hand, didn't need to eat. Spirits gained their sustenance differently than humans. Some spirits ate flesh, others gained strength from the sun or the moon, and some spirits just supped from the universe, never needing anything.

Kull was clearly a spirit that fed on annoyance. That was the only explanation for her shenanigans.

As a cat, Kull sat in the back of the car, never making much noise… which worried Finch. He glanced in the rearview mirror more than once, just to make sure the feline wasn't misbehaving.

When the time on his phone showed 7:48 a.m., Finch went straight for Dr. Colton's house. The doctor was now at the university, and supposedly about to start his class. That would give Finch plenty of time to investigate the doctor's home and disable all the traps.

Finch drove down the road with the orchards and then pulled his vehicle into Dr. Colton's empty drive. After a long sigh, Finch stepped out and headed for the door. Bree and Kull followed shortly after.

"Are you scared?" Bree asked.

The little mischief spirit trotted toward the front door. "Of course not."

"Why? When the traps went off, you couldn't escape."

"Oho! You forget, we have a powerful warlock on our side. And as a spirit, I've found myself in quite a few traps. Sometimes the person who traps you is fun."

Bree frowned as she took her place by Finch. "Being trapped didn't seem like fun," she whispered. Then she reached for the door handle.

Finch grabbed her wrist. Bree flinched and stared up at him. He shook his head, released her arm, and then motioned her away.

"Dr. Colton is clearly using magic to defend his home." He knelt in front of the door. "So we're going to use magic to get inside."

The declaration caused Kull to puff out her chest and hold her head high. Finch ignored her as he placed his hand on the front door. Since she was a spirit of mischief, the ability she imparted to him was one of *making something less secure*—a disturbance ability. It undid locks, loosened knots, and silenced alarms, though that wasn't all it was limited to.

And since Finch had tied her magic to his eyes, all he had to do was visualize the *disturbing* process in order for his magic to work properly. Additionally, magic tied to the core of someone's eyes meant people perceived the warlock differently. As Kull had said—Finch didn't appear on cameras, and he suspected any of his sleight-of-hand trickery would be less detectable.

But he shook away the thoughts. What did it matter if he

was caught on camera or not? All he needed was his *disturbance,* and he would be fine.

Finch pressed his hand into the wood and focused, visualizing everything he needed. His magic seeped into the door, and then traveled to the handle and the doorframe. It struggled for a moment, like a slow car over a large bump, and Finch knew there had been some sort of spell or enchantment on the entrance.

Not anymore.

The handle *clicked,* and the door was unlocked. No traps were triggered.

"Was it dangerous?" Bree whispered. "Did you make it safe?"

"It *was* dangerous, but not any longer."

Finch stood, dusted off his pants, and then opened the door. Bree and Kull both turned to Finch, even though he held the door open for them. When it was clear neither of them would go in first, Finch sighed before heading inside.

Dr. Colton's house remained the same. Dust lingered on every surface. The walls were devoid of personal photos, and instead most of the decorations were replicas of famous paintings. The kitchen table was still covered in ceramic jars.

This time, however, Finch took a moment to sense his surroundings. Magic left a trace, after all, like dust in the air. He crept into the kitchen, and took note of the presence he felt around the jars. They were *all* filled with magic, though some were more potent than others.

Bree stood half inside the house, and half out. She tapped her fingers along the doorframe, her brow furrowed. "Is it okay?"

"You can wait there," Finch muttered. "I'll handle this."

He grazed his fingers across the lids of the many jars. Some were traps, others were filled with bits of magic—the pieces of spirits or something similar. Without opening the jars, Finch wouldn't know for sure, but he had felt enough raw magical energy to know the difference between that and something crafted, like a spell or enchantment.

Unfortunately, Finch was once again reminded he wasn't apt at identification. Just like with the necklaces, he couldn't determine the details of the traps. But did that matter? No. He didn't want the jars, anyway—he just wanted to disable all Dr. Colton's tricks before the man arrived back home.

So Finch grabbed the nearest jar and gripped the lid. With Kull's *disturbance*, Finch prevented the trap from triggering. Then Ke-Koh's fire surged from his grip. Now that he wasn't enraged or panicked, the flames worked exactly as he wanted them to. The heat soaked into the jar and broke it apart into ash. The magic inside was set ablaze, and everything was destroyed without ill effect.

Finch did that with the other twenty-eight jars on the table.

One by one, he turned them into smoldering piles of embers and ash.

As soon as he finished, he walked into the kitchen. Dr. Colton had pulled a gun from a drawer, and Finch turned his attention to that location immediately. He opened it and found the gun inside, along with a spare magazine. It was interesting, only because Finch was certain Dr. Colton hadn't purchased this gun for himself.

Someone had given it to him.

Finch knew only because of the magazine. No one purchased bullets already loaded in a mag. They purchased bullets by the box and then loaded their own mags. But there were no bullet boxes around. The handgun was in the drawer, one mag next to it, like someone had *handed* it to Dr. Colton in case of an emergency.

Which only reinforced Finch's theory.

The murderer worked for an organization. And so did

Dr. Colton, though it was clear the doctor was much further down the list.

"Are you all done?" Bree called from the front door.

"I'm going to search the rest of the house," Finch replied. He took the handgun and tucked it into the waistband of his pants.

Then he crept around the small home, slowly making his way down a long hall. He carefully investigated the two bathrooms and bedrooms, making sure to flip up the pillows and open every drawer, even the small ones under the sinks.

The rest of the house reminded Finch of an Amazon warehouse. Boxes were stacked in the corners with most of Dr. Colton's belongings inside of them. The doctor's bed, dresser, and wardrobe were still in the bedroom, but otherwise everything was packed.

Like Dr. Colton expected to leave soon.

Satisfied with his search, Finch returned to the front door.

"It's clear," he said.

Kull sauntered into the house, her feline form carrying a certain amount of swagger. She twitched the tip of her tail and tilted her head. "Hm. Most of the magic in this house has dissipated... You did a thorough job. What a shame."

"A shame?" Finch snapped.

Kull nodded once. "It would've been amusing if you accidentally triggered something. Could you imagine? Legendary PI warlock gets caught in a sticky trap?" She purred a laugh. "You must admit it would make you laugh if it weren't you."

Bree shut the front door and headed for the kitchen. She glanced around. Then she tiptoed over to the drawer with the handgun and opened it.

"F-Finch," she stammered. "The gun is gone."

"I have it," he stated.

"Really?" Bree closed the drawer. "Do you know how to use it?"

Finch couldn't stop himself from laughing. He patted his chest as he quickly calmed himself. "Oh, yes. I'm quite familiar."

"How come you don't carry a gun around normally, then?"

Finch thought back to his apartment. He had two handguns and a rifle tucked away in his hall closet. They were secured in a safe, all their ammo alongside them. He and Carter had taken them whenever they investigated dangerous locations, but having them sometimes caused average citizens to panic—especially in California.

"If it makes you feel more secure, I'll start carrying one," Finch stated.

Bree half shrugged. "N-No. I was just curious."

"Since I bonded with Ke-Koh, it's been less of a priority." Finch curled his hand into a ball. The heat in his fingertips lingered. "He's a powerful destructive force."

Noises from the front porch silenced everyone. Kull sat perfectly straight, her ears pointed toward the door. Bree glanced between Finch and the entrance, her eyes wide.

Was Dr. Colton home already? That was fine by Finch. He glanced at his phone.

8:01 a.m.

Harsh banging rang throughout the house. Someone was knocking.

Which meant it wasn't Dr. Colton. Who knocked on their own front door? It was someone else—someone without much patience.

Finch rubbed his hands down his coat before pulling open the door. A strange man stood outside, his arm up, like he was ready to knock again. He wore a pair of ripped jeans and enough metal piercings to compete with a hardware store. Earrings and studs jutted from every protruding or dangling bit of flesh on the man's face.

The sides of his head were shaved short, with his dark hair on top, kept long, hanging limply to the side in the world's saddest mohawk. And the man's eyes were so far apart, it was as though they were trying to escape his face.

The ratty black T-shirt and scruffy boots weren't really helping the man, either.

A slight amount of magic wafted around the man like a perfume.

"Who're you?" Finch barked.

The man scratched his scalp. "You're Dr. Colton, yeah? I'm here for the traps." He thrust his hand forward, palm up. "I'm runnin' errands for the Haggin Coven. C'mon, c'mon. I don't got all day."

"I'm not the doctor." Finch shut the door.

Or at least, he *tried* to shut the door. The weirdo man slammed his foot between the door and the frame right at the last second. Finch hadn't been soft about his dismissal, and the man outside yelped.

Reluctantly, Finch opened the door again, and the man stomped his way halfway into the house.

"I said I'm here for the stuff," he said as he slicked back his limp mohawk. "Did you not hear me, *Doc*?" He shook out his foot and then shoved through more of the door.

Finch didn't move. Both men stood less than a few inches from each other. Although the man reeked of smalltime aggression, Finch suspected it was more bluster than bravery.

"What's your problem?" The man glared, his hands shaky. "I'm a *warlock*, asshole. If you don't give me what I came for, this is gonna get ugly for you."

"What's your name?" Finch asked.

"Seth Rivers."

Finch had never heard of him, and given the tiny amount of magic that swirled around Seth's body, Finch was certain he was a beginner warlock at best. This was a petty criminal with some slight magical abilities that probably made him "top dog" among the magicless. Mundane uses for extraordinary abilities could get someone far—but never great.

"I'm not the doctor," Finch said again. "You should come back later." He remained tensed, ready to fight the punk—he couldn't let his guard down—but out of all the things he wanted to do, this was near the bottom of the list. *Note to self,* he thought, *don't enter Dr. Colton's house until 9am in order to avoid this lunatic.*

Seth pulled out a switchblade from the pocket of his jeans. The three-inch blade popped out with a *shick.*

Out of instinct, Finch took a step back and reached for the handgun tucked away at his waistband. The thug stepped into the house, brandishing his weapon like it could kill upon contact.

Finch sighed, and held back the urge to roll his eyes. Why did this have to happen *now*, of all times?

"Adair?" Bree whispered from the kitchen. She poked her head around the corner and stared at the man brandishing a knife. "What's going on?"

Kull sat on the table, watching with bright yellow eyes. She said nothing, maintaining her disguise as a cat. However, if this man worked with a local coven, he was already in the know, and could potentially sense her magical nature. Finch wasn't sure.

"Stay back, Bree," Finch stated.

She frowned. "Who's that? Why is he here?"

"What is this?" Seth huffed out a fake confident laugh. "Who's this kid? I was told the doctor lived alone."

"I'm *not* the doctor," Finch stated again, his volume rising. "I'm a detective with the Stockton PD."

Seth slashed his knife through the air, though he never stepped any closer. Bree gasped and then cut off the sound by gritting her teeth. She didn't run or hide—she remained firmly planted in her spot, her knuckles white as she held on to the doorframe of the kitchen.

"What's *your* name?" Seth asked.

"Adair Finch."

After another laugh, the goon said, "Is that supposed to be funny? Adair is *dead*, fuckface. You can't fool me. I know everything about this town."

"Apparently not."

"I'm *really* a warlock." Seth tightened his grip on his weapon. "And the coven said I can do whatever it takes to get those traps, so if you want your money—and your life—you'll give them to me without any more bullshit."

Bree glanced between the thug and Finch. Then she said, "He's with my mum's killers, too. You should use your fire, Adair. He doesn't deserve mercy."

CHAPTER
EIGHTEEN

Seth thrust his switchblade forward, his stance pathetic, his grip weak.

The whole fight could've been measured in heartbeats.

Finch grabbed the man's wrist, twisted hard, and then kicked Seth's dominant ankle. The man dropped his weapon, yelled, and then fell to the floor. Finch slammed his knee into Seth's back, pinning him. Then Finch withdrew the doctor's handgun and dug the barrel into the man's spine.

Like riding a bike, he sarcastically thought, though he took note of how much slower he had gotten. If Carter had been here, his brother would've thrown in a few punches for good measure, and Seth would've been out cold, rather than just pinned.

Those were the good ol' days, though.

Now Finch had to hold Seth to the floor.

"O-Oh, shit," Seth stammered, his face already dappled with sweat. He placed his hands palms-down on the floor. "I'm not resisting! I'm not."

Splayed out on the living room floor, Seth barely

struggled as Finch shifted his weight into a more comfortable position. He remained tense, waiting for the "warlock" to use any sort of magical ability, but nothing happened.

Unfortunately, that told Finch that Seth was hiding a trick up his sleeve. The moment Finch dropped his guard, Seth would do something stupid. It happened every time.

Bree stepped out of the kitchen and crept closer. "You got him?" she asked.

Kull leapt off the table and landed next to Bree. "This warlock is weak. I'm surprised he even tried to fight. A smarter man would've run." The spirit sniffed Seth's leg. "Hm. His intelligence parallels his level of magic…"

"Can you tell what he's bonded with?" Bree asked.

Kull sniffed Seth a second time. "Marijuana."

"F-Fuck you," Seth shouted, his spittle coating the floor in front of him. "You're all gonna regret messin' with the coven. You should just give me the stuff, or else you're gonna get cursed and… and…"

Bree fidgeted with her oversized coat. Then she hardened her expression. "Adair—ask him about my papa. Maybe he knows something."

"Do you know anything about Liam Blackstone?" Finch asked.

Seth squirmed, but it was halfhearted. Finch suspected the man was just testing the waters.

"You can go to hell," Seth said into the wood floor.

Seth said nothing afterward, but his breathing remained deep and ragged, betraying his anxiety. The man was a terrible liar. Well, he was a terrible gofer, too. And a terrible warlock. Also, a terrible dresser. Really, there was nothing Finch had seen from the man that he wouldn't immediately categorize as "desperately needs improvement."

"You should burn him," Bree said, her tone cold.

Finch glanced over, his eyes narrowed. "You sure?"

There was a moment's hesitation before Bree stiffened her posture. She held her hands together in front of her as she whispered, "Yes. He… tried to kill you. We shouldn't let him get away with that. So…" Bree didn't finish the sentence.

The man on the floor said nothing.

Finch exhaled. People in severe physical pain tended to say whatever they needed to in order to escape the situation. Seth would lie as soon as the pressure was applied, there was no doubt in Finch's mind. But if it would make Bree feel better—if it would give her a sense of control—perhaps it would help her.

Carter wouldn't have approved, though. Finch practically heard his brother's words in his ears. Carter never wanted unnecessary violence.

But perhaps if he had, Carter would be alive today.

"All right," Finch muttered. "If that's what you want, kid. We'll burn him."

Silence.

Bree said nothing, she just waited.

Kull twitched her tail, and did nothing else. She didn't pretend to be a cat and cause some minor destruction, or even make a little quip to defuse the situation. She watched intently.

The thug didn't add anything, either. Seth gulped down air, his dark eyes shifting from Finch to Bree and back again. He was waiting for a moment to use his *one and only magical trick*—Finch knew. He was willing to bet every penny he had to his name.

But he would deal with that when it happened.

Finch stared down at Seth. "Well, you heard the lady. Better start talking. Or else."

Seth half laughed. "You're not gonna do shit, old man.

You're a pussy. I can tell by the way you're draggin' this out. The little girl has more balls."

"Uh-huh." Finch kept the gun in the other man's spine, but with his own hand, he touched the living room floor. The grain of the wood felt rough to his touch. "Do you know what *immolation* is?"

Seth had to mull it over for a few seconds. "N-No."

"Immolation is the process of killing someone by burning them to death."

Finch's palm heated. The floor burned under his fingertips, the heat so controlled, it didn't spread to any area Finch didn't want it to. When Finch's emotions were completely under control, Ke-Koh's abilities were easy to use. He just had to maintain his calm, so he didn't accidentally go too far.

Smoke wafted up from his hand.

Then Finch lifted it, revealing the blackened scorch mark he had left behind. It was a perfect match for his hand, right down to his fingertips.

With smoke still streaming from his palm, Finch grabbed Seth's sleeve. "But I'm not going to kill you. Instead, I'll just burn your arm." His fire spread to the shirt. The heat transferred to Seth's skin, reddening it like a piece of slowly roasting meat.

Seth squirmed harder. He thrashed his shoulders, and tried to stand, but Finch held him down. "H-Hey!" Seth shouted.

"I wouldn't move if I were you," Finch growled. "The fires of Ke-Koh are volatile."

The name caused Seth to stop moving, which meant he probably wasn't a *complete* idiot. Every warlock who knew of Ke-Koh probably had had some formal training.

"If you do that again, the fire could get out of control," Finch stated.

"But... you made a pact with Ke-Koh?" Seth asked in disbelief.

"Hold still. Or else."

Seth breathed heavily into the wooden floor. "What're you going to do, man?"

"First, I'll start by cooking your arm. Your skin will flake, your muscles will harden into charcoal, the nerves will burn out, making you useless... and at the end of this whole awful process, your arm is going to be mere decoration."

Finch grabbed the man's bicep, Finch's fingers still hot from Ke-Koh's magic.

The smell of cooked meat filled the air.

Which was odd, because Finch hadn't yet *burned* Seth. He glanced over and made eye contact with Kull. The little feline smiled back at him, her whiskers twitching.

The smell was her doing.

What a trickster.

"S-Stop," Seth said. "I'll talk!"

Finch tightened his grip. Seth screamed louder than Finch had been expecting. At the highest of octaves, Seth shouted, "*Stop! Please!*"

Finch maintained his hold and said nothing.

"*Stop!* Oh, god—*please*! I have a d-daughter! A family! Please!" Seth took in a ragged breath, tears streaming down his face. "P-Please! I'm sorry!"

His words devolved into incoherent blubbering. Seth cried out, his wails worse than his words.

"Adair, stop!"

Finch glanced over.

Bree had covered her face with both her hands. She, too, was crying. "Stop—you don't have to hurt him anymore." She turned away, her shoulders shaking.

Finch released Seth's arms and almost laughed.

Two seconds into the "torture" and *everyone* had folded faster than a cheap suitcase.

And the worst thing that had happened was the thug warlock had a sunburn in the shape of a palm. That was it.

Kull snickered, her feline eyes alight with utter amusement. "I can't believe I got to watch this for free."

Finch stood and tucked the handgun away. He sighed as he stared down at the sobbing man. None of this had to happen, yet somehow everyone had been too stubborn to listen to reason.

"W-What did I even do to you, man?" Seth said as he cradled his arm. "I *need* my arm. I need it."

"Your arm is fine," Finch growled. "Stand up and answer my damn questions. This circus show is getting embarrassing."

Seth cut his sobbing short and then glanced down at his arm. He rotated his shoulder, and rubbed at the slight red marks where Finch's hand had been. When he realized he wasn't injured, he leapt to his feet, his body still shaky. "You... You really are Adair Finch, aren't you?"

"That's right."

Once it was clear the situation wasn't as previously imagined, Bree turned back around. She rubbed at her red eyes, her lips turned down in a powerful frown. "You *didn't* hurt him?"

"Everyone is fine," Finch said with a groan. "I'm fine. He's fine. We're all fine." He walked over and placed a steady hand on her shoulder. "No crying. I just did what *you* wanted, remember?"

Bree shook her head. After taking in a shallow breath, she whispered, "I didn't know he had a family... All I could think of was his daughter. What if... What if she lost her parents, too? I didn't want that..."

Did Seth really have a daughter? Or had he shouted that

in a moment of panic? Finch wasn't sure—but now he was going to ask some questions. He turned on his heel to face the thug, but that was when his guard was down.

And Seth had been waiting.

The wannabe warlock lifted his hand. *"Get wrecked,"* he yelled as he unleashed a burst of blinding light that flooded all of Dr. Colton's house.

CHAPTER
NINETEEN

Temporarily blinded, but not surprised, Finch lifted the handgun and fired. The Glock 22, like every Glock Finch had ever fired, was utterly reliable. He shot at the top of the front doorframe—or at least in its general direction. The shot rang out throughout the tiny house, and splinters of wood clattered to the floor in the wake of the bullet's destruction.

Bree yelled. A cat meowed.

And just as Finch had suspected, Seth yelped and threw himself to the floor. The man had all the swagger and courage of a mouse wearing the skin of a lion.

Finch lowered his weapon and rubbed at his eyes. Black spots formed across his vision, but so did vague shapes of his surroundings. Seth crawled toward the door, worming his way along. Finch leapt on him, slamming his knee once again into the man's back.

"You thought that would work?" Finch asked, chuckling. He wasn't even mad—just hilariously disappointed. He had thought the wannabe warlock would've had something more useful. "What did you make a pact with? A flashlight?"

"A-A... A will-o-wisp."

Finch smacked his own forehead. Those were weak creatures of trickery and isolation. They barely demanded anything in their pact, but they also offered little in return. A blinding flash of light? What a terrible power.

It took at least another minute before Finch's vision returned enough for him to see things clearly.

Bree furiously rubbed her eyes and blinked several times afterward. When it was obvious she could see again, she hurried over to Finch and Seth. She said nothing, though she did give the man on the floor a few sad glances.

"Why are you here?" Finch barked, his voice almost as loud as the handgun. He pressed the weapon into the man, though he had little intention of firing it.

"I... I..." Seth swallowed some air. "I told you. I'm here to buy the traps."

"Why?"

"Man, I told you! The Haggin Coven wants them. *They're in a war.* It's crazy."

"War?" Finch asked, furrowing his brow. "Like a witches' feud?"

Seth took in a deep breath. "Y-Yeah. With the Swenson Coven. You must know about it."

Although Finch was vaguely aware both those covens existed, he knew nothing about them anymore. He had been too out of touch, lately. Most of the time, covens didn't fight with one another—they had their own turf, and as long as no one intruded, they left the outside world alone. But when covens *did* fight, it was to the death. Witches had little mercy when it came to magical creatures they had a feud with.

"They've been killing each other?" Finch asked.

"Yeah." Seth scratched the tip of his nose. "They're hiring every warlock to help them fight. You *must've* heard about it. Mortals have died. Even a couple cops."

"Damn," Finch muttered. Then he mulled over the last few sentences. "Several police officers? They were caught up in the witches' feud?"

"Y-Yeah. It was on the news. The mortals blamed their deaths on a *gang fight*."

Finch held his breath. He thought back to Detective Jenner, and his animosity toward anything with magic. "How long ago did this happen? When did the officers die?"

"A… A few weeks ago?"

That would explain the tension. If the witches in Stockton were fighting, and their war was consuming everything, even the mortal police, everyone would be on edge, especially the detectives.

Then another thought crossed Finch's mind. Was Vera's death collateral damage? Had she gotten caught up in the witches' feud? There hadn't been any evidence of that, though… No magic at the crime scene, all her brews still in the house…

"Why is Dr. Colton selling these traps?" Finch asked.

"I don't know," Seth replied, indignant.

"Do you know anything about Liam Blackstone?" Bree interjected. She knelt next to Seth. "He's my papa. He's a warlock, and he's missing."

Seth screwed up his oily face. After a short moment, he said, "I've heard of Liam. Some… crafter warlock? But I don't think he ever agreed to help covens. He's married to a waning crescent witch."

Witches came in five varieties—full moon, half moon, waxing crescent, waning crescent, and new moon. Their designation came from the time that a witch reached her full magical potential. If she did so during a full moon, she was a full moon witch, and if during a waxing crescent, she was a waxing crescent witch, and so on. Each type of witch had their own proclivities, influenced by the phase of the moon.

Waning crescent witches never joined covens. They were solitary and independent, and most of their magic involved creating things, either plants or brews. Every old fairy tale that involved a single witch out in the woods was likely about a *waning crescent witch* just doing her thing.

That was why Vera didn't belong to a coven—and it was also why none of the covens would bother her.

And since Vera's killer was a man, Finch was growing more confident the witches' feud was a red herring. But he couldn't be certain. There was a possibility he would need to question local witches.

He also needed to speak with Dr. Colton to really understand what was happening. The magicless man was deep in the conflict, whether he wanted to be or not.

"Can I get those traps now?" Seth asked.

"Wait," Bree said as she held up a hand. "Do you really have a daughter?"

"Yeah."

His quick and confident response told Finch there was probably some little girl somewhere who called this man *father*. It almost made him sad, but then again, at least the man was in the girl's life.

Bree had no follow-up questions. She just stayed by the man's side, kneeling and pondering.

"I destroyed all the jar traps," Finch finally stated.

Seth exhaled and then pressed his face into the floor. He practically deflated, as though the world had failed him.

"What's wrong?" Bree asked.

"Matilda will kill me," Seth said straight into the wooden floorboards. "I've already messed up one too many times."

Finch sneered. "Matilda *Wriedt*?"

"Yeah."

If waning crescent witches were the loners of the witching world, full moon witches were the popular kids.

They were the leaders of covens, and the ones with the most potent magical powers. They tended to have abilities that destroyed or controlled—no one wanted to tangle with a full moon witch.

And Matilda Wriedt was one of the worst.

Finch had dealt with her many years ago, before she had formally joined a coven. The experience had left a bad taste in his mouth.

"*Literally* kill you?" Bree asked.

Seth didn't respond.

With giant blue eyes, Bree glanced up at Finch. He already knew where this was going, and he didn't like it at all.

"No," he preemptively said.

"Please?" Bree scooted closer to him. "He has a daughter. We shouldn't let him just get killed."

"None of this *is real*, remember?" Finch spoke his emphasized words with a single-handed air quote. He kept his other hand on the gun, pressing the barrel into Seth's back. "Once I reset things, this warlock will be fine. Everything will be fine."

Bree motioned to the house. "But Seth will arrive when Dr. Colton is away. He won't get his traps. And what if he tries to break into the house? The front door was dangerous, remember?" Her frown deepened. Then Bree grabbed Finch's coat sleeve, her fingers twisting into the rough fabric. "We shouldn't let him get hurt."

Finch pinched the bridge of his nose, completely flabbergasted by the turn of events. First the dog, and now some random warlock? What was wrong with this girl? Did she need to save *everyone*?

"Oh, I know," Kull interjected. She leapt onto Seth's back and then kneaded the space between his shoulder blades. The man flinched, but otherwise said nothing. "After we save the dog, we'll come here, break in, disarm the trap on the front door, and then leave to complete the rest of our day."

"No." Finch shook his head. "We're not doing that."

Seth turned his head, and with one eye, glanced up at Finch. "What's going on?"

"Shut up. This doesn't involve you."

Bree furrowed her brow and leaned onto Finch. "Please? It won't take much time. We can make sure he's not hurt, and that Matilda doesn't kill him."

It seemed no one listened to him. Finch sighed, his ever-growing frustration replacing all other emotions. Did he really want to continually repeat the exact same steps every morning just so a dog and a random stranger could continue their day injury free?

And Finch didn't want to change the time of his mark until *after* he had saved them. What if the killer was boarding a plane right now? He still had the option to stop them. But if Finch changed the time of his mark to something later, perhaps he would lose that chance.

"Fine," Finch muttered. "*Fine*. We'll save the stupid dog *and* the stupid warlock. Are you happy now?"

Bree's smile could've brightened the darkest corners of hell.

Without warning, she wrapped her arms around Finch's neck. Flustered, he stood and unhooked her arms. "Okay, okay. Enough of this." She continued to beam up at him. Finch didn't know what else to say.

Seth scrambled to his feet, knocking Kull off in the process. He dashed for the front door and then fled the house as quickly as possible. Finch didn't care if the man left, though he was worried Seth would somehow prevent Dr. Colton from returning. If that were the case, Finch would just have to try again.

Kull licked her paws and then smoothed her fur. "That

was invigorating. Now what? Shall we break into some more people's homes for giggles? I've always wanted to steal every left shoe someone owned, just to see their reaction."

"We're going to wait for the doctor," Finch stated. He motioned to the living room and the kitchen. "I want us to be *right here* when Dr. Colton walks through that door."

"You think that weak warlock will find the doctor and alert him to our presence?"

"That man couldn't find his way out of a wet paper bag." Finch half chuckled as he threw himself onto the couch. "And from the looks of it, he doesn't even know Dr. Colton. He thought *I* was the doctor, remember? I think we're safe to just wait here until the doc is done with his classes. Then we'll question him until there's nothing about the man we *don't* know."

CHAPTER
TWENTY

9:32 a.m.

Finch paced the small house. He wasn't expecting any intruders, but after they were visited by a random warlock, he didn't want to take any chances. He closed the blinds, locked the doors and windows, and remained vigilant.

He also mulled over the details of the case.

Vera had been murdered sometime around 1 or 2am by a man who had used no magic. Vera's husband, Liam, had been taken soon afterward, but Vera's daughter had managed to escape.

Liam had been making necklaces. He and Vera had argued about this—Vera had wanted Liam to stop. The necklaces allowed someone to see through minor illusions and invisibility and cats were being killed to mass-produce them. Liam had done most of his work at the University of the Pacific, but it was obvious he had taken some of it home, which was likely why Vera had become upset.

Liam's coworker, Dr. Colton, knew of the necklace

production, and tried to hide it the moment he knew Liam was missing. The doctor's actions indicated Liam's buyer—or handler—would not be pleased if their identity was known.

Dr. Colton also wasn't *important*. When confronted in the parking lot, the doctor was shot, along with Bree.

Bree…

Finch stopped pacing in the middle of the living room.

Bree was the only witness to Vera's murder. Was that why she had been shot in the parking lot? The murderer who had gotten Vera had obviously not wanted to kill Bree—since he likely could have—but the shooter hadn't hesitated. The shooter was a clean-up man. Someone meant to tie up all loose ends.

But there were random facts that weren't adding up.

Who would want such pathetic magical necklaces?

Did the witches' feud have anything to do with this? Could Liam have been working for either the Haggin Coven or the Swenson Coven? Perhaps a rogue agent for the covens was the one who had hired Liam, and become angry when Vera tried to convince her husband to stop.

That would at least be a motive for the killing…

And perhaps the murderer had left Bree alone because she was a witch. It was typically against coven law to kill young witches who had yet to drink from the moon. But then why would the shooter kill Bree?

Finch rubbed his chin.

The identity of the murderer still wasn't adding up.

Sizzling from the kitchen caught his attention. Finch glanced at his phone.

10:12 a.m.

He crept into the kitchen, his hand poised over the butt of the handgun. Instead of an intruder, Finch found Bree standing at the stove, with Kull up on the backsplash. The little spirit swished her tail from side to side, her yellow cat eyes large as Bree stirred a pan filled with bacon.

"What're you doing?" Finch barked.

Bree practically leapt out of her skin. She whirled on her heel, her shoulders bunched at the base of her neck. "O-Oh. Adair." She exhaled and relaxed. "I was making food because I'm hungry. I-It doesn't matter, right? We're not stealing because all Dr. Colton's food will return to him?"

Finch narrowed his eyes. After a short sigh, he stomped over to the stove. "You're doing it wrong." He motioned Bree to the side and then lined up the bacon strips so they were all perfectly side by side. "You don't move bacon around. You let it sit and get crispy. You turn it over once, and that's it."

Bree smiled and nodded along with his words. "You know how to cook? Really? I never would've guessed that."

Holding back a sarcastic retort, Finch stood in front of the pan, watching as the bacon crisped.

"Humans love bacon," Kull said matter-of-factly. "I know. I've seen your commercials. I've studied them, in fact."

"What could you possibly glean from studying commercials?" Finch asked with a forced laugh.

"Well, I've learned a wide variety of things, actually. First off, children are always sad until they've eaten cereal. Yogurt makes women extremely happy. If you want a car, you need to buy one on Sunday, Sunday, Sunday. Women menstruate blue liquid. And—most importantly—bacon can literally be paired with any other food and humans will regard it as ambrosia."

Bree shook her head. "I don't know if it can go with *any* food…"

"There are bacon-wrapped hot dogs, bacon in chocolate bars, bacon mayonnaise, bacon peanut brittle, bacon ice cream—"

"*Stop*," Finch snapped. "We get it. Bacon can be in everything."

Kull nodded her head. "So, obviously, humans *love* bacon." She leaned down and sniffled at the sizzling pan. "I must learn its secret. I must become more like *bacon*."

After a short burst of giggling, Bree smiled wide. "Why do you want to be so much like a human, Kull? Being a spirit, and changing your shape all the time, seems really fun."

"I want to be the perfect human. Once I have a body, I'll live a life so full, I'll welcome death at the end of that short road." She purred and licked her lips. "Oh, what a time it will be."

"But… why?" Bree's tone turned into something like earnest bewilderment.

The cat leapt away from the stove and trotted along the counter. Then she sat at the corner and stared at the table across the room. Her yellow eyes never blinked, but her gaze was unfocused.

"I met a human once," Kull whispered, her quiet voice filled with melancholy joy. "His name was James Hershaw, and he was a painter."

Finch flipped the bacon. "Uh-huh. I knew it."

"Knew what?" Bree asked.

"Spirits only want to be humans after they've met one who they really like." Finch gave her a quick glance. "They fall in love or some nonsense."

Bree walked over to where Kull sat on the counter. "D'aww. Is that what happened, Kull? You're in love with a man named James?"

She flicked the tip of her feline tail. "I met James in Philadelphia, 1842. He had just arrived in the United States of America. It was easy to play tricks on the immigrants. They were all on edge and scared of their new home. It was fun. For months I played at those docks. Until James arrived."

"Wait…" Bree knitted her eyebrows together. "Is he… dead?"

"Oh, yes." Kull finally glanced over. She tilted her head like any normal animal. "But a few days after I met him, I saw one of his works of art. He had painted *me*. And… I loved it."

"Can humans see spirits?"

When no one replied to Bree, she glanced between Finch and Kull.

Normally, spirits had to reveal themselves to the magicless. Mundane humans didn't have the capability to see spirits, demons, and anything else mostly made of magic, which was what prevented most humans from ever becoming warlocks. If a human wasn't trained in magic, they rarely discovered it accidentally—though it did happen from time to time.

Occasionally, spirits took a liking to someone. If a spirit revealed themselves, the human could make a pact, but since they were untrained, it often resulted in terrible things. People being accused of witchcraft or demon worshipping. They had been killed in the past.

And then there were the cases of demons who managed to contact malevolent humans…

Finch shook his head. It wasn't really the time to discuss such scenarios.

"Sometimes people can see spirits," was all Finch said in response to Bree's question.

"I *had* revealed myself to James." Kull purred as she added, "And he painted so many dazzling works of art, I couldn't stay away from him. Day and night, I watched over his home… and eventually his family. For years, I did. I…" Kull lowered her voice as she said, "I loved them all."

The crackling of the bacon was almost so loud it drowned out her quiet words.

Finch pushed the pan to the side. It was ready to eat, but he would wait until the cat finished her tale.

"But I'm a spirit," Kull said, raising her voice again. "And sometimes I had to go away to do *spirit things*." She snickered at her own joke. "But I always returned to his home. Year after year. Decade after decade."

"That long?" Bree asked, her eyes widening.

"I never failed to return. Even after... Even after James died. I watched over his family, you see. His little children, to his grandchildren, to his great-grandchildren." With a smile, Kull lifted her head. "And they passed down stories of me. When I showed up, they knew who I was. Some of them called me their *family guardian*. I was so pleased. So happy."

But the last two words were some of the saddest Finch had heard from the spirit.

Her tail and ears drooped. Then her gaze fell to the floor. Even her whispers seemed to hang heavier than ever before.

"But then one day, I returned and... no one remembered me." Kull went silent for a moment. "They had forgotten," she eventually said. "And I'm a spirit—I've never been afraid of death or dying, or even thought it would be a terrible fate—but in that moment... it *felt* like I had died."

The kitchen was colder than before.

It was difficult for spirits to feel anything. They were beings of specific desires. Kull was one of *trickery*. Whenever they felt something more powerful than their baser urges, it changed them. That was when they wanted to be human—to feel the full spectrum of wants, desires, and emotions.

Bree stroked Kull's black fur but said nothing.

"You don't have to pity me," Kull muttered. "I just know now that there are fates worse than death." She perked up as she said, "But once I'm human, I can experience someone else's love for me. I can make my own family, and grow old with someone. We will perish together, after we experience everything there is to experience." She purred again as she concluded, "And then this ache in my chest will die with me."

The ache in her chest...

Finch rubbed at his own sternum. Some aches never went away.

After a deep breath, Finch searched through the kitchen. He grabbed two plates, some silverware, and then took a handful of eggs out of the fridge. He placed the bacon on one plate, then prepared an omelet in the leftover grease. Dr. Colton had some cheese, and Finch used that to decorate the top of his yellow omelet.

Once everything was ready, Finch brought it over to the table. There was only one chair.

He pushed it over to Bree and then walked back into the bedroom. Finch had seen another; he would just drag it to the table. He did so without a word. There was too much to think about, and now his mind was flooded with thoughts of Carter.

The ache in his chest, left in the wake of his brother's death, never left him.

Ever.

Perhaps Kull felt the same way. But Finch didn't want to discuss it.

He pulled the new chair up and then ate a few strips of bacon. Bree ate some as well, equally quiet. Then she dug into Finch's omelet, a slight smile on her face.

"This is how Papa makes it," she said.

"Good," Finch answered with a grunt.

"Are you okay, Adair? You don't look well."

"I'm fine."

Bree nibbled another strip of bacon. Once she swallowed, she tapped her fingers on the surface of the table. Kull leapt over the counter and landed with all the grace and silence of a ghost cat.

"Are you sad?" Bree whispered.

"I said *I'm fine*," Finch yelled, his voice echoing through the tiny house.

He regretted the words the moment he spoke them, but at the same time, his anger wouldn't leave him, not even when his guilt surfaced.

"I'm sorry," Finch quickly stated, his words curt and his volume still elevated. After a deep inhale, he repeated in a quieter voice, "I'm sorry."

Kull lay down on the table. "Hm. Humans are so strange. Sad stories make them all sad. I suppose that must be your empathy."

"Yeah," Bree whispered. She poked at the edge of her omelet. Then she sat a little straighter. "Oh, Adair! I meant to tell you. I found some board games in the hall closet! Have you played games before? They're so fun. I used to play them with Mum and Papa all the time."

Kull got to her four feet. "Oho! We only play *Monopoly* if I can be the person who slams the game off the table once I land on someone else's hotel."

"That's not part of *Monopoly*," Bree said, lifting an eyebrow.

"According to my research it is."

Finch ran a hand down his face. He turned his attention to the front door. Dr. Colton still hadn't arrived. Then he glanced at his phone.

10:59 a.m.

And while he didn't want to play any board games—he didn't care for any games, really—he also knew he couldn't tell Bree no, not after he had shouted for no good reason. One game wouldn't kill him.

"Fine," he said. "One board game. That's it. Then I'm going to do my own thing while we wait."

Bree leapt from her seat and ran for the hallway. She

practically danced all the way back to her seat at the table and then presented Finch with a game he had never seen before.

The Settlers of Catan.

"What is this?" he asked, frowning.

"It's so *good.*" Bree opened the lid and placed a bunch of tiles until they formed an island. "You don't know how to play?"

"No."

Bree smiled even wider as she snapped her attention to Finch. "Really? So I'm the one who gets to teach *you* something this time?"

"Hm. Don't let it go to your head."

She hurried and dumped out the rest of the box all over the table. "This will be so fun! We can gather resources, and trade wood for sheep, and build cities, and whoever has the biggest settlement wins."

"Wait." Finch held up a hand. "Back up. Did you just say we trade *wood* for *sheep*?"

The phrase baffled him. What did it even mean?

What the hell were kids into these days?

Bree giggled. She bit her lip as she set up stacks of cards. "Okay, you need to pay attention. *And no using magic*, okay? I'll be blue. You'll be white. Kull will be yellow."

"Fine," Finch said as he leaned back in his chair and crossed his arms. "But you better get to the part with the wood and sheep quickly."

CHAPTER
TWENTY-ONE

"Okay, so I pay three ore and two wheat, and that means I get to upgrade my settlement into a city," Bree confidently stated. She took her little settlement token and replaced it with the much larger city token. "And that means I win that game."

"How does that mean *you win?*" Finch asked, glaring at the island board.

Bree giggled as she pointed to all the pieces. "Remember? Whoever makes it to ten points first wins. Settlements are worth one point, but cities are worth *two*, so I went from nine to ten."

"It's simple math, really," Kull said with a feline smile.

Finch shot her a glare. "Don't talk to me about *simple math*, spirit. You've been changing your token pieces on the board this whole damn game."

"Hm. I must be losing my touch. I didn't think you would notice."

After glancing at his phone—11:48 a.m.—Finch returned his attention to the game. "Okay, how about the best of three? Set it up again. I know what we're doing this time."

"You want to play again?" Kull twitched her ears. "After *that* loss? So brave."

Bree chuckled as she grabbed all the pieces off the board and placed them in their starting positions. The sheep, the wood—everything was managed into neat little piles. Then she glanced over and smiled.

"Are you feeling better now?" she asked.

"What's that supposed to mean?" Finch growled.

"You got so mad earlier, and out of nowhere." Bree gently tapped her fingers on the table. "Did playing this game help? Papa says board games make people feel better."

Finch caught his breath. Had the girl brought up the games so quickly just because he had yelled? He leaned back in his seat as the realization settled over him.

The stillness that followed Bree's statement made it feel as though time had stopped. Even Kull refused to joke or make a move, as though she didn't want to disturb the conversation with her presence.

"If you don't want to talk about it, that's fine," Bree eventually said as she tucked some of her brown hair behind her ear. She pushed all Finch's game pieces into place. "We can play another round instead."

"Talking about it isn't going to change anything," Finch stated, no emotion in his voice.

"It helped me to voice the events of my past." Kull tilted her head to the side. Then she smiled. "It might help you to tell us what's weighing so heavily on your heart."

Finch exhaled, his anger building. Ironically, it was easier to speak when he was mad, like the rage gave him the courage just to blurt everything out.

"It's my fault Carter died," Finch said—the first time he had ever said it to anyone other than the reflection in the mirror.

Bree's eyes widened, but she didn't reply.

"You killed him?" Kull asked.

"*No*," Finch snapped. "I didn't kill him. I just... I should've prevented his death." He sat up in his seat, his blood hot. "We were investigating a series of disappearances. It had led us to a place in Paris—the catacombs beneath the city. Most people consider them a tourist attraction, but a coven of witches had unsealed a tunnel and made their home there."

When Finch closed his eyes, he remembered the foul experience of the catacombs—the stagnant air, the walls adorned with human bones, and the icy chill that never left him.

"The witches weren't normal. They were turning themselves into vampires. Sick, twisted vampires. But I didn't care. I got cocky." Finch lowered his voice as he tilted his head back and rested it on the chair. "Carter went first. It was dark, and... there was something else in the catacombs. Something sinister and vile."

After a few deep breaths, Finch managed to bleed some of his mounting stress.

"I should've marked the time," Finch whispered. "But we just barreled in. And then... the witches did *something*. We couldn't use our magic. No one could. Not even the witches themselves."

Finch remembered the moment well.

Having his magic suppressed felt like he was drowning in insects...

The skulls in the walls...

Pillars made of human teeth...

The darkness so thick, he couldn't see...

"There was a monster in the catacombs." Finch opened his eyes and stared at the ceiling. He didn't want to picture any more of the story. "It came for us," he said, his throat filled with cotton ball dryness. "Carter fought it. I couldn't see. I wanted to help, and I chased after them, but the catacombs were a labyrinth."

Even staring at the ceiling, Finch saw the inky shadows of Paris's underbelly.

The images never left his mind.

"I somehow found myself back on the streets," he said, his voice gruff. "I was… free of the witches' magic. Then I tried to activate Chronos's ability, but it was too late. It had been over twenty-four hours since I made my mark. The magic… it had ended minutes before. *Minutes.* I couldn't reverse time anymore. The only thing I could do was make a new mark."

Finch made the last few statements without feeling anything. They were empty words.

He'd had the same hollow feeling upon his revelation in Paris.

"But if you had marked the time before going into the catacombs, you *could* have reversed time?" Bree whispered.

Finch didn't reply. The answer was obvious.

And the realization that his brother had died simply because Finch hadn't been more diligent wore on him like no other mistake in his life.

Carter…

"I know of the monster you mentioned," Kull stated, her tone light and airy.

Finch sat straight as he snapped his attention to her. "*You do?*"

Kull tilted her head. "Well, yes. I mean, I don't know it personally, but I know it roams the lands. No spirits get near it, you see. It has a *presence.* Something that nullifies life."

"What is it?" Finch asked, breathless.

"Oh, I don't know its name. I've merely felt it before. It *is* a terrible beast. I see now why your brother lost his life."

Finch grabbed the edge of the table and held back the urge to yell. He forced himself to breathe deep. It wasn't the spirit's fault. The mischievous cat was just adding to the conversation in a way she thought meaningful.

Still...

Finch had never discovered the identity of the monster, nor had he learned the names of the vampire witches in the coven. All he knew was it was a coven of exclusively full moon witches—power-hungry lunatics who specialized in blood magic, and were somehow making a new clan of bloodsuckers. The witches made sacrifices of human flesh in places where many people had once died. It was their *schtick*.

Finch *had* managed to save the missing people of Paris. The witches had fled after he and Carter confronted them, and Finch had returned to the tunnels for revenge. He'd only found the missing individuals, however. Finch had rescued them, but there would never be a chance to rescue Carter.

And Finch had never discovered why the coven was in cahoots with such a vile beast, either.

That all had been over a decade ago...

"Ah." Kull perked her feline ears. "*That's* why you made a pact with Ke-Koh. You wanted *fire*—the most powerful flames you could get your hands on."

Again, Finch didn't reply. This answer was also obvious.

But Bree furrowed her brow. "Why fire?"

"Both witches and vampires are susceptible to the destructive powers of fire," Kull stated. "They light up faster than a puddle of oil in a firework-testing facility. And witches who become vampires are so flammable, they'll catch fire while pouring themselves a bowl of cereal."

Bree nodded once. "Oh. No wonder..."

"I don't know if they're still in Paris," Finch muttered. He pinched the bridge of his nose. "Or if they still have their monster, but if I ever find them, I'll make sure their whole coven is nothing but ashes."

He had promised Carter that was what he would do.

The rumble of an engine killed the entire conversation. Bree leapt from her chair, her eyes wide. Finch stood, his hand on the Glock, his attention on the door. Kull snickered as she leapt onto the floor.

A car parked in the driveway.

Finch walked over to the kitchen window and peeked out. A black Nissan had pulled up to the house.

Dr. Colton.

Then he glanced at his phone. 11:57 a.m.

"Finally," Finch whispered to himself. He glanced over his shoulder. "I think you should wait in the hall. Or one of the back rooms."

"Why?" Bree asked, her voice equally quiet.

"Just in case he has some traps on him. I'll handle this."

She nodded once and hurried into the hall. Then she glanced around the corner, eyeing the situation from afar. Finch knew there was no point in trying to stop her from spying. He just wanted to make sure she wouldn't be caught in another *Witch's Web*. The girl had gone through one too many traumatizing things already.

Finch moved to the front door, careful not to make much noise. He "hid" himself against the wall, where the door would swing open. The doctor pushed open the door and hurried into the house, huffing as though caught in an asthma attack. Dr. Colton didn't even glance over his shoulder as Finch stepped out from behind the door and lunged for the man.

With one powerful shove, Finch slammed Dr. Colton into the living room wall. The doctor had been carrying paperwork in his arms, but he yelped and dropped everything in a minor explosion of pens, stationery, and folders.

Finch grabbed a fistful of the man's hair, shoved his face into the wall, and then dug the barrel of the handgun into his spine. He sensed no magic from Dr. Colton—he definitely wasn't a warlock or anything of the like—but when Finch focused, he detected a slight hint of sorcery in the doctor's clothing.

"Empty your pockets," Finch commanded, his voice loud enough to echo throughout the small house.

"O-Oh, god…" Dr. Colton flailed a bit, and even blubbered something of an apology, as he grabbed the contents of his pockets and tossed them all onto the floor.

He had a cellphone…

And one of the illusion-defeating necklaces.

That was it.

Finch was tired of this man. It wasn't really fair to *this* Dr. Colton, since this doctor had never triggered a trap on him, or inadvertently drawn the attention of the sniper, but Finch still blamed him for all the alternate timeline events. With barely restrained rage, Finch pulled back on the man's hair and slammed the doctor's face into the drywall. Dr. Colton's glasses broke, and blood exploded from his nose, splattering downward across his muddy brown clothes.

When Dr. Colton yelled and flailed—trying to spin around—Finch hooked his ankle and shoved him to the floor. The thin doctor hit hard on one elbow and let out a sharp *yelp*. Now bloody and cradling his right arm, Dr. Colton stared up at Finch with wide and wild eyes.

"Wh-Who are you?" he asked.

Finch checked to make sure the trigger was forward. Then he casually, with no emotion at all, said, "I'm the *quiz master*, and from here on out, I'm only going to ask you questions. If you *don't* answer, I'm going to shoot you, and if you do answer, but I think it's a lie, I'm going to shoot you twice. Understand?"

CHAPTER
TWENTY-TWO

"-I don't know anything," Dr. Colton stammered. He glanced over at the kitchen table, his gold-rimmed glasses awkwardly slanted to the side, the glass cracked, the bridge of the nose digging into his flesh. There were no traps on the table, and his face paled. When he returned his attention to Finch, he swallowed hard. "Who are you? Really?"

Finch pointed the handgun at the man's kneecap. "Do you know who killed Vera Blackstone?"

Dr. Colton shook his head as quickly as he could. His words came to him in bursts, as though his throat could barely unconstrict. "N-No. I don't know. *I swear!* Vera was m-my friend."

For the most part, Finch believed him, but he wasn't done questioning the man.

"Why was Liam making those necklaces?"

"H-He told me they were for a client! It was a job... Just a job. I wasn't involved."

"Why did you have so many witch's traps?"

"I..." Dr. Colton rubbed his elbow. "Vera made them for

me. It was p-payment for not talking. A-About the necklaces. I wasn't supposed to tell anyone. I had to keep them hidden."

Vera had been in on the necklace scheme?

"Why did you want the traps?" Finch asked, lifting an eyebrow.

"To sell! That's it. Other witches and warlocks were buying them, and it was easy money. And… and also to protect myself, just in case some magic-wielding freak came into my house."

The irony.

Finch tightened his finger on the trigger. He knew the next question was going to cause the doctor to hesitate. "If you could call someone to tell them what was happening here, who would it be?"

The question was no doubt bizarre and abstract from the doctor's point of view, but Finch had seen Dr. Colton call someone after using the Witch's Web. Who had he called? Finch hadn't determined the caller's identity before exploding the whole house in fire.

"I… I would call…" Dr. Colton gulped down air. "Liam's employer. He said his name was *David,* but he never g-gave me anything else. I think it's just an alias. David said if anything went wrong—if any warlocks or witches came to my house asking questions—I was supposed to call or text him right away."

Finch cursed under his breath. *David* did sound like a cheap and lazy alias, but it made sense. Dr. Colton wasn't discreet. Why would anyone risk their association with the man by giving him their real name?

"You have *David's* phone number?" Finch asked.

"Y-Yes. In my phone. I, uh, texted him this morning. He told me… he told me to move the necklaces."

Which meant David knew all about the killing.

"What else did he tell you?" Finch asked.

"To tell him if, uh, I found Liam's daughter."

Bree? That was the strangest bit of information so far. Why would some random magic-wielding lunatic want to know Bree's whereabouts? And why tell the magicless professor to keep an eye out? Was it because Dr. Colton was a friend of the family? Did *David* think Bree would go to him if she were in trouble?

Bizarre.

Finch motioned to the gun he held. "Who gave you this?"

"L-Liam." Dr. Colton wiped the blood from his upper lip with a shaky hand. "He said I might need it." His volume fell as he made the statement. He gazed down at the red splatters across his vest.

"Get your phone out," Finch commanded. "Text David. Tell him Bree is here."

"W-What?"

Bree poked her head out from the kitchen, her eyes wide. "Are you sure, Adair?"

He shot her a sideways glance. "Just stay over there. I know what I'm doing."

The doctor whipped his attention from Finch to Bree and then back to Finch. Blood wept from his nose at a fierce rate, and he started using his coat sleeve in an attempt to keep the crimson liquid from pouring into his mouth.

"That's not Bree?" Dr. Colton asked, his face twisted in confusion.

Which meant he couldn't see through the illusions of the coat. He had before—back in the parking lot—but only because he had been carrying a necklace. Since he didn't have one anymore, Dr. Colton couldn't see Bree for who she really was. All he could see was some nondescript, random individual.

"Just do as I say, or else I'm going to blow out your kneecaps," Finch said, his tone equal parts calm and cold.

"R-Right."

The doctor pulled out his phone. With a shaky blood-coated hand, he poked at the numbers. He left fingerprints across his screen as he slowly—with only one hand—typed out a message and sent it.

"Let me see," Finch growled.

Dr. Colton turned his phone to face Finch.

There were no prior conversations in the chat, which was odd considering Dr. Colton had said he'd texted David earlier in the morning. Was he erasing his chat conversations after having them? What a paranoid man. Or perhaps David had told him to do that. The contact listed at the top of the chat was "Liam's David."

The text message read: teh gril is her

Thankfully, David could read *typo*, because the man replied within a few seconds. A text popped up on the screen that read: Where are you?

Finch motioned with the gun. "Answer him. And use both your hands this time. Tell him we're here at your house."

Dr. Colton nodded once. He glanced down at the phone and tapped out a reply, his thumbs trembling. He deleted and retyped several words. Then he showed Finch the screen a second time.

His new message read: She's at my house

David replied within a couple seconds again. His message: Keep her with you, and ask if she saw anything last night.

Ask if she saw anything? Finch reread that part several times before motioning for the doctor to take the phone. "Text him back. Tell him Bree is upset, but she saw nothing. It was too dark."

Although it was obvious the doctor had no idea what was going on, he constantly glanced up at Finch, his brow furrowed, as if troubled by the command. As Dr. Colton wiped blood off his upper lip for the thirtieth time, he asked, "Did that girl say you were... Adair *Finch*? Is that right?"

"That's right," Finch stated. "But don't you say a word of that to our good friend *David*, understand?"

Dr. Colton nodded once. His nose had finally stopped pouring blood, and the doctor nervously adjusted his broken spectacles. "Vera said you were the best warlock she had ever known..."

Finch didn't reply. That was what Bree had said as well. He wished Vera hadn't gone around saying that. If she had seen how he had lived his life for the past few years, Finch was certain he would've disappointed her.

After he was done with the text message, Dr. Colton flipped his phone around to show Finch. His text read: Bree didn't see anything, it was too dark

David replied in quick fashion. His message read: Did she hear anything? Can she recall any details?

The insistence bothered Finch. Why would it matter to "David" if Bree had seen anything? Finch had been around the business of crime long enough to have a few guesses, but he wanted to know a little more first.

"Tell him Bree knows nothing," Finch stated. "Say she was scared. It's all a blur to her."

Dr. Colton did as he was instructed. When he showed Finch the phone again, the screen was a mess of bloody fingerprints, and it almost blocked out the text. The last message read: She knows nothing, too scared, she's shaking, I'm going to watch her

Finch silently applauded the doctor for playing the role. David replied within seconds. He said: Keep her with you. Don't leave your house if you value your life.

That was interesting. *A threat*. Which meant this David fellow was likely friends with the murderer. Or maybe the murderer himself. Finch wasn't certain, but he knew he couldn't be allowed anywhere near Bree.

"Tell him *okay*," Finch muttered.

Dr. Colton did just that.

"What's going to happen?" the doctor asked. "If we wait here, and he comes to see Bree, I think… things will get violent."

"More violent than they are now?" Finch asked, cocking an eyebrow. The blood on the wall, Dr. Colton's clothing, and the floor made everything seem like a murder scene. All they needed was some yellow police tape and their décor would be complete.

"Liam was afraid of this man. He couldn't stop making the necklaces. He thought something terrible would happen. And now Vera… I think it already has."

Finch clenched his jaw.

That was why Liam and Vera had been arguing. Liam was being forced to make the necklaces, and Vera had wanted him to stop. Had the murderer been there to force Liam into jewelry production? Had Vera gotten in the way? Was that why she'd died?

That would explain why Liam had been abducted right after the fact. It was *his* magic the killer needed to make the necklaces.

The doctor's phone buzzed with another message. Finch pointed the gun at him, and Dr. Colton presented the screen as quickly as possible. The new message from David read: I'll be there later tonight to pick her up.

Pick her up?

The mysterious *David* was extremely concerned about Bree and her whereabouts. And now he thought he could just come get her? Finch wanted to talk with the man. No level of violence could save David from Ke-Koh's fire. And even if that wouldn't work, no one was outside time's trappings. Finch would make this man talk.

"Tell him that's fine," Finch said. Then he motioned to the couch. "And take a seat. We're all going to wait for this man *together*."

Dr. Colton swallowed again as he got to his feet. With hesitant steps, he went to the couch. As soon as he was done texting, Finch ripped the cellphone from his grasp.

"I'll give this back to you once everything is over. Or if you need to make any more responses."

"A-All right." Dr. Colton fidgeted with his broken glasses a second time, trying to get them into the perfect position. Unfortunately, some of the broken glass popped out and clattered onto the wood floor.

Bree ran out of the kitchen, Kull in her arms. The cute little black cat eyed Dr. Colton once she was close, but then she glanced away, clearly uninterested.

"What a meek little human," Kull said as she swished her tail. "I don't want a body like his. So forgettable."

The doctor's eyes grew giant. He shivered on the couch and back away. With a deep frown, Dr. Colton muttered, "That isn't some sort of demon, is it?"

"Kull?" Bree held the cat close to her chest, and she smiled. "*No*. She's a spirit. What's wrong with you? Can't you see how cute she is?"

Bree obviously didn't see the way Kull flashed her fangs at the doctor, her eyes becoming red for a split second. Dr. Colton gasped as he moved to the corner of the couch. He grabbed a pillow and held it with a white-knuckled grip, like he would need it as a weapon at any moment.

Finch wanted to laugh. The little trickster spirit really wanted to mess with the man. Kull even snickered as Bree set her on the floor.

"Everyone, get comfortable," Finch stated. He tucked the

handgun into the waistband of his pants. "We're going to wait for our friend to get here. Then we're going to question *him* about what's going on."

———

Bree and Kull sat on one side of the couch, while Dr. Colton sat at the far end, a full cushion's worth away from them. He kept his back pressed hard up against the furniture, and his attention on the muted TV. The news played with captions at the bottom, but the doctor was clearly having a difficult time reading them with only one side of his glasses.

Food wrappers littered the coffee table and the carpet around the couch. Bree and Kull had raided Dr. Colton's house in order to snack while they waited.

Finch glanced at the time.

7:02 p.m.

The mystery man, David, had yet to arrive. If he didn't show up by 4am, Finch would have to rewind time no matter what. He had a twenty-four-hour window, and he wasn't going to risk losing it by waiting for this one man. If David didn't show, they would find him some other way.

"And warlocks can bond with *anything*?" Bree asked the black cat.

Kull nodded her head. "Anything with magic."

"What about demons? Are they really bad? Mum said they were powerful."

Kull's fur stood on end as she narrowed her eyes. "Demons are the worst. They have powerful magic, but they taint your cores. If you bond with a demon, and it ties itself to your heart, you're forever demon-marked. Your heart will only ever accept the magic of demons from then on out."

Bree's eyes widened. "Oh, really? Wow." She pulled on the long sleeves of her gigantic coat. "Um. When you bond with something, do you get the creature's magic forever? Or is it only until you complete the pact?" Bree pointed to Finch. "What happens when Adair gets you a body? Will he lose your magic?"

Dr. Colton snapped his attention to the conversation the instant Bree muttered, *"gets you a body."* Then he glanced at Finch, a deep frown on his bloodstained face.

Finch sat in an armchair away from the others. He met Dr. Colton's gaze and just shrugged. The hour felt long, and Finch was tired. He hadn't gotten a full night's sleep, and waiting for yet another person to show up to the same dull house was testing his ability to just stay awake. He was almost tempted to play another damn board game.

"Warlocks keep the magic until they release it," Kull said matter-of-factly. "So... a warlock *could* keep the magic forever, but most don't. One of the advantages of being a warlock is the flexibility of their magics. Unlike witches, who fill their cores with their own magic, eliminating the possibility of bonding with other creatures, warlocks can change their bonds, and thus, gain new abilities."

Bree nodded along with Kull's words. She brought her knees up to her chest and bit at her lower lip. "What about angels? I've always thought they were so cool with their white feathery wings."

"Oh, this is awkward." Kull laid her ears back. "They, um... How to put this... Don't look like that. They're more *eyeball* than body in many cases."

"What? Ew!" Bree turned to Finch. "Is that true? Or is Kull just tricking me?"

Finch slowly turned his attention to her. "Hm? I don't know. Just watch TV."

Bree frowned. "Adair? Are you okay?"

"I'm fine."

"What're you thinking about?"

"I'm wondering how much Pine-Sol I would have to drink to put myself in a coma," he said, dry and sarcastic. "Now just… watch TV. Let me sit here. I don't care about angels and demons. Their pacts always require you to fight one or the other anyway, so they're terrible creatures to gain magics from—unless you want a lifelong feud."

"I can't believe this is a real conversation," Dr. Colton muttered under his breath. "Liam never told me about *this*."

"Do you have anything else to eat?" Bree grabbed a bag of chips from the coffee table and sighed. "I don't like most of your food."

"It's all gluten free," the doctor replied.

"No wonder it's gross," Finch quipped.

Kull leapt from the couch and onto the coffee table. Then she leapt over to the TV stand and stared at the screen, mere inches from the images. "Hm. Seems we have a problem."

"What problem?" Finch rubbed his temples. "We don't have any problems. Stop talking so loudly."

"Look. Read this."

Everyone turned their attention to the news. The sound was still muted, but the images were bright and loud. There was a car in the middle of a field, flames billowing from the windows and gushing out from under the hood. A helicopter with a camera circled overhead, filming the wreckage. The words scrolling along the bottom read:

Liam Blackstone, suspected of murdering his wife earlier in the day, was found moments ago in his vehicle. Blackstone, age thirty-eight, had locked himself inside before catching the vehicle ablaze. The Stockton PD has yet to make an official statement, but officers on the scene have confirmed Blackstone was alone and attempting to avoid officers. They suspect suicide.

The time was 7:11 p.m.

"*Papa?*" Bree said with a gasp as she leapt from her seat. She jumped over the coffee table and also stared at the screen.

The scene of the car on fire played on a loop.

Finch stood from his chair, his heart hammering. The murderer had killed Liam as well? Had the warlock run out of usefulness?

Bree's bottom lip trembled. She touched the screen and held her breath.

She really shouldn't be seeing this.

"It's not real," Finch said in as soft a voice as he could muster. "Don't worry. I won't let this happen."

But Bree didn't seem to hear him. Silent tears streamed down her cheeks. With a curse under his breath, Finch rewound time.

Everything froze. The colors in the room faded. Then all the objects broke apart.

The killer…

Really didn't want anyone to know his identity. And Finch had a damn good theory about everything now.

CHAPTER
TWENTY-THREE

F inch threw himself out of bed, headed for the front door, and then yanked Bree into his apartment. Her unfocused gaze, and trembling shoulders, told him everything he needed to know about her mental state. He brewed his last bag of midnight raspberry tea, gave it to her, and then guided her to the same ol' chair as always.

Then he opened the window, pulled in Kull, and slammed it down after her.

He wasn't even thinking about his actions, he just did them completely on autopilot.

Then Finch grabbed a Sharpie and drew his Marks of Chronos, all while his mind went a mile a minute.

"Are you feeling well?" Kull asked. She perched on the back of his favorite recliner. "You have a wild look in your eyes akin to that commercial about the raccoons in the attic. You know the one."

"I've seen this before," Finch said as he hurried into his room and rummaged around for clothing. He pulled on a dirty shirt, a semi-clean pair of jeans, and then his trusty coat. He practically put everything on inside out; he just couldn't focus on the immediate.

"You've seen *what* before? This day? Because, trust me, we've *all* seen this before." Kull huffed. "Frankly, I'm starting to think I'll never see the weekend."

"This scenario," Finch said. He smoothed his wrinkled clothing and then grabbed his shoes. "The killer is very concerned about someone learning his identity."

"That seems logical," Kull muttered. She licked a paw and rubbed her ear afterward. "No killer wants to get caught, obviously."

"No. You don't get it. The actions this man is taking—or maybe this whole organization—are extreme. I get it now."

"Killing people is extreme, yes."

Finch stopped and faced the cat. Then he glanced over at Bree. She had the oversized coat already on her shoulders, the sparkling stripe of magic glittering on one sleeve in gaudy fashion. She stood straight, her expression more determined than before. The tea did wonders, but she was obviously ready to face the reality of the situation.

"Do you know who killed Mum?" Bree whispered.

"Let me walk you through the facts," Finch stated. He paced the room, unable to stifle his restless energy. "Dr. Colton has a method of communicating with the killer—or his buddies. When we confronted the doctor in the parking lot, he saw Bree. And do you know what he did?"

"Got confused by your hobo appearance?" Bree asked.

Finch shot her a mild glare. "No. He texted someone. At the time, he said it was his teaching assistant, but now I know it was a lie. He was texting *David*."

"Oh." Bree took in a small bit of air. "Oh, wait… That was when I was shot."

Finch snapped his fingers and pointed at her. "Exactly. Dr. Colton said he found you. But that's not the key bit of information. The key bit is that you said you saw the murderer. You told that to the doctor. And you know what he did?"

Kull's ears perked upward. "He told David."

Finch snapped his fingers twice and smiled. "And then *David*—sweet guy that he is—either shot Bree himself, or had someone shoot Bree."

The room felt colder than before, but Finch's heart was racing. He knew the conclusion he would draw, but he was worried about voicing all the pieces.

Bree stepped closer to his pacing path. "But how does that tell you who the murderer is?"

"Because in the scenario where we go to the doctor and he tells David you *didn't* see the killer, your father is clearly murdered. Why? Because *he* knows who the killer is. And once the killer got whatever he needed from Liam, he disposed of him to keep his identity a secret."

"O-Okay," Bree whispered. She held her hands together. "But I don't understand. How does that tell us who the killer is?"

Finch held up a finger and smiled to himself. "In my experience, there are two types of people who continue killing in dramatic fashion to hide their identity. Assassins and *good guys*." Finch used air quotes for the last two words. "And when I say *good guys*, I mean people close to the murder victim who were trusted, or who want a reputation of *trustworthiness*."

"Oh, no," Kull whispered.

"You see, trustworthiness only comes from a reliable reputation." Finch chuckled to himself. "You wouldn't hire a bodyguard who killed their former employer, would you? No. So if a bodyguard killed their boss, they also have to kill everyone else who saw in order to maintain their reputation."

"But Mum didn't have a bodyguard," Bree said.

Finch stopped his pacing. "No, that was just an example. But what's the next closest thing to a bodyguard? Who *needs* to maintain their reputation of trustworthiness, even if it means the lives of several people?"

When no one answered, Finch finished readying himself. Bree watched with wide eyes.

"Who is it?" she asked. "Who did this?"

"We should speak with the shooter," Finch muttered as he gathered the keys to his car. "His identity will confirm my suspicions."

Bree stood and tapped the tips of her fingers together. "Does that mean I need to get shot again?"

"No." Finch reached into a cupboard and withdrew a few vials of witch's brew. These particular brews caused hallucinations, which was perfect. "We're going to get him to fire on us, but you won't be hurt."

He headed to the door, and then stopped before opening it. Although Bree seemed hesitant, she hardened her expression and ran to his side. Kull meowed softly as she pranced over.

"You know, we can use my magic to trick the shooter," she said.

Finch smirked. "I'm glad you suggested that, because that's exactly what I had in mind."

"We can't let Cauldron get hit by a car," Bree said, holding up a finger. "And we can't let Seth get hurt. We have to help them first."

Finch took a deep breath. He inhaled and then exhaled, and finally nodded. "Fine. Let's hurry and get those over with as quickly as possible."

———

The beautiful Friday morning was becoming a constant. No change in the weather. It was always foggy in the morning, and sunshiny in the afternoon. The traffic was always the same, and so were the people of Stockton.

Finch tried not to think about those facts. Carter would often get depressed if he thought about the stagnant situation too long, and Finch wanted to avoid that.

Time would flow normally as soon as he had the killer.

Finch drove like a madman over to Cauldron's bush. He left the engine running as he leapt out of the vehicle, grabbed the pooch, and then hurried him straight to Ceija's home. Again, the moment she opened her door, Finch thrust the dog into her arms, muttered something about finding him, and practically laughed to himself when she stared at him with gigantic eyes of utter confusion.

Then Finch jogged back to his vehicle, jumped in, and jetted toward Dr. Colton's home. Bree sat on the edge of the passenger seat the entire time, smiling wide.

"I like that we're saving everyone," she said.

Finch replied with a huffed grumble and that was it. He wasn't happy about the fact they were doing the exact same things over and over again, but at the same time, he knew Carter would approve.

When they arrived at Dr. Colton's house in the middle of the orchards, Finch parked his Toyota on the side of the road. Then he stepped out of his vehicle and headed for the front door. Bree leapt out of the car as well and followed behind him.

"You can wait," he said. "This will only take a moment."

"What if Seth doesn't hurt himself on the traps set in the door, though?" Bree hurried to his side. "If he doesn't get hurt, we don't need to disarm the door every morning. Maybe we should watch to see if anything happens?"

Finch exhaled as he glanced at his phone.

7:10 a.m. Seth would bang on the door at 8:01 a.m. That meant they didn't have to wait long, but it *did* mean Finch would need to rewind time again after they tested this door theory.

"Fine," Finch said. "We'll wait." He pointed beyond Dr. Colton's yard, to the first set of trees just behind the fence. "Let's just stand over there, out of sight, and see what happens to our chump of a warlock."

Together, they walked around the fence and then ducked in the orchard. Finch could peer through the cracks in the wooden fence—enough to see the front door, anyway. Bree knelt beside him, her hands on her knees.

A pleasant breeze whistled by, taking the smells of the farms nearby and scattering them around. Finch rubbed his nose, irritated.

"I've made a decision," Bree whispered, her tone filled with a giddy confidence.

"Oh?" Finch rubbed at his eyes. "Like, what you want for lunch?"

"No. I mean, I made a decision about my magic." Bree held her knees tight. "I want to be a warlock—like you."

Finch huffed a laugh as he gave her a sidelong glance. "You're a witch. Stick with that."

"But I don't want to be a witch. I want to be a warlock. I want to make pacts with all sorts of creatures. I want to be the only other person who has a pact with Chronos. That way, I can be a detective, too."

When Finch turned to give her his full attention, she was staring at him with joy-filled blue eyes. She hadn't ever been *this* happy since Finch had known her. The sight caused him to swallow some of his words. He wanted to tell her it was foolish—who would want to be like him, anyway?—but he couldn't bring himself to dash her happiness against the jagged rocks of reality.

"I'm not a detective," Finch eventually muttered. He returned his attention to the hole in the fence boards, his eyes on the front door, though he wasn't really focusing on anything. "I'm a private investigator. There's a difference. And you should really understand the difference if you're going to throw terms out there like that."

Bree nodded once. "Detectives work with a police force? Is that it? And PIs get to do whatever they want?"

"PIs have private clients," Finch corrected.

"Will you teach me how to be a great PI?"

Again, Finch huffed a laugh. "Don't bet on it." He exhaled as he added, "After we find your mother's murderer, and save your father, I plan to go back to my own life."

Bree tapped her fingers on her knees. Her gaze fell to the dirt. "Oh." Then she perked up, her lips turned up in a coy smile. "What if I was one of your private clients? I could pay you to train me!"

"Heh. What're you going to pay me with? Sheep and ore from your board games?"

"Well, I could, uh…" She tapped the point of her chin. Then her eyes widened. "I could help you find those vampire-loving witches. My mum taught me a lot about different kinds of covens, *and* I'm a witch, so maybe I could do things you can't."

"You won't be a witch if you become a warlock."

Bree pressed her lips together. Then she said, "That's right, but I'll still know things, and Mum taught me how to make brews. We can be a crime-fighting duo and—"

"*No*," Finch snapped, cutting her off. He inhaled, his chest tightening with anger. When he exhaled, he shook his head and calmed his voice. "It's not… that simple. I have a debt to settle. And it's dangerous. Too dangerous for a child."

And in Finch's mind, too dangerous even for him. He had vowed he would destroy the vampire coven—even if it meant his own life. How could he bring Bree into that? It wasn't her vendetta. It wasn't her grudge.

Finch couldn't take her as an apprentice.

He couldn't take anyone.

"Oh, you two look grim," a playful voice said.

Finch whirled around. Kull sat on the branch of a nearby tree, her black fur speckled with light that had filtered through the branches. She offered him a feline smile.

"What're you doing here?" he asked.

"Did you really think I would wait *in the car*?" Kull snickered and stretched. "Silly, silly human. I'm a mischief spirit, not an obedient spirit."

"Don't ruin this for us," Finch growled. He slowly turned back to stare through the fence gap. "I've got enough on my plate as it is."

Bree said nothing. She hugged her knees tight against her chest, her attention also on Dr. Colton's front door. Her blue eyes seemed unfocused, her thoughts clearly inward. Finch tried not to think about it. It really was better if she just forgot he existed once this was all done.

Several long, and strained, moments passed. Finally, 8:00 a.m. rolled around.

Seth parked his vehicle—a Dodge Neon—on the dirt road. With a huff of his breath with each step, he made his way to the front door. The man, right at 8:01 a.m., knocked as loudly as he could. Obviously, no one answered.

"I have money on his inevitable death," Kull whispered from the tree.

Bree held a finger to her lips. "*Shh*. He might be okay." She lowered her hand and added, "I want him to be okay…"

The wannabe warlock sighed, and then went for the window. Seth placed his hands on the glass and peered inside, though it was difficult due to the many potted plants on the front porch. He was supposed to wait for Dr. Colton, but Seth was visibly antsy. After a short moment of investigation around the side of the house, Seth returned to the front door and grabbed the handle.

The resulting *shock* was so sudden, bright, and loud, that Finch flinched and backed away from the fence. It was as if a bolt of lightning blasted from the wood.

Seth flew eight feet backward and then hit the ground on his back, dust puffing in a cloud around him. The palm he had used on the handle was black, and his legs twitched.

A long minute went by. Finch glanced at his phone to make sure.

Seth didn't get up. If he were in a dead fish contest, he would probably take the gold.

He should've waited for the doctor.

"Oh, someone owes me *money*," Kull sang like a jingle from a commercial.

Bree frowned. "Oh, no," she murmured. "We really *do* have to help him, Adair. He shouldn't die."

Goddammit. "Fine," he replied.

"Thank you." When Bree turned to him, it was with a wary smile.

He didn't respond.

Instead, Finch rewound time. Everything froze. The colors drained, and then the objects melted away as well. Everything was a swirl of nothing before he awoke in his bed.

4:34 a.m.

CHAPTER
TWENTY-FOUR

Finch got up, let Bree into his apartment, gave her tea, allowed Kull into his apartment, drew the Mark of Chronos on the both of them, got dressed, gave Bree her coat, and then grabbed the witch's brew for hallucination before heading out the front door.

They drove straight to Cauldron.

Saved him.

Then they sped all the way to Dr. Colton's house and disarmed the magic on the front door.

Which effectively saved Seth from being magically electrocuted to death.

As Finch huffed his way back to his vehicle, he glanced at his phone. 7:01 a.m. Plenty of time to reach Dr. Colton in the parking lot of the university. But before they went there, Finch headed to Bree's home on the outskirts of town.

As Finch turned down a quiet frontage road, Bree faced to him. She brushed her brown hair behind her ear and said, "So, whenever I had a disagreement with Papa, he said we should *evaluate what works, and what doesn't work.*"

"What?" Finch practically barked, utterly confused by the direction of the conversation.

"Papa said it was to help solve problems." Bree laced her fingers together in front of her, as though she were a banker examining a stack of paperwork. "And I think we should do that here."

"What's there to evaluate? Someone *died*. We're going to figure out who did it and bring them to justice. The only *problem* we need to solve is how hard we should kick their ass once we find them."

Bree lifted both her eyebrows. "Oh, I'm not talking about the murder. I was talking about me becoming a warlock." She leaned closer. "Because now that I know how it works, I'm going to do it no matter what. But I really want you to teach me everything you know. So… I think we should talk about *what works*, and *what doesn't.*"

"None of this works," Finch growled.

Kull, from her seat in the back, purred a soft chuckle. "What an opening position. I can see these negotiations going well."

"W-Well, let's pretend all the vampire witches were dead." Bree held up a finger to keep Finch from speaking. "Would you teach me how to be a PI warlock then?"

"Hypothetically," Finch said, a gruff edge to his voice.

"So, there isn't a problem teaching me, just a problem with the witches. See? We're already solving things." Bree clapped her hands once and smiled. "How about we compromise? You'll teach me for a few years, and *then* you'll go find the awful coven."

"No," Finch said.

"What? But this is a perfect compromise."

He shot her a glower. "Just having you as my apprentice would put a target on your back, kid. I can't have that. And if I get a whiff of that coven's location, I'm not going to finish my training with you before leaving—I'm going to take off right away. This is a no-win situation."

Bree shook her head. "But you can control time! Just... I dunno... Train me all in one day! You can keep rewinding the time, and telling me everything I need to know... It'll be easy."

Finch opened his mouth, ready to tell her *no* for the hundredth time, but then he swallowed his words pre-tirade. Technically, her suggestion would work. Unfortunately, that would mean being stuck on the same day for years.

Years.

No one wanted that, even if it would be efficient. Reliving the current day was already grating on Finch's patience.

"You can get any warlock to teach you," Finch finally stated. "You don't need me. I'm a—"

"A bum?" Kull interjected.

Finch glanced over his shoulder and glared. "No one was talking to you, *spirit*."

She twitched her feline ears and tilted her head. "I'm an expert on humans, thank you very much. And humans who avoid responsibilities, and make excuses to avoid everything, are considered bums." When no one replied to that, she licked her paws. "Applauding for my vast wealth of knowledge is an acceptable response."

"You're not a bum, Adair," Bree said. When Finch glanced over, she continued, "You're the greatest warlock of all time, remember? That's what Mum said. And if *you* train me to be a warlock, that means *I'll* become great, too. So, I don't want a random warlock."

"You don't?" Kull asked. "I'm sure Seth would take your money."

Finch actually laughed at that comment. Imagining Seth teaching anything was preposterous. The man would struggle to guide someone through a sandwich making process.

"I want to be an amazing warlock." Bree held her hands together in front of her. "Papa also said, *Never make an important decision right away.* Think about it, okay, Adair? I'll be the greatest apprentice of all time!"

Finch said nothing.

"I don't think you should discount Seth," Kull said from the back, her sarcasm evident. "It would at least make for a hilarious scenario worthy of a sitcom."

The moment Finch arrived on the road to Bree's home, he motioned to the surrounding area. Bree glanced out the passenger-side window, her eyes wide.

"Why are we here?" she asked. "I thought we were going to confront the shooter?"

"The morning the shooter bothered us, we stopped by your house first." Finch parked a few houses down, away from the police cars. "You went with me to the front door, and I spoke to the detective on the scene. We're going to do that, just faster than normal."

"Why?"

Finch killed the engine. His first response was to tell her to trust him, but Finch had hated it whenever Carter did that. After a long exhale, he said, "My working theory is that the shooter is here. I believe he saw me here, and followed me to the University of the Pacific."

Bree nodded along with his words. "Really? But why?"

"When we searched the university tower for the shooter, we didn't find anyone." Finch met her gaze. "That means he isn't there. We *did something* to cause him to set up there. And I believe it's our presence here first."

Kull stood on the seat and then leapt to the center console. She stretched—her front legs way out in front of her —and then meowed. "Well, we aren't going to see if you're correct unless we get out there and do something. Come, come."

"Why are *you* in such a hurry?" Finch grabbed his badge from the glove compartment, opened the door, and then stepped out. Bree followed quickly afterward, but Kull leapt out the driver's side.

"The faster we catch this killer, the faster you'll get me a human body," Kull said matter-of-factly. "And while this is all entertaining, I can't help but feel I'm missing out on some human emotions with it all. I won't know until I have my true body—the one I'm meant to grow old in."

"Maybe you'll get a child body," Bree said as she shut the door of Finch's vehicle. "Wouldn't that be fun? Maybe a little baby."

"Human babies are defenseless and soil themselves." Kull held her nose in the air. "Zero out of ten, not my cup of tea. I want something with more *oomph*. Or at least something that can eat solid foods and not suckle from a tit."

"*Hey*," Finch barked. He shot the cat a glare. "Watch your mouth. She's just a kid."

Bree hurried to his side. With a frown, she muttered, "I told you. I have the internet. That's not the worst of what I've heard."

"Especially when sites like *Pornhub* exist," Kull said with a feline snicker.

Finch kept his gaze on the trees around them. The edge of Stockton was filled with woodlands, orchards, and farmland. The early morning fog still lingered, and Finch was halfway convinced the shooter was using it as cover. Finch shoved his hands into the pockets of his coat as they approached the police tape.

"Do what you did last time," Finch said under his breath. He glanced down at Bree. "Understand?"

She nodded.

"What should I do?" Kull whispered.

"Pretend to be a stupid cat until we return."

As Finch ducked under the tape, a dozen beat cops leapt to stop him. He flashed his badge, and the magic on Bree's ugly coat obfuscated her identity. The cops saw her as someone who belonged—Finch's assistant.

The two of them walked to the front door, and Bree stopped.

"I waited here last time," she whispered.

"Then wait here again." Finch walked into the house, and then turned left at the T intersection of the hallway. The click of the clock on the wall reminded him that he shouldn't waste time. Dr. Colton would be at the University of the Pacific in roughly forty-five minutes.

The kitchen murder scene was just as Finch remembered it—grim and unfortunate. The bloodstain on the floor, the island in the middle of the room, and the gaggle of forensic officers collecting evidence.

Detective Rhett Jenner paced around, his eyes on every detail. When he lifted his gaze and spotted Finch, he froze.

"*You.*"

"In the flesh," Finch quipped for the third time. But before the detective could say anything more, Finch held up a hand. "Don't worry, I've almost discovered the identity of the killer. I'm just here as a formality."

Detective Jenner furrowed his brow and sneered. "A… formality?" Then he shook his head and motioned to the door. "Listen, *you*. We don't need your kind around here. We can solve this ourselves."

Your kind? Finch almost snorted.

The bizarre wording garnered the attention of the other officers. Since they weren't in the know about magic, and had no idea Finch was a warlock, it no doubt appeared like a strange conversation. If Finch had been part of an apparent minority group, he was certain others would've taken offense. As it stood, everyone just stared with expressions of bafflement.

"Look, the next time I see you, it's going to be with a pile of evidence and an explanation of what happened here," Finch stated. "So just keep that stick in your ass until I get back, got it?"

"*Hey*," the detective barked.

But Finch didn't care. He turned on his heel and headed for the front door. Although he had stayed in the house longer the first time he arrived in the kitchen, Finch was willing to bet whoever had seen him had done so from the outside. Now he just needed to head to the university and catch a shooter in a study hall.

When Finch made it to the front door, he spotted Bree hovering around the porch and a group of police officers standing near the yellow boundary tape. Most of the officers were bent over, their phones in their hands. Some of them laughed—one even giggled—and Finch narrowed his eyes as he stomped over.

He already knew what was going on.

"Oh, look at how cute she is!" one officer said with a coo.

Another officer took a few pictures. "So adorable. Do you think she has an owner?"

Finch pushed his way into the gaggle of officers only to find Kull rolling around on the ground. She had her tongue poking out of her mouth, and her eyes practically staring in two different directions. The black cat rolled onto her back and exposed her tummy, her feet cartwheeling in the air.

"I think she has brain damage," one grumpier officer muttered from the back of the group.

Finch scooped the mischief spirit up into his arms. She meowed and then swiped with a paw at his chin. After a short growl of irritation, Finch huffed off toward his vehicle.

"Is that your cat?" an officer shouted.

"Unfortunately," Finch called back.

As Bree chased after him, she nodded to the police. "Sorry! She's our super special investigation cat. We'll bring her back if we can."

A few of the beat cops smiled and waved, but others seemed sad the bizarre cat had vanished from their lives. Finch couldn't believe the cat had made such a scene. He glared down at the animal.

"What was that?" he hissed under his breath.

"You told me to act like a stupid cat," Kull replied. She playfully chuckled. "I was following orders."

Finch immediately regretted all his words to her. He *had* said that. Once he reached his car, he opened up the back, placed Kull inside, and then went for the driver's seat. Bree was already buckled into the passenger side, her eyes wide.

"Are we going to beat up the shooter now?" she asked.

Finch ignited the engine. "You bet we are."

CHAPTER
TWENTY-FIVE

As they drove for the university, Bree fidgeted in her seat. She tugged on the long sleeves of her oversized coat, and then glanced at Finch with worried blue eyes.

"What's wrong?" Finch asked, trying not to sound irritated with her silence.

"I'm not going to get shot, right? You promise?"

"I promise." He gave her a sidelong glance. "If my theory is correct, the shooter will be following us to the parking lot. We're going to park, pretend to speak with the dwarf, and then head for the tower."

Hopefully, no one would get shot in that scenario, though Finch wasn't entirely certain. He was banking on his assessment of the situation, but things could go wrong.

"Maybe you and Kull should wait by the trees where the dwarf dwells while I handle everything," Finch muttered.

Bree nodded along with his words. "Hm. Yeah. We'll make sure the dwarf is okay."

He almost laughed, but he kept that to himself. The dwarf

wasn't in any real danger, but if Bree and Kull wanted to "protect him," that was fine by Finch.

He parked his vehicle in the empty parking lot and glanced at the time. 7:36 a.m. Since Finch had gone to Bree's house at a slightly different time than before, there was always a chance this was all pointless—they had missed their opportunity to attract the shooter's attention.

But Finch was still hopeful.

The three of them exited his car. With slow and purposeful steps, Finch headed for the small cluster of trees around the dwarf's hole. The hairs on the back of Finch's neck stood on end as he imagined a man carefully sneaking into the abandoned study hall. He couldn't see the front door from his position in the parking lot, but his mind filled in all the blanks.

The shooter was likely carrying a case with the rifle. Soon he would be climbing the stairs to the highest window…

Bree leapt to the edge of the dwarf's hole and then stared into it. With a frown, she glanced back at Finch. "Do we need to speak to him?"

"No," Finch muttered. "Just pretend you're doing something for a few minutes. We need to give our bloodthirsty friend a few minutes to set up."

Bree tapped the tips of her fingers together. "Um, Adair?"

"Yeah?"

"*You* aren't going to get shot, right?"

"I won't," he said, cold and confident.

Bree hesitantly smiled. "Oh, okay. Good. Because I don't like the thought of you getting hurt." Her gaze slid down to the ground. "I don't want anyone else to get hurt because of these bad guys."

"Don't worry," Finch said with a groan. "We saved the dog, we saved that loser breaking into the doctor's house—

no one else is going to get hurt. We're about to wrap up this whole case."

His statements immediately brightened Bree's mood. She smiled wider than before. Even Kull seemed somewhat pleased. She silently walked around Bree, her black tail high in the air. The three of them waited in relative silence after that. The morning wind rushed by, bringing with it an ominous chill, but Finch shrugged the shivers away.

As soon as he thought enough time had passed, he turned and headed for the building. With each step, his heart beat a little faster and harder. It wasn't fear—but anger. Whoever was here was the one who had shot Bree and Dr. Colton, seemingly for the crime of knowing who the true killer was. Or at least, having *seen* the killer.

Finch couldn't wait to get to the bottom of this.

When he reached the door, he glanced at the plaque mounted to the wall. STUDY HALL D. The same as before. But when he reached for the door handle, he found it unlocked.

Which was vastly different.

The shooter was inside.

With a cruel smile, Finch let himself in. Dust swirled in the air as he crept to the stairwell. Morning light streamed through the barred windows, casting dark stripes of shadow across the floor. Finch didn't need to turn on the lights to know where he was heading. He climbed the stairs two at a time until he reached his destination.

The third floor.

There were only two rooms that faced the empty parking lot, and Finch had searched them before, albeit in a different time cycle. However, everything was as he remembered. The abandoned space, mostly covered in dust, was easy to navigate. When he approached the first room, he tensed.

The door was ajar.

Inside, the echoes of breathing, and the slight rattle of equipment, bounced around the room. Finch smiled to himself. He reached into his coat pocket and withdrew the witch's brew.

The one-time-use brews could do a wide variety of things, depending on the magic of the witch and her talent for brewing. The most skilled of witches could make brews so potent, they could kill, if so desired. This brew, however, was just a hallucinogen, but in Finch's experience, it was a valuable tool, which he had used time and time again to render his opponents helpless.

And this was the perfect situation.

Finch unplugged the small glass bottle, and then threw it into the room without disturbing the door. The instant he heard the glass shatter on the ground, he grabbed the handle and slammed the door shut.

"*What the?*" came the voice of a startled man.

Finch held the door shut as tightly as possible.

Most witch's brews had fumes, but this one specifically became a gas when it mixed with the air. Although he couldn't see it, Finch already knew the room was filled with a putrid-smelling green vapor.

The stomp of boots told Finch the man was attempting to leave. The shooter grabbed the door and yanked. Finch held steady. He even placed his foot on the wall to brace himself against the pulling.

"What's going on?" the man shouted.

Finch didn't reply.

The man pulled harder and harder. And then he started shouting. Nothing specific—just shouting. The hallucinations often took the form of disturbing, but nonsensical, objects. Carter had always compared it to the *pink elephant scene* from a certain movie Finch couldn't remember.

"Let me out!" the shooter shouted.

The man yanked on the door, but Finch managed to keep him in.

The hallucinations often caused people to just panic and act without reason. Finch worried the man would grab his rifle and fire at the door—that would be the logical thing to do—but instead, the man released the door and started trashing the door. Finch heard the crash of objects hitting the floor, and the distinct sounds of someone slamming the window open and then closed.

"Help!" the man shouted. "*Help!*"

Finch didn't care if the man drew attention. All Finch cared about was identifying him. In a few moments, the brew's vapors would settle to the floor, and then Finch would enter the room.

The entire time, the man thrashed about, clearly distraught. Once he stopped, and Finch glanced at his phone to make sure at least three minutes had passed, he opened the door.

It looked as though a tornado had swept through the abandoned study room. The empty bookshelves were toppled over, the desk on its side, and a frightened man pressed back-first into the corner, his eyes wide and unfocused. His hallucinations would last a while longer.

On the floor, below the windowsill, was an M24 sniper rifle. Finch recognized it immediately—they were rifles used by military and police forces only. They weren't technically allowed for civilian purchase.

Which only confirmed what Finch suspected.

He stomped over to the delirious man in the corner. The shooter wore a plain shirt, and a pair of jeans—nothing immediately identifying him—but Finch grabbed him by the collar and then went for his pockets. Finch withdrew one of Liam's necklaces and a brown leather wallet.

Sure enough, next to credit cards, his ID labeling him as Mack Krom, and a wad of cash, was the man's police badge.

Finch dropped the wallet and released the man. The shooter, Officer Krom, sputtered something incomprehensible and jammed his body back into the corner of the room.

The reason the killer had been so keen on keeping his identity hidden was because it would be a shitshow for the whole city to discover a *cop* was the one who had murdered an innocent witch.

CHAPTER
TWENTY-SIX

Finch grabbed the shooter by the front of his shirt. "Who did it?" he growled. "Who killed Vera?"

The cop's eyes didn't focus on anything in particular. His pupils were dilated, and his gaze flitted from one place to the next with a tweaker's energy. Finch shook the man, and the crooked cop shook his head.

"There are monsters everywhere," Officer Krom said. He thrashed an arm off to the side, knocking one of Finch's hands away in a violent blow. "*Monsters!*"

Finch exhaled through gritted teeth. Then, in a softer tone, he said, "They're illusions. If you want out of this, *you'll answer my questions*. Who killed the witch, Vera?"

"Make them stop!"

Again, the crooked cop flailed around, terrified by phantoms only he could see. Once he stopped waving his arms—no doubt he felt nothing—Finch placed a hand on his shoulder. Krom hesitated, his breathing ragged.

"They won't leave until you answer me," Finch stated.

Officer Krom didn't like that, but his heart hammered so thoroughly, Finch felt it through the shirt.

"I don't know who killed the witch." Krom grabbed Finch by the wrist and held him close. After a hard swallow he said, "Sergeant McGregor gave the order. All witnesses need to go. They're all with the occult bastards. We can't... we can't trust them."

Occult bastards?

Finch released the man and then stepped away. He stared at the floor as he mulled over the name. He had heard it before. Where? It had been a few weeks—for Finch, anyway—but then it clicked. Sergeant McGregor was the man in charge of Vera's murder investigation. Finch hadn't met him, but he had been at the scene of the crime, just outside.

Had the sergeant killed Vera? Or was he covering for someone else?

"How deep does this go?" Finch asked. "Is the whole police force in on this?"

Stockton, the city, was known for a wide variety of things. It had the most trees per capita in California. It once went bankrupt. And the crime was off the charts. Stockton PD was always mired in problems. The only saving grace was that Police Chief Harding—who was a known hero in the community—was an upstanding individual who wanted nothing more than to help the city. He was just recently elected to be the new chief.

Hopefully this wasn't Harding's idea.

Krom smacked himself in the face, his eyes growing wider as the hallucinations worsened. He couldn't seem to stay still. "What's happening?" he asked, panic in his voice.

"*Answer me*. Does the chief know?"

"I... It's not..." Officer Krom grabbed at his hair. "The sergeant deals with all matters *occult*. It's his division."

"Does the chief know?"

"I... I don't know. I don't think so. We don't directly

report to the chief. We're ordered never to report up past the sergeant."

"And no one asks questions?" Finch demanded, his voice so loud he was sure someone in the parking lot could hear him.

"Th-That's how it always is with the occult. We can't leave records!"

That was true. Any official business that dealt with witches and warlocks—or anything of a magical nature—was always off the books. It would be easy to keep corruption a secret in the special division of the police if the head of that division was the source of the corruption. Who were the beat cops and detectives going to report suspicious activity to? Unless they knew the really higher-ups in the feds, they would be stuck with their sergeant.

But that didn't mean Finch liked any of this.

"You're killing innocent witches?" Finch asked. Each word he spoke was icier than the last.

"They started it," Krom said. He rubbed his eyes and then his temples. "*They started it.*"

"What're you talking about?"

"Those occult bastards. *Killing cops.* Starting turf wars. They started it—we're just not going to deal with their shit any longer."

Finch held his breath.

The dead cops…

That wannabe warlock had mentioned that. Several cops dead as collateral damage in the witches' war. But Vera hadn't been involved in that, so why had she been killed?

"You targeted Vera?" Finch asked.

Krom shook his head. He kept his eyes scrunched tight. "I can't stop… seeing things… Hearing things…"

Finch grabbed his shirt again and shook. "Why target Vera? *Answer me.*"

But Krom just continued to shake his head more than a bobblehead figurine. He couldn't focus, and Finch suspected the auditory hallucinations were causing the man to think poorly. Krom probably didn't know what was really happening, either. It was obvious from his responses that he wasn't the killer—he was just a gunman for someone in charge.

And he thought killing *occult bastards* was some sort of praiseworthy duty.

In another timeline…

Officer Krom had even shot a little girl.

Finch couldn't forgive that, even if *this* Krom had done nothing of the sort. So, instead of helping the man recover from the effects of the witch's brew, Finch just left him there. Krom would have to deal with the illusionary monsters for several more hours—or at least until Finch rewound time.

Then Finch exited the abandoned room and headed for the stairs, his focus entirely on the case.

If the police chief didn't know, Finch would have to report it. If the chief *did* know, Finch would have to take evidence to the special division of the FBI—specifically, the FBOI, the Federal Bureau of Occult Investigation. But Finch hated dealing with them. First off, if Finch dragged Officer Krom to them, Finch would *also* be arrested. Torturing someone for information was always frowned upon, even if the torture was all in the person's head.

Secondly, Finch had constantly gone around the bureau's back to do several things in the past, and they had never forgiven him. If he didn't bring them squeaky clean evidence this time, they would find an excuse to throw it out. Or arrest him.

Once Finch reached the ground floor of the study hall, he stormed over to the front door, slammed it open, and headed straight for his vehicle. Bree and Kull spotted him from across the way and hurried to his side. As a trio, they made it to his Toyota and piled in, not a word exchanged between them.

The moment everyone was seated—Finch as the driver, Bree as the passenger, and Kull lazing around the back seat— Bree turned to Finch with wide eyes. "What happened? Did you beat up the shooter?"

"Yeah," Finch muttered absentmindedly.

"R-Really?"

"It was practically the finale of an action movie in there." Finch tilted his seat back so he could stare at the ceiling of the cab. His tone reeked of disinterest, and his thoughts dwelled only on the problem.

He hated the thought of fighting cops.

They were supposed to be the good guys. And in situations where there were crooked cops, Finch knew there were always good people mixed up in everything. One corrupt sergeant could get a whole department fired and their careers ruined.

But he couldn't let them get away with killing innocent people.

"Tell us the details," Bree said as she leaned closer. "Did you break his nose and stuff? Did you interrogate him? *What happened?*"

Finch didn't even know why he was making things up, it was just better than voicing his complicated thoughts. "It was a real brawl. First an arm bar, then a rear naked choke. Then he spilled the beans."

"Eww," Bree said.

Which was an odd response.

Finch glanced over. "What *eww*? Nothing I said warranted an *eww*."

"You choked him while he was naked?" Bree narrowed

her eyes and sneered. "I just… Why would you do that? Eww."

"A *rear naked choke* is the name of an actual fighting move," Finch said, heat in his words and his cheeks. "It has nothing to do with *being naked*." He ran a hand down his face, his jaw clenched. "What do they even teach kids in school these days?"

"I don't know," Kull said as she swished her tail. "That move sounds made up to me."

Finch shot her a cold glare. "You know damn well it's real. Stop playing dumb. You're confusing the girl."

The little black cat purred out a chuckle.

Bree held out her hand. "I don't have my phone. Can I use yours to Google it?"

"*No.*" Finch fixed his seat so he sat upright. "We both know that would result in trauma for the both of us. Listen— we need to focus. The man in the study hall was a cop."

Bree's eyes went even wider. She used both hands to cover her mouth.

Kull twitched her whiskers. "I knew it."

"He didn't know who killed Vera, but it's obviously someone in the police force. My money is on Sergeant McGregor. And if it's not him, he'll know who did it."

"Why was he going to shoot us?" Bree asked.

"Apparently, since witches have been killing cops in the city, all the officers are on edge. He thinks we're with the enemy—any witnesses to the crime are somehow associated with the criminal occult."

"Okay, so let's bust into McGregor's office and explode him with fire," Bree said as she smiled. "You can do that, right? He won't stand a chance."

Finch gave her a sidelong glance. "Listen, if we just wanted to nuke him, and the whole police department, our mission would be easy. But that's not going to get us anywhere meaningful. I need evidence I can hand over to higher authorities so all of Stockton PD can be purged of corruption."

The information took a few moments to settle over Bree. She slowly nodded as her eyes slid over to the dashboard. She didn't focus her gaze on anything for a long time.

"Why did someone kill Vera?" Kull asked.

Finch sighed. "I'm not sure. It has to do with the necklaces Liam was creating."

The moment Finch spoke those words, Bree perked back up and returned her attention to him. "Oh, that's it! We just need to save Papa. He was probably helping the police by making the necklaces to see through magic, that way they could catch criminals easier. *They're the ones who kidnapped him.* I know it. *I know it.*"

That was it.

Finch turned to her, the realization fast and invigorating. That made perfect sense. Liam was a good man—*of course* he would help the Stockton PD if they came asking. He had probably made them a few necklaces, but then they had demanded more.

Why wouldn't Liam make more?

Perhaps he was busy, or he didn't want to kill any more animals to make his items. There was *some* reason. And then the police didn't like that. They came to strong-arm the man into making more. Perhaps even threatened him with criminal charges.

But why kill Vera? Had she just been in the way?

Finch grabbed the steering wheel with both hands. He tightened his grip. "Liam knows everything," he muttered, more to himself than to Bree. "And if we save him, and bring him to the chief, or even the FBOI, he'll have all the relevant information we need to put everyone behind bars."

"Really?" Bree asked. Then her expression soured. "But... Papa is going to get killed... Remember?"

Finch hadn't forgotten. The news report still played in his mind. The cops wanted to get rid of him *specifically* because he knew too much.

So they *had* to rescue Liam Blackstone, no matter the cost.

"We should also find out who the killer is," Kull said as she groomed herself. With another purr-laugh, she added, "I mean, if *one* corrupt cop gets burned to a crisp, that isn't too big a deal, right? So long as Liam is saved?"

Bree clapped her hands once. "Yes! I think that's the perfect plan." She smiled at Finch. "Right, Adair? We can do that?"

He smiled to himself. "I don't see why not."

Just as Finch was about to drive away from the parking lot—and head toward the police station—he realized something peculiar about his vehicle. It was more magical than before. He hadn't realized it at first, because he had been too preoccupied, but now that his thoughts were clearer, the sensation was rather obvious.

Finch slowly turned his attention to Bree.

New magic radiated from her.

They stared at each other for a prolonged moment.

"Y-Yes?" Bree asked, hesitation in her question.

"You're a warlock," Finch said as the realization came to him. "*What have you done?*"

CHAPTER
TWENTY-SEVEN

"I just made a pact with Kull," Bree quickly stated. She nervously tapped the tips of her fingers together. "It's no big deal. I didn't think you would know."

Finch glowered at her. "You thought *I wouldn't know*? What kind of hack-fraud do you think I am? Of course I can tell!" He turned around in his seat, reached into the back, and grabbed Kull by the scruff before she could scurry away. "What have you done, spirit?"

"Hey, hey!" Kull twisted her body and then changed in an instant. With almost a *pop* of magic, she puffed into a pigeon. She flapped her wings and landed on the center console. "Having multiple warlocks bonded is quite an honor for a spirit like me, thank you very much."

"What kind of pact did you make with her?"

"Nothing complicated." Kull fluffed her feathers and shook out her tail. "And I don't have to tell you. Spirits never have to reveal the pacts they made with other warlocks."

Bree held out a hand before Finch could continue his tirade. "It's okay! Kull was really nice. She said—once she gets a human body—I just have to help her with her wardrobe. S-So, I don't even have to do anything unless *you* succeed, and that won't be for a while, right?"

Finch took in a deep breath.

And then exhaled.

He glanced away, allowed his anger to bleed out of him before he said anything else. Kull's pact was a generous one. Especially because, once she had a human body, her powers would wane, though not disappear. She wouldn't be able to take anything from Bree—her ability to punish warlocks she made pacts with would cease.

This was a grant of magic without a real consequence.

Why had Kull been so generous? Did she like the girl?

Kull had already fallen in love with a human once before —perhaps it had happened again, though more in a maternal way.

"Adair?" Bree whispered. "You're not too mad, right?"

"I told you this wasn't a good idea," he replied, flat and icy.

"I did everything you said, though. I, uh, even bonded with Kull in the same place you did. The eyes. I thought you could teach me."

"You can't become a full witch until your pact ends." Finch drove the car away from the curb and headed into Stockton. His heart beat with residual anger, but he tried his damnedest to let it go.

Bree leaned away, her head practically on the passenger window. "I told you. I don't want to be a witch. I want to be a warlock."

"You don't know what you're talking about."

She crossed her arms and scrunched her lips into a tight line. After several moments of silence, she finally said, "I'll always have the option to become a witch. But I won't always have a chance to learn to be a warlock from Adair Finch."

Bree glanced over. "The smart move is to learn everything I can right now."

Finch frowned.

Kids these days thought themselves so clever.

Despite that, he didn't really have a retort. Learning magic was often a long process, and finding good teachers was difficult. A talented mentor could be worth their weight in gold.

As he drove, Kull transformed back into a black cat. She leapt into Bree's lap and curled into a ball, her fur glistening in the morning light. While Finch had *intended* to head to the police station, he changed his mind halfway there. Instead, he turned down a narrow road and headed for *Nico's Brew*.

It didn't take him long to reach the sad hole-in-the-wall coffee joint.

Finch parked his car and stepped out. Bree and Kull followed afterward, both a little confused. Before they went for the front door, Finch opened the trunk of his Toyota and rummaged through his own garbage. He pushed aside a tarp and weeks' worth of fast-food wrappers. Finally, he found three padlocks with keys in them. He pocketed the locks and then headed inside, Bree and Kull close to his side.

Nico's Brew was still devoid of patrons, just like the time before. However, Nico—standing behind the bar—no longer remembered Kull's assault on his coffee mug. Nico stared at a flatscreen TV hanging in the top corner of the coffee shop, the news playing, just like before.

Finch took a seat in the nearest booth. Bree sat across from him, and then placed Kull on the table.

"Is that a *cat?*" Nico bellowed. He narrowed his eyes and pinched the end of his thick mustache.

Bree nodded once. "She's my therapy cat. She won't cause any trouble, I promise."

"Don't let it wander around the shop," Nico said with a

grunt. He pointed a large finger at her. "Keep it to yourself." Then he exhaled and returned his attention to the TV.

After a long moment of silence, Bree turned to Finch with a smile. "It's funny seeing people act the same way after time is reset. He practically did the same things! Isn't that kinda neat? And weird?"

"It gets real dull after a while," Finch muttered. Then he dug into his coat pocket and pulled out the padlocks. He set them on the table.

"What're those?" Bree frowned. "And why did we stop? Are you just hungry? You want to eat before we take down all the cops?"

Nico glanced over at that comment. He narrowed his eyes and rubbed at his substantial gut, his lips turned down at the corners in a slight sneer.

"*Keep it down*," Finch said through clenched teeth. He ripped out the keys and shoved the locks over to Bree. "Take these. We're not going to deal with the police until you learn to control some of your newfound magic."

"R-Really?" Bree asked, half a gasp, half a question.

"What did I just say? *Keep it down*."

"Right." With a giddy smile, Bree scooped up the three locks and held them close. She glanced between them and then returned her attention to Finch. "What should I do with them?"

Finch pointed at the locks. "You have trickster magic now. Unlocking things is the simplest of uses."

After a few moments of silence, Bree turned her gaze down to the locks. She played with them in her hands and then arranged them in a line on the table. "How?" She poked one. Nothing happened.

"Listen carefully. First—"

Nico slammed a mug of coffee onto the table in front of

Finch. The dark liquid nearly splashed upward from the force.

"The usual," Nico said, his voice scratchy and gruff from years of smoking. He turned his cold stare on Bree. "And what will you have?"

Kull purred a bit as she swished her tail. Nico's frown deepened.

"I'll have coffee with cream and sugar," Bree said. She sniffed the air. "I bet you make coffee *way* better than Starbucks."

In an instant, Nico's grumpiness lessened. He couldn't seem to stop himself from half smiling. With a delighted huff, he said, "Well, you must know your brews, kid. I do make a mean sweet coffee. I'll fix that up for ya." Nico walked around the counter and headed for his coffeepot.

Finch was almost impressed. Bree remembered what the man had said previously—and had made him go away as quickly as possible.

"Okay," Bree said as she leaned on the booth table. "I'm listening. What do I have to do?"

Although Finch had his reservations about teaching a young witch how to become a warlock, he leaned in closer and took a breath. There was a lot to cover, but perhaps the most basic of information was best to start with.

"There are five cores to your being," he said.

"The crown, the eyes, the heart, the soul, and the loins," Bree rattled off. "I've memorized them. What else?"

"Each core requires a different skill set to use. If you tie magic to your crown, it requires *concentration* to wield. The greater your concentration, the better you control your magic. If you tie magic to your heart, then emotions will be the basis for its use. The stronger the emotion, the more powerful your manifestations. Are you understanding so far?"

"What about for the eyes?" Bree whispered. She stared at him, unblinking. "Do I have to *look* really hard?"

Finch chuckled to himself. "You need to *visualize* the magic. Seeing it work in your mind before using it. That's the key to using magics tied to your eyes."

With a shaky hand, Bree touched one of her eyelids. "What if I were blind?"

"Your magic would be difficult to use, but you could still do it. Blind warlocks can still visualize—it's just different for them. The same can be said if you were castrated or took one too many blows to the head."

For a long moment, Bree said nothing. She stared at the booth table, a slight frown growing. Then she glanced up. "What does *castrated* mean?"

"Tsk. I thought you had the internet and already knew everything?"

"I don't think I've ever heard anyone say the word *castrated* before."

The coffee shop owner, Nico, walked over right as Bree voiced the statement. The man turned to Finch and glared. With a grunt, he slammed down a mug for Bree.

"What're you two talking about over here?" he demanded.

"She's learning about agricultural science in school," Finch replied without missing a beat. He offered Nico an icy glower. "Now mind your own damn business. She has a test, and she needs to study."

That seemed to satisfy the man. He grumbled something under his breath as he turned away, obviously disgruntled. But this was why Finch liked this place so much. Nico kept to himself, no matter how strange things got.

Bree grabbed her mug and pulled it close. "I still don't know what that word means."

"It doesn't matter," Finch snapped. He motioned to the padlocks. "The key to using a trickster's magic tied to your eyes is to visualize the locks being undone, and then push your magic through them. It's a step-by-step process. First, visualize. Then, you execute. Always in that order."

It was simple to explain, but harder to do. Visualizing the locks being undone required some knowledge of how locks were made. If Bree didn't have that knowledge, her visualization would be weak, and so would her magic. Knowledge—or lack thereof—was one of the hardest parts of being a warlock. So many aspects of the business, from creatures to casting, required understanding.

Did a twelve-year-old have that? Finch suspected the whole process would be difficult for her, which was why he hadn't wanted to do it in the first place.

But here they were.

Finch grabbed his phone and looked up the inner workings of padlocks. With a few pictures ready, he turned the screen to face Bree. "Here. Look at this. It'll make it easier to visualize your magic working. See how everything interlocks? And how the key causes it to open?"

Bree took the phone and studied the images. She flipped back and forth, her brow furrowed. After a few minutes, she handed him back his device and sighed.

"They're more complicated than I thought they were," she muttered.

Finch nodded. "That's right. But the spirit's magic will make quick work of it."

Bree grabbed the closest padlock and stared at it with such intensity, she was practically drilling a hole through it with her gaze. She tightened her fingers on the edges and clenched her jaw, but nothing happened. Then she yanked on the top, but still, it remained secured.

She handed it to Finch. "Show me first."

He grabbed the lock. Within a matter of seconds, the lock

unlatched, and the loop on top popped upward. Finch handed the unlocked padlock to Bree.

With wide eyes, she locked the device. "You did it so fast…"

"Visualize and then execute," Finch repeated.

"Okay…"

Bree stared at the lock. Then she glared. After a few moments, she tugged it again.

Nothing.

She sighed as she reached for the second padlock. "Maybe this one will be easier." She focused her attention on it.

"Oh, my," Kull muttered. "Trickster magic isn't supposed to be this serious. Try imagining the look on Finch's face when you succeed. *That* should motivate you."

Bree waved away the comment, never taking her eyes off the device. "Shh. I'm trying to visualize."

"Hm. All right. Listen to some random *warlock* and not the *spirit you made a pact with*. I see how it is."

Finch sipped his black-as-midnight coffee. He glanced over at the TV and watched the news report on a drug bust. He wondered how Cauldron and Seth were doing. What if they were getting into more trouble? Finch cursed under his breath when he realized he might actually be worried for their safety.

It was foolish. Absolutely silly. Why would he be concerned about them?

What was wrong with him these days?

The sound of a harsh *click* drew Finch's attention back to Bree.

With a smile as wide as her face, Bree held up the unlocked padlock. "Adair! Look! I did it."

Nico glared at them.

Bree lowered her voice—but not her smile—as she said,

"Did you see it? I did it! I actually did it." She handed it to Finch, as though for inspection.

Finch turned the lock around in his hand. It was, in fact, unlocked. "Good." He huffed as he locked it and handed it back. "Now do it again."

"What?" Bree grabbed the lock and frowned. "But I got it. Why do I have to do it again?"

"Don't practice your magic until you get it right—practice until you can't get it wrong." He motioned to the other padlocks. "Unlock all of these. We'll keep doing it until unlocking them is as simple as literally turning a key. Got it?"

The moment between them was long and strained.

Finch worried the girl would argue.

But then Bree hardened her expression—her eyes filled with determination—and she gathered up all the locks and focused on them. No more arguing. No complaining. She was ready to practice until there was nothing left to learn.

Which Finch appreciated.

Even Kull seemed proud. She held up her head and purred.

And also, when Bree wasn't looking, Kull licked at her sweet coffee.

CHAPTER
TWENTY-EIGHT

everal hours passed. The coffee shop only had one other patron, and it was an older man. He entered the shop at 12:05 p.m., took a seat at the far end of the shop, had his coffee and a sandwich, and then left at 12:37 p.m., barely saying a word.

Finch kept the details in his mind, but he knew they would likely be useless. He couldn't stop himself, though. Every new event that occurred, his first instinct was to take note of the time. He never knew when something would become useful.

"Okay," Bree said, her tone once again giddy. She pushed all three open locks toward Finch. "See? I can open them so fast now."

Finch grabbed one, locked it, and then lifted an eyebrow. "Catch." He tossed the lock to her.

Bree caught it and fumbled for a moment, but ultimately kept it in her grasp. Once she had a good hold, she focused on the object, and it unlocked. The whole process probably took ten seconds—which was much better than before—but it still wasn't perfect.

"I think you can practice a bit more," he said.

"Don't we have to be going?" Bree placed the padlock on the booth table. "We have corrupt cops to bust, remember? And I have it good enough."

Finch chuckled. "We have all the time in the world. The cops aren't going anywhere."

The mischief spirit rolled around on the edge of the table, her black fur covering most of the booth. "Oh, he's going to use that against you so many times," Kull said with a snicker. "*We have all the time in the world!* We'll be studying and practicing magic for days. By the time we get to the cops, *we'll* have forgotten what we're doing."

Bree grabbed one of the padlocks with a grip so tight her knuckles grew white. "No. I won't forget. Not until we find Mum's murderer." She frowned as she locked everything up again. "I don't care how long it takes. We're going to do this."

She fiddled with the first lock and unlatched it within eight seconds.

Although Finch felt for her, he didn't want to run around with a warlock who didn't understand anything about her powers. He observed her as she went through the padlocks, undoing them one by one. Once they were all open, Bree locked them again and repeated the process.

Finch recalled his first time studying magic.

It had been very similar…

But he had been so impatient. Only Carter had kept him on track. Without his brother, Finch was certain he never would've been any good. Finch would've been no better than Seth, running errands for deadbeat covens.

He tried not to think about it any longer.

———

After another couple hours, Bree could unlock the padlocks within a few seconds. She was tired, though, and her father's death was fast approaching. It was already 5pm, and his death would be announced on the news at 7:11 p.m.

Finch reset time.

Then he did his morning chores, which included making tea and drawing marks. But, unlike the mornings before, Finch hesitated. He went for his fridge, found an old container of salami at the back of the lowest shelf, and pocketed it away.

When they went to save the dog, Finch parked his car, and approached the shrubs with the salami in hand. He held out a piece and said, "Cauldron? C'mon."

Instead of biting and barking and fighting back, the little black dog poked his snout out of the bushes and wagged his tail with so much power, he knocked off some of the leaves. The pooch leapt from the shrubs and went straight for Finch. It was easier, this time, scooping up the animal and carrying him to Ceija's house.

Finch even petted the dog as he went. "Don't tell anyone about this," he whispered.

Ceija was just as confused as ever when she answered the door, though. Finch handed her the animal and said, "He escaped." Then he turned on his heel and left without another word, even as Ceija scrambled to utter a *thank you*.

For some reason, Finch felt better about the day. Even when they went to disarm Dr. Colton's door—so Seth wouldn't hurt himself—Finch enjoyed the morning. It felt unusual.

Once finished with his many daily tasks, he got into his car and then handed his phone to Bree.

"What do you want me to do with this?" she asked.

Finch drove away from the doctor's house and headed straight for the police department. "Now that you can undo the padlocks without trouble, I want you to look at all those images. They're door locks." He took the fastest route to the station, his thoughts only on the task at hand. "Memorize those as best as possible."

"Some of these are old." Bree swiped through the pictures with a frown. "Who uses a fat key to unlock their doors anymore? I thought that stuff was only for old-timey movies."

Finch narrowed his eyes and huffed. "It's not *that* old. Just look at the damn photos and remember what you can. You'd be surprised what kind of doors and locks you stumble across when you're a PI."

His last statement caused Bree to whip her attention over to him. Her eyes were wide—so was her smile—as she said, "Are you going to teach me how to be a PI, too?" Before he could respond, she lunged over the car's center console and hugged his right arm, her grip surprisingly tight. *"Thank you, thank you, thank you!"*

"I never said that," Finch snapped. And although he could've shoved her away, he didn't. He just sighed, glared at the road ahead of him, and regretted even uttering a phrase that indicated he would teach her anything.

Who wanted to be a private investigator? It was a difficult and lonely career that often involved terrible crimes, cheating spouses, and witches who wanted to spy on their previous covens to make sure they weren't doing as well now they had left.

Sure, it had been fun once upon a time, but those days were long dead.

Again, Finch found himself trying not to think about it.

Bree eventually released his arm. "I'm going to try my best. I promise." Then she sat back in her seat. With a happy hum, Bree flipped through the pictures of door locks and studied each of them as though she were about to be tested.

"I've studied human detectives," Kull said from the back seat.

"No one asked you, spirit." Finch shot her a quick glare. "Don't romanticize this line of work."

"Oh, I wasn't going to romanticize anything. I was going to say I've seen several die horrible deaths. Good thing you can abuse time, hm?"

Bree stopped her humming.

For a brief moment, Finch thought about backing up Kull's statement with personal anecdotes. After all, Carter wasn't the only one to die while out on the job. Whenever it came to the occult, there was always something deadly lurking around every corner.

Perhaps it would dissuade Bree from pursuing the line of work.

But…

Finch couldn't bring himself to scare the girl with talk of death. At least, not now—not today.

Instead, he said, "Whenever a warlock fills one of their cores with the magic of a creature, they get inherent benefits. The type of benefits depends on the core of magic."

"What do you mean?" Bree whispered.

"Because the mischief spirit's magic is in the core of your eyes, cameras won't see you. Additionally, people will notice you less. Makes it easier to sneak around."

"Oh." Bree held Finch's phone with both hands as she asked, "What if I filled my crown core with mischief magic?"

"You would be able to tell lies much easier," Kull said, interjecting herself into the conversation. "The crown core deals with the mind, and mischief magic and the mind combine to make anything sound plausible. You could tell someone you saw aliens, and even the most hardened of skeptics would believe you."

Bree laughed as she swiped through the photos again.

Then her gaze hardened as she asked, "What about the spirit? That's a core, right? How do you use magic from that core? If concentration, emotion, and visualizing are for the others?"

"It's the most difficult of cores," Finch said as he turned down a road and headed for the downtown police station. Stockton was a city of grime. The closer they got to the heart of the municipality, the worse it became.

"How do you use it?" Bree asked.

"Magic in your spirit can only be used when you're calm and tranquil—when you have faith in yourself. Remember how I told you warlocks usually only bond with three creatures? It's because they don't want too many pacts to fulfill, and because some cores are too difficult to use magic from. Most warlocks never bind things to their spirit."

Bree nodded once. "Faith in yourself?"

"Yeah," Finch muttered. "It's unusual to find someone at peace with their decisions. Guilt, depression, and self-doubt all lessen the potential of that magic."

"Oh."

Kull snickered as she said, "And based on the number of therapy and antidepressant ads I've seen recently, that core has become quite the rarity!"

"What about *loins*?" Bree asked. "How do you use that core and—"

"You'll need to ask your father," Finch stated, cutting her off. "That's just another core most warlocks have trouble using properly, understand? Good. Good." He shot Kull a glower. "Right, spirit? We're not talking about it. Not now. Not ever."

She used a cat paw to motion zipping her lips and then throwing away the key. It almost made Finch laugh to see it. Cats weren't supposed to move like that…

"How come magical items take the life span of creatures?" Bree asked. She stopped looking through the phone. "And why only creatures with spines? Is there a reason? I want to know all the details about magic."

"The spine connects the cores of a being's magic," Finch stated matter-of-factly. "All the cores of magic flow through it, from the crown to the... uh... loins. Creatures without spines have a single core, and it doesn't translate well for item crafting. Listen, don't worry about all the complicated magical stuff. Focus on the basics. If you learn too much too fast, you won't get it right."

The words settled over Bree in a matter of moments. She nodded before returning her attention to the phone.

Finch drove through several one-way streets decorated with graffiti. Trash collected in the gutters, acting as the city's perfume. Stockton was so classy, their main police station was across the street from a McDonald's-gas station combo.

Finch parked his vehicle in the guest parking lot. When he stepped out, he took in the huge building and sighed. An impound lot was positioned off to the side, and a statue of an eagle over the Stockton PD logo was next to the front door. While most of the city rotted, this building remained intact. It was clearly a place where taxpayer dollars went to die.

"What's the plan?" Bree asked as she hopped out of the car. She carried Kull all the way over to Finch's side. "Do you think we can just enter the police station and ask about Papa?"

She handed Finch his phone, which he pocketed.

"I have a badge," Finch muttered.

"Oh! Right. You work for the police. Kind of."

"But I have a feeling they're not going to let me into the back." Finch shoved his hands into his pockets. "It's a Friday, and there was a recent homicide, so I'm sure the place is bustling with beat cops and detectives. And since some of them probably don't want me snooping around, I imagine we're going to get a lot of pushback."

"Maybe you could make a pact with something that will give you *invisibility*," Bree said, both eyebrows rising for her hairline. "Or maybe illusions! Or teleportation."

Kull twitched her ears and frowned. "Who is Adair bonding with in order to get all that? A superhero?"

"Remember how I *just* told you that the soul and loins were the worst cores to bond things with?" Finch sighed. "They're my only cores remaining, and I don't feel like calling another creature to get a quick fix for a minor problem. Besides, the last time I did that, the creature never went away, and my patience only goes so far."

"Hey, I resemble that remark," Kull quipped.

"Can you get more than one magical ability when you make a pact with something?" Bree asked.

Finch nodded. "I already told you. There are innate powers you get for filling your core with outside magics. And the powers you can *use* are often different than anything *latent*."

"Oh, neat." Bree stared at the asphalt. "I hope I can remember all this…"

"Let's go into the civilian lobby. We'll scope out the place, get a feel for what's going on, and then make a plan. If we need to, I'll just reset time and we'll try a different tactic."

"All right."

As a group of three, they entered the police department.

CHAPTER
TWENTY-NINE

The civilian lobby was exactly like Finch remembered —cramped, sad, and pungent. Hundreds of people made their way through the lobby every day, and most of them didn't want to be there. They were either stressed or drugged, both of which produced high levels of body odor that never seemed to fade, no matter how much cleaning solution the police force used.

The walls were adorned with faded posters of long-forgotten safety campaigns and dusty plaques recognizing outstanding officers from over a decade ago.

The area was rectangular with several counters. Large plastic bulletproof windows attached the counters to the ceiling, with only small windows to allow for receptionists to speak with the civilians.

A single door led deeper into the department, but it was locked at all times with a special keycard reader.

Finch stepped inside, tense from his toes to his neck. It seemed weird entering the police station when he was here to take down a cop.

He felt like a criminal.

A female officer behind the counter—thoroughly protected by the glass—glanced up from her computer. The other help windows were empty, despite the half dozen people waiting on plastic chairs positioned near the front doors.

There was a man pacing in the corner, his drug-fueled walk as blatant as the needle marks on his arm. There was a pair of sisters, and Finch suspected they were here to pick someone up. An elderly man sat in the farthest chair, and a couple young men kept glancing at their phones. If Finch had to guess, he would say they were here to get fingerprinted for a job.

Bree stood closer to Finch. "Is this how all police stations are?" she whispered.

"Just the ones in California," Finch replied.

Kull squirmed in Bree's grasp. "That's not true. The couple I saw in Louisiana were similar. Just more… interesting. And with more alligator decorations."

Ignoring the commentary, Finch headed for the officer manning the counter. When he approached, the woman regarded him with an icy stare. Her hair was tied back in a tight bun, as was standard for officers with longer hair. Her blue uniform was thick and looked uncomfortable, likely due to the bulletproof vest she wore under her shirt.

"Can I help you?" she asked.

"I'm an independent contractor who works in the special forces division," Finch stated. He pulled out his badge and slid it through the tiny slot of a window. "I'd like to speak with Sergeant McGregor. If he's not in, I'd like to speak with Chief Harding."

The woman took Finch's badge and frowned. "If you're working with the force, you could've used the officer entrance."

"It felt awkward," Finch said.

The woman lifted an eyebrow. When he said nothing else, she glanced at Bree. Her eyes slid over the girl with little recognition. Bree's magic coat worked wonders. She probably looked like nothing more than a young assistant.

But she was still holding a cat.

"What's that?" the officer asked.

"There are a lot of dead cats around the scene of the crime," Finch stated. "We grabbed this one because it had injuries. I'll be taking it to a vet to get it checked out. Maybe we can learn something."

The officer nodded. "I had heard there were a lot of dead cats…"

"I need to talk to the sergeant about it."

"Sergeant McGregor isn't in right now," the officer said. "I can leave him a message, if you'd like."

"When will he be back? I need to discuss some aspects of the homicide that happened earlier this morning."

Although it was completely against protocol to give out officer schedules, the woman sighed as she said, "He'll be back by noon. You can wait or you can come back then."

Finch glanced at his phone.

7:01 a.m.

Perfect. That would give them five hours to search through McGregor's things. Perhaps they would have enough time to raid the evidence lockers or even listen in on some chatter over the radios.

"Thank you," Finch said.

The woman pushed his badge back through the slot. "Next time, use the officer entrance."

"I will."

Finch turned away from the counter. As he slowly made his way toward the front doors, he glanced over at Kull. "You want to help out, right, spirit?"

She twitched her ears. "Do I? I feel like I haven't done enough mischief lately…"

"Detectives have access to the coroner's office and the local morgue," Finch casually stated. "If you help us now, I promise I'll take you to one of those places to look at bodies. Maybe you'll like one."

Kull's ears shot straight up. "Really? You will? Oh, happy days." She purred as she smiled up at Finch. "What do you need from me?"

"I need a pigeon. And I need it to cause a distraction in the lobby."

"Hm! I see. Well, prepare yourselves for an event, as nothing is worse than a frightened pigeon trapped in a confined space."

Bree grabbed Finch's sleeve as they continued their amble forward. "What's the plan? What're we going to do?" They were almost to the front doors, but Finch slowed his pace even further.

"Kull will cause a distraction, and you will unlock *that* door." He motioned to the back door that led deeper into the station. "We'll walk right in."

"Won't someone see us?" Bree frowned. "We'll get caught."

"Not if Kull is enough of a distraction."

The black cat puffed out her fur. "You can't handle my level of distraction."

"I don't know how to unlock that kind of door," Bree whispered. They approached the front doors, and she placed her hand on one. "It's, like, a keycard. How do I visualize that?"

"Like you're a computer, and it just wants to know you're the right person to let through. Trust me, kid—computers are the easiest to trick. You'll get us through."

"Maybe *you* should unlock this, and I'll get the next one."

Finch half smiled. "I thought you wanted to be *the best* warlock? The best don't back down from a challenge."

"Oooooo," Kull said with the tone of a child's playground taunt.

For a long moment, the three of them stood awkwardly in front of the police station doors. Normally, Finch would be concerned about their odd behavior. The whole place was riddled with cameras, from the parking lot to the bathrooms. Anyone watching the camera feed would know they were suspicious...

But thanks to Kull's magic, no one could see them.

So, once they snuck through the locked door, and made it into the depths of the department, it would be smooth sailing. Finch still had his badge—in case anyone asked questions—and he knew his way around the place.

The real reason Finch hadn't gone through the officer entrance was because he didn't want to run into anyone who might try to end him. At least in the lobby, he could ask questions first, and now that he knew when McGregor would be back, everything felt more secure.

"Okay, I'll do it," Bree finally said, snapping Finch out of his musings. "I'll unlock it."

"Good." Even if she *couldn't* do it, Finch knew he was capable. Content that they had a plan, he motioned for Kull to leave them. "Go ahead. Make sure the officer is thoroughly distracted. And then meet us in the parking lot. We'll be out there in an hour or so."

"You have to promise to take me to look at bodies," Kull stated as she swished her tail. "I want a good one. Something that will turn heads. Something you'll *never* forget."

Finch rolled his eyes. "I'll make sure to show you all the bodies with tattoos on their faces. Now go."

The cat leapt from Bree's grip, but before she touched the ground, she had taken the form of a pigeon once more. Her gray-and-blue wings shimmered for a brief moment—then she tore through the air and fluttered around the lobby, cooing with a mad intensity.

The people waiting in the lobby flinched and ducked away.

Kull's presence seemed more like a mild annoyance than a distraction, but Bree opened the front door and snickered. Four more pigeons rushed in, as if drawn to Kull's crazed cooing. They were the dirty Stockton pigeons that Finch was certain carried more than one disease—some of which he couldn't pronounce, they were so bad.

The four real birds swirled around Kull, cooing and spreading feathers.

"What's going on?" the officer behind the counter shouted. She buzzed an emergency switch but didn't leave her post. Finch knew she wouldn't leave—she was the only one in the lobby—but that didn't matter. She just had to pay attention to the birds, and not to anything else.

The pigeons, in classic pigeon fashion, pooped wildly over the chairs and the walls, their yellow eyes big and frightened. Kull cooed the loudest, and even knocked plaques off the wall and slammed into the bulletproof plastic that shielded the officer from the white feces raining across the lobby.

Finch and Bree hurried to the door. Without needing instruction, Bree leapt to the keycard lock. She placed her hand on it and focused.

"Visualize and then execute," Finch whispered.

He was half distracted by the pigeon chaos taking place just twenty feet from them. Never before had he seen those fat little sky rats act so insane. Everyone was trying to either flee or catch them. The officer behind the counter shouted instructions, but the Stockton denizens couldn't care less.

Ten seconds went by, and Bree hadn't unlocked the door.

Finch was tempted to do it himself, but he knew that would demoralize her.

And what did it really matter? If she messed up, he could rewind time, and they could attempt the door again. That mere fact calmed him, and reminded Finch that a good mentor always searched for ways to build up a student, rather than put them down.

That was what Carter had said, anyway.

Twenty seconds.

The lobby was a war zone. People had picked up chairs. Someone had even thrown theirs. The shouting grew so loud, Finch was surprised they hadn't set off some sort of alarm.

Thirty seconds.

The Great Pigeon War was winding down. Two had been caught. One was pecking at the front door. Kull had grown tired.

"Don't stress," Finch stated. "Just visualize."

And just then, the door clicked open.

"Ah!" Bree whirled on her heel and faced Finch, her eyes wide. "I-I did it!"

He grabbed her by the arm and quickly slid into the police department. The sound of an emergency buzz still emanated from the speakers in the walls. Finch ducked down a hallway as a pair of police officers rushed toward the personnel offices and reporting rooms.

The inner workings of the Stockton PD were too vast for everyone to know everyone who worked there. Stockton employed over four hundred police officers, one hundred staff, and countless volunteers and contractors. As long as Finch and Bree blended in, they would be fine now that they weren't in the lobby, looking like civilians.

"I did it," Bree repeated as Finch guided her past the record rooms. "Did you see?"

"Calm down," he muttered.

"But I did it!"

She stopped walking. Finch did the same. He turned to her, half annoyed she would stop and half confused. Her expression was an odd mix of elation and sadness.

Carter wouldn't have been cold with her.

"You did do it," Finch said. He forced a smile. "And once this is all over, I'm going to have to give you an official warlock pendant."

Bree's eyes—which had gone slightly glassy—widened with her smile. "Really? Warlocks have pendants? What do they look like?"

They didn't. Finch had just made that up. It sounded fun.

"You get to design your own," he finally said.

"Oh, wow, that's so cool! Like how Jedis design their own lightsabers?"

"Uh, sure. Whatever, kid."

He guided her toward the sergeant and lieutenant offices. They were beyond the myriad of cubicles used for report writing and analysis. The scent of stale coffee, mingled with the acrid notes of overworked printers, clung to the threadbare carpet, whispering tales of weary vigilance. A sea of computers, paperwork, and pens surrounded them on all sides as Finch navigated the many cubicles, trying not to disturb anyone or anything.

Several officers did their work without glancing up. A few even wore earbuds.

"I've never been inside a police station before," Bree muttered. She matched Finch's quick pace by walking twice as fast as she normally did. "Oh, when I make my pendant, do you think it would be appropriate to put, like, a police badge on it? Since a police station was the first place I really used my magic."

"Sounds great," Finch murmured as he read the many plaques on the wall.

Lt. Cross.

Lt. Gram.

Lt. Sanders.

Sgt. Wells.

And then Finch spotted it. **Sgt. McGregor.** It was the office farthest back—positioned away from the majority of the cubicles. That made sense. If he was in charge of the occult division, he would need to keep his work away from most of the magicless on the force.

"Stay close to me at all times," Finch whispered as he headed for the door.

Bree nodded. Then she tapped his arm. "I think someone is following us, though."

CHAPTER
THIRTY

Finch stopped and quickly turned around.

A woman *had* been following them. She held two notebooks in both her hands, her expression gloomy. With a furrowed brow, she moved closer to Finch and Bree. "I'm sorry, I know you must be busy with an investigation, but I don't think you've signed the book yet?"

She wore a white blouse and a skirt, and Finch suspected she was secretary or perhaps the assistant to the chief.

"Signed the book?" he asked.

"For the families of Officer Pete Gladstone and Officer Joe Manning." The woman exhaled as she handed Finch the notebooks. A pen was tucked between the pages of the first. "If you could write something encouraging about their time on the force, that would be appreciated."

"They're the officers who died?" Bree asked.

The woman clenched her jaw and crossed her arms. Finch suspected she was getting angry—who could forget the death of their brothers-in-arms?—but her expression relaxed after she thought about it. "I'm sorry. I know investigators don't stay in the station long. Yes. They were caught up in gang violence. Everyone here has written beautiful things about how kind both Gladstone and Manning were. It would be great if you could do the same."

Ah.

Gang violence.

Seth had said the witches' feud was being classified as "gang activity." The two officers had likely been caught up in everything by accident. Their deaths had put the whole force on edge, obviously. So much so, they didn't trust anyone with magic.

Finch opened the first notebook and read a few of the messages.

> **MANNING ALWAYS TOOK THE TIME TO BRING DONUTS IN THE MORNING. WE JOKED HE WAS A STEREOTYPE, AND AFTER THE WEEKEND, HE CAME IN WITH A MUSTACHE. ALWAYS A JOKESTER—HIS LIGHT WILL BE MISSED IN THE WORLD.**

> **JOE TALKED ABOUT FAMILY EVERY DAY. NO DETAIL OF HIS SON'S LIFE WENT UNNOTICED. ONCE, HE TALKED TO US ABOUT HOW CLEVER HIS SON WAS FOR SNEAKING SOME COOKIES IN THE MIDDLE OF THE NIGHT. WE HOPE HIS SON KNOWS HOW MUCH HE MEANT.**

Finch wrote something in the notebook. It was a generic platitude, but it didn't matter. When he reversed time, none of this would be real. He just needed the woman to leave him alone.

Once he scribbled a message in both notebooks, he handed them back. "Thank you for handling this."

The woman smiled after his statement. "It's the least I

could do. Thank you for taking the time." She turned and spotted a man across the wide room. With one hand raised, she hurried through the sea of cubicles, dodging unoccupied chairs left strewn about.

"The officers were killed because of the witches in the city?" Bree whispered.

"The witches' feud, yeah."

"That's awful."

Finch returned his attention to Sergeant McGregor's door. It, too, had a keycard lock. A fancy one, to boot. Finch glanced over his shoulder. There were a few dozen people in the room, but most were busy writing reports or signing the notebooks for the fallen officers' families.

"Unlock this," Finch said.

Bree hopped to it. She placed her hand on the reader and stood still for a good ten seconds. Finally, the door unlatched, and she glanced up at him, just as happy as the first time. Bree was smart enough not to shout about it, though. Finch gave her an approving nod.

Her delight doubled.

They both entered McGregor's office, but Finch made sure to securely shut the door the moment he could.

McGregor's office had all the welcoming ambience of a mausoleum. A single fluorescent bulb bathed the room in a jaundiced glow, casting harsh shadows upon the rows of mismatched filing cabinets that sagged under the weight of a million case files.

A large oak desk sat in the middle of the room, demanding all the attention. Its surface, pockmarked with the scars of countless pens and coffee spills, also held a variety of notes. The computer, and tiny keyboard, were pushed off into the far corner.

"This is the sergeant's office?" Bree walked over to a lamp in the corner. She switched it on, banishing the yellowish lighting that had dominated the place moments before. "It's sad in here."

"Criminal law is always sad," Finch said as he ambled around the desk. "It's the unwanted child of valor and cynicism. Keep that in mind, *Miss Future PI*."

"And we know Sergeant McGregor killed Mum?"

"We don't *know* that. All I know is McGregor gave the order to the shooter to tie up loose ends and protect the murderer's identity no matter what. So, either he did it, or he knows who—either way, his office should hold information for us."

Bree nodded. She tapped the tips of her fingers together as she stared ahead. "I hope there are no traps in here…"

Finch took a seat in the sergeant's aging leather chair. It groaned, threatening to give out, but eventually quieted as he rolled it into place. Once set, he pulled the keyboard close and sifted through the files blatantly open on the computer.

"So, if we find Papa, and he tells everyone what the police did to him, they'll all be fired and arrested?" Bree asked. She took a seat in the single chair for guests.

"Only the corrupt cops, and only the ones dealing with occult activities," Finch absentmindedly replied.

"But won't that mean Stockton won't have any police officers to handle the witches' feud?"

"They'll hire outside warlocks to help them. I'm sure they'll manage."

Finch found nothing of interest on the computer. It was mostly report overviews, and emails. Very little that jumped out as pertinent. Finch needed to find something about Liam Blackstone—anything that would indicate his current whereabouts. Obviously, since he was the main suspect in a murder case, they couldn't keep him in any place open or obvious. And if Liam was being held in a public space, he could call for help, which they would want to avoid.

That meant Liam was being held somewhere away from other people. A house on the edge of town. Or a bank basement. Or perhaps a police car parked far from prying eyes. *Somewhere*.

Finch sifted through the paperwork inside the desk.

Anything... He needed anything...

He opened a bottom drawer and found a blue officer's uniform. Finch picked it up, wondering why it wasn't in a locker somewhere. A slight bit of magic radiated from it. Confused, Finch opened up the shirt and found one of Liam's necklaces sewn around the collar. It was half finished, as though someone were attempting to sew fabric over the necklace, so it couldn't be seen.

Ah. Police uniforms that would allow them to see through minor illusions and invisibility.

This was their prototype.

Finch checked the shirt pockets. Inside was a piece of paper with actual handwriting. It read:

HERE IS THE NAME OF A LAUNDROMAT WE COULD USE. IT'S FUNCTIONING, BUT CLOSED FOR ADMINISTRATIVE REASONS. MIGHT WANT TO REACH OUT TO THEM.

Bingo.

This was the lead Finch had been searching for.

He pocketed the note and shoved the shirt back into the drawer. Would Liam be held in a condemned laundromat? Stranger things had happened. Finch was just happy this whole wacky investigation was close to an end.

"But if all the outside warlocks hear they killed a witch, and that the police force hates people with magic, will the warlocks really want to help?" Bree smoothed her giant coat.

Finch shook his head. "What does it matter?" He set the shirt back in the drawer.

"I just, well... Maybe *we* should help the police."

Finch stopped his searching and locked his gaze with Bree's. For a prolonged moment, neither of them said anything. Finally, Finch sighed. "Are you seriously suggesting we solve the *witches' feud* in order to help the police because you're worried about them?"

"Um..." Bree stared at her lap and bit her lip. "I was thinking... There are lots of nice cops. And Papa wouldn't have gotten in trouble if the police weren't scared of the witches. So maybe... We can just stop the *real* problem." She glanced back up. "But also catch the murderer."

That was what Finch had been afraid of hearing.

Why did Bree want to save every damn person? Now she wanted to help the whole *city*.

Finch dragged a hand down his face. "What's wrong with you?" he murmured.

"We have *time* on our side," Bree said with a smile. "I just thought—since you're so powerful—that we don't have to pick and choose. We can do it all."

"Ugh."

Finch pinched the bridge of his nose, irritated that the simple murder mystery had taken yet another turn. It was always like this, though. Once, he and Carter had traveled through three cities just to track down a serial killer. The man had been a feral werewolf. It had been a long hunt, and at the end, there had been someone infecting the werewolf with moon sickness.

Finch remembered hating the case at the time, but he thought back on it fondly.

That was the thing about time. It painted everything in a thick coat of nostalgia.

"I think I might know where your father is being held,"

Finch said as he held up the paper. "Wouldn't you rather just go get him and wash your hands of this whole thing?"

"But people will still get hurt," Bree muttered. When she met his gaze a second time, it was with an expression that betrayed her determination. "Mum wouldn't want that. Would your brother?"

The question caused Finch to catch his breath. He hadn't been expecting her to bring up Carter. There was no answer he had other than—of course Carter would see this through until the end. He wouldn't leave anything undone.

Which covens were in the middle of a feud? Finch thought back to Seth's panicked ramblings. The man had said the Haggin Coven and the Swenson Coven were having an argument over turf.

"You would seriously rather stop the witches' feud before rescuing your father?" he asked, repeating his question.

"We can do it." Bree leapt off the chair and stood straight. "We can save Cauldron, Seth, Papa, and all the witches and cops who would otherwise be hurt. We can. A-And I'm sure Papa and Mum would both want this."

After the longest exhale of Finch's life, he said, "All right." He glanced at his phone.

7:19 a.m.

They still had plenty of time to catch Seth at Dr. Colton's house. The wannabe warlock wouldn't arrive until 8:01 a.m. If Finch drove quickly, they would arrive just in time to question the man.

"Let's go." Finch headed for the door, and Bree bounded to his side, all smiles.

"I think this'll be amazing," she said.

"I think I need to start day drinking."

CHAPTER
THIRTY-ONE

As Finch and Bree made their way to the department lobby, he took note of the disorder. Three police officers had gotten everyone under control, though one civilian was hysterical. He shouted at everything, and gestured wildly at the white smears along the walls.

"Can pigeons even *be* on drugs?" he asked.

Finch chuckled as he exited the building.

Once in his vehicle, with Bree in the passenger seat and Kull the cat in the back, he asked, "Did you have fun?"

The feline purred as she replied, "Oh, yes. What a delightful time. But next time, I think we should record everything. It would've made for a wonderful TikTok."

"Yeah." Bree laughed. "That would be amazing."

Finch drove his vehicle through Stockton as quickly as he could, heading for the orchards around the outskirts of the city. As he went, his mind wandered, but for once, it seemed to settle on pleasant things. When they reached the frontage road, Finch admired the sprawling expanse of neatly aligned trees, their branches heavy with ripe, succulent oranges that gleamed like droplets of liquid sunshine.

It had been a while since he took note of such things.

Finch almost missed his turn. He drove down the road to Dr. Colton's house and parked halfway along. He glanced at his phone. 7:55 a.m. Plenty of time to get to the fence near the doctor's house.

Without a word between them, Bree and Finch exited his Toyota, and then they took their position in the same hiding spot they had before—behind a fence, with a slight view of the front door. Finch had already disarmed the entrance, but now he wanted to speak with Seth. If he stood by the door, he might scare off the man, but if he jumped out, he could catch Seth by surprise.

"Are you okay, Adair?"

He tensed as he turned to Bree. "Hm? Yeah. Why?"

"You seem lost in thought. Are you thinking about the case?" She tilted her head as she questioned him.

Finch shook his head. "No. Sorry." After a short exhale, he added, "Don't worry about me. I might look distant or tired —but I'll always be ready when the time comes."

Bree's smile could give someone diabetes, it was that sweet. She carefully positioned herself behind one board, as though it really mattered. Finch really appreciated her hardworking attitude. The girl never gave up.

Seth Rivers, the sad excuse for a warlock, pulled his jalopy up Dr. Colton's driveway, kicking up dirt as he went. The man parked his vehicle and then stepped out. Glancing over his shoulder several times, he crept to the front door with the demeanor of a burglar.

Although Finch had already disarmed the front door, he stepped around the fence and headed toward Seth. After a few steps, his boots crushed a dirt clod loud enough to draw Seth's attention. His sad mohawk fluttered in the wind, and his too-far-apart eyes widened.

"Uh, this is where I live," he said, gesturing to the building with a jut of his thumb.

Finch resisted the urge to drag his hand down his face. "How many people shout *this is where I live* when someone stops by, fool? *Try* not to act suspicious, Jesus."

Seth stared for a long moment, visibly grappling with Finch's words.

Finch stepped close, tucked his hands into the pockets of his coat, and then sighed. "Where is the Swenson Coven located?"

"Wh-What?"

"You work for the Haggin Coven, right? And they're fighting with the Swenson witches? Just tell me where the Swenson Coven makes their base of operations. I'll handle them."

Seth had to slowly, and painfully, take in all the information. "Wait... How did you know I work for—"

"Never mind. Just answer the question. I have places I need to be."

"Uh..."

"The Swenson Coven is your enemy, right?" Finch rolled his hand, trying to coax out the information as fast as possible. "They're my enemy, too. Just tell me where they are."

"They, uh, work and live at the Delta College. In the astronomy department." Seth combed his fingers through his greasy mohawk. "Why did... you come out here to ask me this?"

Finch didn't bother replying. He knew *exactly* where the Delta Community College was located. If the witches were there, it would be easy to locate them. He headed back to the fence, motioned to Bree with a tilt of his head, and then headed straight for his car down the road.

"Wait," Seth called out. "Who are you?"

Finch ignored that, too. What did it matter? He had all the information he needed.

"The Swenson Coven is our enemy?" Bree asked as she hurried to match his pace.

"No." Finch shrugged. "I just said that so *our friend* would answer me. No coven in the city is our ally. Witches stick to themselves."

The wind picked up just as Finch opened his Toyota and got inside. Bree happily leapt into the passenger seat and buckled up. Kull had waited for them, sunbathing in the one beam of light streaming through the side window.

As Finch started the car and turned it around to head to the community college, Bree glanced over. "Do you have many friends in the city?" she asked.

"Not anymore," Finch muttered.

He drove faster than the speed limit, but slowed when he made it to the main road. They would be heading into a part of Stockton they hadn't thoroughly traveled through yet. He wasn't sure how the traffic would be for their time of day.

"Do you miss your brother?"

The question caught him off guard. Finch slammed the brakes harder than normal as he came to a stop sign. Everyone jolted in their seat, and Kull almost fell to the floor, but after a moment, they all corrected themselves.

"I miss him all the time," Finch replied. He tightened his hands on the steering wheel as he told himself there was no point in getting angry. Not anymore.

Bree turned her attention to the window. "I miss Mum, too." Once the car started again, she happily returned her attention to Finch. "Have you ever fallen in love before?"

"*Fall in love?* Kid, I can barely fall asleep." He snorted and shook his head. "Look, it just hasn't been a priority of mine."

"Maybe you should try a dating app."

"I'd rather have cancer."

"Dating apps *are* a cancer," Kull chimed in from the back seat. "Trust me. I've done lots of research. Most humans dislike the superficial and scummy mentality of most people lurking in the depths of dating apps."

As Finch turned onto a major road—Hammer Lane—he offered Bree a quick glance. "Why these questions?"

"I just realized I didn't know that about you," she said. Bree leaned back in her seat. "Are you attracted to women? Or men? Both?"

As Finch approached a red light, he slowly stopped the car and then rubbed at his temple. Sometimes, he wondered if he just didn't understand the world anymore. Since when did kids talk about stuff like this?

"We shouldn't be having this conversation," he growled. "Save it for your father."

"I think you're ace." Bree glanced back at the window. "Since you're so old and haven't fallen in love yet."

So old.

Finch sighed.

He wasn't *that old*. With a hesitant motion, he touched his unkempt hair and then grazed his stubble. *Maybe I should clean myself up.*

"I think he's just grumpy," Kull chimed in from the back seat. "But he's getting softer. You can tell." She swished her tail. "Well, *I* can tell."

"No one asked you, spirit."

She purred a quiet laugh.

Finch drove to the entrance of Delta College, and turned into one of the many parking lots. Unlike the University of the Pacific, Delta was gigantic. It was one of the largest community colleges in the state, and it stretched across the city of Stockton with such size, it had its own streets. Finch had to follow a series of signs just to get close to his destination—the astronomy department.

Delta was so large, they had their own damn planetarium. It stood in the middle of several classroom buildings, and Finch admired it as he stepped out of his vehicle.

Bree, holding Kull, exited the car a second later.

"You sure you don't want to head to that abandoned laundromat?" he asked. "Your father might be there."

"We came all this way to see the witches," Bree said. "We should at least *see* what's going on."

"They might be dangerous, so stay on high alert, understand?"

She nodded once. "Okay. If things go poorly… will you rewind time?"

"That's right. But still. Don't provoke them. We want information. If they're the ones who killed the cops, we'll need evidence, and we don't want them to know we're investigating them, got it?"

"Yeah. I'll, uh, follow your lead."

With a sigh, Finch headed to the main faculty offices. The time was 9:32 a.m. The campus was a pleasant one, with bright green trees and clean walkways, but he still hated every moment. Messing with a coven was never high on his list. Not since Paris.

He didn't trust them.

At 9:33 a.m., Finch opened the astronomy department door. His eyes were immediately assaulted by an eclectic mishmash of decorations that seemed to have been salvaged from the depths of a forgotten attic. Crystals of all shapes and sizes adorned every available surface, each shimmering under the bright white lights hanging overhead.

Books with weathered spines were piled high on the front desk, their titles evoking a sense of pseudo-intellectual profundity.

Oh.

Finch held back a deep exhale.

These were *new moon* witches.

"Wow," Bree said as she moved over to the tower of books on the front desk. She set Kull on the floor. "Mum never had books like this. I love these. Look, Adair. This one is about healing mental wounds with various types of crystals."

A small woman poked her head around the stack of books. She wore giant, circular glasses as red as roses. Her hair, a messy auburn tangle, was tied into a bun on the top of her head. She radiated a sweet kind of magic that Finch would never mistake. This woman was one of the new moon witches.

"Hello," the witch with the glasses said to Bree. "Can I help you? Are you a student?" She glanced over to Finch and grimaced. "Oh. Sir, we don't have any spare change."

"I'm here to speak with the leader of your coven," Finch said matter-of-factly, hiding all his irritation.

There was no one else in the room, so it didn't matter if he revealed himself as someone with magic. Despite that, the woman held a hand to the collar of her shirt, as though Finch had done something unspeakably rude.

"Do you have an appointment?" she asked, her tone harsh. "Because Professor Landa doesn't speak with just anyone."

Professor Landa?

"Maria Landa?" Finch asked. He knew her. Well, once upon a time, he knew her. "Can you tell her Adair Finch is here? She knows me."

The witch with the glasses narrowed her eyes into a harsh squint. After a few moments of contemplative silence, she stood from her chair and headed to one of the many office doors. "Wait right here." Then she disappeared into a back room, turning around as she shut the door, as though to make sure Finch didn't follow her.

Bree poked the edge of the reception counter. "I don't think she likes us."

"Yeah, I seriously doubt it."

"You seem a lot less tense," Bree muttered. "Do you like Maria?"

He shook his head. "This is a coven filled with new moon witches. I doubt we're in any danger."

"Why's that?"

Kull leapt up onto the desk, and then onto the top of the books. The whole tower swayed a bit with her weight, but with her cat-like reflexes, she stayed on top. "New moon witches have magics centered around healing and knowledge. They're pro civilization and all about the wisdom of the stars." She twitched her whiskers. "New moon witches always find places for themselves in academia or hospitals."

"Hm." Bree turned her gaze to the floor. "Mum liked them, I think. But she really didn't like their books and stuff. She never kept any of this in the house."

"It's because new moon witches preach enlightenment while offering snake oil promises," Finch quipped.

"They seem nice, though." Bree poked at the spines of the books. The tower wobbled, and Kull leapt onto the desk once more. "I mean, all these books are about healing and growing as a person. That can't be all bad."

"From my experience, these kinds of witches aren't for me. Sure, one whiff of their magical lavender will remove stress and leave you feeling calm, but it'll also leave you with an empty wallet. These covens operate to swindle people, all while disguised in *good vibes*. The witches themselves aren't dangerous—they're just the magical equivalent of a used-car salesman."

"Are *all* new moon witches like that?" Bree asked. "I thought they could really heal people?"

Finch rolled his eyes. "A lot of them are frauds. But some aren't. It depends on how skilled they are with magic. The ones who can barely hold it together sell you temporary cures, but the *real* ones are worth every penny you pay them."

"Then you shouldn't insult all of them. That's not really nice."

"Tsk."

The witch with the glasses stepped out of the office with a deep frown. She pointed to Finch, and then to the door. "Professor Landa said she would see you. *But just for a few minutes.* She has work to do."

CHAPTER
THIRTY-TWO

inch, Bree, and Kull entered the professor's office.

A zodiac poster hung on the nearest wall, its colors faded and its edges frayed. The many zodiac signs were woven into crowns and tiaras, as if the artist had taken the grandiosity of astrology and transformed it into a garish caricature.

A large metal filing cabinet, locked with a key, was the largest piece of furniture in the whole room. A window allowed the morning light to stream in, and it was cracked a bit to allow for natural airflow.

Professor Landa's desk, positioned near the back wall, was buried beneath a mound of half-finished star charts and papers with cryptic symbols. A scattered assortment of questionable artifacts lay strewn about—anything from tarot cards to dried herbs, and even a crystal ball acting as a paperweight for the mail piled in its own little box.

But unlike the witch at the receptionist desk, Landa had an aura of power Finch couldn't deny.

"Hello, Adair," the professor said.

Finch stopped a few feet from her desk. He didn't want to anger her.

Landa was taller than most women. Probably six and a half feet tall, though Finch had never measured. Her skin, chestnut and flawless, was strategic. She couldn't sell her magical-youth brews unless she, herself, was youthful. With flowing locks of perfectly coiffed black hair that seemed to possess a life force of their own, Landa shook her head and then offered a pleasant smile.

Few people had her beauty, and she knew it.

"I'm pleasantly surprised," Landa said, her voice lyrical. "I thought you had died."

"Not yet," Finch muttered.

"But soon, from the looks of things."

Finch snorted. Landa hadn't changed at all.

She stood from her chair, her pants suit all white, with her shirt underneath black and marked with star constellations. Her height was more impressive than Finch remembered. The woman wore three-inch heels, and she could practically touch the ceiling, if she jumped just right. When she walked around the desk, Finch spotted the name tag that hung from a lanyard around her neck.

He motioned to it. "I see you're a college professor now. I can already picture your syllabus. *Forget about the rigorous scientific process of clinical trials and peer-reviewed research!* Just trust that these colorful rocks, neatly arranged in a circle, can mend the very fabric of your being and leave you feeling rejuvenated, or at the very least, mesmerized by the aesthetic symmetry."

Landa lifted a perfect eyebrow. "Oh? Bold choice to mock my profession when you walk into my office looking like you do. I already see the ads for your little business. *Behold, a lowly PI, a man draped in a mismatched ensemble of wrinkled garments!* Watch as he solves your petty case, paying no mind to the conventions of fashion or personal hygiene."

The both of them shared a chuckle, but Bree crossed her arms with a huff. "I don't think she should be saying those things about you," she whispered.

Finch shook his head. "It's fine. Landa likes a good riff."

The woman stepped away from her desk and held out her arms. Although Finch wasn't in the *hugging mood*, he knew he'd never be able to convince the witch not to. Landa embraced him.

"I hate this," he awkwardly said as he patted her shoulder.

"I know." Landa held him at arm's distance. "But it's been so long." Then she stepped back and smiled. "Where is Carter? Surely *he* still dresses to impress."

The question left Finch feeling like his mouth was filled with cotton. He exhaled as he said, "Carter is the one who died."

"Oh. I'm so sorry." Landa slowly turned away, her gaze falling to the floor. "Truly. I shouldn't have mentioned it." She walked around her desk and took her seat once more. "Well, then... To what do I owe this visit?"

"Your feud," Finch stated, deadpan and emotionless.

Landa's expression hardened, but her eyes came alive with fierce interest. She sat up in her seat as she steepled her fingers. "Adair, are you working for Matilda? Because we can pay you double whatever she's offering you. I *won't* have one of the Finch brothers working against me."

Talented new moon witches loved to use money to solve problems. Which made Finch curious. Why had Landa gotten into a feud to begin with? This coven seemed entrenched in the college... Were they expanding their territory? Why not just buy off her competition? That's what most witches of her kind did.

"I'm not working for the other coven," Finch stated. "I'm here because a couple of cops died. I want that to stop."

"Ah."

Landa said nothing else. She sighed and tapped a finger on her desk.

"Um…" Bree stepped close to her desk. Kull stayed close to her feet at all times. "My name is Bree. I'm a warlock, like Adair. I was wondering why you're fighting? Maybe we can solve this by helping you come to an agreement with the other witches."

"There will be no agreements with the other coven," Landa stated.

"But… why?"

"The Haggin Coven recently fell apart and then reformed under new leadership. *Matilda Wriedt* is unreasonable, aggressive, and frankly, a lowlife. Her coven creates brews that are little better than meth, and she sells them to whoever is buying. When her witches came onto *my* campus, trying to sell to *my* students, we had a disagreement."

Bree's eyes widened. "The coven was selling drugs to students?"

Landa, obviously restless, stood again. She paced behind her desk, her eyes constantly drawn to the zodiac symbols on the wall.

"At first, I thought the fools selling drugs were just petty human criminals," she said. "Mortals. Magicless and dull. I called the police." Landa walked around to the other side of the desk and sighed. "When it turned out they were witches, a fight broke out. Matilda, the barbarian that she is, killed the officers and then fled."

Finch couldn't stop himself from sighing.

He had a clearer picture of the timeline of events.

Some time ago, Matilda took over a coven and began

selling magical meth. She got into a fight with another coven, and two cops died as a result.

The cops, desperate to stop the witches, pressured Liam into making them magical items they could use to defeat Matilda. For some reason—Finch still wasn't entirely sure—Vera didn't want Liam making necklaces.

Vera was killed, likely because she was in the way.

And then Sergeant McGregor ordered all witnesses to the crime killed, so he could protect the name of his police station and department. Hence why a police officer would go out of his way to shoot Bree, an innocent twelve-year-old girl.

Now Finch had to deal with the feud in order to make sure every loose end in the case was solved. If the feud was resolved, and Vera's murderer brought to light, Liam saved, and the corrupt sergeant of the police station arrested, everything would be perfectly resolved.

Finch just had to end this.

"Where is Matilda now?" Finch asked.

Landa shook her head. "I don't know. I wish I did."

"Do you know anything about her magics?"

"She's insane, and she's grafted a demon to her heart and spirit."

Finch ran a hand down his face as he muttered, "What the hell is wrong with people these days?"

"Is that bad?" Bree asked. She stepped closer to Finch and stared up at him. "Can you graft things to all your cores? Are demons just no good?"

Kull purred as she rubbed against Bree's legs. "Full moon witches typically have powers to *steal* magic from others. They're the most power-hungry of witches, after all. Many capture creatures—spirits, demons, even oni—and then graft their magic onto theirs. Only talented ones make it work.

The untalented witches are driven mad. And there are *so many* untalented witches."

Landa glanced at Kull. Instead of asking why a spirit was with them, she seemed to decide to ignore it. With a frown, she said, "Matilda grafted a chain demon to herself, and now no one wants to get close to her."

"A *chain* demon?" If Finch could throw himself from a cliff instead of dealing with this, he would. He rubbed one eye, trying hard to think of a way to deal with the situation that wouldn't result in actually fighting the witch. "This just keeps getting worse. Are you sure?"

"Very certain," Landa stated. "She used the demon's power to kill the police, and one of my witches. She's a menace."

Bree grabbed the sleeve of Finch's coat. "See, Adair? This is the heart of the problem. This witch was causing trouble for the whole city. Now we have to stop her—we're the only two warlocks who can."

The only two? Finch wanted to point out she wasn't really his "partner in crime," but he didn't have the heart. If she wanted to fantasize, he would let her.

After a long and pained sigh, Finch met Landa's gaze. "I'll handle this."

She snorted back a laugh. "Adair. My old friend. You obviously can't handle taking a shower. There's no way you can handle Matilda."

"Remember how you said that when I told you I'd help your sister?" Finch snapped back. "And everything worked out fine, didn't it?"

Her eyes searched his for a moment. "That was a decade ago. You were more... put together then."

"I'll handle it," Finch repeated. "Trust me. I've gotten back in the rhythm."

"Even if that's the case, a single warlock cannot handle a witch with the powers of a chain demon."

"*Two* warlocks," Bree interjected.

Landa snorted back a second laugh. "One and a half warlocks cannot handle Matilda."

"I just need something to weaken demons," Finch muttered. He rubbed his chin as he thought about his options. The Occultist would probably have something. "My goal is to restrain her and turn her over to the chief of police so they can book her and know the feud is over."

Landa walked over to the massive filing cabinet against the back wall. She pulled the key for the cabinet out of a drawer of her desk. "The moment Matilda became a problem, my sisters and I brewed something to break her demonic powers, but even then—it's suicide to fight her. She would need to ingest this brew, and that would require restraining her ahead of time."

The witch unlocked the cabinet to reveal shelves of books, papers, and dozens of liquid-filled vials. At least six of them glittered a gentle white, and Finch knew from their pristine aura, they were brewed with the feathers—or some other body part—of angels. A quick and easy solution to the demonic powers.

Finch wasn't about to ask where she had gotten the angel bits, though. Angels *never* shared them. To have anything from them was an indication that Landa wasn't on any good terms with the celestials.

Landa plucked one off the shelf and held it in her palm with the flair of a TV salesman. "This is quite potent. Just a sip will render Matilda harmless for at least twenty-four hours. But getting her to drink it will be impossible."

"Maybe we can secretly slip it in her drink!" Bree smiled at her own idea.

"It sparkles with celestial power," Landa said, shaking the vial. "And it'll stay that way, even in coffee, betraying its obvious magical properties. Additionally, the demonic powers attached to her cores will allow Matilda to sense it from a mile away. There will be no tricking her into ingesting this. You'll have to force the issue."

Finch held out his hand. Landa gave him the vial, and he turned it over a few times.

Quite potent, indeed. Landa had become a talented witch. He pocketed the vial.

After a moment's contemplation, Finch glanced around the room. "When did you get in this morning?"

Landa blinked. "Excuse me?"

"When did you get into your office? What time exactly?"

"I think... I arrived at nine, like most mornings. Why?"

Finch walked over to her window. It was cracked open, and it *could* be opened wider to accommodate a person, albeit a small one. "And was this window open before you got here?" He touched the glass.

"I always keep it open a crack," Landa said, her tone growing more suspicious with every word.

"Perfect." Finch turned on his heel and headed for the door. "Thank you for the help. Don't worry about the other coven. It'll be handled before the end of the day."

Landa laughed at his declaration. With a shake of her head, she said, "Adair, I really don't want you to get hurt. You shouldn't face Matilda alone. At least hire other warlocks, or a professional hunter, to help you."

He waved away her comment. "I don't need anyone holding me back. A hunter would just be a hassle. Don't worry about it." Finch slipped out of her office without another word, Bree and Kull close behind him.

Landa attempted to sputter out more protests, but the door clicked shut just as she was mid-sentence.

"She doesn't know you made a pact with Chronos?" Bree whispered as they walked by the receptionist and headed for the door.

"No," Finch replied. "I try not to tell anyone the exact extent of my powers."

"But Kull knew."

"Spirits share secrets," Kull said with a purr-laugh. "You can't keep your magics from us."

Bree nodded along with the words. "The Occultist didn't know your powers, either..."

They remained quiet as they headed for the car. Finch didn't want to tell Bree that—in his original plan—he had intended to not give her the Mark of Chronos on the second to final iteration of the day. If he did that, she would forget everything once he rewound time. And like everyone else, she would never know the extent of his magical abilities.

But perhaps he wouldn't do that after all...

Finch still hadn't made up his mind.

First, he had to deal with a demon witch, which was a statement he never thought he would make when he woke up in the morning.

CHAPTER
THIRTY-THREE

Finch got into the car. Bree and Kull took their usual seats and then turned to him. After a few seconds—where Finch stared off into space, not really seeing the parking lot in front of him—he turned to the others. "I think we need to start the day over."

"Why's that?" Bree asked.

"Because our good buddy Seth knows where to find Matilda."

Kull licked her paw and smoothed some of her black fur. "You want to follow that man into the den of a demon-witch? That's what I call bravery."

"And then we'll fight her?" Bree asked.

Finch pointed to his chest. "*I'll* fight her. *You* will sit on the sidelines and watch."

Unlike every other time, Bree just smiled. "All right. Sounds good."

That was better than arguing over the matter. Finch really didn't want to have to rewind time for four to six months to teach a child the basics of combat. If she didn't know what a rear naked choke was, it would be a long and terrible uphill climb to get her up to speed on submission techniques.

Finch used his magic. Everything around him froze. The leaves falling through the air, Bree, Kull—even the whistle of the wind ceased to be. Then the color drained away, shifting the world until it became entirely black and white. Finally, the shapes fell away, leaving a void of darkness that lasted only a moment before Finch sat up in his bed.

4:34 a.m.

He headed to the front door, less urgently than usual, grabbed Bree, and then went to the window to get Kull. He gathered his clothes, drew the marks, and even brewed the tea for Bree. They didn't speak much, not even as Bree grabbed her oversized coat and pulled it onto her shoulders.

Finch grabbed the brew of hallucinations, just in case, and then exited his apartment. Bree and Kull followed him to the car, where they sped off to save the dog. Once the pooch was secure, Finch immediately went to Delta College.

It was only 6:45 a.m. by the time they arrived in the sprawling parking lot. Bree stared out the window as they parked, her eyes wide. "Why are we here?" she asked.

"We need Landa's brew." Finch stepped out of the vehicle. "Kull, wait here. We'll be right back."

She replied with a sarcastic salute.

Bree happily leapt out of the vehicle and followed him to the astronomy department. Instead of heading inside, however, he curved around into the decorative shrubbery that lined the building. Finch stepped over ferns and half-dead bushes until he reached Landa's office window. And just like before, it was cracked open, just a tiny amount.

Finch grabbed the pane and tugged. The window opened —but not enough for him to fit through. He had been afraid of that. With a sigh, he glanced over at Bree. "It's your time to shine."

"What're we doing?" she asked, clearly baffled.

"You're going to sneak in, open Landa's filing cabinet, and grab that sparkling brew."

Bree smoothed some of her brown hair. "Um, but isn't she your friend? Why don't we just talk to her like we did before? She happily gave you the brew."

"Because that would take too long. We'd have to wait for them to open, then go inside, speak with the receptionist, talk to Landa, explain the situation all over again..." He sighed just thinking about it. "Or we can just take it ourselves, go straight to Seth afterward, and then go deal with Matilda. If we're lucky, we can solve this whole feud before Landa even makes it to work this morning."

"R-Really?"

"That's the plan." Finch sardonically motioned to the window. "But first you need to break into this office."

"You don't think Landa will be mad?"

"She gave me her brew before, didn't she?" Finch waited for his words to sink in before adding, "And we're about to do what she wants, anyway, remember? Everyone will be happy. But first, we need to *break into this office.*"

Bree clapped her hands once and forced a smile. Then Finch gave her a boost into the office through the window. The girl was almost too big herself, but she managed to shimmy her way inside. The coat got caught on the lock, and Bree tugged it free before heading over to Landa's desk.

Bree opened the top drawer, pulled out the key, and then unlocked the filing cabinet. Once inside, she gathered two of the brews, and then hurried back to the window.

"I got them," she said with a laugh.

"Why didn't you use your magic to unlock the cabinet?" Finch asked. He had thought she would be more excited to use her new abilities.

"Never use an ace when a two will do, right?" Bree slid

out of the window and landed in the shrubs next to Finch. "That's what a certain someone taught me earlier."

He huffed and chuckled at the same time. *What a smartass.* Finch patted her shoulder. "Good job. Now let's go visit Seth."

———

Finch parked his car down the road from Dr. Colton's house. It was 7:45 a.m., and they had plenty of time before Seth would make his appearance.

While they waited, Finch disarmed the door, and then went inside. He grabbed the jar with the Witch's Web. Perhaps this would also come in handy? Having every tool available in his arsenal was better than going in empty-handed.

Which reminded him…

Finch also grabbed the Glock. The moment he picked it up, he cursed himself. This model of handgun was the standard issue for police officers. He should've *known* the police were involved when he saw it the first time around, but Finch hadn't wanted to believe it.

He tucked the weapon away and then went outside to meet with Bree. She headed for the fence—as though they were going to hide and wait for Seth—but Finch motioned to the road, where his car was parked.

"Where are we going?" Bree asked.

"Waiting for Seth to take us to Matilda."

"Shouldn't we speak to him?"

Finch shook his head. "That idiot will waste our time. We're just going to wait for him to collect the traps out of Dr. Colton's house, and then we're going to follow him."

"Oh." Bree giggled to herself. "Good idea!"

"And as soon as we know where Matilda is hiding, we won't need to repeat this process."

"Won't you just instantly defeat her?" Bree held out her hand like a superhero shooting a laser beam. "I mean, you have Ke-Koh's fire, right? You'll take down Matilda, no problem."

"Most demons are immune to flame," Finch dryly stated. "When their magic taints one of your cores, you often gain a lot of their traits—that one especially. That's why full moon witches like harvesting their power for their own. So, no. I won't be burning her. The objective is to stuff some of the brew in her face until she drowns in it. Then I subdue her, and take her to the police station."

Once they reached Finch's Toyota, they hopped inside. Kull licked her leg and then rolled around on the back seat cushion. "You took one of the witch's traps? Oh! Tricky. I like it."

"Let's hope Seth doesn't notice," Finch muttered as he adjusted his rearview mirror to get a better look at the doctor's house. "Knowing that man, he probably can't count that high, but still."

They waited in relative silence until about eight in the morning. That was when Seth's jalopy of a car lumbered its way down the dirt road, heading for the doctor's abode. As the man drove past, Finch, Bree, and Kull all ducked below the window line, trying to be as inconspicuous as possible. Seth went by without glancing over.

Once at Dr. Colton's house, the sad warlock went in through the front door, stayed inside for a minute, and then emerged with an armful of jars. He stuffed them into the trunk of his vehicle before climbing back into the driver's seat and heading back down the road. Once again, he drove by Finch's Toyota, never realizing it was full of passengers.

The instant he turned down another road, Finch started

up his car and followed. At first, he did so from a distance, allowing Seth to go several blocks before pursuing, but once they reached Stockton proper, Finch got closer.

The drive was pleasant enough. The fog cleared, and soon Seth took them to a section of the city near a long line of railroad tracks. Bree watched with rapt fascination the entire trek. Kull took a nap, all four paws in the air.

For some reason, in that moment, Finch felt more relaxed than he ever had.

Even if they were about to confront a lunatic witch.

Half an hour of driving led them to a parking lot at the far end of a lonely business district. Seth drove up to the gate of a self-operated storage facility. The hundreds of garages, protected by a chain-link fence, were one of the last places he would've thought to look for a coven of witches.

Seth poked at the keypad. Once the gate opened, he drove his car inside.

Finch pulled up to the gate afterward. He rolled down his window and glanced at the keypad. It was old, with all the numbers worn off the buttons.

He touched the outside, used Kull's magic to disable the lock, and watched as the storage facility's gate slid open at a creaky crawl.

"This is going to be so easy," Bree said with a giddy chuckle.

They drove inside, but Finch parked his car in the first available spot. He didn't want to risk drawing attention to himself. If Matilda was here, he had to speak with her. Perhaps she would turn herself in?

Finch laughed at his own thought.

He would need to speak with her, but he doubted anything would come of it.

Everyone exited the car. The storage facility was just row after row of gray brick buildings with bright red garage doors. Each unit was secured with a rusty padlock, as though they had used the same locks for over five years.

"Witches are here?" Bree asked. "And they're making drugs?"

"Somewhere," Finch muttered.

Kull happily trotted alongside them. "It's like a game of hide-and-seek, but with the added thrill of potential meth lab explosions."

They crept along a row of garage doors, Finch attempting to step softly. He heard nothing, but the acidic aroma on the air told him they were close. Bree kept her shoulders bunched at the base of her neck, her eyes wide.

When they turned down a row, she whispered, "What's a chain demon?"

Kull purred as she replied, "It's a lesser beast designed to guard the gates to the realm of Asmodeus, the Third Archduke. It's basically a demonic homunculus with no will of its own. They're incapable of existing in the world of mankind, but witches steal their magic or their chains fairly regularly."

"What does... any of that mean?"

Finch exhaled as he said, "Forget all that. All you need to know is that chain demons are dangerous to humans. They can render individuals helpless. Their bodies—and chains—taint the spine upon contact. It causes paralysis."

"The spine?" Bree sucked in breath through her teeth. She empathetically rubbed at her back. "I thought you said the spine is super important."

"It is. Which is why chain demons are never a fun tango partner. One touch—from any part of their skin, or claws, or teeth—will cause you to seize up."

Bree relaxed her shoulders a bit. "So a demon isn't going to pop up here?"

With a laugh, Kull said, "Definitely not."

"Oh, okay. Well, I'm sure Adair knows what he's doing."

"I'll handle it," Finch said with a sigh. "Like I said, just stand back and let me do everything."

"I'll take notes!"

"Sure. Whatever, kid. Knock yourself out."

She smiled.

But once they turned down another row, Finch stutter-stepped to a stop. Seth's banged-up car was parked next to a garage door. To a normal person, it would've looked like nothing was here, but Finch felt magic like he felt the wind on his face. When he concentrated, he saw beyond the glimmer of minor illusions.

The garage door was actually half open. Two women stood near the entrance. They weren't suspicious in appearance—both wore jeans and a T-shirt—but they had ears that dangled down past their collarbones, each with a specific set of star designs.

Somehow, in some way, witches always loved to mark themselves as one of the mystical.

After mentally preparing himself for a train wreck, Finch stepped forward. Bree hung back a few feet, and Kull leapt into her arms.

"Good morning, ladies," Finch called out as he stepped close to the open storage unit. Both felt magical, but neither were powerful. "My name is Adair Finch. I'm here to speak with Matilda Wriedt."

CHAPTER
THIRTY-FOUR

The morning sun shone down on the storage unit garages, casting awkward shadows over the asphalt. The two witches regarded Finch with confused glances.

"Who are you?" one of them finally snapped.

For some reason, Finch thought they would've known who he was. Instead, he rolled his eyes as he replied, "I'm a warlock. Matilda is hiring us, right?" That would probably be the easiest way to speak with her.

"I'm a warlock, too," Bree said.

"She's in here." One woman motioned to the storage unit with a tilt of her head. "You can both go in, if you want."

Finch walked over, ducked under the bright red door, and then stepped inside. Bree stayed close, but she didn't go much deeper into the unit.

To his surprise, two walls had been knocked down, connecting the one storage unit to both the others on either side. Now it was a large room with thick brick walls and barely any light. Two floor lamps, one with a flickering bulb, were the only illumination, giving the place all the atmosphere of a horror-movie.

What made things worse was the mark drawn on the floor. It wasn't the Mark of Chronos—it was the Mark of Asmodeus. Again, Finch rolled his eyes and sighed. The mark, since it was drawn on the ground, would amplify the magic and power of Asmodeus's demons in this small area.

Can this get any worse?

The walls of the unit were lined with lab equipment. Everything from glass jars to crappy ventilation systems humming with a high-pitched intensity. The equipment seemed hastily thrown together, and precariously balanced on thin aluminum tables. Everything was on wheels, so it could be moved on a moment's notice.

The police never would've found this. But maybe, with Liam's necklaces, they could've...

Finch pushed the thought out of his mind. Now wasn't the time.

Seth stood inside the poorly lit storage unit, alongside a woman Finch hadn't seen in years.

Matilda Wriedt—the witch who had started the feud that led to dead cops, which led to Vera's murder and Liam's kidnapping.

Her once-flowing chestnut hair hung disheveled in tangles around her thin face. Dark circles haunted the hollows beneath her eyes, and her pale skin seemed almost translucent, as though chemicals had given her a faint grayish undertone.

Her body carried all the signs of neglect and excess. She was gaunt and emaciated, her figure lacking vitality. She wore a sweatshirt and jeans, but no shoes.

This was the madwoman who had killed two cops? Finch wondered if the witch would keel over dead at any moment.

"What do you want?" Matilda asked, her voice as raspy as Finch had imagined.

Her words echoed throughout the storage unit. There were no windows, and only one exit. The stagnant air smelled of chemicals, blood, and panic.

"I love what you've done with the place," Finch quipped. "It has real *illegal chemistry* meets *unbridled laziness* vibes."

Although Matilda had been turned to face Seth, she shifted her weight to give Finch her full and undivided attention. With a cruel half smile, she asked, "You think you're smart? You have real gall coming in here, *to my domain*, just to make jokes."

Seth quietly backed away until his back was up against a brick wall.

"I'm a warlock. Adair Finch. You don't remember me?"

"*Ha*. Everyone knows the Finch brothers died years ago."

That was a shame. Finch remembered her. Matilda had been just as batshit insane before as she was now, but at least back then, she was more… alive.

"Did you come here for a job?" Matilda rubbed a finger along her bottom lip. Cracks in the skin widened, and a thin line of blood trickled down her chin. "You want cash?"

"I want answers."

"What kind of answers?"

"Did you intrude on the Swenson Coven's territory?"

Matilda wrinkled her nose. "What of it?"

"Did you kill a pair of cops?"

"I did. So?" She tightened the muscles of her neck, and veins bulged in odd places. "You have a problem with all that?"

"No, I just want to make sure it's all true before I haul you to the police station."

Matilda cackled. The mark on the floor pulsed, and Finch knew she was agitated and using some sort of ability. He widened his stance and tensed. Her laughter lasted a total of four seconds before she lunged at him.

Claws erupted from the tips of her fingers—slender knife-like extremities meant for rending flesh. Everything about her was like a witch out of an old Grimm's fairy tale. Wicked. Terrifying. Maniacal.

The moment before she reached him, Finch shattered the jar with the Witch's Web on the floor. The invisible webs shot forward in an instant, their reach great enough to hit the back of the storage unit wall. The barbed wire lashed around Matilda, and even Seth, despite the fact the loser warlock clearly wanted nothing to do with the conflict.

Seth was so ensnared that blood practically gushed from thin lines all down his body, starting with a line across his neck.

The Witch's Web…

It held Matilda in place, mere inches from Finch, but the woman literally foamed from the mouth. Her eyes, wild and unfocused, met Finch's. Then she thrashed her arm, her demon-powered claws ripping through the barbed wire.

One of the advantages of demonic magic was a demon's strength. They were beasts of brute power, especially chain demons, and Finch wasn't surprised when the insane woman effortlessly broke free of the trap.

When she swiped at Finch, he tried to step back, but her speed was far greater than that of a normal human being. The tips of three of her claws caught him in the chest and sliced up a few shallow gouges. He tumbled backward and hit the cement floor, winded. Then his back seized up as stiff as a board as he felt the rot of the demon claw its way up his spine.

But unlike when Finch had been trapped in the Witch's Web, he had mentally prepared for this. His concentration, unbroken, allowed him to use Chronos's magic.

He rewound time.

All the color faded.

All the shapes disappeared.

When he opened his eyes again, Finch was back in his bedroom, staring at the ceiling. He had figured something like this would happen, but he had been hoping Matilda wouldn't fight. Now that she had, Finch would have to try again. With a groan, he got up and headed to the front door. The second he opened it, Bree burst into his messy apartment.

"Adair!"

To his surprise, she threw her arms around him.

"Hm?" Finch stared down at her, baffled. "What's wrong?"

Bree broke the embrace and then furrowed her brow. After a careful circle around his whole body, she exhaled. "Are you okay?"

"I'm fine." He glanced at the clock on the wall. 4:34 a.m. "It's the same morning, remember? Nothing actually happened."

"But... your spine?"

"I was prepared," Finch said, his tone thick with apathy. Then he headed to the window and let the mischievous pigeon inside. The bird flew in the moment she could.

"That was quite the show," Kull said as she fluttered over to a chair. "Bravo." She clapped her wings together.

"Maybe we shouldn't do this." Bree rummaged through the dirty clothes strewn about the living room. "Catching Matilda isn't a real priority. We should just head to Papa and forget we even tried this."

Finch grabbed the midnight raspberry tea and actually huffed out a laugh. "Are you worried about me?" With a snap of his fingers, he heated the water in a cup. "Kid, I've been through a lot worse. This is nothing." Once the tea was ready, he walked it over to her. "Trust me."

"I don't like that you were hurt." She took the cup and brought the liquid to her lips. With a frown, she added. "It looked like it was terrible."

Finch recalled hitting the ground. His adrenaline had been so high, he didn't remember the sensation of hitting—just the crawling rot of demonic powers. He rubbed his nose and shook his head. "Don't worry about me."

"Someone has to," Bree said.

That comment struck him. Finch met her gaze, and for a long moment, neither of them said anything. But then Finch sighed. "Look, no matter what happens, I'm going to come through for you. We're going to save your father. We're going to bring down this witch. And we're going to make sure your mother's murderer pays. I mean, I might not be flashy about everything, but I assure you—Matilda isn't a match for me."

Kull cooed a laugh. With a hop off a chair, she transformed into a cat and then landed on all four feet. "Next time you should say that right before she claws off your face."

"You should drink this tea," Bree said as she handed it back to Finch. "Just in case you need the calming effects."

He took the cup. "You don't need it?"

"Not anymore."

He sipped the drink. The tea… He had brewed himself a cup every morning for years. Anytime he woke up with dreams of Carter, he always needed just a sip. The aroma was familiar, and he allowed it to soothe him, just like it had all those other mornings.

"If you don't want to do this, I understand," Bree whispered.

Finch smiled. After the tea was finished, he set the cup on the kitchen counter. "I already told you. I might look tired or down, but I'm always going to step up when you need me to." He offered her a genuine smile. "Let's go catch us a crazed witch."

———

Finch did everything the same way. He drew the marks. He saved the dog. Got himself the Witch's Web, a gun, and Landa's angelic brew—and he even arrived at the storage unit just in time to see the two witches opening everything up for the day.

This time, when he entered, Seth wasn't even there. It was just Matilda.

Bree stood behind Finch, at least ten feet back and near one of the brick walls. She didn't say much, she just watched with wide eyes.

"What do you want?" Matilda asked in the same raspy tone as before.

"I love what you've done with the place," Finch quipped again, trying to inject the same level of energy he'd had before. "It has real *illegal chemistry* meets *unbridled laziness* vibes."

With the same cruel half smile, Matilda asked, "You think you're smart? You have real gall coming in here, *to my domain*, just to make jokes."

"I'm a warlock." He didn't offer anything else. Finch didn't want to repeat that part of the conversation.

"Did you come here for a job?" Matilda didn't rub her bottom lip this time, which Finch found oddly curious, but not worth remembering. "You want cash?"

"I want answers."

"What kind of answers?"

"Did you intrude on the Swenson Coven's territory?"

Matilda wrinkled her nose. "What of it?"

"Did you kill a pair of cops?"

"I did. So?" Again, Matilda tightened the muscles of her neck, and veins bulged in odd places. "You have a problem with all that?"

This time around, Finch had his phone in his pocket, recording the whole interaction. He had already known she was going to confess—which was why he'd had to replicate the conversation, so she would say the same things—so now, when he brought this to the authorities, he would have all the evidence he needed.

"No, I just want to make sure it's all true before I haul you to the police station."

And exactly like before, Matilda laughed. Finch counted the seconds until she lunged. This time, he tried using Dr. Colton's gun. He brought it up right as the demon-witch was pointblank in front of him.

When he pulled the trigger, the bullet barely tore through the woman's wan skin. The demonic power running through her veins gave her improved fortitude, it seemed. The bullet only made it half an inch deep before stopping.

Finch wouldn't be taking the time to pack this useless weapon again, that was for sure.

And then Matilda swiped him with her claws, this time slashing his neck. That was a tad disturbing, but Finch *never* lost his concentration. He had known there was a risk, and he undid time before he even hit the ground.

4:34 a.m.

———

Finch did everything he had before, and on his sixth attempt fighting Matilda, he knew what to look for.

"Did you kill a pair of cops?"

"I did. So?" Again, Matilda tightened the muscles of her neck, and veins bulged in odd places. "You have a problem with all that?"

"No, I just want to make sure it's all true before I haul you to the police station."

Matilda laughed. Finch counted the seconds. Then she lunged. Finch dodged to the right, completely avoiding her claws. When she swiped again, he ducked under it. Her third strike went for his gut, but Finch backstepped, once again completely avoiding everything.

More foam frothed from the woman's mouth. Colors drained from her body worse than before, and Finch suspected the cost of demonic magic was quite high. She was tired. Which was good news for him. If he could last through the fight, he might be able to—

But Matilda surprised him. She spit blood like a damn dinosaur in a *Jurassic Park* movie, momentarily blinding him. *Then* she managed to touch him.

Finch rewound time.

4:34 a.m.

———

Finch did everything he had before, and on his eighteenth attempt fighting Matilda, he was feeling rather confident, but also bored.

"What do you want?" Matilda asked in the same raspy tone she always had.

"I came here to tell you your storage unit sucks and your face is gross," Finch said in a flat tone. He wanted the conversation to go faster, and just straight insulting her rather than making funny quips did the trick.

"You have real gall coming in here, *to my domain*, to mock me."

"I'm a warlock."

"So? You came here for a job? Cash?"

"I want answers." Finch repeated everything like a talentless actor reading his lines from a script. There was no passion, no natural cadence to his words. Even Matilda gave him a strange look, like he was half robot.

"What kind of answers?" she asked, a slight confused inflection to her voice.

"Did you intrude on the Swenson Coven's territory?"

Matilda huffed. "What of it?"

"Did you kill a pair of cops?"

"I did. So?" Again, Matilda tightened the muscles of her neck, and veins bulged in odd places. "You have a problem with all that?"

"No, I just want to make sure it's all true before I haul you to the police station."

She laughed. Finch stared at her like he couldn't be any more bored. When she lunged, he felt nothing, not even the adrenaline of a fight. He dodged to the side, then sidestepped, then took a step back. Matilda attacked with her claws, but Finch's mind was filled only with the steps he needed to take.

Back up. Lean to the left. She's about to spit... There it is.

Matilda coughed up a glob of blood. Finch twisted his body, and the gunk hit the far wall.

The two witches from outside ran into the storage unit. When it had happened the first time—back around attempt eight—that had surprised Finch. But now he was ready. He threw the clay jar on the floor, pointing it in their direction. The Witch's Web shot outward, catching both women before they were more than a few feet inside.

Bree clapped.

Matilda attacked him from behind, but Finch was prepared.

Two steps forward. Quickly dodge right.

Then he got to the end of his previous experiences. Matilda was panting, sweat dripping from every inch of exposed skin on her body. When she threw another swipe,

Finch managed to just dodge regularly. Then he pulled out Landa's brew.

How was he going to administer it?

Matilda leapt for him, both her hands outstretched, her claws pointed at his chest. Finch threw the vial at her face. The brew shattered across her forehead, but nothing made it into her mouth. Instead, Matilda collided with him, her claws and skin soaked with the power of the chain demon, corrupting his spine.

Finch undid time.

4:34 a.m.

———

Finch did everything he had before, and on his *thirty-third* attempt fighting Matilda, he brought along a syringe he had filled with Landa's brew.

Finch and Bree entered the storage unit together, Kull at Finch's feet. Bree yawned.

"What do you want?" Matilda asked, her raspy voice now irritating.

"Did you kill a pair of cops?" Finch asked. An AI could've given more emotion than he did.

"What?" The witch sneered.

"Did you kill a pair of cops?" he repeated, loud enough for his phone's recording.

"I did. And what of it? Are you their dog?"

This conversation—Finch had discovered on his twenty-first attempt—was much faster than the original one. "That's right," Finch said, but before he could get to the final taunt, Bree tugged on his coat sleeve.

"Uh, Adair?" Bree asked.

"What is it?"

"Can I play games on your phone this time around?"

Matilda, utterly baffled, watched the exchange with a permanent bewildered expression.

Once Finch handed over his cellphone, he returned his attention to the deranged witch. "Where were we?" he muttered. "Oh, right. You suck. Your face is weird. And I'm going to haul you into the police station."

This time, she didn't laugh. She never did when the conversation was too awkward. Instead, she just lunged, but she attacked in the same pattern as before.

Back up. Lean to the left. She's about to spit...

The globs of blood hit the wall only a few feet from Bree. She didn't even glance up from the phone. She poked at the screen, beating a level of *Candy Crush* as a deadly battle between a demonic witch and a warlock took place mere feet from her.

The two lackey witches ran into the storage unit.

Finch threw the Witch's Web and caught them instantly.

Matilda attacked him from behind.

Two steps forward. Quickly dodge right. Dodge left.

Finch didn't even see the storage unit around them anymore. He was in his own head, counting the number of steps he had to take, or which way he needed to lean. Matilda, on the other hand, grew more desperate. She was panting and panicking in equal amounts. The more Finch effortlessly evaded her attacks, the wilder her attacks became.

From an outside perspective, it looked as though Finch was a god of predictions and combat—perfectly ducking and weaving and evading, barely keeping his eyes on his target, yet never once getting hit.

And then the moment came.

Matilda swung with a powerful haymaker. When she missed, it left her unbalanced. She wobbled to the side, and that was the opening Finch had been waiting for.

With his syringe, he stepped forward and jabbed her in the soft part of her flesh, just near the armpit. The witch screamed so loud, and so horrifically, Finch was afraid he had killed her.

Instead, she twitched as she fell to the ground, her skin's color slowly returning as she spasmed around.

Bree lowered his phone, her smile returning in full force. "Oh! Did you do it this time, Adair? I knew you would!"

"Hm?" Kull woke up from a nap in the corner of the witch's meth lab. "It's over now? *Finally.* I mean, it was amusing the first few times we were here, but I'm absolutely done with this rodeo."

Finch leaned down and watched as Matilda's mouth filled with more sickly white foam. What was wrong with her? Her eyes glazed over, but she continued to breathe through her mouth. She wasn't dead, though she would need to be restrained.

"Okay," Finch said with a sigh. "That's it. Let's secure her, take her to the police station, and go find your father."

Bree bounded over to him. "This is so amazing, Adair. I can't wait to tell Papa everything. He's going to be so amazed. I just know it."

CHAPTER
THIRTY-FIVE

inch drove to the main Stockton Police Department, the one right across the street from the McDonald's-gas station combo. Matilda, handcuffed and barely breathing, lay in the back, with Bree in the passenger seat, and Kull in her lap. The ride was a tense one. Bree constantly glanced over her shoulder, and Finch kept his rearview mirror pointed back at the demonic witch. But she never got up. Finch wondered if the brew was a little *too* potent.

Maybe I should dilute it a bit if I have to do this over, he thought.

When he arrived at the station at 12:45 p.m., Finch's giving-a-damn about the situation was at an all-time low. He called in the citizen's arrest, making sure he was transferred to the occult division. Then he waited in the parking lot for a half dozen officers to come surround his vehicle and remove the witch. Finch handed over his phone with the recording, along with his badge, and the booking officer recorded everything. But then they had *questions*.

"What, exactly, happened?" the booking officer asked. The

police parking lot was roped off, Finch's car the heart of a scene.

"I was at my storage unit when this witch started yelling at me," Finch said, his hands in his pockets. He was already tired. It had been a long morning, and his back hurt from the fight with the witch, even if she never managed to land a blow.

"And she confessed to killing the two cops?" The police officer was obviously having a hard time connecting the dots in Finch's poorly constructed lie.

He shrugged. "I asked her, she said she did, and then she attacked me. After I subdued her, I brought her here."

"I saw the whole thing," Bree chimed in matter-of-factly.

"Uh-huh. Okay, well, we'll call you if we need any other information." Although not entirely convinced, it was obvious the officer just *wanted* this to be true. And Finch understood. It wasn't every day a known murderer was just brought to the station completely disarmed and ready for processing.

But then the doors to the station opened, and out came Sergeant McGregor. Although Finch had never met the man, his nametag glistened in the afternoon sunlight with the pristine polish of someone who hadn't been out on the streets for years.

Sergeant McGregor walked with a limp, his left leg stiffer than the right. The man exuded an air of grizzled toughness, as if the hitch in his step was a badge of honor. His attire, the standard police uniform with a neatly pressed shirt, barely fit over his large frame and bulletproof vest. His black hair, which matched his polished boots, was slicked back, highlighting his widow's peak of a hairline.

Bree stood a bit closer to Finch as the sergeant approached. Kull, still a cat, regarded the newcomer with the same unconcerned demeanor a normal cat would offer.

"You're the one who caught Matilda?" Sergeant McGregor asked, his voice just as gruff as his appearance would imply. "Adair Finch?"

"That's right," Finch replied.

"She had grafted a chain demon to her. No one just apprehends a witch like that. You had *no help*? No plan? You waltzed up to her and were never touched? *Not once?*"

"I'm fine."

Finch didn't actually want to speak with the sergeant. The man was behind the whole cover up of Vera's death. Sergeant McGregor had ordered the shooter to kill Bree in the timelines they thought she was a liability. Which meant—and Finch kept it at the forefront of his thoughts—McGregor knew who the killer was, or was the killer himself.

"I've heard about your work before," Sergeant McGregor said. He frowned as he added, "They said you were the best. No murder unsolved. No criminal ever escaped. But they also said you didn't do work for the station anymore. What made you change your mind?"

"Vera's death."

The mere mention of her name made the man tense. He rubbed at his thick neck. "I see. Well, we have officers out searching for her husband right now. He's top of our suspect list."

"I'm pretty sure I know where he is," Finch said, unable to keep the icy tone out of his words. "You don't have to worry. I'll have this whole thing wrapped up in a matter of hours as well."

The sergeant stared into Finch's eyes for a long while. He was shorter than Finch—his left leg wasn't the same size as his right, and it took some of his height. That didn't stop the man from glowering, though. It almost seemed like a challenge—like the sergeant thought Finch was bluffing, and wanted to silently call him on it.

But Finch wasn't backing down.

Vera's killer wasn't going to escape. They were caught in Finch's time bubble, and like the inevitability of the heat death of the universe, there was no stopping Finch from finding the murderer and bringing them to justice.

All he needed was Liam Blackstone. The man had all the evidence Finch needed to accuse the murderer—even the sergeant—and get them locked up for life.

"We already have several detectives out hunting for Liam," Sergeant McGregor finally said. "You don't need to worry about finding him. You should be focusing your incredible talents on other dangerous criminals in the city."

Stockton always had *some* problem. But Finch wasn't concerned about those at the moment.

"Well, my assistant and I are going to grab some coffee to celebrate apprehending a dangerous criminal." Finch turned back toward his vehicle. "You have a good day, Sergeant."

As they walked over to his Toyota, Bree took every step as though she were a helium molecule. "I'm your *assistant*?" She smiled wide. "I've gotten a promotion!"

"Don't let it go to your head," Finch muttered.

"Too late," Kull said. "She's already ordered five hundred business cards with her name and new title."

They piled into his vehicle, and Bree practically hopped up and down in her seat. She fastened her belt and then happily stared out the window.

Before Finch started the car, he asked, "The night your mother died... Do you know if the murderer was limping? Can you remember that much?"

For a long while, Bree said nothing. When she glanced back, her expression was neutral. "He wasn't limping," she said. "He was really fast. He grabbed Papa." Then Bree met Finch's gaze. "I don't think it was the sergeant."

"All right."

Once it was obvious the conversation was done, Bree pointed to the road. "Are we heading to *Nico's Brew?*"

"No. We're going to look for your father at a condemned laundromat."

"Do you really think he's there?"

"I think there's a good possibility. And if he's not, I'm sure we'll find some clues to his whereabouts." Finch half smiled as he glanced over at Bree. "Apparently, the cops are using the laundromat to wash their magic-item-laced uniforms. Probably so no one discovers their secret. I'm starting to get the feeling the police didn't want anyone knowing Liam was involved with them at all."

"You mean the necklaces that allowed them to see through illusions and stuff?" Bree rubbed her coat sleeve. The bright, sparkling stripe, garish and striking, marked it as magical. "The shooter had a necklace, didn't he? That's how he knew to shoot me."

"Don't worry about it, because this is all almost over," Finch muttered.

Bree leaned back in her seat. "Instead of a warlock pendant, can I have a coat instead?"

"What?"

"You know. A warlock pendant. You said all new warlocks got one. Can mine be a coat instead?"

Finch huffed a laugh. "What kind of coat?"

"One from *Saint Laurent!* Maybe we can even put the illusionary effects on it, like this coat has. But maybe... the stripe will be somewhere on the *inside.*"

"What is *Saint Laurent?*"

Bree giggled and shook her head. "Don't you remember when you took me to the mall? I got a coat from there."

That had been months ago. Finch barely remembered the extremely overpriced trash that had brought Bree so much joy. "Oh, right. That place. Sure. Once this is over, you can have a *warlock coat* as your prize for doing such a good job."

"Excellent." She glanced back out the window, but a moment later, she returned her attention to him. "You're still going to teach me how to be a warlock once this is all over, right? Because I don't know any of the other cores, and I think I can make a pact with Chronos, too, if you just show me where he is."

Finch huffed back a laugh. The thought of taking a child to see Chronos was preposterous, but he wasn't in the mood to explain why. "I think you and your father are going to need a break after all this. Maybe once you're settled, we can talk about *magic training*."

After a short moment to mull that over, Bree once again smiled and returned her attention to the brightness outside. She seemed satisfied with that answer. Finch just wanted to focus on the last bit of this investigation. Liam was somewhere in the city, but Finch knew he was probably making more work for himself.

Since he had turned in Matilda, the sergeant would likely inform all his officers and detectives that Finch was on the hunt. They would be on edge.

Finch made a mental note to himself. If he had to reset time, he would grab Liam *first*, and then get Matilda. That way there was no difficult overlap.

"Adair…"

Finch glanced over. Bree stared at him, her blue eyes glassy.

"What's wrong?" he asked.

She shook her head. "Nothing. I… I wanted to thank you." Bree rubbed at the corners of her eyes. "Mum said I should go to you if ever there was anything wrong, because you would make it right, and… you did. Thank you."

Finch's throat tightened. He took a moment to force

himself to calm down. "It's not over *yet*. And even when it is officially over, you won't need to thank me."

"You should all be thanking *me*," Kull interjected with a chuckle. "I mean, you really couldn't have solved the witches' feud and murder without my amazing magics."

Bree turned around in her seat to face Kull. "That's true. Thank you, Kull. You're awesome."

The little mischief spirit waved a paw through the air. "Oh, stop." But then she smiled a feline smile and whispered, "But actually keep going. Spirits like me don't usually get praise."

"I'm never going to forget you for the rest of my life, Kull. Or should I say... *Kull-than-tar-rick the Sneak*. I'll even remember your super weird name."

This statement seemed to leave Kull speechless. Then purring loud enough to shake the car brought another smile to Finch's face.

The drive to the laundromat seemed shorter than it really was. Finch recognized the area the moment he turned down the last street. It was a wasteland of litter, stray dogs, and failed businesses. A few places still existed—the liquor stores, which said everything about the area—and Finch drove by two before he reached their destination.

Happy Time Laundromat.

What a bizarre name. The sign had once been a myriad of rainbow colors, but those had faded into a gray oblivion.

The laundromat was a massive building surrounded by rented chain-link fences. The afternoon sunlight was bright, but it wasn't strong enough to pierce the tarps covering most of the laundromat's windows. Finch stared at the building as he cautiously drove up. The place was dark, and separated from everything else.

The perfect place to hold a kidnap victim.

And also clean dirty laundry with suspicious items inside.

Finch parked the car near the gate and then stepped out. Bree and Kull followed suit. The fence wouldn't stop them. Bree touched the brand-new padlock and unlocked it within a few seconds.

"We can go in now," she said.

"Stick close to me," Finch said. "If something goes wrong, you shouldn't go far."

"I thought we're here to pick up Papa?"

Finch slowly glanced around. He didn't see any other vehicles, but he had a bad feeling about the place. No one left their kidnapping victim *unattended*. Someone was here. Finch would bet good money on it.

"If there's a fight," Finch whispered, "I'll handle it."

Kull snickered. "But can you do it in less than thirty-seven attempts? I think the last scuffle you were in was a little boring, to be honest. At least spice this one up with some backflips."

Finch didn't reply. He wasn't in the mood to joke around.

The three of them headed for the front door, crossing the empty parking lot at a leisurely pace. Finch was still sore from the fight with Matilda, and he made another mental note about the order in which he needed to solve things. The fight with her had to be the last thing he did. She was just too much of an irritant.

He pushed open the front door to the laundromat, and it squeaked the entire way. Finch stepped inside, the hairs on the back of his neck standing on end.

The laundromat still had electricity. A distant hum from the back of the building betrayed the fact *something* was on and running.

Bree stepped in after him, Kull in her arms.

Despite the power, the lights were off. Some of the tarps over the windows had holes slashed into them. A few brave stray beams of light trickled in through the holes, barely illuminating the area.

Dozens of washing machines—at least eighty, perhaps a hundred—were packed inside, some stacked one on top of another.

Finch crept forward, glancing around, looking for any sign of life. Broken glass littered the floor. Beer bottles. There was a tent in one corner, along with piles of fast-food wrappers.

Squatters sometimes lived here, it seemed. They were homeless people who broke into condemned buildings and made them their temporary home.

The laundromat was also a professional cleaning service. A giant motorized clothing conveyor rack sat at the far end of the building, one used to hang freshly pressed and dried clothes. Hundreds of empty plastic suit protectors hung from the conveyor, like ghosts all waiting in a line.

"I don't like this place," Bree whispered.

Finch crunched some glass underfoot as he stepped forward. There were office rooms and dry-cleaning spaces. Perhaps they would have to check those…

"I can't believe it," someone said, their voice echoing throughout the building, bouncing off machines and creating an odd ring to their voice. "The sergeant wasn't lying. *Adair Finch* is on the case—and here you are."

CHAPTER
THIRTY-SIX

A man stepped out from behind a cluster of washing machines.

Detective Rhett Jenner.

He wore the same jeans, shirt and black coat he had on at Vera's house when he was "investigating" the case. Jenner always had a permanent glower, and right now was no different. He stepped around some more machines, closing the distance between him and Finch.

"How did you know I was here?" Jenner asked.

"Lucky guess," Finch quipped.

Bree grabbed Finch's arm, her fingers twisting into the fabric of his coat. "It's him," she whispered, her voice barely audible. "His voice... I recognize it."

"Why'd you do it?" Finch asked, his own voice echoing around the dead laundromat. "Kill an innocent witch, I mean."

"*You don't know that,*" Jenner hissed. He slammed his fist into the side of one of the machines, the resulting *bang* as loud as a gunshot. "You couldn't possibly know any of that." As he stepped closer, his piercing glare shifted over to Bree.

"Wait... You have Liam's girl?" He cursed under his breath and then returned his attention to Finch. "She told you, didn't she?"

Finch didn't reply. He grabbed Bree's shoulder and kept her close. Sure, if Bree was hurt, he could undo time, but Finch didn't want the girl to get shot again. It had obviously upset her.

Bree kept her head poked around his side, her attention on Jenner.

"Why'd you do it?" Finch asked again. "You hate witches so much you just wanted to get your rocks off?"

Jenner's boots crunched glass as he stepped around one more machine and stood across from Finch, only ten feet away. "You shut your mouth, *warlock*. I didn't want to kill her. It was an accident."

"You *accidentally* stabbed her five times?" Finch's tone was sarcastic, but he couldn't keep the contempt from his words. "How did that happen, Jenner? Slipped and fell?"

The detective sneered. "She was getting in the way," he said, his voice icy and soft. "Her husband was working with us just fine, but then she made an issue of things."

"What *things*?"

Jenner said nothing, and it made Finch wonder. What was so terrible about the police—about Detective Jenner—that Vera would turn hostile? What was Jenner hiding? Finch had a feeling he was missing one crucial detail.

"You know what?" Finch rhetorically asked. "It doesn't matter. You killed Vera Blackstone, and there's no tale you can spin, or fact you can twist, to make it right."

"Tsk." Jenner clenched his jaw. "We weren't making Liam do anything illegal. He was *helping us* stop the real criminals."

"You mean that deranged witch, Matilda? Don't worry, I already dealt with her."

Jenner waved his hand. "You think stopping *one* witch is

enough? There will always be more. *Always*. In a simpler time, the police only had to worry about perps with guns, or losers in gangs, but when every magic-wielding sociopath has the ability to not only be invisible, but also kill anything they touch or explode a building by *thinking* hard, then we have to adapt."

"What does that even mean?" Finch asked, trying hard not to laugh. How was this one detective going to change things fundamentally? "You think having a few necklaces that let you see through party-trick illusions is going to change the whole game? C'mon. Get serious. You don't even know what you're doing."

"We're not going to sit back and do nothing."

Finch scoffed. "You might not want to admit it, or relinquish control, but other witches and warlocks can handle magic-wielding sociopaths."

"Tell that to Officer Gladstone and Officer Manning!" Jenner slammed another washing machine, but this time he smiled, like he had something up his sleeve—something that gave him confidence, even if Finch thought it unfounded. "They *died* because the number of law-abiding magic sociopaths is *much lower* than the number of law-breaking magic sociopaths."

Finch couldn't argue that point as effectively. Those with magic—witches, warlocks, wizards, and everything in between—often considered the laws of the magicless to be mere *suggestions*. They did consider themselves above all that, especially if they could evade detection with ease.

Illusions, obfuscation, invisibility…

There were hundreds of ways to avoid the mundane.

"Maybe someone else on the force will find a way," Finch muttered. "But it's not going to be you. I'm taking you in for the murder of Vera Blackstone, and then I'm going to report Sergeant McGregor for the cover up."

"You're not gonna do jack shit," Detective Jenner shouted, his confidence never waning. "Sorry, Adair, but I found a way to make sure you magic thugs are put in your place. We're going to purge Stockton of every whack job witch, parasitic warlock, and trash-eating spirit."

A wave of magic blanketed the laundromat.

No.

No.

Not magic. The exact opposite of magic. Finch caught his breath, his heart hammering the instant he recognized the sensation. It was as if a thousand insects had been poured over him—crawling on his scalp, digging at his skin, and burrowing deep into his flesh.

The last time he had felt this, it had been in Paris, the night Carter had died.

This was the power of the magic-nullifying monster.

Finch couldn't use his magic.

"He's a warlock," Kull shouted, her black fur standing on end, her yellow eyes wide with fright. *"He made a pact with the magic eater!"*

Detective Jenner pulled out his handgun—standard police issue Glock 22—and aimed for Bree.

Finch pushed Bree to the side. He wanted to duck out of the way himself, but the fight with Matilda had left him sluggish. The white-hot pain of a bullet shot through his side, momentarily blinding him. Finch hit the concrete floor, but he had no memory of the fall, just the few seconds of agony that came from a terrible, near-instant injury.

"Adair!"

Someone grabbed his arm and tugged. They were too weak to pick him up.

Finch opened his eyes.

Bree knelt next to him, tears streaming down her face. Her panic sent a surge of energy through him. Finch got to his feet, his body numb. Something was terribly wrong, but he didn't have time to think about it.

He had to get Bree to safety.

When he stood, Finch realized he was still in the laundromat. Of course. But he was momentarily disoriented.

Then he spotted Jenner.

The detective was flailing about, cursing so loud his words echoed around the building. A pigeon was swirling around his head, pecking and scratching. He shot twice into the air, but missed the bird with both shots.

Jenner had positioned himself so he stood between Finch and the front door. That didn't matter. Finch backed away, his thoughts jumbled, but he knew every building had to have two exits—it was a matter of law. When he turned, he stumbled, his body not responding like it should.

Finch was injured.

Very injured.

"Adair," Bree said, her lips quavering. "Oh, no…"

Finch grabbed her by the shoulder. When he stepped forward, he had to lean half his weight on her. His right leg… It wouldn't support him. He glanced down. Dark blood soaked his shirt, coat, and the upper part of his pants.

Tears streamed down Bree's face. Finch pushed her forward, urging her to move forward.

"We have to go," he said, his voice smooth, despite the growing panic in his thoughts. "C'mon."

"You're hurt," she whispered. "You're bleeding so much."

"God gave me two kidneys for a reason… I don't need this one." He forced a smile, even if he didn't feel it. He urged her again, and his false confidence seemed to bring Bree back to the present. She nodded once, took in a ragged inhale, and they hurried beyond a stack of washing machines.

The dry-cleaning machine, with its hundreds of plastic

clothing protectors, reminded Finch of the ghostly catacombs.

Detective Jenner…

He had made a pact with the monster…

He had become a warlock? That was why Vera hadn't used magic the night of her death.

She *couldn't*.

That was probably why she had been upset about Liam's involvement. Vera hadn't wanted Liam involved with the nullifying monster. That was why Jenner had needed to kill her. Why he'd had to kidnap Liam and force him.

That was why the necklaces were difficult to identify.

They were partially made with the vile magic of this monster.

And he hadn't known Jenner was a warlock, because his magic was the antithesis of magic. He was some sort of anti-warlock. Finch had never experienced that before, not even in Paris.

Once Finch reached a row of plastic suit covers hanging from the conveyor, he turned.

Jenner and Kull were locked in a scuffle, but it was clear the mischief spirit wasn't herself in this zone of nullification. She didn't transform as fast. She shifted into a cat, but it was nightmarish. Her wings slowly folded into a body, and black fur burst out of the body of a bird.

She leapt from one machine, onto the top of another, and then transformed again.

This time, Kull became the most mischievous of all amphibians…

A strawberry poison dart frog.

Her bright red skin, and blue legs, were distinct enough to see across the giant room. Kull leapt at Jenner's face.

Jenner swung his arms, but failed to hit her before she collided with his nose. Finch suspected Kull had been aiming for the eyes, but missed. A poison dart frog's toxins weren't that irritating to the skin, but they were quite painful if applied straight to an eyeball.

Jenner, in a fit of rage, grabbed the little frog and threw her to the floor.

Then he stomped Kull with his boot, her guts popping outward like the blood from a bloated tick.

Finch's connection to her magic ceased.

"*No!*" Bree screamed.

Normally, humans couldn't kill spirits, but in this sinister aura of monstrous nullification, it seemed Jenner had the ability to snuff out anything made of magic.

Finch yanked Bree behind a row of plastic covers, hiding them from Jenner's view. He gulped down air, his head light, his thoughts scattered. Without his magic, he couldn't rewind time. He couldn't use his fire.

Bree trembled. She ran both her hands through her hair, her eyes unfocused. "She died. K-Kull died."

"Bree, listen to me," Finch said, his voice low. "You need to leave. The exit should be right over there."

Flickering green light from an exit sign on its last legs pointed the way out.

"I can't," Bree said through a ragged breath. "*I can't.* I can't lose everyone. I can't…" She grabbed Finch's coat and held on tighter than she had held anything before. "E-Everyone's leaving me. I can't do anything. I can't. I don't want anyone else to leave."

"*Adair!*" the detective shouted as he stomped through the laundromat. The man wasn't one to keep his anger in check. "*Get out here, you piece of shit!*" He slammed a washing machine as he made his way closer. "What's wrong? *Too scared now?*"

"Bree," Finch whispered. "You need to go. I'll handle this."

Tears ran the length of her face at a steady rate. She was

so choked up, her words came out soft and broken. "I don't want you to leave."

She kept saying it like he was going somewhere, and the significance wasn't lost on him. Finch shook his head. "I promise you. This isn't real. I'll change it back. But you have to go."

Finch would've said anything to get the girl to save herself. He wasn't worth dying over. If Finch could've given his life for Carter's, he would've done so in a heartbeat. And it was the same with Bree. She just had to go.

Perhaps it was his false confidence, but Bree glanced up at him and nodded. She couldn't speak, her crying wouldn't allow it, and instead, she turned and headed through the line of plastic suit protectors, leaving Finch to face the murderous detective.

"*Adair!*" Jenner shouted again, this time much closer than before. "What's wrong? Can't handle my abilities? *Huh?* I don't need crackpots like you anymore. *I can do my job like it was intended now.* I made a pact, how do you like that? With *Gixmoth the Desolate*, some fucked-up beast that thinks it's a god. You can't handle *his* power, can you? Of course you can't."

It wasn't difficult to tell Jenner would find him soon.

"You're going to die here, Adair. And then I'm going to get Liam's girl, and silence anyone who knows about this. *You're a dead man.*"

CHAPTER
THIRTY-SEVEN

F inch clung to a plastic suit cover, his body growing colder with each passing second. His vision tunneled, but he mulled over the information as much as possible.

Gixmoth…

Finch had never heard the creature's name. The monster who killed his brother.

Detective Jenner slammed his way to the massive drycleaning machine. He kicked over a cash register and stomped ever closer.

Finch could make some deductions.

Jenner hadn't bonded Gixmoth to his heart. If he had, the anger he was displaying would've caused the suppressive magic in the area to fluctuate. The powers drew on emotions, and the stronger they were, the more *oomph* they had. The magic hadn't changed, no matter how livid the detective became.

And while it was possible Jenner had bonded the beast to his eyes, Finch was fairly certain the man had bonded at the crown. All "gods" wanted the crown.

And the crown…

Needed concentration for its magic.

Kull had gone for Jenner's eyes, but Finch suspected it was to disrupt Jenner's focus, not to actually disturb the core of Jenner's eyes. The little mischief spirit… had given her life to help them.

As Finch went through the ghostly line of empty plastic protectors, his breathing shallow, he turned his attention to the wall. There was an electrical outlet not too far from his location. Several cords—large power cords—were attached to the motor that powered the clothing retrieval line. Some of the cords were broken, and their rubber coating frayed.

Jenner stomped past his location, heading for the back exit.

Finch couldn't have that. He wouldn't let this madman anywhere near Bree.

Once he emerged from the line of clothing covers, Finch found the controllers for the conveyor. He flipped it on, and the hum of electricity grew louder. A loud groan rumbled throughout the building, and the plastic covers swayed slightly as they moved along.

The crack of a gunshot caused Finch to grimace. He ducked his head. The bullet ricocheted off the wall near him.

"*Adair!*"

Finch crouched behind a service counter, his heart beating hard, his body assaulted by a barrage of lancing pain. Jenner had stopped and turned back around, heading for Finch's location.

"I know you're over there. *Come out.* No amount of hiding will help you."

Finch scooted along the floor, moving closer and closer to the wall with the power cords. He refused to answer Jenner's taunts. Since Jenner's magic wasn't bonded to his heart, there was no point in riling him. Finch just had to make it to his desired destination.

It hadn't occurred to him how bad everything had gotten since he had sequestered himself away in his apartment. Had crime run that rampant? Was a desperate play for power all beat cops and low-level detectives had left?

Finch gritted his teeth, trying to keep his focus on the task at hand.

"Your blood is all over the floor, asshole. You aren't hiding long." Jenner stomped closer and closer. He ripped off plastic clothing covers as he went, throwing them to the floor. "*You're so pathetic*," Jenner growled. "Everyone in the office used to whisper your name like you were a legend, but here you are, hiding in the dark—a decrepit warlock who is *nothing* without his magic."

Finch reached the power cords. A part of him wanted to point out that Jenner wasn't anything special without his magic, either, but now wasn't the time for sardonic comebacks. He grabbed a portion that still had its protective lining and twisted it until the damaged portion broke. The sparks and hum of power were lost in the noise of the conveyor.

When Jenner neared, Finch held the cord tight. His head...

Once this was over, would he even have the concentration needed to rewind time?

It didn't matter. Everything had been done. He had saved the dog. Kept Seth alive. Ended the witches' feud. Made sure Bree was safe. The only thing left—the one *last* checkmark for their list—was to take down Vera's murderer.

Kull...

He shook his head and forced himself to stand, though only one leg would support his weight. Then Finch turned, pressed his back to the wall, and stared at the row of moving suit covers.

"*Jenner,*" he rasped. "I'm over here."

The detective tore his way through the plastic covers. He burst out of the conveyor line mere inches from Finch. With what energy he had left, Finch thrust the exposed power cord forward. He struck Jenner in the side of the neck as the detective brought his gun up. The resulting shock wasn't deadly—it probably wasn't even as bad as a Taser—but it still stung.

And the sting caused Jenner to flinch.

In that half second where Jenner's muscles seized up, his negating aura faded. Finch was ready. His hate, his frustration, his determination—all of it powered the magic— and he wanted Jenner *gone.*

An explosion of fire erupted forward, melting the plastic, wrecking the machinery, and blowing through the laundromat like a dust explosion. The fire burned red, orange, and white, incinerating Jenner's body in the flicker of time that he didn't have his protections.

The glass of several windows shattered outward in the rush of heat and destruction. The floor was blackened, and a spark from a small machine exploding was like the last firework at a grand show.

Ke-Koh, the Ifrit of Rebellion, would've been proud.

The intense inferno had lasted a few moments. It had decimated the inside of the building, leaving a wreckage in its wake. Sunlight from the bright afternoon shone in through the ruined windows, illuminating the once gloomy laundromat.

Finch exhaled, and a line of smoke and embers wafted out of his mouth. The fire ended a few seconds later, quenched. Without Finch's magic, it couldn't sustain. These were hotter flames than what any normal mundane fire could create.

Finch slumped to the floor. Ash, embers, and charred debris was all that was left in front of him. The wall at his back was untouched. He leaned against it, his breathing weak. When Finch glanced down at his side, he considered cauterizing his wound, but what was the point?

He closed his eyes.

The weight he had carried for so long didn't feel as heavy. The smell of burnt hair and meat made his nose tingle, but otherwise, he felt little irritation with the world. For a long time, whenever he was alone, his dark thoughts had acted as a quicksand, dragging him down to the point that everything felt *broken*.

But now…

His thoughts didn't betray him.

Finch exhaled, more smoke and embers leaving his body from Ke-Koh's magic.

Footfalls drew his attention. Finch managed to flutter his eyes open long enough to spot Bree. She had waded through the devastation to reach him. Without regard for his injuries, she flung her arms around his neck.

"Adair," she said, her voice hitching. "*Adair*. I thought you weren't going to make it."

Finch brought a single hand up to pat her back. He didn't say anything.

"Rewind time. *C'mon*. I want to go back, Adair."

He considered telling her there wasn't anything they needed to redo, but he saved his strength. There was no point in arguing with her. When Finch had told Bree to wait in the car, she had followed him. When he had told her not to become a warlock, she had made a pact with Kull. Whatever he wanted, she ignored.

But Finch supposed it wasn't all that bad… He had enjoyed those moments.

Bree grabbed the sleeve of his coat. She looked him dead

in the eyes. "Focus, Adair. C'mon. We have to go back. It's okay. We know it's the detective now. We can do this. We can do it right. *We don't have to give up anything*. We can do it all."

Bree smeared ash across her tear-stained face. Her lips quivered again, but this time she held back the tears.

"Please, Adair. Let's go back. I know you can do it. Mum said you were the best—and there's no way someone like Detective Jenner is going to stop you."

Finch could never really tell her *no*.

"You told me I shouldn't worry if you looked tired. You said you would always be ready to step up. *Get up*. I know you can!"

With a smile he couldn't hold back, Finch tried to concentrate. His blood loss seemed substantial, and he desperately wanted to lie down and sleep, but he thought about how unhappy Bree would be if Kull didn't make it.

And then…

Everything froze in place.

The colors faded.

The shapes disappeared.

Darkness engulfed him. Once Finch managed to open his eyes a second time, his lightheadedness was gone. He stared up at the ceiling of his apartment, his heart hammering.

Finch glanced at his phone.

4:34 a.m.

CHAPTER
THIRTY-EIGHT

inch got up and went to the front door. For a moment, it felt like a dream. He didn't hurt, his thoughts were clear, and he was happier than he had ever been in years.

As he opened the door, Finch smiled.

Bree leapt into the apartment, practically bouncing off the walls with sheer, unmitigated joy. "You did it!" she shouted as she hugged him. "Adair! You did it! *We did it!*" Bree didn't let go. Her embrace tightened. She latched on harder than any barnacle.

Finch held a finger to his mouth. It was four in the morning. Even if everything was amazing, it would still cause mild problems if the neighbors heard. He patted her back until she quieted down, though she continued to giggle and hug him tight.

"Everything is fine," he said.

Bree finally released him, more tears on her face. She rubbed them away with the back of her arm and nodded. "I might need some more of that tea today…"

Finch smiled. "Sure. Maybe we can share it."

Then he went to the window, his anxiety building. Finch hesitated before opening it, for fear a spirit wouldn't return.

But the instant he lifted the windowpane, in flew an exuberant pigeon. Kull fluttered around the living room and then came to a stop on the back of Finch's favorite chair. She preened her feathers and glanced around with her yellow eyes. "I see you all *weren't* lying. You did remember me! Fantastic. I really didn't want to die that way. Not in a *laundromat* of all places."

Bree leapt from her seat and scooped Kull into her arms. Even though the spirit flailed about, her feathers going everywhere, Bree hugged her tightly. "I'm so happy you're okay."

After several alarmed coos, the pigeon relaxed. She laughed a bit as she said, "That makes two of us." With her wings outstretched, Kull returned the hug.

But once it was over, Kull twisted in Bree's arms and revert to her cat form. Bree set her on the back of the chair and frowned. "You were such a pretty frog. You should be that more often."

"It's poisonous." Finch pointed at the cat. "No frog."

But Kull had already begun her transformation. She went from *black cat* to *colorful amphibian* within half a second. "She can look, but no touching?" Kull asked, her voice adorably squeaky to match her diminutive size.

After a long sigh, Finch muttered, "Fine."

Bree clapped her hands.

The frog did the same.

It was rather cute.

Finch rubbed at his chest through his shirt. His bond to Kull was affixed to the core of his eyes, which was a relief. Well, half a relief. He didn't want to find her a dead human body, but at the same time, he was grateful she hadn't died permanently.

"Wait," Bree said, her smiling fading into a frown. "We didn't see Papa."

Finch grabbed his wrinkled clothing, brewed some tea, and then drew marks on both Kull and Bree. "Let's head out right now. I'm pretty sure your father is there at the laundromat."

"We're going back?" Kull's frog eyes bulged. "Right now?"

"Detective Jenner is currently at Vera's house." Finch grabbed the handle of the front door. "He's not there, and if Bree's father *is*, we need him."

It occurred to Finch that Jenner had been *extra* defensive whenever Finch had visited the murder site. Of course. He was the detective "investigating" his own crime. No wonder he had been so bizarre and aggressive when Finch showed up on the scene.

Finch exited his apartment, Bree close behind. Kull, as a bright frog, leapt over to Bree, but midair, she transformed back into her black cat form. As a trio, they made their way back to the accursed *Happy Time Laundromat.*

———

The building was just as spooky—perhaps worse—in the fog of the early morning.

5:23 a.m.

Finch approached the chain link fence with his hands in his coat pockets. The laundromat appeared abandoned, just like before. Bree unlocked the padlock, and then they approached the front door with cautious steps.

"Perhaps I should wait in the car," Kull whispered. She leapt off Bree's shoulders and stood with her back arched. "Spirits don't care for bad memories…"

"Okay." Bree patted her head. "We'll be right back."

Kull scurried back to the vehicle, occasionally glancing

over her shoulder with eyes that gleamed. Finch went inside, confident Jenner was nowhere near them. The laundromat was just as he remembered. Machines everywhere. A terrible squatter's tent in the corner. A smell that reminded Finch of three varieties of mold.

He went straight for one of the back offices. When he found dust disturbed around the door, Finch wasn't surprised. He entered the office to discover a metal desk, several file lockers, and an unconscious man. The man was handcuffed to a pair of exposed pipes that were visible through a hole in the wall. It was like someone had taken a hammer to the drywall. Finch suspected some lunatic searching for copper to resell had damaged the building.

"Papa!"

Bree ran to the man and knelt next to him.

Liam Blackstone, a man who *looked* like someone who lived in a library, took in shallow breaths. He had an open gash on his forehead that wept enough blood to pool around his face. His brown slacks and white shirt were stained with dirt and crimson, and his glasses, crooked and shattered, were somehow still perched on his misshapen nose.

The man didn't have any spare body fat. If Finch had to guess, he would say Liam was the intellectual type who forgot to eat and sleep whenever he was deep in his research.

"Wake him up, Adair," Bree said, her words quick and panicked.

He walked over, knelt, and then slapped Liam a couple times with the back of his hand.

Bree grabbed Finch's arm. "Stop! He's injured."

The man had a black eye, and his neck was red, but he was obviously still breathing. A moment later, his eyes half opened.

"Liam?" Finch asked. "Can you hear me?"

It took a long time for Liam to even tilt his head to the

side. He glanced up, his eyes as blue as Bree's. His brown hair, clumped with blood, reminded Finch of a grumpy hedgehog.

"Adair?" Liam asked, his voice raspy.

Finch touched his handcuffs and used Kull's magic to undo the lock. They popped open, and Liam was free, but he was clearly incapable of walking. He was almost incapable of speaking.

Finch stepped close, hoisted Liam into his arms, and then stood. He groaned as he headed to the door, lamenting the fact he hadn't truly worked out in ages. *I swear, the moment this is finished, I'm going back to the gym*, Finch promised himself. *I'll clean myself up. Get back in shape.*

He carried Liam's limp body out of the laundromat and straight to his vehicle. The college professor didn't say anything, and the way his head jerked to the side and then upright over and over made Finch think he had *just* been assaulted.

And it was probably true. When had Jenner killed Vera? Only a few hours ago. That meant Liam had been dragged here not long afterward. Jenner had probably dropped Liam off, and then gone straight to the crime scene to be the "lead detective" on his own heinous acts.

What an asshole.

Finch placed Liam in the back of his vehicle. After a long sigh, he pictured all the things he needed to do before the day was over. If he did everything *just right*, this would be the last time they lived through the day.

"Will he be okay?" Bree asked, her hands shaky.

"I think so," Finch muttered. "He definitely won't die in a car fire, that's for sure."

Kull, perched on the roof of the Toyota, tilted her head from one side to the other. "I'm sure you could catch your car on fire if you wanted."

Finch ignored the statement and got into his vehicle. "C'mon," he said to Bree. "Let's get this day over with. We have a whole corrupt police department to expose."

Bree happily plopped herself into the passenger seat, and Kull joined her. "All right," Bree said. "Let's do it… One more time."

————

If anyone had been watching Finch for this one day, they would've thought him insane.

After leaving the condemned laundromat, Finch drove like a lunatic back to his apartment. He put Liam on his bed, allowed the man to rest, and then grabbed some stale salami out of the fridge. Then Finch drove without regard for speed limits all the way to a specific bush in an odd part of town. He flew out of his vehicle, lured a small dog from the shrubs with said salami, and rushed the pooch to his owner's house.

Without so much as a *hello*, Finch then turned on his heel and headed for the outskirts of Stockton.

In the orange orchards, away from most people, Finch ran to the front door of a specific house. He placed his hand on it, unlocked it, and then went inside to steal exactly two things. A gun, and a clay jar.

Then he went to the local community college. It was probably the most bizarre stop, because Finch helped Bree shimmy into an unoccupied room while he went to another building and stole a syringe stored in the medicine cabinet of the nurse's office.

After Bree brought back the angelic brew, Finch drove his car to a local pawn shop. Technically, Stockton had five of them, but there was only one Finch trusted: *Stockton Loan & Jewelry*. There was a warlock who worked the back, and that man always had everything.

Finch traded the Glock 22 for a Taser and a pair of fuzzy handcuffs. The pawn shop didn't have *normal* handcuffs, and Finch didn't want to waste time looking for any. So, his "perfect day" included leopard print, which was probably the most embarrassing part.

His equipment secured—long before 10am—Finch drove over to the self-storage units. He parked his car inside, walked down a few rows until he came to Matilda's temporary hideout, and then engaged in an honest-to-goodness battle with her.

Finch broke the Witch's Web jar on her lackeys, and then injected her with the angelic brew with the syringe. It was diluted a bit this time around, and instead of almost dying, Matilda was weakened enough to drag into his vehicle.

Finch had a few spare moments, so he got a haircut, shaved, and even purchased a new outfit. He looked more like his younger self—and he felt like it, too.

Right at noon, Finch brought the demonic witch to the police station. He answered all the officers' questions before they even managed to voice all the words, and specifically spoke to Sergeant McGregor. Satisfied the witches' feud had been handled, Finch returned to the laundromat.

But instead of walking in through the front door, Finch snuck in through the back.

He crept through the rows of plastic suit covers, and eventually made his way to the back-office door. This was the only part of the plan Finch hadn't experienced before, and when he approached, he had expectations of what he would find.

Fortunately, his assumptions were on the money. Detective Jenner was there, and he was searching for Liam. Clearly, the sergeant had warned him, and now he was trying to cover up his own tracks.

"Where did he go?" Jenner muttered as he slammed the metal desk over.

Finch waited outside the office, his nose tickled by the dust lingering on the air. When Jenner stepped out, Finch jabbed him in the side of the neck with his brand-new Taser.

The detective hit the floor, his body locked up as though frozen. After a second, he spasmed, but by then, it was all too late. Finch leapt on top of him, handcuffed the man, and disarmed him.

When he stood, Finch huffed a dry laugh. "Gonna call me a decrepit warlock now, huh?"

Detective Jenner, his face twisted in utter confusion, stared up at Finch from the floor. "W-What?" Jenner rolled to his side, his neck red, his face scuffed from his fall onto the concrete flooring. "How did you... Where did you even come from?"

Finch knelt and grabbed Jenner by the collar. "Where's Gixmoth? What kind of pact did you make with him?"

"What?" It was obvious from the lack of focus in Jenner's eyes that his level of disbelief was too high to form coherent sentences.

"*Where can I find that monster?*"

"I... I don't know. I made a pact with it months ago. How did you even know about—"

Finch punched the man across the face. Then he shook out his hand, his knuckles hurting. Again, Finch reminded himself to get in better shape.

Blood spilled from a split in Jenner's lip, but the man was rather solid. He glared up at Finch, his bewilderment gone and replaced with sheer rage. "You're a piece of shit, Adair Finch. I *wish* I knew where that monster was, because whenever it finds you, it's going to gut you."

Damn. Finch wanted nothing more than to track down that monster and the witches who had allied with it, but where was he even going to begin? It was a mystery for another infinite day, it seemed.

"Hope you like rotting in jail, fuck-face," Finch said as he stood.

"Adair…"

Finch turned, stiff and ready for a fight, but all he saw was Bree standing next to the dry-cleaning registers.

He pointed to the exit. "I told you to wait in the car. You shouldn't have followed me. Something *could* have gone wrong."

"But nothing did. And I need to do something."

Bree walked over and kicked Jenner square in the crotch with all her might. The man yipped and folded into a tight fetal position, his knees practically buried in his chest. Then Bree spit on him, her expression aggressively neutral.

"Okay," she finally said. "I guess we can bring him in to the police." Bree sighed. "You think they'll punish him, right? He won't get away with killing my mum? He'll pay?"

"If they don't punish him, I will," Finch darkly replied.

"Good."

Then they dragged Jenner to Finch's vehicle, and went back to Finch's apartment. With both Liam and Jenner, Finch was finally ready to present all the evidence to the chief of police.

CHAPTER
THIRTY-NINE

7:59 p.m.

F inch stood in the middle of Police Chief Harding's personal office. Out the door and down the hall, the statement room was being prepared for the press. Several officers had been arrested, and although Stockton had seen corruption before, every journalist from here to Fresno wanted a statement about the murder coverup.

The chief stood behind his desk. Finch stood on the other side.

Police Chief Harding had an impressive record. As an officer, Harding had held assignments in the Field Training Program, Violent Crimes Enforcement Team, Gang Investigations Unit, the Child and Elder Abuse Unit, and finally, the Homicide and Crime Scene Unit. Harding had earned himself several awards for his gang busts, and even a medal of bravery when he rescued three kids from an active school shooter.

Harding had been shot twice, both times in the line of

duty, and in one instance, protecting a fellow beat cop from a spray of gunfire.

The walls of Harding's office weren't a shrine to his achievements, like many other cops Finch had known. Instead, Harding hung newspaper clippings chronicling the many successes of the students who had lived through the shooting, and even a few pictures of the gang members who had turned their lives around after completing their drug rehabilitation programs.

If ever there was a man who embodied the motto *protect and serve*, it was Police Chief Harding.

And the man looked the part.

Harding was taller than most—even with a perfectly bald head that reflected the lights mounted to the ceiling. His shoulders were broad, like he both physically, and metaphorically, could carry any burden. And he wore his uniform with pride and respect, everything in place, pressed or polished.

He had brown eyes and a dark complexion that reflected his many hours out in the sun. He had been the chief of police for only a year, but it was obvious Harding was well adored in the community.

"Let me get this straight," Harding said as he walked around his desk. He took each step slowly, saying the words with care. "Liam Blackstone's daughter, a witness to the crime, ran to your apartment for help."

"That's correct," Finch stated. He kept his hands casually tucked into his new slacks. They were crisp, black, and matched his suit blazer. Finch felt like a million dollars in his snazzy name-brand suit. Perhaps he would keep the look.

"Bree's mother—a witch—said you were trustworthy."

"I knew Vera a long time ago," Finch muttered. "Back when I was still an active PI."

"Uh-huh." Harding rubbed at his striking jawline. "And then you *immediately* solved the crime, discovering it was Detective Jenner and Sergeant McGregor in cahoots because of some details you put together."

"That's right."

"It wasn't difficult for you?"

"When you're the best PI in the business, simple murders don't trip you up."

Harding narrowed his eyes as he walked to Finch's side. "And you also, in your spare time gathering evidence, apprehended Matilda, the head of the Haggin Coven, a known criminal."

"That's right."

"Randomly?"

"It needed to be done," Finch quipped.

Harding met Finch's gaze and stared for a long moment, never blinking. "You also rescued Liam, the victim's husband, who is the second witness to Vera's murder."

"Also, I saved a dog."

"Uh-huh. And you did this all *in less than twelve hours?*"

Finch nodded once.

Harding stifled a laugh—but just a single laugh. He seemed both bothered and impressed, as though he wasn't sure what to do with the deluge of information. After a long time, where it was obvious Harding mulled over all the details, he finally said, "I need someone like you on the force."

"I don't work for the department directly anymore," Finch said. "I'll help as an outside contractor, but not as a detective."

"Are you going back into retirement?" Harding asked.

"No. I have a new warlock to train, and I don't think my brother would approve of me hiding out in my apartment any longer."

"What're you going to do?"

"I'll probably open up my offices again. Maybe offer Liam a place to recover for a while. He's a decent warlock, and knows his way around magical items." Finch didn't want to mention anything about the monster Jenner had made a pact with.

He would deal with that in due time.

Harding held out his massive hand, his palms calloused. "Then let me be the first to officially thank you on behalf of the city, Adair Finch. Stockton could use more warlocks like you. Hell, if we had just one more, I feel like this whole city would be cleaned up in a day."

"Maybe," Finch said, his tone cryptically serious. He shook the chief's hand. "In the meantime, I'll do my best to help out as much as I can."

And perhaps, one day in the future, there would be two warlocks—maybe more—who finally cleaned up the city.

Finch was going to aim for it.

THANK YOU SO MUCH FOR READING!

Please consider leaving a review—any and all feedback is much appreciated!

Adair's Finch's story continues in *Chronos Warlock*!

To find out more about Shami Stovall and Adair Finch, take a look at her website:
https://sastovallauthor.com/newsletter/

To help Shami Stovall (and see advanced chapters ahead of time, including Chronos Warlock) take a look at her Patreon:

https://www.patreon.com/shamistovall

ABOUT THE AUTHOR

Shami Stovall is a multi-award-winning author of fantasy and science fiction. Before that, she taught history and criminal law at the college level and loved every second. When she's not reading fascinating articles and books about ancient China or the Byzantine Empire, Stovall can be found playing way too many video games, especially RPGs and tactics simulators.

Shami loves John, reading, video games, and writing about herself in the third person.

If you want to contact her, you can do so at the following locations:

Website: https://sastovallauthor.com
Email: s.adelle.s@gmail.com

facebook.com/SAStovall
x.com/GameOverStation

Made in the USA
Coppell, TX
23 August 2024

36372729R00217